KATIE MacALISTER

Sex and the
Single Vampire

D1513516

HODDER

First published in Great Britain in 2008 by Hodder & Stoughton
A division of Hodder Headline

The right of Marthe Arends to be identified as the Author of the
Work has been asserted by her in accordance with the Copyright,
Designs and Patents Act 1988.

A Hodder paperback

I

A CIP catalogue record for this title is
available from the British Library

ISBN 978-0-340-95198-9

Printed and bound by Clays Ltd, St Ives plc

Hodder Headline's policy is to use papers that are natural,
renewable and recyclable products and made from wood
grown in sustainable forests. The logging and manufacturing
processes are expected to conform to the environmental
regulations of the country of origin.

Hodder & Stoughton Ltd
A division of Hodder Headline
338 Euston Road
London NW1 3BH

I owe many people profound thanks for their support during the time I wrote this book (Kate, Michelle, and Vance – you guys are the best!), but this book is dedicated to my friend Lori Grube, who laughs when I tell her my story ideas, never stops me when I natter on and on about the books, and always drools over the heroes. Writing wouldn't be nearly as much fun without you to share it with me, Lori!

Chapter One

The message waiting for me at the hotel desk was short and concise: *Either you come back from England with bona fide proof of a spiritual entity, or you needn't bother returning to the office. There's no room in UPRA for crackpots and never-beens.*

It was signed by my boss, and the head of the western U.S. division of the United Psychical Research Association, Anton Melrose II.

"Well, isn't that just Jim Dandy fine," I muttered to the message as I crumpled it up and tossed it into the appropriate receptacle, situated at the end of the reception desk, wishing as I did that I could Summon up a demon or two, minor ones, just bad enough to scare the bejeepers out of my employer. "I'd pay good money to see him eat his words."

The woman at the desk smiled as she passed me the key to my room. "I'm sorry, Miss Telford; we're not responsible for the quality of the messages. We have to deliver them no matter what they say."

I smiled back, secure behind the sunglasses I wore everywhere. "That's okay; it's just my life falling apart, nothing to worry about. Is there a computer free now, do you know? I'll only need fifteen minutes."

Tina, the receptionist at the St. Aloysius Hotel in jolly old London, checked the log for the two computers kept in a small, dark room for the use of those businesspeople who couldn't live without an Internet connection. "It's all yours."

I gathered up my bag, ignoring the clinking that came from within, and mumbled my thanks as I limped down the short hallway that led to the computer room. One of the two computers was taken up by a skanky-haired young man of about twenty, who raised one pierced eyebrow as I carefully set my bag down next to the chair of the second computer. The clink of glass bottles was loudly evident.

"It's holy water," I told him when his pierced eyebrow rose even higher. "For the ghosts. Nothing drinkable. That is, you *could* drink it, but I've had it on the best authority that holy water tastes like tap water that's oxidized for a couple of days."

He blinked at me.

"Bland," I explained, then turned my attention to the computer. I waited until he was busy with his own screen before pushing my sunglasses up so I could better see the computer screen, logging quickly into the e-mail account I'd set up for those rare times UPRA had seen fit to send me outside of the Sacramento area (which is to say, twice), just as quickly scanning the six messages collected. "Spam about an herbal product guaranteeing to make my penis grow larger, spam about low mortgage rates, e-mail from Mom, spam about something to do with furry barnyard friends that I'm not even going to open, e-mail from Corrine, and spam asking me if I'm single. Well, it's nice to know I'm missed."

The young man snickered and logged off his computer, pulling up a briefcase that had the name of a major software company embossed on the side. "Do you see lots of ghosts, then?" he asked as he stood and shoved in the chair.

I pushed my sunglasses into their normal position and gave him a little moue of regret. "So many I hardly have a moment to myself. They're very simple-minded, you know. Really no different from a puppy. Just a kind word or two, a little pat on the head, and they follow you around forever."

He stood staring at me for a moment, as if he couldn't decide whether I was serious or not.

I held up both hands to show him there was nothing up my sleeves. "I'm joking. No ghosts to date."

He looked relieved, then managed to twist his relief into a familiar sneer common to all young twenty-somethings. I ignored him as he left, pulling my glasses off as I scanned my mother's e-mail, filing it to be answered later before I clicked on Corrine's.

Allie: This is just a reminder in case you've forgotten—the Dante book signing is at the new Hartwell's store in Covent Garden tomorrow night, 7 P.M. London time. Be there or I'll do something so horrible to you, I legally cannot put it into writing.

Hope you're having fun! I don't suppose you took

my advice and left the shades at home?
   Corrine
   P.S.: Don't forget to give Dante the key chain I made him. Be sure to tell him how long it took me to embroider his name into the warding pattern. And don't forget to ward it! *I doubt if I will* ever *live down the embarrassment of the time you handed over an unwarded key chain to Russell Crowe!*

"Mmm. What a shame. The C. J. Dante key chain was mysteriously left at home," I told the computer as I logged off and popped my sunglasses back on just in case I ran into anyone in the hallway. For a moment I just sat, exhausted, listening to the sounds of the hotel and the noise outside the window of London on a busy winter afternoon. Anton's message did nothing but add to my exhaustion. I had seen the handwriting on the wall for the last six months— "Produce or else" was his motto, and I was lamentably lacking in the proof department.

"This is it, Allie," I said aloud to the empty room. "Put up or shut up time, and I have to tell you, the job openings for an unproven Summoner are pretty slim."

My voice echoed in the room as I continued to sit and dwell on my grim future. It almost seemed like too much trouble to push myself out of the chair and haul my bag of tricks upstairs to the small corner room that had been allotted to me, but a glance at my watch got me up and heading to the bed that promised a few hours of much-needed blissful nothingness before I had to go off to a haunted inn and hunt ghosts.

*   *   *

The dream started even before I felt myself relax fully into sleep. It was dark, nighttime, the air damp and musty-smelling. I walked through an empty house, its walls stained with mold and age and unsavory things that my mind shied away from identifying, my footsteps echoing loudly as I moved from room to room, searching for something, a place, somewhere I was supposed to be. Small black shapes skittered just beyond my range of vision in every room I entered, faint, soft phantom noises trailing behind me like a wake. Mice, or something more disturbing? I wondered as I let my fingers trail over a dusty banister that led me downstairs into a dark pool of inky blackness. Fearless as I never was in real life, I pushed opened the door at the foot of the stairs and saw a man stretched out on a table.

A man? Even in my dream I modified that word. He was no mortal man; he was a god, a perfect specimen of masculinity created just for my pleasure. Long black hair spilled onto the table, a halo of ebony against the light wood. His eyes were open, dark, but not as dark as his hair, almost mahogany in color, rich with browns and reds and even a bit of gold flaring around the edges of his irises. The long, chiseled lines of his jaw and squared chin were still, as if he were sleeping, but his eyes followed me as I moved into the room. He was naked but for a piece of cloth covering his groin, his body striped with what looked to be hundreds of small cuts, blood dripping slowly from the wounds onto the floor beneath the table.

I approached him, wanting to touch his wounds, wanting to heal them, but his voice caught and held me in a net of immobility when he spoke my name.

"Allegra," he said, his eyes dark with torment. "Help me. You are my only hope."

I reached out to touch him, to push a lock of his hair off his forehead, to reassure him that whatever it was he needed, I would do, that I wouldn't let him suffer any longer. I would send him on to eternal rest. As my fingers touched his heated skin, I woke up, gasping for air, sitting bolt upright in the bed in my hotel room, shivering despite the fact that I had cranked up the heat just before I settled down for my nap.

"What the . . . Oh, no, now I'm dreaming in the daytime?" I reached for the carafe of water that I keep at my bedside. I've found that while water can't wash away the foul taste night terrors invariably leave in my mouth, keeping hydrated is an important part of limiting the length of my nightly trial.

Faint whispers of the dream stayed with me as I showered, brushed my teeth, and dressed in a pair of black wool pants and white silk blouse. I frowned at myself as I pinned my ordinary brown hair out of my eyes, and applied the minimal makeup needed to appear in public without frightening small children or the elderly. There were dark smudges under my eyes, making my skin look bruised.

"It's going to get a lot worse if I start dreaming during the day, too," I told my reflection. The Allie in the mirror didn't look any too happy at that thought. I knew how she felt—sleep was precious enough; if the only time I had to catch up on what I missed each night was taken from me, I'd be a walking zombie in just a couple of days.

I poked around the hotel room for a bit, tidying up my bag of tricks (the digital voice-activated recorder needed new batteries, a bottle of holy water had come loose from its cocoon of cotton and was banging up against the thermal-imaging video recorder, and the EMF (electromagnetic force) counter was almost out of its leather case, which would have scratched the front of the ion analyzer). I strapped the motion detectors down firmly, double-checked that the infrared nightscope was secure, and replaced the damaged ultrasonic emission detector with the updated version I'd bought that afternoon.

"Too bad none of this stuff seems to really work," I told the bag sadly. It declined to answer me. I plopped down on the floor beside it, glancing at the clock. There was still an hour to go before I had to head out.

"No time like the present, I suppose," I said as I plucked a thick piece of chalk from the bag. "It can't hurt to give it another shot. What's the sense in being put in a haunted hotel room if you don't get to see the ghost?"

Clearing my mind of everything but the vision of an open door, I traced a circle before me using the chalk. The circle would hold the ghost after I Summoned it, until I either Released it to its next existence, or grounded it into the here and now.

That was the theory, anyhow. I hadn't actually ever successfully Summoned a real ghost, although I did have a nasty run-in with a chill wind in a mansion on the Oregon coast that was supposed to be haunted by a timber baron. Still, as Anton was the first to tell me, a draft does not a ghost make, which left me more than a little desperate. My job with UPRA was at stake, and although I knew England was just teeming with spiritual activity, thus far the ghosties had chosen to stay away from me.

A bit jadedly I intoned the words traditionally used to Summon ghosts.

"It's not going to work," I told my toes as I finished the invocation. "It never works. I'm going to have to go home without one single successful Summoning under my belt, and that'll be the end of my short and less than brilliant career as a regional Summoner. Stupid English ghosts. You'd think the least they could do is to show up for an out-of-town visitor!"

I fingered the vial of dead man's ash that I brought with me just in case. Dead man's ash, for those of you who don't dabble in Summoning, is created by burning tree limbs that have fallen over a grave—there's no actual dead man in it, although I like the colorful name. A witch once told me she'd had great luck using dead man's ash, so I opened the bottle and sprinkled a little of the gray ash out onto my palm, repeated the words of the Summoning as I held it over the circle, then released it with the mental image of a door slowly opening to allow all of the possibilities.

The air within the circle shimmered a little. I squinted at it, waving away bits of ash that were wafting out of the circle and straight toward my nose. Was it just the ash, or was there something forming in the circle?

The air was definitely shimmering, although ever so faintly. I batted at a few more bits of ash that were drifting toward my face and wondered if I should sprinkle more dead man's ash. The air within the circle pearlized, gathering itself as if it wanted to form into something, but couldn't make up its mind just what that was.

I took in a deep breath preparatory to repeating the words of the Summoning, and ended up sneezing out a bit of ash that had made its way into my sensitive nose.

A small, disgruntled-looking three-legged gray-and-white cat stood in the circle, glaring at me with yellow eyes. My jaw hit the floor as I realized I could see right through the cat's hazy body to the bed behind it.

The skin along my arms and back tightened, the hair on my neck standing on end as I realized what I was looking at—a ghost! "I did it! I've Summoned a ghost! Oh, my God, I can't wait to tell them back at the office. You, little kitty, have just saved my job!"

I bounced up and down as I beamed at the cat. "My first ghost, my first real live ghost."

The cat twitched an ear at my voice, and sat down to lick its hindquarters.

"Well, okay, you're not alive, but you're a ghost! A ghost cat! Who'd have thought this room was haunted by a cat? This is *so cool!*"

I reached into the circle to see if I could feel any sensation around the cat, but it wavered and broke up like a bad TV picture.

"Oh, right, I can't break the circle unless I ground you first." I crawled over to my bag, rooting around in it until I found my notebook. "This is just so amazing! I can't believe I did it! A ghost! Anton is going to be pea green with jealousy. Okay, pussycat, just sit tight there and I'll ground you so you can leave the circle. Let's see . . . um . . . grounding, grounding . . . ah. Here we go."

The procedure to ground a Summoned spirit was pretty straightforward: Summoned beings were, by the very nature of Summoning, bound to the person who called them. Grounding them simply meant that they could not slip off to any other plane of existence without the Summoner first Releasing them.

"The forces of life shine strong within me," I told the cat. It looked unimpressed at my prose and continued to lick its rear end. "The power of death binds you to me. Until death overtakes life, you will heed my command. By my words, you are thus bound."

It was short and simple, not much to it at all, but as I spoke the words and traced protective symbols on my left hand and over my right eye, the figure of the cat slowly solidified until it looked like a translucent gray-scale picture of a cat licking its butt. I reached my hand into the circle, and was delighted to note that the cat's image didn't shimmer in the least. "At least I know the grounding works," I told it as my hand scooped through the cat's middle. Other than a slight tingling of my fingertips, the ghost cat felt like . . . well, air. Slightly tingly air.

"Pictures!" I shouted, scrabbling in the bag. I pulled out my digital camera and snapped my fingers a few times until the cat looked at me. Its ears flattened back at the flash, but I got a few shots before it stood up and hobbled off to investigate my shoes. "They are just *not* going to believe this back home," I mumbled as I looked at the back of the camera at the images I'd just taken. The cat was faint and a bit fuzzy, but clearly visible. I could have hugged it, I was so happy.

I was busy with the ion analyzer when the alarm on the clock went off. "Drat it all! Carlos will be waiting for me." I chewed my lip and looked back at the cat. It had limped over to a chair and curled up on a pillow, turning its back to me as I used every machine I had to record its presence. I wanted to stay and continue recording it, but it had taken me three months' worth of begging and pleading e-mails to arrange for a local representative of the Society for the Investigation of the Paranormal to show me one of the most haunted spots in London. I couldn't cancel.

I got to my feet and collected the lighter version of the dark glasses I wear during the day. A quick look in the mirror confirmed what I had known— my eyes hadn't changed during the miracle of the Summoning. I glanced one more time at the cat, but it was apparently sleeping. According to the rules of Summoning, it shouldn't be able to leave without my Releasing it, but maybe there was an expiration date or something that meant I had only a little time with it.

"Just stay put, kitty, and I'll be back as soon as I possibly can," I told it as I shoved my glasses on and grabbed my purse. The Do Not Disturb sign swung from the door handle as I closed the door and headed downstairs.

The guy slouched over a magazine at the reception desk was the evening clerk; I recognized him from the last couple of nights when I had slunk out of the hotel on my ghost-hunting missions.

"Hi. I'm in room one-fourteen. I'm going out for a bit; will you take any messages for me? Oh, and I left some equipment out, very fragile and expensive equipment, so I don't want anyone going into my room."

"Not a problem," the clerk said without even lifting his eyes from his magazine.

I hesitated a moment, then decided to throw caution to the wind. "Um . . . I've heard that the room I'm in is supposed to be haunted."

He looked up at that, frowning at my dark glasses.

"Eye condition," I told him with a wave at my face. "My eyes are . . . uh . . . sensitive."

"Oh."

"Do you happen to know anything about room one-fourteen? Who it's supposed to be haunted by, that is?"

His frown deepened. "If you'd like another room—"

"No, no, it's not that; the room is fine. I was just curious about the ghost that's supposed to haunt the room. I love history, you see, and thought there might be an interesting story connected to the room."

"Oh," he said again, his gaze slipping down to his magazine. "Supposed to be an old lady and her cat. Died in the room in a fire."

"The old lady or the cat?"

He shrugged and moistened a pudgy finger to turn the magazine page. "Both."

"Ah. When was that, do you know?"

He shot me an annoyed look. "What's it to you, then?"

It was my turn to shrug. "Just casual interest."

12

He eyed me suspiciously for a moment, then returned to the magazine. "I heard the old lady died sometime during World War Two. This hotel was blitzed. Everyone made it out but her and the cat."

Interesting. I wonder why my Summons drew only the cat and not the human ghost? Maybe I didn't use enough dead man's ash. Or perhaps I just didn't have enough strength to Summon a more complex spirit as a human. Former human.

I nodded my thanks to the desk clerk and limped off to find a cab. When you have one leg shorter than the other, riddled with scar tissue that has defied even the most dedicated of orthopedic surgeons, you hesitate to spend long hours on your feet, let alone walking anywhere that can easily be reached by a comfy cab. I used the short cab ride out to the building located near the Southwark Bridge to muse over whether or not the successful Summoning of a ghostly cat meant I'd have luck at the haunted inn.

"Maybe just a smidge more dead man's ash," I mused aloud before realizing the cabdriver was giving me a worried look in the mirror. I smiled in what I hoped was a suitably reassuring manner and kept the rest of my musings to myself.

Ten minutes later I limped around to the back of a tiny old building dwarfed by a nearby sports complex. About three hundred years ago the small building had been an inn, but had most recently been used as headquarters for a trendy decorating shop. Now it was empty, reportedly due to the unusual and unexplained "phenomena" that was connected with the inn's distant past. A thin man of medium height

13

stood shivering by the door, waving his flashlight at me as I hobbled up.

"There you are, thought you'd never come. I'm freezin' my arse off here!"

"Sorry. I take it you're Carlos?"

The man stomped his feet, nodding as he pulled out a key and unlocked the door. "I can only give you twenty minutes. There's a show everyone from SIP is going to, and it starts at ten."

"A show?" I asked as I followed him into the building, pulling the ultrasonic emission detector from my bag and flipping it on. "What sort of a show?"

Our footsteps echoed eerily as we walked down a corridor paved with broken flagstones, our breath little white clouds of air that puffed before us. I sniffed, then blew out a disgusted breath. The air was thick with stink from the nearby Thames—the whole building clearly suffered from damp, long fingers of mildew creeping up the wallpapered walls. In addition to the smell of a musty, closed-up building, the sharply acidic note of rodent droppings made it clear that although humans might shun it, four-legged residents found it an entirely suitable abode.

"It's not really a show, per se, more of a test for psychics. It's sponsored by a very powerful medium, Guarda White. She's holding nightly Summonings for a week, trying to assemble a group of proven psychics. Everyone in SIP is mad to try out for a spot on her team."

It sounded like a bunch of hooey to me. Dedicated Summoners did not perform in theaters for the amusement of the masses. Still, Carlos was my host. It probably was best I not ridicule his excitement.

"Why is she assembling a team of psychics?" I asked as we climbed a dark staircase. I had my own flashlight out now, my sunglasses pushed up as I alternated between scanning the ground in front of me for debris and checking the walls of the common room that stretched before us. The ultrasonic detector was quiet. I paused long enough to pop it back into the bag and pull out the ion detector before hurrying to catch up with Carlos.

". . . creating the greatest team of paranormal investigators that Britain has ever seen. It's all pure research, of course, the team being sent out to hot spots to locate and verify entities and disturbances. The team will be paid from a private fund set up by Mrs. White."

In other words, it was a pet project set up by another fan of the unexplained who likely had more money than brain cells. *Ah, well,* I thought to myself as we climbed to the top floor of the building, *her little group of devotees certainly can't hurt the cause, and might actually do some good if she uses scientific methods to obtain proof that would shake even the most skeptical of critics' arguments against the existence of ghosts, poltergeists, and other until-now unexplained phenomenon.*

"This is the top floor," Carlos said, the light from his flashlight sweeping in an arc around the area at the top of the stairs. "That room over there has had recorded temperature drops of ten degrees. The door at the end of the landing leads to the room where a pig farmer was murdered. He's seen only on nights with a full moon, so you probably won't have much luck there. Across the hall is the room where a vicar named Phillip Michaels was set upon by thieves, and left hanging. And to the left"—he turned and shone his light beyond me. I turned my face away. There was no need to scare him—"is the room where the Red Lady is seen."

"That's the one who jumped to her death rather than submit to her bridegroom?" I asked as I pulled out the infrared scope, juggling the ion detector, flashlight, and scope not too successfully as I headed to the left.

"That's the one."

I set my bag outside the door and took a reading at the door. There was nothing. Cautiously, so as not to scare any spirits who might be lurking within, I opened the door. It creaked open in suitably eerie fashion.

The room had a couple of broken pieces of office furniture and a strong smell of mice, but nothing that looked even remotely ghostly. One by one I checked my detectors and got no reading. Carlos stood in the doorway, shifting uncomfortably from foot to foot as I dictated a few notes on what I was seeing and feeling (cold, and a distinct aversion to mice) to my voice recorder.

I glanced at my watch and realized I had only seven minutes left to examine the rest of the building. I gnawed my lip for a minute, trying to decide what to do. I really didn't want to be left alone in the building, but I did want to try a Summoning after my success earlier this evening. The question was, how much did I want it? I took a deep breath and reminded myself that although I'd seen lots of strange things in my time—not the least of which was a three-legged semitransparent cat currently sleeping in my hotel room—at no time had I ever felt physically threatened. I was a Summoner, after all. I had wards. I was in control, and no one could take that from me. I traced a protection symbol in front of me and said, "Um . . . Carlos, why don't you go on to this séance thingy you want to see? I'll close up here when I'm done."

I peeked at him through the screen of my hair. He looked hesitant for as long as it took him to realize that the sooner he left, the sooner he'd be warm. "If you're sure you don't mind being here by yourself?" He looked around and only just suppressed a shudder.

"No, no problem. I don't mind these sorts of places. They're usually very peaceful." They were until I'd successfully Summoned my first ghost, that was. My palms prickled at the thought of what I might accomplish in a really haunted building like this. "If you just set the keys next to my bag, I'll lock up on my way out, and drop the keys by your office in the morning."

He hesitated for a moment. "You're sure?"

I swallowed hard and waved him away without looking at him. "Absolutely. I'm just going to try my hand at a spot of Summoning; then I'll check out the rest of the rooms. It's only the top floor that's supposed to be active, yes?"

"That's right."

"Okay, then, I'll check out these rooms, then toddle back to my hotel. Have a nice séance."

He was gone before the words left my lips. I sat quietly and listened to the sound of his footsteps as they retreated down the stairs, then the faint percussion of the back door closing behind him. I took an admittedly shaky breath, looking around the room. I was alone. By myself. In a building that was supposed to be one of the most haunted places in London.

Sometimes I'm not very bright.

An hour later I rose from where I had been kneeling in the room supposedly haunted by a murdered pig farmer. My leg was stiff and sore from sitting on hard wooden floors, my fingers were almost numb with cold despite my gloves, and I had lost all feeling in my nose.

"So much for one of London's most haunted buildings," I said sourly to the empty room as I gathered up my equipment and started for the stairs. The feeling of uneasiness that had first claimed me when Carlos left hadn't dissipated, but I haven't fought for control of my life to let a little thing like fear rule me. So even though the hair on the back of my neck was standing on end the entire time I checked out the upper rooms, I gritted my teeth and conducted four Summonings, none of which brought me anything more than a desire for a thermos of hot coffee and a really big piece of key lime pie.

"And there's no chance of either materializing in this place," I said aloud as I limped heavily down the stairs. My voice echoed strangely as it reached the second floor. I got a severe case of goose bumps, but nothing showed up on either of the two detectors I held, or on the more efficient scanner that made up my personal sensitivity to otherworldly happenings. I stopped at the bottom of the stairs and held my breath, opening myself up to the building, imagining myself slowly walking through the rooms. There was nothing on this floor that disturbed me, and nothing on the ground floor below it, but deeper in the earth, in the basement, there was a shadowed area that made me shiver uncontrollably. I couldn't penetrate the darkness to determine what was there, but I could feel its awareness, a sense of blackness that went beyond the mere absence of color.

Something soulless was down there.

And whatever it was, it knew I was here.

Chapter Two

"Okay, Allie, do not panic. This is exactly what you've been waiting for," I told myself as I fought to keep my feet from racing down the stairs and out the door. "This is what you studied for, what you swore you could do when Anton hired you. This is your job. Failure is not an option. You know what'll happen if you don't investigate this!"

Oh, I knew. Everything I'd worked the last seven years for, every bruise I'd suffered, every small success from learning to balance a checkbook to getting a job, every triumph over the monster who had dominated my life would be dismissed, eradicated, wiped out, and I'd be the failure that Timothy so often screamed I was. Not good for anything, too stupid to ever survive on my own.

A freak.

I lifted my head and squared my shoulders, holding my bag close to me as I slowly walked down the stairs. There was nothing on this earth that could frighten me as much as the life I had once been trapped in; if I was strong enough to leave an abusive husband, I was strong enough to face a little sentient darkness.

I held that thought until I started down the stairs to the basement. Then all sorts of warning bells and whistles went off in my head, not to mention the voice of sanity, which was screaming to hell with my honor; I needed to get out of there right then, before whatever was behind the door at the bottom of the stairs got me.

A cold wave of sheer and utter terror washed over me, stopping me dead on the middle of the stairs, my feet refusing to move anymore, my hand gripping the dusty banister in a manner that would take a crowbar to release it. I couldn't breathe, so oppressive was the blackness beyond the door. I couldn't swallow, I couldn't blink, and I seriously doubted if my heart was beating. A faint noise, a distant, soft, muffled beat from the room throbbed along the edge of my awareness.

"Heartbeat," I croaked through lips numb with fear, then instantly regretted the word as I felt the darkness beyond gathering itself, turning its attention to me. "Oh, crap," I whispered, torn between the need to escape, and the knowledge that I would fail my life's calling if I didn't confront what was in that room.

My heart suddenly resumed beating, racing now, making me dizzy with the sudden flow of blood to what passed for my brain. I was light-headed and disoriented, but suddenly the choice was made.

I would resist the urge to flee danger—it's a pow-erful instinct, and a difficult one to deny. I used my free hand to pry my fingers from the banister, and whimpered ever so softly as I shifted my legs until they took a step down.

"One," I counted in a voice so soft that even a feather hitting the ground would drown it out. I took another step down. "Two. Three left to go. Three. Two left."

My stomach roiled, making me regret drinking the water earlier. "Four. One more, Allie. You can do it."

My breath got caught up in a strange panting sort of rhythm, which I used to distract that part of my brain screaming at me to flee. I made it down the last step, and stood in front of the closed door.

I could feel whatever was beyond the door now, without even trying to open myself up to it. In fact, I did just the opposite, throwing up as many barriers between my mind and the thing as I could create. It didn't help much. Inside the room I could feel a howling wind of torment, anguish, pain so deep it had no beginning and no ending. And everywhere there was darkness, blackness, an absolute void of light. Hopelessness filled that room, and reminded me of the antique maps where cartographers had penned images of monstrous sea creatures with the notation that "Here be dragons."

Somehow I had a feeling that a dragon would be much easier to face.

I sketched protective wards around me to all four compass points, made a Herculean effort to calm my panic-stricken mind, and with one quick continuous move that didn't let me think, put my hand on the doorknob and threw the door open.

The light from my flashlight didn't seem to penetrate the darkness within at first; then the faint *pat pat pat* noise caught my attention, and I turned the light to the left side of the room.

The light glinted back from a wooden table. Lying on the table was a dark shape, a bulky dark shape, a human dark shape. Recognition suddenly filled my mind as I stepped forward hesitantly, then dropped my bag and raced into the room. It was the man from my dream, the man who'd suffered some horrible death. His ghost was here, trapped in this room, lying in eternal torment and suffering, waiting for someone—me—to release him from his earthly bondage.

"Oh, you poor thing," I said as I stood over him, clutching my hands. I wanted to touch him, but I knew that to break the spirit's cycle was not a good thing. Although his eyes weren't open, as they were in my dream, I knew he was aware of me. "Don't worry; I'm a professional. I'm going to help you, to send you on, so you'll be at peace at last. Oh, boy, that blood looks really realistic. You must have suffered terribly before you died. Just hold tight there, and let me get my book, and I'll take care of everything."

I hurried back to my bag and dug out my notepad, the chalk, and the powdered ginseng that a wizard friend of mine swore would be great in a Release. I stood over the body of the man, the faint *splat* of blood dripping from the table to the floor making the only noise. "Um . . . Releasing a spirit, Releasing a spirit, where is it, I know I—Oh, here it is." I tucked the flashlight under my chin and used one hand to open up the stopper on the ginseng, the other to trace a symbol of protection over the ghost. Poor man, he needed all the help he could get.

Plop, plop, plop went the drip of blood. *Sprinkle, sprinkle, sprinkle* went the ground ginseng over the ghost. *Tickle, tickle, tickle* went my nose.

"Go. Away."

I looked up from the notebook where I was reading the procedure to Release a ghost to stare at the man lying before me. Had he spoken, or was it my own overheated imagination that made me think he had? The ghost was lying as still as ever; not even his chest moved. I leaned closer and couldn't help but notice that the man I saw in my dream, the god, the perfect embodiment of masculinity, was nothing compared to him in the flesh.

So to speak.

Despite having every visible surface (and I had the worst urge to peek under the cloth draped over his crotch) mutilated by cuts, he was breathtakingly gorgeous. His skin was tanned and looked—other than the cuts—to be firm and invitingly touchable. The muscles that banded his chest and marched down his stomach were well defined without being too obvious. His arms, crossed over his belly, were covered in a fine dark hair that matched the hair on his chest. I skipped over the covered bits, and mourned that someone had so tortured such a delectable man. He clearly belonged to an age at least a hundred or so years in the past, if the thick muscles of his thighs—what my mother used to call horseman's thighs—were any indication. But it was his face that drew my attention, a strong face made up of harsh angles and a stubborn chin.

"You really must have been something before you were tortured," I said, my fingers itching to push back the lock of sable hair from his brow. His face alone was unmarked, and I wondered what horrible event had brought him to such an end. I tore my gaze from his lips—really, really nice lips—and reminded myself that it wasn't polite to ogle the ghosts.

"Must have been my imagination," I told him, then set the chalk down on the ground next to me so I could make the protection symbols as I spoke the words of Release.

"Go away. I don't want to be Released."

I dropped my notebook. "What? Who said that?"

I spun around, pulling the flashlight out from where it was clamped beneath my chin. "Carlos? Is that you?"

"Go away now."

I turned back to the ghost. The voice—low, beautiful, and smooth as silk floating on water—came from him. As I peered closer at him, one eyelid cracked open and a beautiful brown eye glared at me.

"Um," I said.

"Leave now," the ghost said, his words coming from his clenched jaw and thinned lips as a sibilant whisper.

"Don't worry," I said reassuringly, wishing like the dickens I could pat him. "I'm going to make sure this torment you've been caught in for so very long is ended."

The eye closed for a moment, then opened back

up. There was a strange quality to the iris that made me feel as if I were being captured in its mahogany depths. "Now. Leave now. Right now."

I nodded and bent to pick my notebook up. He was in a hurry to be Released. I didn't blame him one bit. If I were dripping blood all over the place, I'd be in a hurry too. "I'm going as quickly as I can. You just have to be patient for a couple of minutes longer; this is a bit new to me. I haven't had much practice doing this, and I don't want to mess something up and have you on my conscience. Oh, poop, now I've lost my place. Just a sec, I won't be a moment; then you can leave."

I flipped through the notebook, absently wiping on my leg the wet substance that coated the front of the notebook.

"If you do not remove yourself from my presence and this building in the next thirty seconds, your conscience will be the least of your worries."

He was looking at me with both eyes open now, glaring at me really, his hands clenched into fists on his belly, his body unnaturally—or rather, supernaturally—still. I dragged my mind from the wonder and joy that was his voice—a voice that had a delightfully sexy European accent—and back to more important matters.

Like his attitude.

"I beg your pardon?" I closed my notebook and rubbed my fingers together. The floor must have water seepage because the notebook was wet. "Now let's just get a few things straight here, shall we? I am here to help you. You are here to be helped. Copping an attitude is not going to do anything but tick me off and delay the aforementioned helping. So why don't you just lie there and be quiet, and I will get on with the Releasing, okay?"

The ghost's eyes rolled in a realistically annoyed fashion; then he rose up on one elbow and scowled at me. I stepped back, alarmed that he was too close to me, that if some part of his ethereal, albeit extremely solid-looking body touched me, it would break his cycle.

"I am trying to tell you to leave me. What is so hard to understand about that? Leave, I said, and all you do is nod and go on with your silly Release spell. I don't want you to Release me; I want you to leave. This building. *Now!*"

"You are a very rude ghost," I said, poking my notebook at him.

"I'm not a ghost."

I snorted. "You are, too. You're lying there dripping blood from some heinous torture you underwent before you died. I know a ghost when I see one, and you can take it from me, you're dead. Finished. A corpse. An ex-person."

Now the ghost was grinding his teeth. It was amazing the difference between a human ghost and the semitransparent cat. This man looked so real I had to fight a constant battle to keep my hands off him. "I'm going to say this once more. I am not a ghost. I do not need to be Released. I do not want your help. I *do* want you to leave me alone and go back to wherever you came from. Is that sufficiently clear?"

"I am a Summoner," I said with dignity.

"Brava. Go Summon elsewhere."

"I know ghosts. Okay, you might be the first fully

human ghost I've seen, but I know ghosts. Many times the deceased are confused about their status. The first thing they teach you in Summoning school is that not all ghosts are willing to admit they're dead. Clearly you're in that category. Now if you will just be quiet for three more minutes, I will finish the Release and you can go on your merry way."

The ghost leaped up off the table and stood glaring at me. I couldn't help but look at where the cloth had fallen from.

"Eep," I said, my eyes close to bugging out of my head.

He snarled something and grabbed the cloth from the floor, wrapping it around his hips. "By all the saints, will you just leave me in peace?" Oddly enough, that beautiful, silky voice didn't lose any of its charm even when it was bellowing at me.

I dislike being yelled at, however. It takes me back to the days when I was married and didn't have enough brains to know that I didn't have to take either the verbal or physical abuse. For that reason, I tend to be a bit snappish when someone starts lighting into me. "That's what I'm trying to do, give you peace, you stupid spook! Now lie down and shut up!"

I had dropped my notebook again when he leaped off the table, and bent down to pick it up, secretly amused by the stunned expression on the ghost's face. My amusement died when I picked up the notebook. It was sticky with wetness. I flipped it open and noticed that everywhere I touched I left red smears.

Smears of blood.

I stared at my hands for a second, then down at the floor where the ghost's blood had collected.

"What is . . . Is it ectoplasm?"

The ghost raised his hands to the heavens. "In all my years I have never been so plagued as I am at this moment! No, it is not ectoplasm!"

I touched a wet spot on my notebook, then looked at a cut on his chest that was slowly seeping blood. Hesitantly I reached out and pressed a finger against his flesh. It was warm, firm, and felt like the softest velvet over steel. I instantly wanted to touch more, much more.

Then I realized what it meant. I blinked. I swallowed. I cleared my throat. "You're not a ghost."

The nonghost seemed to be breathing hard, which made his wounds seep blood all that much faster.

"I am not a ghost," he acknowledged, his teeth still apparently doing the grinding thing. "I have told you that at least six times now—"

"Twice."

Breath hissed out his really nice lips. His eyes darkened until they were obsidian. His fingers clenched. "Twice what?"

"You said you weren't a ghost twice, not six times. Must be the blood loss making you a bit woozy."

Muscles in his chest rippled. I tried not to notice them, feeling it was rude to stare at such a magnificent—if bloody—chest when its owner was clearly in need of deep psychiatric and immediate medical care.

"I have never been spoken to as you have spoken to me."

"Is that so?"

"I do not like it," he continued, just as if I hadn't

said anything. "You will cease it immediately and leave."

"Leave. As in . . . now?" Clearly he wasn't thinking straight. It behooved me to try to calm him down before he did any more damage to himself.

"Yes, now," he answered me, a muscle in his jaw twitching. "You need to leave right now, before you ruin—" His lips clamped down on the words, cutting them off.

"Ruin what?" I couldn't help but ask. "I realize it's a bit nosy of me, but I don't often find naked men slowly bleeding to death in the basement of haunted inns. Call me silly, but I think you still need help. It can't be good for you to slice yourself up like that and then lie around in the damp and drip blood everywhere. I'm sure there are some very nice doctors who would be happy to take care of you—"

He said something in a language I didn't recognize, but which sounded suspiciously like it was swearing, then froze and looked at the doorway. There was a soft noise from the upper level that sounded a whole lot like someone had just closed the back door.

"*Peste,*" the man snarled, whirling around to leap back on the table. His voice deepened until it felt like the richest velvet brushing against my skin. "I command you to go now, without allowing the others to see you. You will forget everything you have seen here tonight."

"You know, I was married to an arrogant, domineering, tyrannical sort of man who thought he could control me. You can just take it as a given that the high-and-mighty act isn't going to cut any ice with me."

The man banged his head on the table twice. I winced for him. The table sounded awfully solid.

A faint echo of a voice reached me. I turned my back on the crazy man and rushed to the door. "Hello? Is there someone up there? Listen, I need some help down here. There's a guy who needs a doctor and . . . uh . . . a policeman. Hello?"

Hushed voices whispered to each other for a moment.

"You know, there's some really bad karma to be had from refusing to help someone when they're injured," I yelled up the stairs. "If you don't want to come down here and help me restrain this guy, the least you can do is call for—"

A hand wrapped itself around my mouth and pulled me backward against a warm, hard body.

"Now listen carefully," the man said in my ear, the silk of his voice doing all sorts of naughty things to me. "You will heed my words and do as I command."

It was the word *command* that did it. Ever since Timothy, I react badly to it. Without even the merest thought about the repercussions of my actions on an obviously insane and badly wounded man, I stomped my boot down on his bare foot and slammed my elbow back into his belly. He grunted in pain and doubled up as I lunged forward and raced up the stairs. I knew it was the sheerest folly to leave a lunatic with a bag full of expensive equipment, but I had no choice. Whoever he was waiting for, whoever had left without having the decency to help, clearly wasn't going to call the police or medical aid. I leaped up the stairs, ignoring the pain in my leg and the stitch that instantly formed in my side as I ran down the hallway to the door. I had remembered seeing a callbox down the block. I'd call for help, then sneak back into the inn and keep an eye on the poor, handsome, utterly deranged man.

It was raining—a cold, nasty, sleety type of rain— as I galloped awkwardly down the road to the call box. It took me three tries to dial 999, but at last I was connected with an emergency dispatcher. Two minutes later, having described where I was and what the problem was with the man, I headed back to the old inn at a slower pace, worried that my escape might have sent the poor man over the deep end.

I crept into the hallway and stood with my back to a moldy wall, keeping an eye on the stairs to the basement. It seemed like it was an hour before the sound of a police car siren Dopplered against the building, but according to my watch it was only eight and a half minutes. I greeted the two policemen, explained quickly what I had seen, and followed them down the stairs to the now closed door. They switched on powerful flashlights and cautiously opened the door.

The room was empty.

Not only was the room empty, the table was gone, and the pool of blood on the floor had vanished. My bag and piece of chalk and flashlight were still there, but everything else was gone.

"Wait a minute—I . . . There was . . . He was right here! How could he . . . And the blood, it was right there—that table must have weighed a ton! How could he have moved it so quickly?"

"Madam," said the smaller of the two policemen, shining his flashlight right on my face. I heard him gasp as I turned away so I was in profile. "Madam," he said again, his voice a bit shaky. "Are you aware of the fact that it is a crime to call the police out on a nonemergency situation?"

"But . . ." I looked around the room, keeping my head tipped so they couldn't see directly into my eyes. There was nothing here but an empty room, two cops, and my bag of tricks. "He was here! I swear to you, he was here! Bleeding all over the place, and naked as the day he was born."

The taller policeman took a deep breath. It didn't take any psychic abilities to know I was in for a lecture. I gathered up my things as they took turns telling me what happened to tourists who turned in false alarms. By the time I explained what I was doing there, reiterated that I wasn't given to phoning in prank calls, and heard their second round of lecturing, they hustled me upstairs. I was more than willing to believe that I'd had some sort of weird episode in the inn, something related to its spectral inhabitants, and imagined everything with the handsome, if troubled, man.

Until I reached in my bag to pull out the key to lock the door behind us. Then I saw my notebook.

There were bloody fingerprints all over it.

I spent the rest of the night writing up my experience, in between watching the ghost cat sleep, groom itself, and hobble around the room poking into things. It didn't seem to be thrilled to see me, and after trying unsuccessfully to convince it to lie on the bed next to me (so I could take a picture of the two of us together), I ended up more or less ignoring it as it ignored me.

By the time dawn lightened the gray layer of clouds enough to indicate it was morning, I was exhausted and cranky, unsure whether I had witnessed some amazing spectral encounter with a ghost that could manifest a physical presence, or if I was delusional.

I fell asleep wishing the former. At least then I could touch him.

"No messages, Miss Telford," Tina the receptionist said that afternoon as she handed me the room key. I waited to see if she had anything else to add, anything along the lines of a complaint about the three-legged semitransparent feline that was inhabiting my room, but she just smiled and turned to deal with another customer.

"Curiouser and curiouser," I said as I limped over to the elevator, my bag clinking and rattling. I shifted it to the other shoulder and wished I were in a line of work that didn't require so much equipment, equipment that had to be taken everywhere, just in case it was needed. My day trip to a haunted abbey turned out to be one of the times when it was nothing more than a heavy albatross hanging off one shoulder. I punched the number for my floor, and wondered if the Summoning had faded enough to let the cat return to its previous existence. Maybe the maid hadn't seen the cat because it was gone.

"Oh, hello, kitty," I said as I unlocked my door. It

was sitting on the windowsill, staring out the window. "I thought you'd gone. I'm glad to see you haven't, although . . ." I tugged on my lip. Between the tests I'd conducted early the evening before, and the ones I'd done during the dark hours of the night, I had about as much data as I could conceivably collect. Pictures, video, infrared and ultrasound readings, ion analysis, you name it, I had it, enough to give the analysts back at the office an orgasm. Perhaps it was time to Release the cat.

"You want to go home, kitty? I think it's time. I really don't want to have to explain to the housekeeping staff just what I've been up to in here, and although you really are the almost ideal pet—no shedding, no litter box odor, no finicky eating habits—I get the idea you aren't wild about being here either."

I laid out the necessary tools in front of me, and after sprinkling a bit of ginseng over the cat, started reciting the words of Release.

I had to stop midway through to pinch the bridge of my nose. The powdered ginseng was tickling my nose, making it scrunch up and my eyes water with the urge to sneeze. I waited until the urge passed, completed the Release chant, made the protection symbols, and unguarded my mind to envision Releasing the spirit to another plane of existence.

The cat twitched an ear at me and started licking its shoulder.

"Uh-oh." I gnawed on my lower lip and considered the cat. Maybe I didn't use enough ginseng? Or maybe my stopping in the middle of speaking the words threw it off. I'd try it again, this time taking care not to breathe in the ginseng.

As the last word of the Release left my lips, the cat moved on to licking its sole back leg.

"Poop. Something's not right here. I wonder if the ginseng wasn't fresh enough?"

I spent the next hour and a half trying variations on the Release, adding and subtracting amounts of ginseng, even adding a dollop of dead man's ash in case that was the secret ingredient to a successful Release.

Nothing worked.

I was starting to get a bit worried. I knew by the rules of Summoning that if I didn't Release the cat, it would be bound to me for all my days, and while it had managed to escape being seen by the maid, I couldn't count on it achieving that feat every day.

Not to mention how I was supposed to get it home to my apartment in northern California. I hated to think what I was going to have to write on the customs form: *One translucent feline, dead fifty-some-odd years. Vaccinations up-to-date.*

The alarm on my watch started pinging, signaling something I was supposed to do.

"Oh, that stupid book signing. Drat. It would have to be now, when I'm busy with something important."

I thought of brushing it off, but Corrine had begged and pleaded with me before I left for London to attend this book signing.

"Honestly, Cory and her vampire romances," I scoffed as I started repacking the bag. "So some hot-shot author has a book signing. Big deal. I have a job to do! But no, I have to go stand in line and wait for a smug author to sign a copy of a book she could get back home. I have to suck up and make nice just so he'll write something pleasant that she'll forget five minutes after she reads it. I have to spend my evening standing on my bad leg in a line that's sure to go for miles because Mr. I'm So Important Dante can't be bothered to do more than one book signing a year. Well, fine, just fine. Make me give up trying to Release my ghost cat. Boy, she's going to owe me for this!"

I finished tidying the bag, popped on my evening sunglasses, told the cat to behave itself, and headed out to find a taxi to Covent Garden. On the way there I ran over the mental list of who in the area I could consult about why the Release wasn't successful.

"Let's see . . . there's Carlos at SIP, but he's not a Summoner. There is that witch who Ras mentioned supposedly Summoned the ghost of Karl Marx, but I don't have her address, and besides, I'm not sure I want to hang out with someone who actually wanted to spend time with a dead Marx who wasn't Groucho. Um . . ." I tapped my lip, watching as the dark, damp streets of London passed by the rain-splattered window. "Oh! That hermit that the woman at the SIP office mentioned. That might be a possibility."

"SIP as in Society for the Investigation of the Paranormal?" the taxi driver asked me.

Rats. I was talking to myself out loud again. It's a habit that I can't seem to break myself of. I smiled at the driver and nodded, hoping he wasn't one of the religious fanatics who seemed to delight in lecturing me as to the sinful nature of my job. "Do you . . . um . . . know about them?"

"My wife and me go ghost hunting with them a couple of times a year. Just last August we spent the night in the Tower."

The Tower of London was said to be the most haunted spot in all of England. It was a paranormalist's version of Disneyland.

"Did you? See anything interesting?"

He shrugged. "Couple of orbs, a hand coming from the wall, and we felt one or two cold spots, but nothing we caught on film. You a Summoner?"

Normally I don't admit to my job to laypeople, but the driver seemed to be copacetic with the whole idea of ghosts and ghoulies, so I nodded again.

"Thought you might be. What's with the dark specs?"

I waited until he was stopped at a light and lifted the glasses to my forehead for a moment.

His eyes widened as he whistled. "That natural?"

I laughed a harsh, bitter little laugh. "It's nothing I want, believe you me."

He looked thoughtful for a moment. "I guess not. Must make for some odd looks, eh?"

And odder responses, responses like people screaming and dropping things, claims that I was doing it just to get attention, and worst of all, accusations that I was a freak.

The rest of the ride was conducted in silence. I looked out at London at night and wondered if my optician wasn't wrong—the last time I'd tried contacts, I'd managed to wear them almost a week before my eyes started ulcering. That had been over a year ago. Maybe now they could handle the contacts. . . .

As I left the taxi, the driver pushed a card into my hand. "In case you ever need a chauffeur to take you outside of London. I do that as well."

I thanked him and joined the throng of people streaming into the new bookstore.

"How many copies do you want?" a harried bookstore employee asked me a few minutes later as I shuffled forward in a line so long it was guaranteed to leave my leg aching.

"One of whichever is the latest book."

"One?" She looked me up and down as if I were an insect that had donned human clothing. "Just one? *One*?"

"Oh, you want more than one, dearie," the woman in line behind me said as she tugged my arm. "They're ever so good."

"I've never read them. I'm just doing this for a friend."

"Never read them!" The woman gasped as I accepted a hardback book from the store employee. "Never read them! Well, you just have to read them. Here, you, give this lady another copy. You'll love it, you truly will."

"No, thank you," I said as I pushed the second copy back to the employee. "One's fine. I'm sure they're very nice, but I'm not into this sort of book."

The woman's eyes narrowed. "What do you mean, *this sort of book*?" She shook the three copies she held at me. "These are beautiful books, wonderfully written and full of dark, brooding men and the women who save them!"

"And the sex is good, too," a woman behind her added.

The woman behind me nodded emphatically. "Just lovely love scenes, very creative and hot enough to melt your knickers. Here." She shoved a book into my hands. "You take this. Read it. You'll be a believer in no time. The way Dante writes . . . it's positively *unearthly*!"

I lifted my glasses just enough so she could get a good look at my eyes. "Trust me, I don't need to read a book to know what unearthly feels like."

She choked and hurriedly dropped her gaze from mine. I pushed my glasses back down and gently returned the book she'd shoved in my hands, turning around to face forward in the line. I hated calling attention to myself in that manner—my limp was enough to make people stare—but if there's anything I dislike, it's a rabid fan.

Those were my thoughts until the line slowly snaked its way down the rows of bookshelves, close enough for me to see the group of people gathered around a table situated in the middle of the store. Bodies shifted and moved in an intricate dance of color and pattern. I stood, bored, mentally drawing warding spells to protect me from overeager readers, until suddenly every hair on my arms stood up on end. The person directly at the front of the signing table shifted and moved far enough to the side that I could see the man who was sitting behind a stack of books, his head bent over a copy as he signed it.

Long, shoulder-length black hair had been pulled back into a ponytail, but a strand had escaped and framed one side of a hard jaw, a jaw that led down to a familiar squared chin. The man looked up at the person he was signing for and smiled. I staggered back as if I'd been punched in the stomach, literally feeling as if all the air had been sucked from the room.

It was the man I'd seen first in my dream, then later in the inn, the crazy man who had cut himself all over his really nummy body and then disappeared . . . or had that been a fantasy, nothing but the deranged ramblings of an overtired mind? I rubbed my forehead, unsure of whether that whole episode had been imagined, or if he was . . . My mind came up with a blank as to an explanation, if he really had been at the inn. No one could have cleaned up that room and gotten rid of the table in the ten minutes I was gone. No one human.

C. J. Dante, famed vampire author, the man who came to me in my dreams and begged me to help him. A tormented man, one whose anguish I could feel without even opening my mind up to him. A man who sliced himself up like a loaf of bread, then got testy when I tried to help him.

"Just who—or more to the point, *what* . . . is he?" I muttered to myself.

Unfortunately, I had no answer.

Chapter Three

As I saw it, I had two choices. I could either assume that the past evening spent in the presence of a mentally disturbed individual who thought nothing of inflicting horrible tortures upon himself was not real, something my mind dredged up for some purpose or other, or I could rip that black sweater from Dante's manly chest and look for healing cuts, calling loudly for the police and the nice guys in the white suits.

In the end I decided to take my cue from the man himself. If he recognized me, I'd know the episode was real. If he didn't, I'd know that I had the most vivid and realistic vision I could ever possibly imagine, one that had left red fingerprints all over my notebook.

As the line slowly crept forward, I kept myself hidden by the chunky woman in front of me, just in case

Dante spotted me and started making a scene. One of the store employees was escorting people to him, handing him the books to be signed, then making sure the fan was hustled off so the next one could take her spot. I looked behind me, then back to the front. Every single person in line was female. *Hmm.* I peeked around the shoulder of the woman in front of me and studied Dante. He was every bit as handsome as I remembered him, more so because he wasn't dripping blood everywhere.

"Some men look really, really good in black," I said without thinking. The woman in front of me turned and nodded her head emphatically. I gave her a cheesy smile in return. I felt something behind me, a sort of rippling in the air, and turned to see a tall, very pregnant woman waddle past the line of people waiting. She was accompanied by a short woman with one of those pretty heart-shaped faces that I had always secretly coveted. Both of them grinned and circled around behind the table to greet Dante. He stopped signing long enough to kiss both their hands, and speak with them for a few minutes before apologizing to the person who was waiting for her book.

So he has groupies, I told myself. *So what? You can't expect a man to go around looking like he does without having great huge hordes of women falling all over him. Means nothing to you, unless of course the slice-and-dice scene last night was real; then you have to do something about him before he starts cutting up others.*

I gnawed my lip and tried to decide what to do as the line snaked ever so surely forward, but in the end

I just kept myself hidden behind the chunky woman until I was next in line. The bookstore woman grabbed my book from me.

"Just signed, or inscribed to someone?"

"Um . . . inscribed, please. To Corrine. Two *R*s, one *N*."

The woman nodded and turned back to look at Dante as the chunky woman giggled and told him he was no better than he should be. He smiled and the bookstore woman handed him Corrine's book, leaning forward to give him the information. He bent over the book, writing with an elegant hand that reminded me of Victorian copperplate.

"I hope you enjoy the book," he said as he signed his name with a flourish, his voice as beautiful as I remembered it. It slid over my skin like silk, raising the hairs on my arms with the pure, rich tone. He looked up and smiled as he handed me the book, then froze like a pointer spotting a pheasant.

"Christian?" The pregnant woman looked between the two of us standing still as statues.

I stopped breathing. Even through my dark glasses I could feel the pull of his eyes. It was as if I were being sucked into them, teetering on the edge of an abyss.

"Christian?" The woman touched his arm.

Without being aware of it, I unguarded my mind and felt myself plunge down into the depths of his eyes, down into a blackness that surrounded me, filling me with grief and anguish and hopelessness without end. I was overwhelmed with his pain, filled with it, unable to catch my breath under its suffocating presence.

"Christian, are you okay?"

Desperately I tried to reguard my mind, bringing down as many mental barriers as I could to keep him from filling me with his torment.

"Who are you?" I asked in a whisper that was all I could manage after the experience of looking into his mind.

His eyes darkened.

"More important, who are *you*?" the shorter woman with the pretty face asked. She looked at me curiously, eyeing me from toes to nose before turning to Dante and whapping him on the shoulder. "I *told* you this was a good idea! See? We got her after only a half hour! Good. Now I can go home."

The bookstore woman nudged me, and when I didn't do anything but stare at the man in front of me—who, it should be noted, was staring right back at me, his eyes dark with mingled surprise and pain and no little amount of speculation—she took the book from his hand and shoved it at me, giving me a little push to get me going. I stumbled forward, unable to tear my gaze away from Dante's until the pregnant woman put a hand out and touched my shoulder.

"You're probably going to think this is very strange of me, but I wonder if I could talk to you for a few minutes?"

I blinked and dragged my gaze off Dante's tortured eyes to look at the woman standing next to me. She was a few inches taller than me, and had pleasant eyes and an aura of friendliness that I could feel without dropping my guards.

"Um . . ." I said, still feeling more than a little bit

dazed. I mentally shook my head and gathered my wits. Summoners were in control at all times. To be out of control was a dangerous thing; it opened the Summoner up to all sorts of horrible eventualities. I couldn't let a little thing like a meeting with . . . My eyes drifted back to where Dante was sitting. He was watching me even as the woman before him prattled on about how much she loved his books. I took a deep breath and turned back to the woman, who was also watching me closely. I had at least a thousand questions to ask about Dante; his groupies were likely to be a good place to start. "Sure, I can spare a few minutes."

The woman smiled, warmth glowing around her like a halo. "Good. Rox?"

"Right with you," the smaller woman said, grabbing my arm. "Let's go to the espresso stand. I don't know about anyone else, but I could sure use a latte right about now. It's hard work, hunting Beloveds."

I peeked at her out of the corner of my eye. She must have noticed, because she grinned and tugged me forward until I was frog-marched between the two of them, feeling like nothing so much as a prisoner being escorted to a cell.

The tall one stopped after a few steps and glanced down at my leg. "I'm sorry; I'll walk slower."

I shrugged off her concern and limped forward. "It's okay. My leg doesn't like it if I stand around too much."

"So what's with the shades?" the smaller woman asked as she walked next to me. "You got an eye condition or you just like to look cool?"

"Roxy! Don't be so rude! You'll have to forgive

46

her," the pregnant woman said as we stopped before the in-store latte stand. "She was dropped on her head when she was a baby. Several times, as a matter of fact. Two double tall skinny lattes, and . . . what would you like?"

"Americano," I said, wondering just what sort of man attracted such strange groupies. And was that his baby the tall one was carrying? More important, why did I want so much for it not to be his?

She gave the order. "And I'll take one of those lemon muffins, and that piece of pastry with the cherries on it, and . . . um . . . that mocha brownie." She turned to us. "Do either of you want anything?"

"You're going to explode if you eat all that," the smaller woman said with a pointed frown at the pregnant belly. I shook my head, then allowed myself to be herded over to a nearby table.

"I expect you're a bit curious about this," the tall one said, giving me a reassuring smile. "First off, I'm Joy, this is my friend Roxy, and you are . . . ?"

"Allie. Allegra Telford."

"You're American, too?"

"Yes." I squirmed a bit uncomfortably in my chair, wanting for some reason to go back to Dante so I could stare at him a bit more.

"Cool," Roxy said. "The big question, of course, is do you believe in vampires?"

"Roxy!"

She turned to her outraged friend. "What? It's important!"

"Yes, but you don't just blurt it out like that! You work up to these things cautiously, carefully. Most people get all weirded out if you start talking about vampires and Dark Ones and all that. You have to approach the subject with kid gloves. I'm sorry, Allie; she has no delicacy or tact."

Delicacy? About the paranormal? Around me? Laughter burbled up inside of me until I couldn't keep it in any longer. I whooped until my eyes streamed, forcing me to grab a napkin and mop up under my glasses. Both women stared at me as if I had a ghost of a three-legged cat standing on my head.

"Sorry, it just struck me funny. What you said. In answer to your questions, Roxy, yes, I have an eye condition, although it's not sensitivity, if that's what you were thinking. If you really want to see, I'll show you, but most people find my eyes . . . unnerving. And I'm not weirded out by stuff like vampires, Joy, although I have to admit I've never seen any proof that they exist. You don't happen to know what a Summoner is, by any chance?"

Both women shook their heads, then Roxy, on my left, leaned in close and squinted to see in behind my glasses. I rolled my eye toward her. "Ooooh, cool, you have really light eyes. What is that, gray? Silver? Yeah, it's a bit strange to have eyes the color of a full moon with a dark ring around the outer edge, but I don't see what's so unnerving about them."

Joy, on my other side, tipped her head to look in the right side of my glasses, then frowned. "She doesn't have light eyes, you idiot! They're kind of a hazely gold with patches of a darker brown. That's interesting how the color varies within your iris. Still, I have to agree with Rox—it's different, but hardly unnerving."

I sighed and made sure no one was near, then pulled my glasses off. Both women gasped.

"Oh, that is so totally cool! Your eyes are two different colors! Are those contacts?" Roxy asked, leaning close to peer at my eyes.

"No."

"You were born like that? Very cool!"

I couldn't help but smile at her. She was the only person I'd ever met who thought my eyes weren't creepy. "It's a condition called heterochromia irides. It's fairly rare, and most cases don't have the extreme variation in eye color that I have, but it's not, as some people believe, a sign that I'm marked by the devil."

"Well, of course not," Joy said. "Personally, I like the effect. It makes you look . . . unique."

I snorted. "Unique, that's a nice way of saying it. The silver eye would be bad enough by itself, but coupled with the dark eye . . ." I shrugged and put my glasses back on. "Most people get nervous around me when I'm not wearing my glasses."

Roxy peered in the side of my glasses again until Joy smacked her arm and told her to behave. "It's unusual, Allie, but not unnerving. Don't feel like you have to hide your eyes from us."

"So what's a Summoner?" Roxy changed the subject abruptly as the waitress brought our drinks and Joy's food.

I chewed on my lip for a moment. Something was bothering me; some vague sense of unease was growing. I took a long look at the two women next to me, but the feeling wasn't coming from them.

"A Summoner has the power to talk to ghosts." I turned my head to scan the people in the espresso area, my gaze moving beyond to the line of people visible waiting for Dante to sign their books. The line was smaller now, just twenty or so people left, but something nagged at me, pulled at my mind as if I were missing something important.

"Cool!" Roxy breathed. "And you're one? You can talk to ghosts? Do you use a Ouija board or something?"

"Wait a minute," Joy said, her brow furrowed as she tapped out a tattoo on the tabletop. "I think I read something about that in one of Christian's books . . . isn't a Summoner someone who can raise the dead?"

I gave the line one last worried look, then turned back to shake my head at Joy. "Not really, no. We can only call those spirits who are already present, tied to a location, not ones who have passed on to another existence. But once we call them, they stay bound to us until we release them. Summoners are used primarily in cases of hauntings that trouble the living, poltergeists and the like. The spirit is Summoned, then Released to move on to where they were meant to go."

"We? So you're a Summoner?" Roxy asked, her eyes big.

I nodded.

"Wow. Can anyone do it? I mean, is it a matter of just a few magic words and voilà, you got yourself the ghost of Great-Grandpa Joe?"

"Don't be so flippant, Roxy; this is a serious matter. If Allie is Christian's—" She stopped and gave me a toothy smile. "Well, regardless, I'm sure she is uniquely qualified to do what she's doing."

"Oh." Roxy eyed me. "Yeah. I see what you mean."

"I don't," I replied, looking from her to Joy. "I take it Christian is C. J. Dante?"

Both nodded at me.

"Would either of you happen to know if he's riddled with at least a hundred cuts on his torso, arms, and legs?"

As if they were in unison, both their mouths dropped open in surprise.

I sighed. "I'll take that as a no. Right. So what does Christian have to do with me, other than—" It was my turn to stop in the middle of sentence.

"Other than what?" Roxy asked, just as I knew she would. "Have you met him before? He never told us he met you, and I think he would, don't you, Joy?"

"Yes," she said, her dark eyes considering me as she munched on a lemon muffin. She licked crumbs from her lips and glanced at Roxy. "Christian is a very dear friend of ours. We promised last year to help him find . . . someone."

"Someone? Like a blind date?"

Roxy snorted.

"Not quite," Joy said, popping another piece of muffin in her mouth.

I didn't believe her. She was trying to match Christian up with someone; I could feel her concern about him. Still, that had nothing to do with me, nothing unless it turned out he really was in that inn last night, and then I had a few questions for him, questions like what on earth he was doing cutting himself up like that, and who were the people he was waiting for, and how did he get rid of everything so quickly without me seeing him. . . . Suddenly the word *vam-*

pire echoed in my head. I blinked. "He's a vampire?"

"Shhh!" both women shushed me, looking around to see if anyone was within hearing distance. Only one person was, and I unguarded my mind a moment to see if she believed what she heard. She didn't.

"You're kidding, right? I realize that he's a bit . . . well . . . intense, but a you-know-what?" They both looked back at me with serious, unblinking eyes. I shook my head, glancing again at the line before turning back to the two women next to me. "Ladies, the world of the supernatural is my business. I'm a Summoner; I work for an international organization that investigates paranormal activities in an attempt to prove and explain them. I know about ghosts, poltergeists, demons, both minor and major—"

"Demons?" Roxy asked. "You mean there are really such things as demons? Holy cow!" She turned to her friend. "Bet you five bucks our ninth grade algebra teacher was a demon."

Joy ignored the interruption. So did I. The feeling of doom was growing, creeping up on me, making me restless with the need to be doing something. I gnawed my lip for a moment, scanning everyone left in the book line, but without unguarding myself—something I didn't want to do with Christian sitting over there thinking who knew what—I couldn't pinpoint the source of my concern. I took a deep breath and returned to what I was saying. "I know witches and wizards, have sat in a Wiccan circle, and seen things that would make most people pee their pants."

"So've we," Roxy said with a grin. Joy frowned at her.

"But I've never, ever seen a vampire. Nor have I ever heard of anyone mention seeing one. There are just some things like were-whatevers and vampires and the Loch Ness Monster that have more basis in myth than reality. I realize your friend is a bit unusual, and heaven only knows what he's told you, but I can assure you that he's not . . ."

The skin on my back tightened uncomfortably as my head was flooded with strong emotion. I jumped up from the table and ran toward the line of people, my leg stiff and sore and slowing me down so I didn't think I was going to make it in time. I saw the gun even before Christian did, and shouted out a warning. The bookstore employee standing next to the customer grabbed her, turning her so that the gun was pointed away from Christian . . . directly at me.

I tried to make my body move sideways down one of the aisles, tried to stop my headlong rush right at the madwoman who had intended to shoot Christian, but I was too slow. Her finger tightened on the trigger even as the bookstore employee struggled with her. Just before the bullet exploded through me, there was a rush of air, and suddenly I was lying on my back in an aisle between two rows of bookshelves, my breath knocked out by the heavy body lying on top of me. I blinked and stared up into the eyes peering down at me.

"You have mismatched eyes," Christian said, almost against my lips. "You have the Sight."

I was suddenly filled with the overwhelming desire to tip my chin up enough to taste his mouth, but instead I pulled a hand free and felt my face. My glasses had been knocked off when I was pushed aside.

"How did you do that?" I asked, extremely aware of his body resting against mine. His hair had come loose from its ponytail, flowing around our heads like a silken curtain. "How did you move faster than a bullet? Your name isn't really Clark Kent, is it?"

He frowned. All sorts of spots on my body started tingling, especially the parts of me that were pressed against parts of him. "I believe a better question is how long you knew that woman was intending to shoot me?"

"Oh, my God, are you two all right?" It was Joy, standing at our feet.

"Are you implying I had something to do with that?" I ignored her question to ask him. "Because if you are, you can just think again. In case you've forgotten, I tried to help you."

His eyes narrowed. "The store manager would have noticed the woman in time, even without you yelling in such a very convenient manner."

"Christian? Allie? Are either of you hurt?"

"Oh! I like that! I go out of my way to save you—twice—and you act like it's all my fault. What an ingrate!"

"Twice? Ingrate?" His breath fanned out over my face, combining with that smooth voice to drive me nigh on mad with the desire to grab his head and kiss him despite the horrible things his delectable lips were uttering.

"You seem to be talking, so I'm going to assume you're both all right, but really, Christian, it might be better if you were to help Allie up. There's a bit of a crowd gathering."

"Twice," I said with emphasis, ignoring the fires starting all over my body at his touch. "The first time was last night, when you were bleeding all over the place, making me think you were a ghost."

"I never made you think—"

"Are they okay? What are they doing? Why is Christian lying on Allie?"

"Ha!" His eyes darkened from mahogany to ebony at my snort of disbelief. "I'd like to know what else you'd think if you came across a man bleeding to death in the basement of a haunted inn. Which reminds me, just what *were* you doing there?"

"I think they're arguing about something. Allie doesn't seem to be too happy about something Christian said."

"Oh. It looks to me like he's going to kiss her."

"All I am at liberty to say is that you quite successfully ruined my plan; you'll have to be content with that," he said, looking at me for a moment. His eyes, already black as night, darkened even more; then his mouth touched mine for a brief, brief, way too brief moment before he pulled himself away from me. All of the flames his nearness had started inside my traitorous innards turned into an inferno at his featherlight kiss, which made me more than a little surprised at finding my body whole and complete, if sprawled out in an ungainly manner. Christian rose and offered me his hand.

"See? I was right. He did kiss her."

I ignored Roxy to frown at Christian. What did he mean, I ruined his plan? What sort of a plan involved him slicing himself up and lying around in a damp basement? And come to think of it, what did he mean by saying I warned him in a convenient manner? Was he implying I was an accomplice to the woman with the gun, and just trying to make myself look innocent?

My frown turned to a red-hot glare as I ignored his hand to get (painfully and with less grace than I would have liked with an audience) to my feet. I heard a couple of familiar gasps of horror, and started searching the ground for my glasses.

"Here," Roxy said, pushing them into my hands. "They were at Joy's feet, but she can't bend down anymore."

I popped them on. The world retreated to a darkened, familiar place that made me feel protected. Which is surely an odd feeling for someone who was just pushed out of the path of a fired bullet.

Joy, who had been speaking in a low voice to Christian, turned and took my hands in hers. "Are you all right, Allie? Christian didn't hurt you?"

"I saved her life," he protested.

"And I saved yours," I snapped. What sort of a person did he think I was? Clearly the man had some trust issues.

"That is a subject open to debate," he said as he brushed himself off.

The nonchalant way he treated me rubbed me the wrong way. All I can say is that the combination of pain from my leg, and a smug, arrogant man pushed me beyond what was polite and accepted in such a situation.

I put my hands on my hips and upped the wattage

in my glare. "You really are obnoxious, you know that? I can't think of one other man who wouldn't be on his knees in gratitude for having someone care enough to save him, but you have to twist it all around and make snide insinuations instead of being thankful I took the time to save your rotten life."

"My life would have been entirely safe without your meddling," Christian said in a low, beautiful tone that I swore I could feel slipping along my skin.

"They're arguing," Roxy said to Joy.

"Fine," I said, poking him in the chest. "The next time someone tries to kill you, I'll just let them, shall I? Then I can wait until you're dead and Summon you to make your apologies. And trust me, you're going to be apologizing for a very long time!"

Christian took a step closer to me, his jaw tight. "You are not at all the type of woman I like. You are aggressive and independent, and you seem to feel it is your right to insult me without cause."

"They aren't supposed to be arguing, are they?"

I snapped my fingers and waved away his comments. "As if I care what sort of woman you like. And you're damn right I'm aggressive and independent, and if the insult fits, wear it."

"I mean, that's not right, is it? Them fighting like this? Isn't it against the rules?"

"I don't know," Joy said, her eyes worried. "I thought it would have been impossible, but . . . maybe we're mistaken."

Christian glanced at Joy, snarled something I was sure was rude in what sounded like German, then stalked off. The police rolled in at that moment, pushing the chaos of the store up several levels. I had to describe what happened to three different police-men, skating carefully around the question of how I knew the woman had a gun and was intending to kill Christian when I was seated more than thirty feet away with my back to the signing table.

I couldn't keep from looking for Christian, no matter how hard I tried to ignore him. Most of the time I found he was watching me, but once I saw him arguing quietly but vehemently with Joy. She gestured in my direction and said something to him that he didn't like. He shook his head repeatedly, making gestures of denial with his hands. Finally he snapped something at her and turned on his heel, storming away from her. From the look of surprise on her face, I guessed he wasn't normally that rude.

To her. Me, he all but accused of being a partner in crime with the gun-toting woman. Not to mention messing up some suspicious plan that involved carving himself up for who knew what reason. Maybe he was into some strange blood-sport sex cult. He certainly was sexy enough for five men; I wouldn't put it past him at all to be the sort of domineering, assured, self-centered man who loved to have women fawning all over him. Men! If I weren't so partial to them—sometimes, under certain circumstances—I'd give them up completely.

By the time the police were through interrogating everyone who witnessed what happened, I was exhausted. I could barely stand; my leg felt like someone had used it as a knife-throwing target, even after a nice policewoman got me a chair. I got to my feet and staggered a step before I got my leg under control. Christian's head whipped around from where he was talking to the officer in charge; his eyes narrowed and became almost black. I bared my teeth at him in what I hoped passed for a reasonably polite smile, and limped toward the door. I felt his gaze burning me every step of the way.

"Allie! Wait a minute; I'm not as fast on my feet as I used to be."

"You were never fast on your feet. Admit it, Joy, you're an Amazon. A fat Amazon."

"I'm pregnant, you annoying short person. I'm allowed to be fat." Joy puffed her way up to me and held out a card. "Come for tea tomorrow. We have a lot to talk about."

I looked over her shoulder to where Christian was still watching me with a narrow-eyed glare. "Thanks, but no, thanks. I don't think your friend there likes me overly much."

Joy tipped her head to one side while Roxy grinned.

"Christian won't be there. He's never up that early. It'll be just us three. And possibly Raphael."

"That's her fiancé," Roxy added helpfully.

I couldn't help but glance at Joy's very pregnant stomach.

Roxy shot her friend a pointed look. "I *told* you that you guys should have gotten married as soon as you knew you were preggers. What that poor child is going to have to go through if you don't tie the knot in time. . . ."

"Come to tea, please," Joy said, exuding warmth and happiness that slipped past all my guards. I hesitated, then took the card. Joy's smile grew wider.

"You think we should tell her about the steps?" Roxy asked Joy.

"Steps? I prefer elevators, thank you. Easier on the legs."

Joy looked thoughtful. "I hadn't thought of that, but you're right. Christian just completed the second step. If that doesn't convince him, nothing will. Now he *has* to believe me."

"What sort of step? Convince him of what? Believe what? Why do I feel like you guys are talking about Eskimos, and I'm trying to explain how to make fudge?"

Roxy nudged me with her elbow. "You're going to love the third step. Trust me on this."

"Third step of what?" I asked them both.

Joy rubbed the small of her back, grimacing as she did so. "We'll tell you about it tomorrow. Four o'clock. We have lots to talk about."

I had a feeling that was going to prove to be the understatement of the year.

Chapter Four

By the time I made it back to my hotel room, it was too late to call the SIP offices and try to get the name and address of the hermit (man or woman, I wasn't sure which) I thought might be able to help me with my Release problem. I took a long bath instead, soaking my leg until I was all pruney, then got into a pair of soft sleeping shorts and a T-shirt, wrapping myself up in an oversize lumpy green bathrobe. With my scarred leg and odd eyes and decidedly frumpy nightwear I might not be a fashion plate, but I was certainly comfortable.

"Well, Mr. Kitty, it looks like it's just you and me again tonight. I hope you do your disappearing act tomorrow when the maid comes in. I'll send you on as soon as I can, but don't hold your breath until then. I need to talk to that hermit first."

I spent some time writing up notes on the evening's events, then pulled on my sweatpants and shirt to pop downstairs to leave Corrine an e-mail saying I had her book and would bring it home with me. That done, I hung around the lounge for a bit, but eventually the strange looks I was getting (sweatpants and sunglasses were evidently not considered haute couture) were enough to send me back up to the privacy of my room.

"I see privacy is a relative term in London," I commented as I closed the door behind me. Christian was in possession of the sole comfortable armchair in the room, his legs crossed with casual elegance, the fingers of one hand rubbing his chin as he watched the three-legged cat roll on its back and bat with ineffectual paws at the fringe of the bedspread. "How did you get in here, what do you think you're doing, what was your little game last night, who were those people who ran off, how dare you think I knew anything about that madwoman with the gun, and are you or are you not a vampire?"

Sleek sable eyebrows pulled together as he rose gracefully to his feet and made an exquisite bow. "I don't believe we've been formally introduced. I am Christian Johann Dante. Your name is . . ." He frowned. "Allie?"

"It is. It's short for Allegra."

"Ah. I dislike diminutives; they are so common. I will use Allegra."

My hackles went up instantly. I crossed the room to snag the wooden seat sitting before the dressing table, hauling it into a position from which I could more effectively glare at him. "Is that so? Well for your information, Mr. Stuck-up, my twin brother gave me that nickname. My brother who died eighteen years later in the same accident that crippled my right leg. So you'll have to pardon me if I don't find it at all common."

He stood watching me for a moment until I made an annoyed sound and told him to sit down.

"I am sorry that you lost your brother. I, too, lost a dearly loved brother in my youth. It took me many years to forgive myself for living when he died."

I glanced up at him, startled that he felt the same way about his brother's death that I did when Leslie died.

"Tell me of this accident. How old were you when it occurred?"

I slammed the guards on my mind down tight against the gentle probes I could feel him sending out. No one played in my head without an invitation. "Why don't you try answering a few questions before you start asking them? Namely, how did you get in here?"

He shrugged, an elegant move that matched all of his other elegant moves. Even though he was dressed in a simple black sweater with simple black pants, I had the strangest sense that I wasn't seeing him as he really was—he should be dressed in silk shirts with ruffled fronts and lace on the cuffs, I thought, with those colorful vests that men wore a couple hundred years ago, and tight breeches and boots that reached to his knees. And a riding crop—he looked very much like a riding crop kind of guy.

"I wished to speak with you. I had no idea that your room was already occupied." This he said looking at the cat, now engaged in licking its belly, "or that you would find my presence so objectionable. I felt that after the evening's deplorable event we had some unfinished business to settle."

"Uh-huh," I said, not in the least bit convinced. "Unfinished business like just what were you doing last night? And how did you get out of there so quickly? Wait a minute—answer my last question first: Are you a vampire?"

His eyes glittered mahogany and gold at me, but other than the slight incline of one eyebrow, he didn't look at all perturbed to be having this conversation. "I am Moravian, what is commonly referred to as a Dark One."

Well, that was a big help. "So you're a vampire?"

His fingers made an elegant gesture that left the question unanswered.

"Okay, let's try this: Do you drink people's blood to survive?"

He sat extremely still. "Yes," he finally answered, the velvet of his voice giving the word a power I'd never felt before.

"Are you immortal?"

Again the hesitation. "I can be killed."

"Most living beings can. Let me rephrase that—what year were you born?"

His gaze never left my face. "In the year of our Lord eleven hundred and twelve."

I did a bit of quick mental subtraction. "That sounds pretty immortal to me. Do you burn to a crisp in the light of the sun?"

A slight smile played around on the corners of his lips. I suddenly wanted to be that smile. "Burn to a crisp? No, but I do not find sunlight particularly healthy."

"Fine. So you"—I ticked the items off on my fingers—"drink blood to survive, are more or less immortal, and avoid sunlight. Well, you know, that sounds like a vampire to me!"

"Dark Ones are frequently referred to as vampires," he allowed.

"I hear a 'but' in there."

The smile grew, making me feel a bit too warm in my comfy sweats. "The mythology of vampires and the history of Dark Ones is similar, but not identical."

"Oh. So you're like, what, a benign vampire? A quasi-vampire? Vamp light? Do you go around doing good deeds? Or are you merely a vampire with a really big chip on his shoulder who likes to push people around and slice himself up for fun and profit?"

He actually had the nerve to look martyred at my words. "You are the most irreverent woman I have ever met."

"And you're changing the subject."

"I shall do so again: Why do you have the spirit of a cat in your hotel room?"

"Can you think of a better place to keep it?" I asked, then immediately regretted the retort. "This room is supposed to be haunted. I was trying to Summon the ghost who resides here, and got her cat instead."

"Is that what you were doing last night at the old inn?"

"You haven't finished answering *my* questions."

"I believe a conversation is traditionally made up of give and take. I have given; now I expect to take."

It was the way he said it that made me feel both

extremely turned on and furious at his high-handed arrogance. I stood up and fisted my hands on my hips. "Yes, I was at the inn last night to Summon ghosts. It's what I do, I'm a Summoner. I didn't have any success, if that is your next question. This cat is the sum total of all the ghosts I've managed to Summon, so I'll thank you to be a bit nicer about him. He may not be great, but he's all I have. And besides, I've tried to send him on, but something's screwed up in my Release invocation."

He smiled again, and once again my body (pro-Christian) warred with my mind (definitely anti-Christian). "So you couldn't have Released me last night had I been a soul in torment?"

I threw my hands up, then let them fall to my hips. "How do I know? I haven't tried to Release a human spirit! Now, I've given; it's your turn again. What were you doing there last night?"

The smile faded as he got to his feet, taking two steps until he was close enough to me that I could feel the heat from his body. He pulled my dark glasses from my face, examining first one eye, then the other; then his finger traced the line of my jaw. I wanted to pull back, to move away from the strange attraction that he held for me, but I couldn't. His eyes were warm and dark on mine, his finger stirring little frissons of fire down my neck, blossoming out to every conceivable part of my body.

"Joy believes you are my Beloved, the woman who is meant to spend her life with me."

"Oh," I breathed, not wanting him to stop touching me, but not allowing myself to fall under his spell. I knew what it was to give power over oneself to a man; I'd never make that mistake again. With an effort, I stepped back. His eyes were shuttered as he dropped his hand.

"I think Joy has the wrong woman."

He looked at me strangely for a moment, then nodded. "I believe you are correct. I would know my Beloved the moment I saw her, and she likewise, yet I have no awareness of you unless I am in your presence. I fear I must disappoint Joy with the truth."

"I'm sure she'll recover," I said, my voice a bit hoarse. "I know I will strive to."

The half smile reappeared on his lips again; then suddenly I was in his arms, pressed up against his chest, his thighs hard against my legs. "Then it cannot matter if we put the question to a brief test, can it?" he asked just before his mouth swooped down to capture mine.

I will say one thing for the man: living more than nine hundred years had taught him how to kiss. His lips started out all hard and domineering, then suddenly turned soft. His tongue probed, then slid in, doing things I'd never imagined a tongue could do. I let him kiss me for about a minute before he pulled away enough to speak without his tongue in my mouth.

"You are not helping?"

"Give the man a cigar."

He pulled away even farther so he could glare into my eyes better. "You are attracted to me; I can feel it. You enjoy looking at me. Your heart rate speeds up when I am near you, yet you do not allow yourself to take pleasure in a simple kiss?"

"Look, Romeo, I'm attracted to a lot of men, that

doesn't mean anything other than that I have a healthy libido. And I doubt if anything, even a kiss, is simple where you're concerned."

He looked oddly pleased with that statement. "We will try it again, and this time you will join in."

I stepped back. "Thanks, but I think you've checked my teeth aplenty tonight."

His eyes turned ebony.

"Oh, stop doing that, you big show-off!" I pushed him back and went to get a few tools from my bag. If I was going to have to entertain a vampire in my hotel room, the least I could do was take some readings on him.

That was what I told myself. My brain, however, knew that I needed to put some physical distance between us before I threw myself on him and kissed the fangs right out of his head.

When I turned back to him he was leaning against the wall, one long finger rubbing against the lovely curve of his lower lip. My mind rebelled for a moment and flashed glorious Technicolor, wide-screen memories of what it felt like to have those lips caressing mine. I told my mental projectionist to take the evening off, and started checking out Christian's ion levels.

"Why do you wear the clothing of a man?"

I ignored the question and switched on the thermal-imaging recorder.

"I do not want my woman to ape masculine habits. Women should be feminine, soft, giving. It is your role in life, yet you are none of those things."

"Which is probably why it's a good thing I'm not your woman," I answered, giving more orders to my mind to stop imagining what it would be like to be with him. He might be sexy as hell, but he was also domineering and arrogant, two traits that can be very dangerous.

"I said that you were not my Beloved; I said nothing about you *not* being my woman."

I shivered at the undertone of dark promise in his voice. I thought I remembered reading somewhere that vampires could seduce with their voices alone—of that I had no doubt. I clicked on the digital voice recorder. Maybe someone back at the UPRA offices could analyze his voice and see what made it so beautiful and evocative. "So were you born this way, or did another vampire snack on you and turn you?"

"You are also too independent and obstinate, and you lack self-confidence."

I ground my teeth and turned on the EMF counter, making notes of the readings. I would not let him goad me into—*Hey!* I squinted my eyes at him in the meanest possible manner. "Obstinate? Lacking self-confidence? Well, aren't you just full of the insults?"

"They are not insults, just statements."

"Fine, well, let's try on a few more for size, shall we?" I set down the EMF counter and limped over to him, poking a finger into his chest. He captured my hand with his, refusing to let it go. I ignored the wonderful things his touch did to me, and let him have it with both barrels. "For your information, Dracula, women have been emancipated. We can think on our own, make our own choices, and even—heaven forbid!—live our lives in comfort and happiness without any know-it-all males telling us what to do. Furthermore, I am a Summoner. It goes with the territory that my mind is strong. Strong is *not* obstinate. And as for self-confidence, I'm very confident in myself and my abilities. Just because I haven't had a lot of success Summoning doesn't mean that I can't do it. I can, I know I can, but it's not an exact science and there's a lot of elements that come into play when you're dealing with ghosts."

"I wasn't speaking of your self-confidence relating to your skills; I was referring to the fact that you find your appearance lacking."

"There's nothing I can do about my appearance," I snapped. "I'm well aware of my shortcomings, if that's what you mean. I don't consider dealing with what I've got as best I can as expressing a lack of self-confidence."

"You hide your very feminine body behind the cover of shapeless male clothing just as you hide your eyes behind dark glasses."

"I wear pants because they're a heck of a lot more comfortable when crawling around haunted houses than a skirt and heels. I wear dark glasses because being called a freak gets a bit wearisome after the fiftieth time. Any more questions, Sherlock? Or can I get on with taking a few readings?"

"You hide your attraction to me behind denial."

I grinned and checked him for any ultrasonic emissions. "Oh, so now we get to the truth of your complaints. You're just pissed because I didn't respond to your kiss. Your smug masculine pride has been hurt. Poor little Christian, used to swooning maidens whenever you lay a lip on them, is that it? I guess the real test of a man's attraction comes down to what he can do *without* the enhancement of a little mental push to aid a seduction, eh?"

In hindsight, I saw that baiting him was not the wisest course of action. Lesson to the smart: Never challenge a vampire's masculinity unless you're made of marble, or are dead. You just can't win.

He was on me before I could take a breath, my body slammed up hard against his, his arms immovable and impossibly hard behind me. But it wasn't his arms that worried me; it was the look of determination in his beautiful (now a rich walnut) eyes.

"You are impossible," he said against my mouth, his body quickly becoming aroused. Mine answered the call despite my sending out the fire department to extinguish all the delightfully tingly fires he started. "You mock me, you abuse me, you do not respect the power that I hold, and yet you make me feel things I've not felt for centuries."

For a moment he slipped into my mind, and I felt myself go soft against him at the recognition of his need. I hadn't forgotten the torment I'd felt both in the dream about him and in the inn, but I had assumed it was greatly exaggerated in my mind. Now I knew it wasn't; Christian was a deep well of desperate need, the need for the purity of love to salvage his soul, to pull him from the abyss of anguish and despair that filled him. I closed him out of my mind more as a self-preservation tactic than anything else, and rallied my strength to resist the lure of his lips just as his mouth closed on mine.

This time there was no softness in him. He was all dominance, quickly overpowering any resistance I had until I had no choice but to allow him into my mouth. He was consuming me, overwhelming me, and I knew in a desperate part of my mind that if I didn't do something, he would take everything I had and leave me empty, drained, a shell of what I had been. Struggling was not an option, nor was I sure I could. Even as I feared his control, pleasure burned bright in every touch of his lips and tongue. Instinct saved me, instinct and the desire I felt that he would not allow me to deny. I melted against him, tempering his hard body with my softness, feeding his power with my own. Miraculously the kiss changed from dominance to something erotic, a joining of our desires that quickly went beyond a mere touching of mouths. Without even thinking, I took his pain into my body and returned it with warmth.

He tore his mouth from mine, suddenly releasing me.

I swayed against him for a minute, then regained control of my body. "All right," I said, turning away so I wouldn't have to see the triumph in his eyes. "You've made your point. You're the world's champion kisser. Fine. I'll have a plaque made up in the morning. Now will you just leave me be? I have work to do."

I gathered the necessities and eased myself down on the floor. The cat was curled up underneath the armchair, sleeping. Christian remained silent as I traced a circle with chalk. I finally gave in and glanced at him. He stood watching me, the expected look of triumph strangely absent from his eyes. Instead he looked almost . . . vulnerable. I quickly returned my gaze to the circle. An arrogant, dominant Christian I could deal with. One that looked as shaken as I felt by our kiss was a beast of a different color. I ached, I positively ached to comfort him, to take him into my arms and kiss that look of sorrow and pain from his face, but I knew well how a man of his domineering mien would react to such a gesture—he would take my heartfelt offer and twist it into a way to control me. *Never again*, I vowed, and traced the wards of protection on my left hand and over my right eye.

"What are you doing?"

His voice skimmed my skin like a sultry breeze. I reinforced the circle, worried that his presence had distracted me enough to leave the circle open (and thus useless). "I'm a Summoner; hence, I'm Summoning."

"Why?"

Evidently he had recovered from our kiss. I hadn't. I was still quivering inside, but not so much that I couldn't slide him an annoyed look. "It's what Summoners do. If I'm boring you, feel free to leave."

He leaned back against the wall again. "My questions was not why do you Summon, but why are you doing it now? I thought you tried earlier and only raised the cat?"

I thought about saying something about persistence and not giving up, then figured he'd turn that against me by crowing over the effect he had on me. Instead I opened up the dead man's ash and tried to clear my mind. "I'll continue to try to Summon the human ghost until I have to go home."

Before he could speak I said the words of Summoning, opening the door in my mind to all possibilities, sprinkling the ash liberally over the circle. As before it floated all over, some in the circle, other bits drawn by my warmth to float around my face.

"That looks rather messy. Isn't there a more efficient way to Summon a spirit?"

"Comments from the undead are entirely optional," I told him as I waved away the ash, peering into the circle. Just as it had all four times at the inn, the circle wasn't doing anything. "Dratted"—I pinched the bridge of my nose—"ash. Gets everywhere. Oh, no, I think I'm going to . . . to . . ."

I sneezed. When I opened my eyes Christian was standing next to me, staring intently at the circle. Within its confines the air gathered itself, slowly turning opaque, until the form of a short, hefty woman in a bathrobe, with a headful of fat sausage curls, emerged from the mist.

I stared up at the ghost, the hairs on my arms standing on end as I realized that I'd done it; I'd Summoned my first human ghost! All by myself! *Woobah!*

A tanned hand (how did a vampire get a tan? Were there undead tanning salons?) appeared in front of my face. I took it and allowed him to pull me to my feet.

I looked at Christian. He cocked an eyebrow at me, and looked back at the ghost. I looked at her, too. She was dressed in what looked suspiciously like my comfy green bathrobe, and a neck-to-ankles flannel nightgown. She must have been sleeping when the hotel was bombed.

I grounded the spirit and opened the circle. "Um . . . hello. I take it you're the lady who died in the fire."

She stretched and patted her hair. "Well, I don't

remember a fire, but I was staying in this room. Esme is my name, Esme Cartwright. And you are?"

"My name is Allie. Allegra," I corrected, sliding a glance toward Christian. "This is Christian Dante."

"It is the utmost pleasure to meet you, madam," he said, bowing in the deliciously foreign way he had.

"Oh, my, a Dark One!" She tittered at Christian and made what I'd have called (if she hadn't been dead more than fifty years) eyes at him. Then she turned back to me with a perky smile. "You have excellent taste my dear. He's quite easy on the eyes."

"Oh, he's not mine," I protested.

Christian wrapped one of his steely arms around me and hauled me up to his side. "We are trying to work out the exact nature of our relationship."

"No, we're not," I said, elbowing his side until he released me. "There is no relationship and nothing to work out."

"Oh, a lovers' spat!" Esme said happily, clapping her hands. I glared at her. "I have several young friends, and all of them say I give the best advice. You must turn to me in your time of need, child."

It was a battle to keep from rolling my eyes, but I won. Eventually. "Thank you, Mrs. Cartwright. I'll keep your offer in mind."

"Esme, dear," she gently corrected me. "First names are so much more convivial, don't you think? And now you must tell me what I'm doing here, for the last thing I knew I'd just decided to take a long sleep after that horrible episode with the newlyweds who took umbrage when I popped in to offer them a bit of helpful advice."

At last! The moment I'd been training for, the moment that I'd mentally rehearsed for long, long hours. I cleared my throat and ignored Christian's disturbing nearness as best as possible. "I have called you forth to further mankind's knowledge of the life that is found after death. With your permission, I will take a few readings, ask you a few questions, and then it will be my pleasure to Release you and send you on to your next destination. If you feel you have any tasks left you would like accomplished before you move on, I will be happy to undertake them to the best of my abilities. Be aware, however, that you passed over more than fifty years ago, so the likelihood of my being able to contact loved ones is very slight."

It was a lovely speech, it truly was, delivered from the heart, but Esme didn't seem to hear much of it. The cat, evidently disturbed by the Summoning, emerged from under the chair. She took one look at it, then rushed over and scooped it up in her arms, squealing and kissing it and spinning around as she clasped the poor thing to her ample breast. "Woogums! Mummy's widdle Woogums!"

"Hmm," I said as I pulled out my notebook to make a notation. "Interesting. Ghosts Summoned at the same physical location can interact physically with each other."

"Evidently," Christian replied, a faint grimace on his lips as he watched Esme rain smacking kisses down on the cat's head.

"What, haven't you ever had a pet?" I asked.

"Several. They all died."

I glanced up at him, struck once again by the pain that darkened his eyes. "What is it you want from me?" The words were out of my mouth before I could stop them.

A smile quirked his lips, lightening his eyes to a middling oak color. "Would salvation be too much to ask?"

I clamped down on the smile that wanted to answer his. "Probably."

"I see. In that case, perhaps you will join me tomorrow evening? There is an exhibition that I think you might find interesting."

"Woogie woogie Woogums! Did oo miss Mummy? Mummy missed her Woogums!"

"What sort of an exhibition?"

"Perhaps a better term would be demonstration. A local medium is hosting a series of Summonings, open to the public."

I wondered how Christian knew about the psychic shindig, then figured he must have had an ear to the paranormal grapevine. "I heard about that. I suppose it might be interesting, although I'm at a loss as to why you want to take me there. After all, I'm not in the least bit feminine or submissive or docile, and of course, I have this great huge problem with my self-image."

He took two steps forward and held my chin between his thumb and forefinger. Little flames of desire licked down my neck at his touch. "You are also a very talented woman, intelligent if rather distant emotionally."

The flames froze solid. I smacked his hand away, ignoring Esme's horrified gasp of surprise. "You are just about the rudest man I've ever met. You've done nothing but insult me ever since you came here—

uninvited, I might add—and now you have the balls to tell me I'm frigid?" I took a deep breath and pointed to the door. "Don't let the door hit you in the butt as you go out."

"Allie," Esme the ghost shrieked. "Child, that is no way to speak to your man! Firm, yes, but never, ever demanding. It isn't ladylike."

Christian smiled at me—smirked, really, a knowing, full-of-himself smirk that made my hand itch to slap it off his face; then he made another one of those old-fashioned bows that would have looked ridiculous performed by any other man, but which fit him perfectly. "I shall call for you at eight of the clock."

"Out!" I snapped, stabbing my finger at the door.

"Esme, it was a distinct pleasure. I hope to see you again, but if Allegra determines what is wrong with her Release spell and I am unable to, *bon chance*."

"Oh, my! Christian, you really are the charmer, aren't you? I'm sure I will be around for quite some time. I can see that Allie needs a guiding hand, a mother's helpful advice."

"Esme, you're not my mother. And you are dead. Those are just two reasons why advice from you is not needed."

Her lower lip quivered, and her eyes filled with ghostly tears.

"I hope you are pleased with yourself. You have made a spirit cry."

I glared at Christian for a moment. "Weren't you just leaving? Oh, Esme, I'm sorry; I didn't mean to hurt your feelings. It's just that . . . well, I have a mother. She's very much alive, and she's full of good advice, so although I appreciate your concern—"

The ghost sniffed and pulled a handkerchief from her pocket, blowing her nose. I made a mental note to record the fact that ghosts' noses got stuffy when they cried. "But you're American! She must live in America, surely? You need a mother figure here, child. You obviously have a great deal to learn about men, and since I've had four husbands, I'm just the person to tell you what's what. Now you run along, Christian," she said, tucking her handkerchief away, a smile once again brightening her face. She made shooing motions toward him. "Allie and I have a great deal to talk about, and none of it is fit for a man's ears."

"Oh, Lord, what have I done?" I moaned softly to myself.

Christian's amused smile turned into an out-and-out grin. He inclined his head toward Esme. "You have my full permission to—how is it said?—whip her into shape."

His words fell like shards of glass on tender flesh. I wondered if he had ever been whipped. I had. It wasn't an expression I used lightly.

The smile faded off his face as his gaze shifted to me. "Allegra? Is something amiss?"

I could feel him testing the guards I'd sent on my mind, searching for any cracks that would allow him in. I forced down the pain that had risen at his words and stretched my lips into a smile. "Everything's fine. Good night, Christian."

He continued to stare at me for a minute, probing my mind gently, but my will was strong. Closing my mind to others was the first step in self-preservation that I'd learned. It was a hard lesson, but one that was instinctive to me now. He nodded abruptly, then turned and went out the door.

I closed it behind him, leaning against it as I blew out a whoosh of breath. I hadn't realized just how he upset the balance of my mind until he'd left. I felt drained, unfinished, almost as if part of me had walked out the door with him.

"Fancies, sheer and utter fancies." I shook my head at myself and straightened my shoulders. Disturbing influence or no, I had work to do. I would not let a handsome man with wicked eyes and seductive lips interfere. No matter how hard he tried to dominate me, I would remain in control. I kept my smile firmly attached as I turned to the waiting ghost.

"Just a word of advice, dear. Your smile should be representative of your inner beauty, of your natural gentleness. It should shine from within, and should warm the heart of the one you're smiling at, not make that person think of death's-heads and grinning skeletons."

I let the smile fizzle off into nothing. Sometimes I had to wonder if being a Summoner was really worth it.

Chapter Five

"Dear, you are a young woman. You have a dashing young man. Why don't you put your hair up in papers? It would do wonders for it."

I ground my teeth and made note of Esme's EMF reading.

"And your clothes—really, I understand that they're comfortable, but you have your future to think of! What man will want to marry a woman who wears loose athletic trousers and baggy jumpers? You have a very nice figure, I'm sure. Don't be afraid to show it off!"

The point of my pencil broke against the notebook. I threw it away with a muttered snarl and reached for a pen.

"And your posture—I realize this is a different age than when I was a girl, but my mother would have swooned if she'd seen me slouching as you do.

Shoulders back, child, back straight, head high. A lady never sits like a lump."

The pen gouged a hole in the paper. I closed my eyes and took a deep breath. There were just a few more things to record; then I could send Esme on to her reward, leaving me in blissful quiet. Two hours of her nonstop, if well-meaning advice had just about worn my nerves raw.

"You know, I think if you tried a different sort of eyeliner, it might help tone down your eyes a wee bit. I realize there's nothing you can do with them, but you do want to maximize what you have, in a minimal sort of way, if you know what I mean. A lady doesn't look like a painted trollop; she just looks . . . enhanced. Subtlety is the key with cosmetics."

I picked up my digital camera and switched the settings to manual. "Could you hold . . . um . . . Mr. Woogums for a minute? I'd like to get a few pictures."

"Photos! Why, of course, I'd be delighted. Come here, my little Woogy-woogy man."

I focused, checked the flash settings (I'd found that flashes made ghosts all but invisible to the camera), and snapped a few shots.

"Now you must do one of my left side," Esme said as she struck a dramatic pose in profile. "I'm told it's my best side. You must cultivate your best side, dear. Always keep your man on that side, so he will have only the best of you to look at. And we must have a word about your eyebrows! Young ladies nowadays simply have no idea of the proper way to groom their eyebrows."

"My eyebrows are just fine, thank you. Now how about a couple of shots of you next to the wall? I want to see if you show up better with a dark background."

"Oh, I'm sure I do," she said as she obligingly moved over to the wall, which was covered in dark blue silk. She struck a pose that reminded me of Hollywood starlets in the 1930s. "And as for your eyebrows—tsk, dear, tsk! You cannot mean to have them looking like great hairy caterpillars clinging to your face. Eyebrows are meant to be delicate little swoops that draw attention to the eye."

I looked at her over the top of the camera, one great hairy caterpillar cocked in question.

"Yes, well, perhaps your eyes demand an eyebrow with a bit more substance, but they do need help. Lots and lots of help."

"Mmm. Just a couple more shots and then I think I'll be finished with you. I can Release you so you'll be free to move on to the next level of existence."

She held her smile until I lowered the camera, then shook her head, fat iron-gray curls bobbing madly as she walked over to me. "Oh, I couldn't do that, dear. I'm not ready to move on yet."

I made a note of the conditions of the pictures, camera settings, and day and time, then tucked the camera away in the bag. "Oh, right, you have some unfinished business. Well, I can't guarantee I can fix it, but I'll do my best. What do you need done?"

She smiled and reached out to pat my shoulder. My arm went numb. "Why, it's you, dear. You are my unfinished business."

I goggled at her. "Me?" I squeaked. "What do you mean, I'm your unfinished business? You didn't even know me until I Summoned you!"

Her curls bobbed as she nodded. "Exactly. As soon as I saw you, I said to myself, 'Esme, that young woman needs your help. This is why you were meant to stay in this room all those years.' And I was right; you do need my help."

I thought madly over everything I'd learned about Releasing a ghost. Was it possible to send one on if it didn't wish to go?

"Poop," I snarled, knowing full well the answer was no. It wasn't possible to Release a ghost without its cooperation.

"Allie! Language! We are judged by the quality of our language. It behooves a lady to strip from her vocabulary any of those words deemed uncouth. Oaths are definitely a no-no. Gentlemen do not wish their wives to have a mouth like a sailor!"

I sat down in the chair with a half sob caught in my throat. "Esme, I know you think I need your help, and I appreciate your kindness in giving me such—" *unwanted . . . useless . . . dated* "—*helpful* advice, but I can honestly say that I'm very happy in my life. I have everything I've ever wanted: a great job . . . well, great now that I have evidence of two successful Summonings . . . a nice apartment, a couple of friends—"

She tipped her head to the side. "And what of Christian?"

I tried to smile, but was just too tired to make the muscles of my mouth work properly. The lightening of the perpetual gray outside indicated that dawn had come. "Christian doesn't fit into my life picture. He's just an acquaintance. So you see, much as I'd like to keep you with me just for the pleasure of your company"—a little white lie never hurt anyone—"it would be greedy and selfish of me to keep you from the reward that waits for you."

"Don't be ridiculous, dear. How could I enjoy myself without knowing you and that darling man have worked out your differences? No," she said, settling down on the bed with the cat in her lap. "I'll just stay with you until everything is set right; then you can send me on."

"But, but . . ."

It was no use. I tried for an hour to get her to agree to a Release (assuming I could do it), but she remained adamant that she couldn't leave until she saw me happy. I explained three more times that my happiness was not tied up with Christian, but she countered every excellent point I made with criticism of my wardrobe, my hair, and everything else from my attitude toward men to the color of my socks.

By eight o'clock I was exhausted, worn out from lack of sleep and the energy needed not only to Summon Esme, but most draining, to listen to all of her advice.

I gathered up my jammies, told her I was taking a bath, and used the bathroom as a quiet zone, somewhere I could relax and not worry that my eyebrows or underwear or choice of sleeping apparel would be cause for comment.

It lasted all of two minutes.

"What a cozy little scene this is," she said, drifting in through the closed door. "I always did like this room; it has the best view of the park. The room proper, that is, not the WC. Dear, a word of advice—

women who do not have large bosoms should never hunch their shoulders forward. It minimizes, and you want to maximize."

I sank my minimized bosom below the water and considered continuing on until my head was under as well, but if I drowned in the tub, no doubt my spirit would be trapped with Esme's, and the thought of eternity with her raised goose bumps on my arms.

"Esme, I'm taking a bath," I said finally, water lapping at my chin. I waved my sponge around. "See? Water. Bubbles. Tub. Me."

"Oh, don't mind me, dear; I'll just make myself comfortable over here. Now, what shall we talk about? Oooh, is this your cosmetics bag? Now, cosmetics I know. Just let me look at what you have. I can advise you as to what colors will look good with your skin tone and . . . erm . . . eyes."

Just what I needed, a motherly ghost.

"No, no, this shade of eyeliner is all wrong for you. Well, it might be fine for the dark eye, but it's much too harsh for your white eye."

"It's not white; it's silver. Or gray, if you prefer. The doctor said my left eye is actually just an extremely light version of gray, while the right is ordinary brown."

Esme looked up from where she was poking through my cosmetics case. "Allie, dear, your eyes are anything but ordinary."

"Well, the left one is a bit spooky, but the right—"

"Has color variations that just aren't human."

I dropped my chin into the water and made a face into the bubbles, where she couldn't see it. While I'd heard comments like that all my life, it didn't make them hurt any less.

"Oh, my, now I've hurt your feelings. That was unkind of me, Allie; please accept my apology."

I lifted my chin so I could speak. "Esme, you're standing in my legs. While I know you don't feel anything, you're making me lose all feeling in my toes."

"I won't move until you tell me you forgive me for that unkind comment."

"I forgive you. Believe me, I've heard worse."

She stepped through the edge of the tub and patted my head, making my vision go squirrelly for a minute. "Don't listen to anything unkind that people tell you. It just shows they're jealous. And ignorant. That's what caused me to say that cruel thing, I'm ashamed to say. Why don't you tell me about your eyes, and then I'll understand."

I had to give her credit; she was truly sorry she'd said what she did. It was hard to stay hurt when she felt so bad about it. I explained about the heterochromia irides, and tried to leave it at that, but she prodded and pushed until I spilled how hard it was to grow up so obviously different from anyone else.

"But that just makes you unique, dear! You should celebrate your differences, not hide them!"

"Easy for you to say; it doesn't make people skittish when they see your eyes coming."

She smiled and winked. "Now that isn't in the least bit true."

I laughed at her mischievous face and reached for the towel as I got out of the tub. "Oh, trust me, I've heard tales about the ghost of room one-fourteen. I know you like to pop out at couples when they are arguing, and you have a tendency to rearrange towels."

She made a little moue. "Girls these days have no idea how to properly fold a towel."

Eventually I managed to impress Esme with the fact that I needed to sleep, and she faded off into the nothingness that I gathered was a ghost's state of sleep. Before she dissolved away, I begged her to not bother the maid when she came in later to clean the room. She fussed about that for a bit, but in the end promised that she would make no untoward appearances.

Six hours later I was heading out the door to meet with the hermit. The SIP office had been reticent to give me her name and number (at least I knew it was a woman now), but promised to pass along my information. Ten minutes after I'd hung up, the hermit called and made an appointment to meet me at the British Library.

"I thought the whole purpose of a hermit was that they shut themselves away from everyone, not gallivanted around one of the most popular research libraries in the world," I told the then-quiet room. It didn't answer back.

The British Library is now housed in a huge building at St. Pancras, more than fourteen floors of books, manuscripts, periodicals, and other literary items. I had arranged to meet the hermit in the John Ritblat Gallery (which contains, amongst other things, the Magna Carta), as I didn't have a reader's card and couldn't access the reading rooms.

I wandered through the gallery looking at the missals and Leonardo da Vinci's notebook, and was about to join a demonstration of what a scribe's workshop was like when a middle-aged woman in a tweed skirt and jacket approached me.

"Allegra Telford? I'm Phillippa. I spoke with you this morning."

"Oh, hi. You must be the—" I stopped. I supposed it wasn't entirely appropriate to call a woman wearing a tweed suit and expensively coiffed blond hair a hermit.

"I'm a hermit, yes," she nodded, then waved toward an exit. "Why don't we go into the restaurant and have a cup of tea? We can talk about your problem there."

I followed her through the piazza to a well-lit restaurant. We collected two little pots of tea, and seated ourselves in an out-of-the-way corner table.

"Phillippa, you'll have to forgive me, but I've never met an honest-to-God hermit before. What . . . uh . . . what exactly does a hermit do? If you're not comfortable being here, around so many people, I'd be happy to go somewhere a little quieter."

She looked around the room. "No, this is fine. I spend many hours at the library. Oh, I see what you want to know—why am I a hermit when I don't hide myself away in a dank cave?"

I nodded.

"In my case, the hermit status applies on a metaphysical level only. I spend most of my time mentally cloistered, doing research. I do sometimes take on apprentices, and even more rarely offer my services to penitents such as yourself who seek to gain greater knowledge."

I gnawed on my lip a bit. "I see. You're kind of a mental hermit?"

She grimaced and sipped at her tea. "For lack of a better term, I will accept that. Now what is the problem you're having with Releasing spirits?"

I explained what had happened the day before with the cat.

"I tried every variation I could think of, but none of it worked. I thought perhaps there might be something different about English ghosts, and that's why I couldn't send the cat on."

"Hmmm." The hermit poured more tea into her cup. "You warded yourself before you spoke the words of Release, yes?"

I nodded. "Left hand, right eye."

"Just so. And the ginseng? It was ground by a stone mortar and pestle? No metal touched it?"

"Ground it myself."

"You haven't been raising demons lately, have you? I've found that even the weakest of demons can wreak havoc on ginseng."

"I didn't know that, but no, I haven't raised any demons, ever. I'm really not interested in the dark arts, just the Summoning side of things."

"Hmm. Very bizarre. Now, if it were a human spirit, I would say it had some unfinished business, but a cat . . . surely a cat cannot refuse to be Released. What do you know of the cat's owner, the one who died in the fire? Perhaps the cat is bound to her, and that is keeping it from transferring."

"The ghost is a woman. She refuses to leave, too. She told me she's not leaving me until she sees me happy with a . . . well, with a certain man. It's not going to happen, so I have no idea how I'm going to convince her to move on."

The hermit set her cup down carefully. "You didn't tell me you'd Summoned a human spirit."

"Oh. Sorry. I did, last night . . . er . . . early this morning."

"And does the cat seem to be bound to her?"

I thought about Esme kissing that poor cat's head. "Oh, definitely. She calls him her woogie Woogums. I think that just about says it all."

"Indeed!" The hermit looked horrified. "Well, then, that is your answer. The human spirit has bound the cat's spirit to hers. If she refuses to leave, the cat will not be able to be sent on."

"But I tried to Release the cat before I Summoned the other ghost."

She shrugged and adjusted the string of pearls she wore over a blush-pink blouse. "It is still bound."

I took notes on some suggestions she had that might help in future Releases, then looked up when she asked, "Tell me about this spirit refusing to be Released."

I sighed heavily. "Oh, Esme. She's— Oh, my God! What are you doing here?"

I stared in horror at the translucent image of a woman in a ratty old bathrobe with fat gray curls, holding a three-legged cat. "Good afternoon, Allie. You called?"

"Go away!" I hissed, waving my hands through her in an attempt to dissipate her ghostly form as I peered around us to see how many people were witnessing a completely unplanned spectral visitation. I was thankful no one was looking in our corner of the

room, but it would be only a matter of a few seconds before someone noticed that the third person at our table was floating approximately six inches above the chair.

Esme looked mildly insulted at both my words and my actions.

"You didn't seal the ghost to her room?" the hermit asked in quiet surprise.

"Are we having tea? What a lovely idea. It's been ever so long since I enjoyed a good cuppa. How do you do? I'm Esme Cartwright, Allie's friend. I see you are a Summoner, as well."

"Seal her? I grounded her, if that's what you mean. Esme, go away! Fade! Dissolve! Make yourself invisible! Someone is going to see you!" I had my head in my hands now, peering out over the top of my glasses to see if anyone was looking toward us.

"You have to seal a spirit to a physical location," Phillippa lectured, eyeing both Esme and the cat with a distinct lack of enthusiasm. "That keeps them bound to one location. Otherwise, as the Summoner, you have the power to bring the spirit to you simply by invoking their name."

"Oh, God, I didn't know! Esme, will you *please* disappear!"

"Mmm, Earl Grey, I always did enjoy a nice cup of Earl Grey. Who is your companion, Allie?"

The crash of crockery hitting the hard stone floor and a loud, feminine shriek indicated that someone had at last looked our way.

"Her name is Phillippa and she's a hermit and please, please, please fade away, Esme. You're about to get me into a very sticky situation."

"Well, as you asked me so nicely . . ." She faded away until there was only a faint shimmering of the air where she'd been.

"Oh, thank God she's gone," I moaned, banging my forehead against the palms of my hand, sending out the only kind of mental push I used—one to muddle the memory of Esme in the mind of the woman who was hysterically telling her friends what she'd seen. She quieted down immediately.

"I'm not gone, dear; I'm still here safe and sound. Do you want me to rematerialize?" Esme's voice might have been disembodied, but it could still be heard loud and clear.

"No!" I shrieked, then lowered my voice and hissed through my teeth, "Just stay the way you are, and don't move. Phillippa, what am I going to do? How do I get you-know-who back to our room? I can't have her coming with me—I have things to do this afternoon, and she's likely to—" I waved my hands around to indicate a person's form.

"I won't be any trouble, dear."

"No," I said firmly to the shimmering air, then turned back to the hermit. She opened her mouth to speak.

"It's been so long since Mr. Woogums and I have been anywhere," the chair intoned mournfully.

"Another time, Esme."

The hermit waited a moment to see if there would be a reply, then tapped her fingers against the teapot. "Do you have any keepers on you?"

"Keepers?" I looked down at my sweater and jeans. The sweater was the most feminine thing I had, worn because I had a nasty suspicion that Christian was going to make an appearance at Joy's tea. The sun set shortly after five o'clock, so it wasn't out of the question that he'd pop in. I didn't relish the comparison that could be made between frumpy little me, the statuesque and obviously pregnant, very feminine Joy, and the petite, pretty beauty of Roxy. All of which goes to explain—at more length than anyone probably cared to know—why I was at that moment wearing a cream, pink, and gray sweater in a rose trellis design, with little yarn bobbles accenting each of the rose stems. "Um. I don't think I have any keepers. I'd know, wouldn't I?"

The hermit sighed. "A keeper is a talisman, something you inscribe with the power to bind an unsealed spirit. It is a way for you to contain the spirit and move it without its becoming visible."

"My name is Esme Cartwright," the chair said indignantly, trembling a little. "I am not an *it*."

"Ah. I must have missed the class on keepers. What do I need to make one? Some sort of a bottle or something with a lid?"

The hermit shook her head. "No, any object will do. The spirit doesn't go inside the keeper; it becomes part of it, bound to it until you release the spirit from it."

I looked around me. "Okay, so . . . how do I go about making a keeper? I'll take a few notes now and make some up later tonight."

"Allie, I would suggest you think about this before you take such a radical action. You don't really know this hermit woman. I am quite happy to stay invisible for however long you desire, and I can assure you that both Mr. Woogums and I will be no trouble as you go about your day. Now I think on it, I can see a benefit to you in having us along with you, a great benefit. I will be able to offer you such advice as you may need when you next meet Christian. I know you are very nervous about your date tonight, and I would be happy to act as a chaperon if it will make you feel more comfortable. I shan't leave you alone for a minute."

I pulled a fuzzy bobble off my sweater. "Now," I said to the hermit in a tone of voice that had her raising her eyebrows. "Tell me how to do it right now!"

She showed me the wards to trace over the keeper, followed by the words of binding. During the whole time I was preparing the keeper, Esme first pleaded with me not to do such a cruel thing, then threatened to make herself visible if I didn't stop. I rushed through the last few words as the air over the chair started to thicken, growing milky white and solidifying into a familiar form, then hastily cleared my mind and visualized the sweater bobble trapping Esme's spirit.

"I'm warning you, Allie, I'll not be treated like some sort of spectral good luck chaaaa*aaaaaaaaaaa*—"

The bobble trembled in my hand for a moment, glowed with an inner light that is not normally found in a yarn bobble, then settled back into normal, albeit slightly tingly, bobbleness.

"Whew! That was close. Thank you for your help. I don't know what I'd have done without you."

The hermit accepted my thanks with a nod, then glanced at her watch. "I must be leaving; I have an herbal to translate. Do not leave your keepers lying about; they should be carried with you at all times."

I looked at the bobble resting on the table. "Oh? Why is that?"

"Possession of the keeper grants control over the spirit within. If it is destroyed or damaged, the spirit is destroyed with it."

"Oh, yeah, I suppose that isn't too good."

"Good?" She stood up and gathered up an expensive-looking briefcase. "Such an event would rend your soul in two. As the Summoner of a spirit, your soul is bound with it. To destroy the spirit's soul is—"

"—to destroy mine," I finished, feeling a little sick as I carefully tucked the bobble away in my inner coat pocket. "Gotcha. Thanks again. Once I can convince you-know-who to be Released, I'll let you know if your suggestions help."

She traced a protection ward on my forehead, and left with a brisk good-bye. I sat at the table, feeling a bit drained by the creation of the keeper, not to mention all the worry that Esme's unexpected appearance caused. I made notes on the keeper process, and half an hour later limped out to find a taxi to take me to Jamaica House, where Joy and her fiancé lived in a top-floor flat.

Luckily it had an elevator, so I could stand composed and dignified as I rang the bell, rather than gasping for breath and clutching my bad leg.

"Oh, it's you. She's heeeeeeere," Roxy bellowed over her shoulder, grabbing my wrist and pulling me inside. "Did you have any trouble finding the place? It's a bit out of the way, huh? I told Raphael and Joy that, but they like it. It's an historic building, you know. Used to be some sort of a coffee shop, one of the old-timey ones, not a modern one. Johnson and his dictionary and all that. I wonder if it has any ghosts. Hey, maybe you could look around and see? Here, let me take your coat."

Roxy started tugging my coat off just as Joy and an extremely large man with yellowish eyes (no wonder she didn't find my eyes that strange) emerged from a sitting room.

"Allie, how nice to see you again. This is Raphael, my husband-to-be. Roxy, let her get her arm out of the coat before you take it."

Somehow—and I swear that someone who shall be nameless had a hand in this—as I was reaching to shake Raphael's hand, Roxy jerked my coat from my left arm, and the Esme'd bobble bounced onto the floor. Roxy started forward toward a coat stand. I shrieked.

"Oh, my God, stop! You'll crush Esme!"

A name has power, thus the ability to Release, bind, and enchant a spirit by means of the entity's name. As I had seen in the British Library restaurant, speaking the name of a spirit bound to me had the effect of calling that spirit forward, bringing it to wherever I was. Hence the need, the hermit had explained, for sealing a spirit to a location if one did not want it to come running everytime its name was spoken.

True to form, the second Esme's name left my lips she was released from the bobble, just a scant nanosecond before Roxy trod upon it.

The appearance of a middle-aged ghost in a bathrobe, holding a three-legged cat, did much to stop conversation. In fact, it was a pretty fair bet to say that you could have heard an individual atom of oxygen hit the floor.

I closed my eyes for a second and wondered why I couldn't have a nice, normal life with nice, normal ghosts.

"Good afternoon, everyone. Allie, you didn't tell me we were going to pay calls. I'm all at sixes and sevens today. Is that scones I smell? I haven't had scones in *years*! I do hope you make the kind with dates in them, not sultanas. Sultanas give me the wind. Just let me freshen up a bit and I'll be ready for a nice little chat."

Three pairs of extremely surprised eyes turned to look at me. I did my utmost to rally a smile. "Are we early?"

Chapter Six

"I know there's nothing she can eat, but I feel terribly rude not even offering her a cup of tea," Joy said a few minutes later, after we had survived the introductions. Raphael, on his way out to do some work with the security firm he owned, looked more than a bit startled, but all in all, everyone took Esme's presence pretty well.

Roxy was in seventh heaven, sitting next to Esme on the couch, grilling her as to what life after death meant. Esme had met her match in Roxy—for every morsel of helpful advice that was offered ("Petite women should never wear horizontal stripes; it makes you look like a munchkin"), Roxy parried with yet another pointed question about the afterlife.

"What was the first moment you knew you were dead? How come you look like you did shortly before you died, rather than at the moment of death? I mean, if you burned to death, shouldn't you be all smoldering, blackened flesh and gooky stuff? Did you see a light at the end of a tunnel? And what's the deal with angels—are they real, or is it all just a bunch of hooey?"

I turned away from Roxy and Esme and made an apologetic face at Joy. "I'm really sorry about this. I realize you thought you were just getting me when you invited me to tea. If Esme makes you uncomfortable, I'll just turn another bobble into a keeper and tuck her away."

Joy, sitting with her hands resting on her ample stomach, eyed my sweater. "You keep your ghosts in sweater bobbles?"

"Sometimes," I said cautiously. "But really only in cases of emergency. Not to change the subject, but could you tell me what this step business is that you and Roxy mentioned last night? I meant to ask Christian about it, but what with him making snide comments at me, and then there was Esme and the two of them ganged up on me . . . well, it just kind of got pushed aside."

Joy's mouth hung open for a minute before she snapped it shut. "I have no idea what you're talking about, but I'm sure it's going to make a fascinating tale. The steps, oh . . ." She looked over at Roxy, who was sweeping her hands through Esme's midsection, much to the latter's delight. "Well, the steps are part of the Joining. Do you know anything at all about Moravians?"

"Other than that they are not quite vampires, no."

Joy leaned toward me a little. "You know, you really should read Christian's books. Much of what he writes about is actual Dark One lore, although, of course, he presents it as fiction. I will be happy to lend you my copies."

I gnawed on my lower lip. "I'm not really much of one for romances," I said carefully.

She smiled, her eyes dancing with inner laughter. "Trust me, you'll like these. And anything you don't understand, you can ask Christian about. Now, the steps . . . we were talking about that. Let's see . . . well, each Dark One is born having one true love, his Beloved. That's Beloved with a capital B, by the way. Anyhoodles, a Dark One's Beloved is his soul mate, the woman who was born to redeem his soul and balance his life. We had thought that there was only one Beloved for each Dark One, but . . ."

She looked uncomfortable. I couldn't tell if the baby was dancing on her bladder, or if it was something she was about to say, but I suspected the latter.

"It's really not important in the least. I don't want you thinking that it is, because it isn't, not truly."

I blinked. "Okay."

"And I don't want you thinking that there's anything between Christian and me, because I love Raphael more than anything on this earth, and I always will. Christian was just a little confused about me for a short while, and took things a bit hard, but in the end it all worked out well, even though Raphael did get fired, and he does have a scar, but at least the tattoo is safe, so that's good."

I opened my mouth to say something, then thought better of it.

"But I did promise Christian, you see. I swore to him that I'd help him find his Beloved, and then Roxy had this crazy idea about writing a book to draw her out, and I knew that wouldn't work, but I thought if Christian did a book tour to a number of countries, that might stand a fair chance of working, and Roxy came over just for the book signing because she said Miranda—that's a Wiccan friend of ours—Miranda said the goddess told her that Rox was needed in London. And it worked, because here you are!"

Finally, something I could understand. "Wait a minute, if you're talking about my being Christian's main squeeze, I have to correct that misimpression. I talked to him about this last night, and he himself told me that I wasn't his Beloved. He said he would break the news to you." I took in her crestfallen expression and gentled my words. "I see that he didn't bother to do that."

"I haven't seen Christian since he saw us home after the book signing," Joy said, pinching worriedly at a ginger cookie. She frowned for a minute; then her face cleared. "No, he's wrong, that's all."

"Who's wrong?" Roxy asked as she scooted forward to snag a handful of cookies.

"Christian. He told Allie she wasn't his Beloved."

"Oh, is that all. Sure, he's wrong. He was wrong about you being his Beloved; makes sense he'd be wrong about her, too. Poor man is a bit stunted in the Beloved-recognition department," she told Esme in a confidential tone of voice.

"Really? And he seemed so nice."

"Wait a minute." I held up my hand, feeling like the conversation was getting beyond my control. "Can we back up a minute? Christian thought *you* were his Beloved? Is that what all that 'I don't want you to think it's important' business was about?"

Everyone started talking at the same time, Roxy to tell me that although Christian was a pussycat and she loved him dearly (in a purely platonic way, since she had a husband she adored), he was still a man, and everyone knew men were idiots, Esme to inform me that girdles worked wonders where nothing else could; and Joy to add that Christian had been just a little confused, but that was all straightened out now.

I let them all talk, sitting back and closing my ears to the noise while I mulled it over.

Christian had thought Joy was his Beloved. She clearly was in love with the big man named Raphael, but just as clearly Christian was a very dear friend of hers. I suspected from the warmth that lit the edges of his eyes when he spoke of her that the feeling was returned.

The question was, did his feelings for her go beyond those of a close friend? Was he hiding a broken heart behind a façade of friendship? Or worse, was he on the rebound, willing to cling to any warm body to ease the pain of his unrequited love? I didn't know enough about the Dark Ones to know just how this whole Beloved thing worked, but I gathered that it was a pretty serious matter, and Christian thinking Joy was the woman meant to redeem his soul had to mean he had some pretty strong feelings for her.

That said, why did that thought bother me so much?

"Okay, enough, I get the idea," I said, trying to bring some order to the chaos around me. "Now maybe one of you can explain these steps. What exactly is a Joining? I don't think I've ever heard of that."

Joy looked worried, and absentmindedly ate six cookies. "The steps are steps to Joining. A Dark One Joins with his Beloved—that is, they have to complete the seven steps, and then they are Joined."

I had a horrible suspicion I knew what she was driving at. "You're talking about sex, right?"

Joy choked on her cookie. Roxy reached over and pounded on her back a few times until Joy stopped sputtering and coughing.

"If you wouldn't be such a pig, you wouldn't have this problem. Sex is the fifth step, but the others don't have anything to do with it," Roxy said. "Well, the third step does, but that's just kissing, so I don't count that."

I rubbed a weary hand over my forehead. I felt more than a little like Alice in the company of people who spoke only in riddles. "What exactly are the steps? Maybe if I know what they are, I'll understand this Joining better."

"Oh, that's easy," Roxy answered, counting off her fingers. "First step: the Dark One marks his Beloved. I assume Christian's already done that with you, yes?"

I gnawed on my lip. "Marked how?"

"Have you had any visions recently?" Joy asked. "Any times when you felt as if your mind had merged with Christian's?"

I smiled a grim little smile. "No one gets into my mind without my permission. Guarding my mind from others was the first thing I learned."

"Really?" Joy looked at Roxy. Roxy looked back at Joy. Esme looked at her cat. Mr. Woogums licked his butt. "Well, I don't know what to say in that case. With me, everything Christian felt and saw, I felt and saw. And . . . er . . . likewise."

I felt a stab of something that bore a remarkable resemblance to jealousy. I squelched the feeling immediately. I was not jealous of Joy. Christian did not mean anything to me. "I did have a dream about him. Dreams are often the only way to get to someone with a strongly guarded mind. We ward ourselves as best we can before we go to sleep, but there's a certain lack of control when you're sleeping." Which was one of the reasons I seldom slept at night. Nighttime was traditionally the domain of those creatures who sought control over Summoners' minds.

"A dream? An erotic dream, you mean?" Roxy asked.

I laughed. "Hardly. He was covered in blood and had a hundred cuts all over his body. I thought he was a tortured spirit when I first saw him."

"You saw him?" I nodded to Joy. "Oh, well, then, that definitely is a marking, wouldn't you say?"

"Definitely," Esme answered for Roxy, nodding her head vigorously. Her little sausage curls bounced around as she beamed a happy smile at all of us.

"The second step is protection from afar," Joy said.

"And we saw that well enough last night," Roxy added.

I made a noncommittal face. Two out of seven was statistically still a coincidence. I'd seen much stranger things.

"The third step's the good one—exchange of bodily fluids."

"Ew!"

"It sounds gross, but it's not," Roxy reassured me. "Really, it just means kissing. You know." She tipped her head toward Esme. "Enchfray issingkay."

"My third husband was very good with his tongue," Esme told her. "He could tie a cherry stem into a knot."

There just wasn't much any of us could say to that.

"The fourth step," Joy said as she rested a teacup on her belly, "is when the Dark One entrusts the heroine with his life by giving her the means to destroy him."

"Hey, wait a minute, I want to find out if Allie and Christian have been doing the tongue waltz."

"Roxy! That's none of your business!"

"Look, sister, I flew all the way over here just to help you help Christian, leaving my darling husband to fend for himself for seven whole nights. It is too my business. So . . ." She turned to me. "Have you guys locked lips or not?"

"I . . . I . . ."

"She's blushing," Esme said to Roxy. "I would hazard a guess that is a yes. And after what I saw of Christian last night—such a nice boy, even if he is a Dark One—I can't blame her. If I were thirty years younger, I might try taking him away from her."

There's nothing so annoying as a ghost who exudes coyness.

"The fifth step," Joy said firmly, giving her friend a stern look, "is the second exchange."

"Bet you can't guess what that means." Roxy sniggered.

"Stop it, Rox; you're being obnoxious. You don't have to embarrass Allie. The sixth step is where the

Dark One seeks his Beloved's assistance to overcome his darker self, and the final step, the one that redeems his soul and ends his torment is the final exchange—a blood exchange—after which the Beloved offers herself as a sacrifice so that he might live."

"Don't worry; Christian won't actually let you sacrifice yourself. You just have to make the effort. That's what Joy did, anyway, and it worked."

I stifled the little voice inside me that said I'd heard just about enough of Joy and Christian's relationship for one day. "It all sounds rather . . . oh, I don't know, epic somehow."

"It is in a way, isn't it?" Joy agreed. "There is a strong element of selflessness and absolute love to the whole thing that makes it seem like one of those lengthy medieval romantic poems, but I can assure you that it is a very serious matter to Christian. He is, for lack of a better word, wounded, and can't be healed until his Beloved agrees to save him."

"Ah. Well, that's fascinating, but I have to say, all this drives home the point that Christian is absolutely right. I'm not the epic story type. I'm not Beloved material. I'm a Summoner, pure and simple, and any . . . er . . . feelings of a warmer nature—which I don't have—are purely coincidental."

"Uh-huh. No warm feelings, eh? Is that why you blushed so hard over the kissing question?"

"Roxy, stop teasing her." Joy looked at me with a puzzled frown. "Perhaps we're wrong. Perhaps you really aren't Christian's Beloved, although I could have sworn . . . Well, it doesn't matter. If you are, you'll find a way to work things out, and if you aren't, we'll simply keep looking for the woman who'll save him."

Something twinged deep within me. I ignored it just as I ignored all of the rest of the strange things my mind was trying to tell me. "Would you mind if I asked why you're so involved in finding this Beloved person? I mean, isn't Christian really the best person to do that?"

"Yes," came a familiar, deep, beautifully resonant voice from the door behind me. I didn't bother turning around to look at him; I was too busy telling my body it was not going to leap up out of the chair and throw itself into his arms.

"Christian," Joy cried in delight. She peered over her shoulder at the window. "Is it dark so soon?"

"Not quite; there are another twelve minutes until sunset," he answered, setting a black fedora, black silk scarf, and ankle-length black coat on a table before advancing into the room. "Good evening, ladies. Joy, you look glowing as ever. Roxy, I see the fine hand of your husband in that lovely gown. Please tell him again what exquisite fashion taste he has. Esme, what an unexpected delight. You are charm personified."

He turned to look at me. I crossed my arms over my chest and waited. He took his time letting his gaze travel down from my hair—pulled back in a scrunchy—to my rose-trellis sweater with the yarn bobbles, and farther down to my jeans, which I suddenly realized had a big old mud splash on the ankle. I tried to cross the clean leg in front of it before he saw, but I could tell by the sweep of his eyebrow

108

as it swooped up his forehead that he'd seen anyway, drat it all.

"Allegra, that is a very pretty, very feminine sweater. Dare I hope you wore it on my account?"

"No, you dare not. I wore it because it had bobbles that it turned out I needed today. You had nothing to do with it."

"Put in my place, and very handily, too," he said with a smile that melted every single one of my traitorous internal organs.

"Christian, I don't understand. How can you be out if the sun hasn't set?" Joy was back to looking worried again.

He glanced at me, then seated himself in the chair next to hers. "I awoke early. After I dined—"

"He keeps a whole ton of servants in his London house just so he can feed off them," Roxy leaned forward to whisper to me. She must have seen the horrified look on my face, because she quickly added, "Oh, he wipes their memories clean, so they don't remember a thing about it. They don't suffer at all."

"—I decided I would accept your kind invitation as Allegra and I have plans for the evening. I assure you I was well protected against the elements for those few seconds I was exposed to sunlight." His gaze dropped to my jeans. Unwittingly I brushed at my legs, then stopped when I realized what I was doing.

"If you keep cocking your eyebrow like that, one day it's going to freeze in that position," I snapped. "You needn't look at me as if I'm a reject from the ragpicking farm. I don't have any girl clothes with me, so if jeans and a bobble rose-trellis sweater don't meet your exacting standards, I'll be happy to go sit in St. Paul's Cathedral and see if I can't Summon Sir Christopher Wren."

"Really?" Roxy asked. "You can do that? Cool!"

"I was joking," I said.

"Oh, you poor thing, of course you don't have any nice dresses with you. I forgot that you're just visiting, and unlike some people I can name"—Joy thinned her lips at Roxy—"I bet you don't travel with a metric ton worth of luggage. I'd be happy to let you borrow one of my dresses, but I'm sure they're much too large for you. Roxy?"

Roxy eyed me. "I think she's too big for anything I have."

My cheeks flared up at the implication. "No, please, it's not that I didn't have room in my bag for any dresses; I just don't own any."

"It's true, I've seen what's in her wardrobe. Nothing but blue jeans and those dreadful shapeless athletic trousers. I've tried to tell her the importance of a proper lady's wardrobe, but she became very snappish with me. Why, the state of her undergarments alone would drive off any man of taste." Esme suddenly realized who was sitting next to her and smiled a barracuda smile at Christian.

His eyes did an amazing little twinkling thing that pooled heat deep inside me.

I slumped my shoulders in defeat. When my bras and undies became the topic of polite conversation, I knew it was time to go book myself a room in the Old Summoner's Home.

"Gotcha," Roxy said. "I understand completely.

The only reason I wear dresses is because Richard—that's my husband; he's a doll—likes me in them. But if I had my druthers, I'd be just like you, slouching around in comfy old clothes and not caring how bad anyone thinks I look."

"I just can't take you anywhere, can I?" Joy asked as she threw a muffin at Roxy. "Apologize, you idiot!"

"For what?"

"Nothing. It doesn't matter. If you don't mind, I think I'll be taking Esme and Mr. Woogums home now." I looked at Christian and gave him a toothy smile. "I have a pair of black wool pants, if that will soothe your delicate sensibilities. They're the dressiest thing I brought."

He rose when I did. "I will be happy to escort you to your hotel, and thence to a restaurant for a little dinner before we got to the theater."

"Oooh, dinner and a show! How come you never take us to dinner and a show?"

He smiled at Roxy. "I would spend the entire evening fending off the hordes of your admirers."

She fanned herself and grinned back at him. "You gotta love all that suave debonairness!"

I decided not to comment on that. "I'm quite capable of returning to my hotel by myself."

"I have no doubt that you are. I will feel more comfortable, however, if I were to see you safely there before we leave for the evening."

"We would be delighted to have your company," Esme told him as she stood and adjusted the tie on her bathrobe. "A gentleman's protection can never be undesirable."

I snorted. "Regardless, I will survive without his attendance."

"I insist on accompanying you."

"You can stuff your insistence where the sun doesn't shine," I said sweetly.

Esme gasped. "Allie! A lady never refers to a gentleman's rectal area, no matter how provoked she might be!"

Christian turned to Joy with his hands spread wide. "You see what I must put up with?"

"Oh, my, he shouldn't have said that." Esme shook her head. Joy and Roxy both nodded their agreement.

"Put up with?" I stalked over to where he stood and glared up at him. "Put up with? No one is asking you to *put up with* me, Count Chocula. In fact, I'm willing to bet you I could live out the rest of my life quite happily without ever seeing you again, so you can take your *put up with* and stick it alongside your insistence!"

"Dear, as I mentioned, a lady—"

Christian took a step closer to me, his eyes lit from within with something that felt a lot to my guarded mind like unadulterated fury. His breath fanned over my face as his voice wrapped me in unbreakably strong silken bonds. "I have tolerated your abuse only because I realize how insecure you are regarding your appearance, not to mention frightened of what I represent, but I will entertain your rudeness no more. You have done considerable damage to my plans without offering an apology, you have pushed yourself into my life without my express desire that you do so, and you have met every kindness on my part with uncouth retorts and juvenile remarks. Enough! It is at an end. You might not be my Beloved, but there *is* a bond between us, even if you will not admit to it. Because it is the way of Dark Ones to protect their women, I *will* escort you to your hotel, and about that there will be no further discussion."

Have I mentioned that I detest bossy, controlling men? Really, it was his verbal attack on me that prompted me to do what I did. I'm not proud of it, but I am a survivor. I lived once in the control of a man, terrified to do anything even remotely against his wishes lest the repercussions (almost always involving physical pain) fell upon me, and I had made a solemn vow as I stood over Timothy's lifeless body that I would never again give anyone that sort of power over me.

I thanked Joy for the tea.

"I'm sure we'll be seeing more of you," she answered with a quick glance at Christian. He raised an eyebrow at her. I ground my teeth at the obvious wordless byplay that was going on between the two of them, then stopped when I realized what I was doing.

I plucked a bobble from my sweater.

"Say good-bye, Esme," I said as I made the keeper warding signs over the bobble. I turned my back on everyone to silently speak the words (I hate being watched when I practice my art), then turned back when the bobble glowed with Esme's light. Gathering up my coat, I ignored Christian when he did the same. Roxy chattered beside me as we walked to the front door. With my right hand hidden in front of me,

I sketched a series of confining symbols on the door. I walked through the door, holding my breath and praying that the simple spell would work on a vampire as it did on others.

Christian stopped at the door, the oddest expression on his face. He frowned and tried to push through the barrier my spell had woven.

"Christian? What's the matter?"

His eyes narrowed on me as I smiled. "What have you done?"

"Me? Juvenile, rude, insecure, frightened little me? Whatever can you mean?"

His voice dropped to the sexiest growl I'd ever heard. It sent little shivers of delight traipsing up and down my spine. "You have done something to the door, Summoner. Something to keep me from passing through it."

I flashed a few more teeth in my smile as I leaned in close to him. "Never, ever think you can tell me what to do. I have a mind and a will of my own, and never again will I allow anyone to take that away from me."

I turned with a cheery wave to a worried-looking Joy, and made my way out of the building to the drizzle-damped streets. A few minutes later I sat back with a sigh in a taxi I'd been lucky to find disgorging its occupants, wondering how long it would take Christian to realize that my limited spell-casting power—Summoners usually know only those spells that are related to their own personal protection, or have to do with the binding of spirits—applied only to the front door of Joy's flat, and not any of the other means of exit. I suspected it wouldn't take him long to figure it out.

"I hate it when I'm right." I sighed as I closed the hotel room door. Christian stood before my wardrobe, poking through the clothes contained therein.

"Esme was also right. The state of your underthings is deplorable. Why do you not wear silk and satin, as other women do?"

I set Esme's bobble down on the small desk that graced a corner, and peeled off my coat. "Look, I realize we both said some things better left unsaid. For my part, I apologize for telling you to shove your insistence . . ." I waved my hand toward his midsection. "You know. That was rude of me, and I'm sorry for it, but you have to understand that I just do *not* like dominating, arrogant men."

He walked to me, wrapping his hand around my neck and tipping my chin up with his thumb. I fought the urge to strike back, and just stood there, passive, letting him examine my face.

"You did not tell me that you had been treated ill in your past. Who was the person who took your mind and will away from you?"

I thought about lying to him, but decided those all-seeing eyes of his (now a lovely reddish-gold mahogany) would know I wasn't telling him the truth. "My husband."

His jaw hardened.

"My ex-husband," I qualified. "Or rather, my late almost ex-husband. I had left him and filed for divorce by the time he died, and no, if you were going to ask, I didn't kill him, although I wanted to. He was shot by the police trying to set fire to my house. While I was asleep inside."

Christian's eyes were slowly darkening, deepening in shade until it seemed as if his pupils were absorbing all the color in his eyes. "This man, this husband abused you?"

"Abused, controlled, tortured, killed my brother—all that and more, yes."

Onyx eyes bored into mine. "You said your brother was killed in the accident that injured your leg."

"You're hurting my neck."

The tight sting of his fingers was gone, replaced by warmth and heat and something erotic that skittered along the surface of my skin as his lips kissed away the ache in my neck.

"My brother—" I stopped as he kissed a particularly sensitive spot near my ear. "My brother was killed in a car accident. Timothy . . ." Another pause as teeth gently nipping my earlobe made me shudder in delight. To keep myself from responding to him, I concentrated my thoughts on that horrible night, filling my mind with the memories of it. The blackness spilled out of me, making my voice thick with unspoken pain.

"Timothy was driving. He was drunk—he was always drunk—but he thought it would be funny to see if he could drive through some woods that ringed one side of our yard to reach the house. Leslie died when he wrapped the car around a tree." Christian had stopped nibbling on me and was now looking at me with dark, shuttered eyes. For a moment I felt a pang of regret that my ploy had worked, a pang that was firmly pushed aside. "My leg was injured in the crash, broken in four places, I later found out. But we had no insurance, and Timothy was driving drunk without a license, so he dragged me to the house and left Leslie dead in the car. He buried him later, after he sobered up enough to realize what he'd done."

"You did not report him?" Christian asked, something in his face that made me want to throw myself into his arms and let him protect me from the world. I pushed that feeling down, too. I hadn't learned to stand on my own two feet just to hand my independence over to the first man who showed me a bit of sympathy.

"I couldn't. Timothy splinted my leg and kept me mindless for a long time on drugs, painkillers mostly, a small mercy. By the time I started hiding the pills he gave me, and realized that he was lying about Leslie having gone away, it was too late. I had no proof, and I was crippled, unable to walk for six months. I don't know if you've ever found yourself at the mercy of someone who doesn't know the meaning of that word, but years of experience had pounded into me the fact that I had no hope of escaping him."

His fingers returned, this time to touch my cheek and brush away the tears I hadn't realized were there. "But you did escape this monster."

I nodded, closing my eyes for a moment at the warmth his touch brought me. "He tried to kill me a year later. I ran away from him, and kept running. I ended up in a women's shelter. One of the women who volunteered there was a witch, and she saw the power in me that I'd long since learned to hide. She helped me understand what Timothy had done to me, and how to break the cycle. She taught me that I did not ever have to give control over myself to another human being. She taught me how to be strong, how to fight back rather than to be a victim. She made me realize that men are not happy unless they are in a dominant position of control, and that the way they deal with someone who challenges their authority is to overpower and bully them." I raised my chin and let my determination fill my eyes. "I will never let another man do that to me."

To my surprise, he nodded. "I am glad you have survived your ordeal, and have been tempered by your tragic experiences. A woman should not be helpless, should not be a victim." His fingers tucked a loose strand of my hair behind my ear. "I never thought you were anything but strong, Allegra. I would not want you to be anyone but yourself. Your past has shown you only one side of power, however—abuse. It does not follow that all men are made in such a fashion."

I stepped back. "I notice you don't deny the fact that men aren't happy unless they are dominant and controlling."

He shrugged that elegant shrug of his. "It is a part of what makes a man a man. Males are naturally dominant, females are—"

"Subservient? Subjugated? Passive little doormats whom men trample over?"

He smiled, his white teeth flashing. "I was going to say nurturers. A woman may become dominant, but only in order to care for those she loves. It is not a natural state."

I snorted (again—it was becoming a bad habit around Christian). "Do me and every other twenty-first-century woman a favor and get over yourself. Women can be just as dominant as men, only we do it without trampling over everyone."

His smile turned into a frown. "Women only use dominance to prove to themselves they are equal to men in all things."

I squinted my eyes at him. "Oh, you do *not* want to go there. In fact, this whole conversation is pointless. You're one of the caveman throwbacks who thinks he has the right to push everyone around for their own good. You're not in the least bit reasonable or open to a sensible debate, so I'm just going to stop talking to you." I strode over to the wardrobe and grabbed a handful of clothing. "Esme, you can come out now. Feel free to entertain Nosferatu here with tales of how a lady acts. I'm going to take a shower. Alone," I added with emphasis.

"The conversation is far from over, Allegra," Christian said mildly.

"Allie, I must lodge a complaint about the manner in which you insist on transporting Mr. Woogums and myself." Esme shook out her bathrobe while the cat sat at her feet licking his shoulder. "I really must insist that you carry us somewhere other than your coat pocket. I felt positively smothered in there. Good evening again, Christian; it is always a pleasure to see a man with such gentlemanly manners."

I rolled my eyes and stomped off to the bathroom, working off a smidgen of my frustration—and I'm sad to admit, a goodly chunk of it was sexual in nature—by slamming the door behind me.

Esme came in to the bathroom a few minutes later, but I ignored her and concentrated on washing my hair. Twenty minutes later I emerged from the steamy bathroom. "I meant to ask you earlier, but you were being pompous—how did you get through my spell?"

Christian had his martyr face on—a face I admit I secretly enjoyed—but he answered my question civilly enough. "I went out another door."

I smiled, pleased that my spell had held up against him. I felt compelled to be honest, however. "The spell probably wouldn't have lasted too long. I'm not very good at spell casting. Summoners don't need to use them often, and it's too easy to screw them up, so I try to get by without them. Still, it's nice to know I can hold a fully grown Dark One if I need to."

Christian's face took on a new level of martyrdom.

"Okay, I'm ready to go to dinner. Esme, you stay here and behave if a maid comes into the room."

"Dear, you wouldn't think about taking us—"

"I think you've had enough jaunting about for a day," I said gently but firmly. I turned to Christian. "Where are you taking me to dinner?"

Both his eyebrows rose at that. "Me? You expect me to act in a domineering, arrogant male manner and presume to pay for the dinner of an independent woman who detests being treated in such a patronizing way?"

I pulled my coat on. "Seeing as you probably have oodles of money lying around gathering dust, and as I am here on my own dime, quickly running through all my savings, I will this once allow you to pay for my dinner." I paused as I opened the door and looked back at him. "If you ask me nicely, that is."

"Do you know," he replied with a thoughtful look on his face as he followed me out the door, "we almost had a civil conversation going. There might be hope for you yet."

I smacked him on the arm and, after hesitating a moment, took the hand he offered me, twining my fingers through his and smiling secretly to myself. Hope? Not for me, but maybe for . . . *Hmmm.* What an interesting thought.

Chapter Seven

Our unspoken truce lasted through dinner, during which I watched with fascination while Christian did *not* eat his food.

"How do you do that?" I asked when I looked up to find yet another bit of his prawns gone.

He smiled. "The hand is quicker than the eye."

"Oh. You've never been able to eat?"

"Food? No."

I thought about that for a minute while I ate some lemon-roasted chicken. "How exactly did you end up"—I looked around us—"as you are? Were you born that way or did someone turn you?"

His long fingers toyed with the rim of his wineglass. "There are two types of Dark Ones: those who were born to it, and those who were created. I am in the former group."

"Really? So your parents were vamps, too?"

He nodded. "All males born of an unredeemed Dark One are the same as their father."

Something didn't sit right. "Wait a minute, you said that when you guys find your Beloveds, they save you and redeem your soul, right? So how can an *unredeemed* Dark One have children?"

"The same way any other man does," he said with more than a hint of a grin. "There are many of my kind who never find their Beloveds, but that does not mean they do not take solace where they can in relationships with mortal women."

"Oh." Which, of course, made me want to ask, "So do you do that too? Take solace, I mean?"

His eyelids dropped until he was giving me a look so steamy it could have cooked carrots. "Are you inquiring for general knowledge, or is there a purpose to your question?"

I made an attempt to stifle the parts of my body that were responding (with much enthusiasm) to the effect of that smooth, beautiful voice, not to mention his bedroom eyes. It wasn't easy, but finally I could look back up to him and speak without grabbing his head and kissing the dickens out of him. "Let's just say it's general curiosity."

His eyes darkened to a deep walnut. "Why do you do that?"

I blinked and tried to summon my innocent face. "Do what?"

"Struggle against the attraction you feel for me. I feel the same and yet I do not struggle; it would be pointless. It is not something one can control—it either is, or it isn't. Yet you deny the passion that beats so strongly within you, I can sense its presence even when I am not near you. Are you so threatened by me that you cannot stand the thought of physical intimacy?"

"I'm not threatened by you," I said in a low whisper, not wanting our conversation to reach the ears of others. "And I'm not passionate."

He laughed a smooth, seductive sort of laugh that felt like velvet touching my skin. "*Malý váleèník*, you are."

"I am not. I've been told often enough that I lack any sort of connubial warmth to disbelieve you. In fact, the words *cold fish* were used at one point. And what did you call me?"

He ignored my question. "Was it your ex-husband who told you this?"

I shifted in my seat and wondered how he could know I was struggling with myself not to respond to him. I had a very tight control over my mind; not even Christian's probes had been able to penetrate my guards. "Well . . . yes, but I know for a fact it's true. I'm neither a virgin nor a prude, Christian. I'm thirty-one years old. I have been with men. I know I'm lacking the passion other women have because I've never particularly enjoyed sexual acts, and from the dissatisfied looks on my partners' faces, the feeling was obviously mutual. So you needn't bother trying to seduce me in order to gain a little solace. You won't find it in my arms."

"No? Let us test that theory, shall we?" He held out his hand for me. "Come here."

I stared at his hand like it was made up of boiled spiders. "What?"

"Come here. Sit next to me."

I looked around us. Although we were in a rather secluded spot in the restaurant, our table was clearly visible to at least a half dozen people. "No! People will see us!"

One sable eyebrow rose. "Does that thought arouse you?"

I frowned down my nose at him. "Not in the least."

He sighed. "I can see I will have much to teach you. Come here, Allegra. Sit next to me. Prove to me that you are a cold fish."

"I am not going to fall for such a weak example of reverse psychology," I told him with an annoyed roll of my eyes.

"Ah, so you are too afraid of me to prove what you say?"

"I'm not afraid of you," I answered. "I don't have to prove anything."

He made an elegant gesture that spoke volumes— volumes about him proving his point, and me being too chicken to correct him.

"All right," I snarled, standing up as I threw down my napkin. I walked over to his side of the table and plopped myself down in his lap, ignoring at least five pairs of eyes that I could feel on my back. "You want me to prove that I'm passionless, I'll prove to you that I'm passionless. Be prepared to be bored to tears."

I clamped my hands onto his shoulders, mashing my mouth up against his, purposely grinding my lips hard against his teeth. He tolerated that for a moment, then gently cupped either side of my jaw and tipped my head back at a different angle. "We will try this again, but without the show of brute strength, yes?"

I looked into his eyes and knew I was in trouble, serious, deep, fathomless trouble. His eyes were dark wells of desire—a desire for me, something I'd never seen in a man's eyes. I felt myself falling into them as his lips teased mine, feathering soft little kisses along the length of my mouth, tantalizing me until I could no longer deny the truth.

I wanted him to touch me. I wanted him to kiss me. I wanted to taste him again, to have him taste me. I fought a desperate fight to maintain control over my desire, but the first stroke of his tongue against my lips tolled a death knell for my good intentions. My lips softened on his. I allowed him to surge into my mouth, and with that intimate touch the last of my barriers were destroyed. I moaned into his mouth as his tongue become more aggressive, stroking mine, demanding, not asking for response. I slid my hands into his hair, pulling the leather thong that bound it free so that his hair hung loose to his shoulders. The satiny length of it poured over my fingers like cool water, making me shiver in response.

I felt his touch in my mind, felt the whispers around the edges of my guards, and was overwhelmed with a curiosity to know what he was thinking. It was the sheerest folly to allow myself to receive his thoughts, for I knew he would be able to receive mine as well, but the fire that flamed within me at his touch was too strong to be quenched. He deepened the kiss as I opened my mind to his, allowing the sensations he was feeling to join with mine. His thoughts were wordless, formless images of pleasure, of need and desire and a desperate hope that were bound together until it was impossible to separate them. I responded to the need, knowing I shouldn't, knowing it would lead to disaster, but unable to keep from taking his darkness within myself and returning it with all the light I had.

His power surrounded us, permeated us, bound us together in a manner I did not understand, or even wish to examine. Rather than be stifled by it, I gloried in it, allowing his power to blend with mine just as our thoughts merged. His arousal fed mine; my desire fired his to greater heights. His tongue was everywhere in my mouth; then mine was in his, tasting him, learning him, aching for something that I couldn't quite reach.

This is not the way of a cold fish, malý váleèník, the thought echoed in my head.

I sucked his lower lip into my mouth, nibbled on it for a bit, then slowly pulled my mouth from his.

What does malý váleèník *mean exactly?*

I could feel the smile in his thoughts. *Little warrior.*

Warrior, hmm? I could live with that. What worried me was the ease with which he settled into my mind. Slowly, gently, I shut him out, replacing my mental guards. I was shaken, more shaken than I wanted to admit even to myself at just how tempting it was to throw down my guards altogether, but as I stared down into Christian's midnight eyes, I reminded myself that even if he was immortal, he was still a man. I couldn't risk trusting him with that sort of power over me.

I pushed myself off his lap and stumbled back to my chair, reaching with a lamentably shaky hand for the water glass.

"So"—I cleared my throat to try to lower the level of huskiness his kiss had generated—"what do you know about this medium Guarda White? One of the SIP people mentioned her. I'm curious as to how you know about her."

Christian touched a finger to his lush lower lip. "You will not concede defeat?"

I picked up my fork and speared a chunk of chive-roasted potato. "I wasn't aware we were engaged in battle."

He smiled and inclined his head. "Touché. It was not a battle, merely"—his gaze dropped to my lips. Instinctively I licked them. They felt sensitive and tender, as if they were swollen—"an experiment with a most interesting outcome. I begin to think I have been overly hasty in my conclusions."

My entire body went up in flames at the longing in his eyes. I tried desperately to gather the shreds of my control around me. "Please, Christian . . ."

He ignored my whispered plea, taking my hand in his, his thumb stroking circles on the back of my hand. "Why do you struggle so? Why do you fight to wrap shields of indifference around yourself when I can feel within you all the ardor you stir within me? Why do you deny the passion that fills you at my touch?"

I pulled my hand from his slowly and tucked it away in my lap. Unreasonably, I felt close to tears, but didn't know if was for him I wanted to weep, or me. "I'm sorry, Christian," I told the remains of my chicken. "I just can't allow any man to have that sort of power over me."

Christian was silent for a time, a long enough time

that I finally had to look up at him. His eyes, always an indicator of what he was feeling, glistened brightly in the glow of the candle on the table. His voice was low, pitched only for my ears, and skimmed along me like a pair of lover's hands. "It will be my distinct pleasure to show you that not all men use power to inflict punishment."

I said nothing. There was just nothing to say.

The theater rented by the Association of Research Mediums and Psychics Investigation Trust (known by the dubious acronym ARMPIT) for their cattle call of psychic talent was a small, intimate space located in the basement of an old building that looked to date back to the late eighteenth century.

"According to this," I read out of the pamphlet that had been shoved into my hands as we entered the theater, "Guarda White and someone called Eduardo Tassalerro, head of Milan Psychics, Limited, are forming a sort of brain tank of psychics 'in order to further knowledge of spirits, and spectral activity in Britain today.' Hmm. I wonder what they think they can do that we in UPRA can't do."

"UPRA?"

"It's the organization I work for. The sister organization in England is the SIP, both of which are more than fully capable of furthering knowledge about spirits and such."

"Perhaps the brain tank has another purpose?"

I slid a glance at Christian. It wasn't what he said so much as how he said it—with a sense of controlled excitement that even in my guarded state I could feel. I wondered idly if some of his mind was leaking into mine.

That was all I needed, a man so handsome he made my bones melt and my blood boil with just a look slipping in and out of my mind whenever he wanted. I glanced at Christian again. His head was tipped as he read the pamphlet, his long hair once again tied back. He was wearing a suit tonight, midnight blue with some sort of shadowy pattern woven into the cloth. The cream shirt and dark tie were common enough, but the vest he wore was a work of art. It was a deep sapphire satin that rippled and moved with each breath he took, embroidered with tiny, detailed silver stitching that traced out great birds of prey, eagles and falcons in full flight, heads thrown back and claws extended. It was beautiful and chilling at the same time, and I wanted badly to tell him how much I admired it on him, particularly how it hugged the contours of his chest, but his ego was inflated enough. The man certainly didn't need to be told he was just about the sexiest thing on the face of the earth.

Christian smiled lazily at the pamphlet. I dragged my gaze back to my own, chewing on my lip and wondering if it was just a coincidence. What was I thinking; of course it was! My guards were solid. I'd had almost thirty years to perfect them.

Which didn't explain the fact that Christian's smile grew.

I wrestled my mind away from the fascinating topic of the man whose leg was pressed nonchalantly against mine, and back to the theater. Carlos was up in the front row with two women I recognized from SIP, one of whom was the director. The theater was about half-full, most of the people wearing badges with local ghost-hunting groups' names emblazoned on them. A few people had laptops set up and were typing fast and furious; others wore that peculiar geeky look that dedicated paranormalists often had. I fretted with a bobble and wondered if I looked just as geeky as they did.

"Good evening, esteemed colleagues, dedicated researchers, ladies and gentlemen." The woman standing in front of the curtains had a clipped, faintly Germanic accent that matched her short silver-touched blond hair and no-nonsense build. She looked every inch a hausfrau, but the aura of power she exuded was anything but normal. "I am Guarda White, the president of the Association of Research Mediums and Psychics Investigation Trust. I welcome you to this our sixth of eight trials to be held in the London area. For those of you who are new to the trials, we will take volunteers from the audience who wish to participate in a group Summoning, often referred to in lay terms as a séance. Those members who we feel show a particular gift for the paranormal will be invited to join the trust. My associate, Eduardo Tassalerro of Milan Psychics, Limited, noted physical medium, will join us at the table. Will we require ten more volunteers. If you wish to be considered, please raise your hand and one of the attendants will take down your name and particulars."

The curtain behind Guarda opened to display a large round table surrounded with twelve chairs. The lights on the stage were subdued, limited to a single spotlight. I wondered why anyone would want to perform on the stage for a group they knew nothing about when they could join any one of a number of legitimate research groups. I turned to whisper my question to Christian, only to find him with his arm in the air.

"What do you think you're doing? You're a vampire; you can't Summon ghosts!"

"True, but you can."

"Me?" I looked around us and saw with horror that a young woman in a tight miniskirt was beetling straight for Christian. I had the worst urge to put my hand on his leg, just to let her know he was taken. . . .

"Drat," I snarled at myself.

"Is something the matter, Allegra?"

Oh, yes, something was the matter. Christian was not mine; I did not claim him. I forced my snarling lips into what I prayed looked like a cheerful, "casual acquaintance minding my own business, not in the least bit interested in the man next to me" sort of smile.

Christian's lips quirked as he dropped his free arm over my shoulders.

"You wish to volunteer?" the miniskirted hussy asked breathlessly, her eyes all but devouring him. I stopped trying to shrug his arm off my shoulder and wondered how bad raising a minor demon could be.

"Alas, I do not have the skills that are required to sit successfully in a Summoning circle, but my companion does. She is very interested in the trust and would be delighted if it were possible for her to be one of the chosen ten."

I glared at him and decided two demons were in order.

The woman glanced quickly at me, her brow furrowed in doubt. "I can't guarantee that your friend will be chosen. Mrs. White reviews all of the information and makes all of the decisions about who is to sit with her."

Christian's voice—always beautiful and velvety smooth—achieved a new level of polish that made his words so slick they positively skated off his tongue (and I'm ashamed to admit that a tiny little fire started in my groin at the thought of that tongue). "Is there nothing you can do to ensure that my companion will be chosen? I assure you she is more than worthy of that honor."

The woman's brow smoothed out under the close-range influence of his words. She nodded vehemently. "I'll do what I can."

She quickly took down my name, occupation (I just told her I worked for UPRA), and a brief sketch of my experience.

"You are all that is gracious," Christian said with a smile so bright it made me want to offer the young woman my sunglasses. She staggered off with a sunstruck look on her face.

"Okay, Mr. Persuasion, now you can tell me just what you're up to. Why do you want me in that circle so badly?"

His brows rose in a protest of innocence. "What makes you think I have a reason for you to join the demonstration?"

A group of four chattering twenty-somethings sat down behind us. I lowered my voice. "Call it a hunch. You of all people don't want more attention on the realm of the paranormal—I'm sure it's only a short hop from proof of the existence of ghosts to great hordes of men with torches racing through the countryside armed with stakes and necklaces of garlic. Come on, Blacula, dish."

He got that martyred look on his face again.

"You know, there's nothing you can do to make me go up there if I don't want to," I pointed out to him in a whisper. "If you want my help with something, you're going to have to spill it first. By the looks of things, you have about ten minutes before they start calling people up. You can either hem and haw and delay until it's too late, or you can tell me now and give me as much time to prepare as possible. The choice is yours."

Christian sighed, tightening his arm on my shoulder. I fought between the unhealthy desire to snuggle into him, and the unwelcome knowledge that I should stop him before he got the wrong idea. "It is, perhaps, inevitable that you should learn of my suspicions. You would find out in the next day or so anyway."

"Really?" I gnawed my lip as I looked at him. "Why?"

The look he gave me could have cooked cement before it cooled down into something dark and troubled. "Three months ago a friend of mine, Sebastian, a Moravian like myself, disappeared from his home in Nice. After a month when he did not answer any of my calls, I became worried and ventured out to determine whether he had felt the need to leave Europe in haste, or if something unthinkable had happened to him."

"Unthinkable?" Two of the ARMPIT assistants swooped down on the group of four behind us. I leaned into Christian so they wouldn't see my hand (that's my excuse, and I'm sticking to it) as I mimed a stake through his heart. "You mean that kind of unthinkable?"

He grimaced, and captured my stake-stabbing fingers in his free hand, absently stroking his thumb over my fingers as he spoke. "You are an unusually bloodthirsty woman. Oddly enough, I find that to be one of your charms. There are other ways to kill a Dark One, but yes, I was concerned that some fatality had befallen him. Sebastian was not the type to go off on his own without alerting me or another of our kind as to his destination. I tracked him first to Paris, then to London, then to a small house just outside London."

"Don't tell me—Guarda White and Signor Tassa-whatever were at the house."

He looked thoughtful. "No, but it was leased by Mrs. White's trust."

He was silent for a few minutes until I nudged him with my elbow. "So? Was Sebastian there or not?"

The ARMPITs moved off. Christian's finger stopped rubbing circles on the back of my hand. "He had been there. He left a message for me, a message that indicated he was being held prisoner and had little hope of gathering enough strength to escape."

"A message? What sort of a message?"

His mouth looked grim. I chanced a glance up to his eyes and quickly looked away. I hoped that whatever else happened in my life, Christian never had cause to look at me like that. "It was a message written in the manner of the Dark Ones."

I swallowed back a lump. "A message written in blood?"

He nodded. "Protected to keep it from the eyes of everyone but the person for whom it was intended. In this instance, me. Sebastian knew I would search for him once I realized he was missing, and although he was weak and had little strength, he used up a precious amount of his blood to leave me the message."

I thought about that for a minute as I watched the last few stragglers meet up with the assistants. People throughout the theater were talking in low, hushed voices that echoed like soft little brushes of a bird's wing against the high ceiling. "Um, I may regret asking this, but I've felt the power that flows through you. How do you hold a Dark One prisoner against his will?"

His eyes turned a flat, lifeless black. "There are ways."

I shivered at the bleakness of his voice and decided not to pursue that particular avenue of thought. "Okay, so you think that Guarda and Eduardo are holding Sebastian prisoner somewhere, and you'd like me to get chummy with them so I can find out where. What makes you think I'm the least bit inclined to help you?"

His eyes positively caressed my face. My body melted at that look. "I have few resources available to me here. It was my hope that I could appeal to your curiosity and your desire to help those who are unable to help themselves."

I raised my chin. "That sounds like quite a different description than independent, stubborn, and lacking in self-confidence. Give me one good reason why I should help you."

His eyes never wavered from mine. "Because I am asking you most humbly for your assistance in locating my friend."

My innards melted even more at the sincerity and hope in his voice. I told my guts to get a grip on themselves and thought about it. Helping Christian wasn't in my game plan. I had only three weeks in London, and already five days had passed. If I got involved in this weird trust thing, it would severely cut into my time trying to Summon more ghosts. On the other hand, it would be good research to present to UPRA, and might go far toward keeping me employed. I glanced at Christian as I gnawed on my lip and, with an internal sigh, admitted the truth that it wasn't for job security, or even for Christian's helpless friend that I would accept his request; it was for him and him alone.

"All right, I'll help you, but I have a few conditions."

He rolled his eyes. "Why did I know there would be conditions?"

I grinned at him. "Because you're a bright boy, despite all that macho posturing. Condition one: You have to lighten up a bit. No more of this ordering me around. I don't *take* orders, I *consider* requests."

His martyred look returned; his jaw was so tight it didn't seem to want to move when he spoke. "It will be difficult, what you ask, but I will make an effort to temper my natural tendency to express my desires in the form of orders. Will that suffice?"

"Barely, but I'll accept it. Condition number two:

No more wisecracks about my clothes."

"Agreed."

"Condition number three—"

"How many conditions are there to be?" he interrupted.

"This is the last one. Condition number three: You have to stop peeking into my mind."

He looked startled.

"Oh, don't give me that look; I can feel you hanging around the edges of my thoughts. And you smile when I think about you being—" I stopped. He was smiling now. "Since I know my guards are good and strong, it means you're pulling some weird Vulcan mind trick on me."

"Not Vulcan, Moravian."

"Aha! You admit it!"

"I admit nothing. If there is a sympathetic connection between us, it is nothing of my doing."

I looked at him suspiciously. He looked me dead in the eye. I couldn't see any signs that he was lying, and I'm a pretty good judge of that. "Well, okay," I said grudgingly. "But you just make sure you stay out of my mind unless I invite you in!"

His thumb commenced back-of-hand rubbing. Three more people trooped down the aisle, but judging from their matching black T-shirts, they were all ARMPITs.

"You have to explain a few more things to me, too. For one, I don't understand why people interested in proving the existence of ghosts would keep a vampire prisoner. I mean, it's like apples and oranges."

"You are operating under the assumption that the goals of the trust are as Guarda stated. In reality, I believe it has a much more sinister purpose."

"Really? What would that be?" I asked.

"Allegra Telford? You have been chosen. Would you come to the stage, please? Steve Ricks, you have been chosen; please come to the stage. Arundel Roget, please come to the stage."

The list of people called to the stage continued as the miniskirted woman trotted up to Christian for a bit of praise and to shoo me toward the stage. I half expected her to beg to be petted, then decided that was too catty a comment for even me to be thinking, and surreptitiously sketched a protection ward on her as penance.

Christian stood to let me pass, pressing my hand in a manner that more gave strength than asked for help. I gave in and squeezed his in return, more than a little reassured by the warm solidness of his presence.

I shook off the odd sense of reliability that his touch had inspired, and followed the miniskirt to the stage, where I was handed a piece of colored chalk.

"No, thanks, I have my own," I said, pulling out the chalk that, with the dead man's ash, I'd made a habit of keeping on me while I was in a city filled to the brim with historic sites, and even more historic ghosts.

I was pointed to a chair. I walked across the stage, neck-pricklingly aware that someone was watching me intently. I glanced to the side and saw that Guarda had me in her sights as she spoke to one of her flunkies. I gave her a weak little grin and took my seat. A short, balding man with a serious perspiration problem took the seat to my left, while a young, cocky woman with a thick cap of curly blond hair sat on my right.

"I'm Diane," she said, introducing herself. I shook her hand, told her my name, and turned to the man on my left.

"Peter Dunwich." He had a soggy hand, but I managed not to let him see me wipe it off on my pants. I fervently hoped Guarda wasn't the type who liked to form circles made with physical contact between the participants. Holding Peter's hand did not promise to be a pleasant experience.

Guarda and the tall, olive-skinned man she'd introduced as Eduardo joined the table. The lights clicked off in the theater, leaving only the one spotlight on us.

"Showtime," I murmured, then took a deep breath and focused my attention on calming myself and preparing for the ritual of Summoning.

Chapter Eight

Guarda looked around the table slowly, eyeing each of us intently before she spoke. I blessed my dark glasses as she studied me, since they allowed me to present an unintimidated and tranquil expression.

At last she clasped her hands in front of her and addressed the table, her voice picked up by one of the six microphones scattered around the table. Lights clicked on as three women and a man in ARM-PIT T-shirts fired up their digital video cameras, all trained on us. "As you probably know, we chose this building because of its unusual spiritual activity. There have been at least six separate entities identified here. Three have already been Summoned. Three remain. Usually we begin the circle by clasping hands and combining our power to bring forth any spirits who might be residing in this building, but as we have two experienced Summoners with us tonight, I believe we will instead work individually. We will start with a supplication to the spirits. If you all will please place your hands flat on the table, your fingers touching those of the person on either side of you, we will begin."

I've always thought the supplication was a bit of nonsense, a silly, showy bit of fluff that impresses the uninformed, but serves no real purpose to Summoners. Still, it was better to just have the tip of my little finger touching Peter's rather than having to hold his entire hand, so I spread my hands out in front of me, joining them with Peter's and Diane's. Guarda went through the supplication while I tried to get a feel for the building we were in, opening myself up to any of the three spirits who remained. I caught a faint impression of one very close, in the theater itself, but no others. I tried to focus on the spirit, but couldn't do more than pinpoint the location to a small room behind the stage.

"As Allegra and Steve are the experienced Summoners, perhaps they would care to take the first circles, and allow the rest of us to watch and learn from them."

It was an order, not a question, with Guarda's pale blue eyes resting on me in something very like a challenge. An odd wave of hostility rose in me in response, an emotion I quickly squelched. There's no room for any negative thoughts when you are trying to Summon a ghost.

Steve, a young man in a black turtleneck and pants who in no way came close to achieving the dashing figure that Christian had made wearing a similar outfit the previous evening, chose to make his circle right there at the table. I was uncomfortable being the focus of so much attention, so I walked over to the dimly lit far side of the stage until I found a spot I liked. I sat down, cleared my mind, ignored the couple of volunteers and two of the camerapeople who'd followed me, and, using my piece of chalk, made a circle.

The actual Summoning procedure was the same as the other times I'd performed it, but this time I had barely spoken the words over the ash when the air in the circle started to thicken and move in an agitated way. I waited, my mind focused on the spirit I'd felt in the back room, willing it to come forward. The shimmering started to die away.

"Oooh," someone directly behind me breathed in disappointment. She was quickly shushed, but the damage had been done. My concentration was broken. I rubbed out a bit of the chalk, breaking the circle, and looked over to where Guarda sat at the table.

"I'm going to give this another shot. I don't need to have absolute silence, but I'd appreciate it if everyone kept from breathing down my neck."

A small woman with a birthmark on her forehead made a grimace. "I'm terribly sorry. It was so exciting there for a minute, I thought you were going to do it. I promise I'll be quiet."

I smiled at her, then glanced out at the audience, but couldn't see anything between the combination of the darkened house and my glasses. I took a deep breath, cleared my mind, drew the circle, made the wards, and intoned the words over the ash.

Bits of it drifted on the currents of air on the stage,

some floating to land on a man who sat on the other side of my circle, other bits floating toward me (it *always* seemed to float straight for my nose). The air started shimmering again, thickening and twisting around itself as if it was trying to form. Suddenly my nose twitched and I sneezed. Twice.

"Wooo-hooo!" The birthmarked woman leaped up and shouted, pointing at my circle. I stared up, stunned by what I saw. Standing in the circle was not one, but two ghosts. One was a small, unhappy-looking young man in black breeches and a dirty cream-colored shirt with a black coat cut in eighteenth-century fashion, wearing a dingy pow-dered wig; the other was a really ugly old white-haired woman, her face crumpled up like an ancient apple gone bad. She had on a tight, shiny black floor-length dress and apron that emphasized every bulge and protuberance, and there were a *lot* of protuber-ances.

"Glory hallelujah," I said softly.

"Amen," someone said behind me. I stood and looked at my ghosts. Two! I'd Summoned two! By . . . *sneezing*?

"This is amazing, absolutely amazing," Guarda said as she hurried over to my side, walking around the circle as she examined the ghosts. "I have never seen two spirits Summoned at once. I have never even heard of such a feat! This will go down as a momentous day in the history of psychical studies!"

I rubbed my nose, feeling it tickle again. There was no need to show off and Summon a third spirit.

"You must ground them quickly, so we might take readings and ask them questions." Eduardo pushed his way past a couple of people and eyed the ghosts critically. I got a bit annoyed at that. They were *my* ghosts; I wasn't going to put them on display for anyone. I didn't mind people taking a few readings, but I was not going to have them treated like freaks at a freak show. I'd Release them just as soon as the readings were taken.

Somewhat reluctantly I grounded them. As soon as the last word left my lips, the old woman started in with a harangue, shaking her finger at me and complaining in an annoyingly scratchy voice.

"What's she saying?" I asked Peter, standing next to me.

He scratched his bald spot. "I'm not sure. I think it's Welsh."

"Welsh? Whatever would a Welshwoman be doing in this building? How old is it, anyway?"

"Approximately two hundred and fifty years old," Eduardo answered as he scooped his hand through the sour old woman. She turned on him and gave him the rough side of her tongue. Although she had no physical presence, just her appearance and demeanor were enough to make him back up a couple of steps.

I stifled a snicker.

"What is your name?" Guarda asked the young man's spirit. I looked closer at him. His face was marked by pimples, and his clothes had a hand-me-down look about them. His powdered wig, once probably white but now stained yellow and rust with age and who knew what, didn't quite fit his head, listing to the left and leaving a swatch of black hair uncovered.

The ghost looked at Guarda with a surly frown and shoved his hands in his breeches pockets. "Don't 'ave to answer."

"Now look here, you—"

"That's right," I interrupted Eduardo and smiled at the ghost. I judged him to be about fifteen. "You don't have to tell us anything you don't want to. I'm here to help you, to Release you from your bondage and send you on. You'd like that, wouldn't you?"

He stuck out his lip. "Mebbe. Mebbe not. Who're you lot?"

I introduced the few people I knew names for, and explained that we'd like to take a few readings, and then would be happy to send both him and the old woman on.

"A moment of your time, if you please, Allegra," Guarda said as she pulled me aside, away from the cameras. "This is a very exciting and important moment in the history of paranormal research. While I applaud your intention to Release the spirits to their reward, I feel that much good can come of a continuing, ongoing study of them. Just think of the research grants that will be available to us if we are able to show sponsors actual proof of spirit entities!"

"But at what cost to the ghosts themselves?" I asked. "As a Summoner, it is my job to Release them just as soon as adequate readings have been taken. Keeping them hanging around indefinitely while a bunch of corporate sponsors stare at them is hardly my idea of a worthy reason not to allow them to move on."

"Think of the research you and others will be able to do," Guarda said smoothly. "Based on your expertise, I am most happy to offer you a position on the trust team. There is a generous honorarium, of course, and you will find yourself working with the keenest minds in paranormal research. In addition, think of the fame you'll achieve as you write definitive paper after paper on every aspect of the spirits' life after death. You'll be famous both in and out of paranormal circles! There will be books, television shows, lecture tours, sponsorships—all of that will be yours, and for only the highest and purest of reasons: research. You can see why it is more important that we resist our natural inclination to Release the spirits, and instead use this unique opportunity to gain as much knowledge as we can from them."

"Um," I said, not wanting her to realize that with every oily word she spoke, I became more and more sure something was extremely rotten in Denmark. I slipped my hand into my pocket and felt around for what I had in there that could be used as a keeper. There were only a few coins, and somehow I had a hard time imagining binding a spirit to a coin. A couple more bobbles would have to be sacrificed.

The question was how I was going to create two keepers without someone noticing what I was doing.

"I knew you would see reason on this," Guarda said suavely as she turned back to the ghosts. The old woman had stomped away and plumped herself down in a chair, and was glaring at everyone. The young man was staring openly at one of the ARMPITs who had a spiky hairdo, a pierced eyebrow, and tattoos covering both forearms.

"Just a second—what happened to the other three

ghosts that were Summoned? Are they being studied now, too?"

Guarda smiled and patted me on the hand. "One is, yes. The other two, unfortunately, were lost to us."

"Lost to you?" The only way a Summoned spirit could be freed was if the Summoner Released them . . . or if the Summoner died. "Lost how?"

"It was an unfortunate accident; it won't happen again, I can assure you," she answered before turning back to the circle. "And now, please, everyone, if you would stay back, the trust members will take some preliminary readings."

"I haven't completed my circle," the Summoner named Steve whined.

"Yes, yes, you must do that, there is one spirit left unaccounted for," Eduardo said.

I decided I needed a distraction to make the keepers, but before I could do that, I had to find out my ghosts' names. Names, as I've mentioned, have power, and I didn't blame them for not wanting to let everyone know their names. As I was their Summoner, however, they were obligated to answer any questions I put to them. I moved back until I was in the darkest part of the stage (several of the stagelights had been turned on as soon as my ghosts appeared) and locked my eyes on the old woman. I focused on her, opening a tiny part of my mind to her and asked softly, "What is your name?"

Her head turned to look over to where I was standing. Her mouth moved. "Alis Owens."

Guarda looked over to her with a frown. I crossed my fingers that she hadn't heard what the old woman had said.

I looked at the teenage ghost, focused, waited until he turned his back on one of the camerapeople who'd rudely shoved her camera in his face, and asked my question.

"Jem Hopkins."

Guarda heard him; I'm sure she did. She oiled over to Eduardo and tipped her head toward him, speaking urgently and shooting occasional glances my way.

Rats. I'd have to act quickly, before it was too late. I moved out to the front of the stage, then pushed a hand away from me and swayed, moaning soft little moans and trying my best to look like someone who was about to pass out.

"Christian?" I mumbled pitifully. Several of the volunteers turned toward me, but Christian could move very fast when he wanted to. He was there in an instant, one arm draped around my back to support me. I swayed into his chest.

"I just feel a bit faint. All that power used Summoning," I said weakly into his neck, thoroughly enjoying being held against his body. I couldn't help breathing in the faint spicy scent that clung to him, a scent that seemed to permeate me and sink into my blood.

Christian repeated my words to the people who had come to see what was wrong with me. Someone pulled a chair over for me, but I shook my head and remained clinging to Christian. He brushed his lips against my forehead.

What is it you want, malý váleèník?

I stiffened in his arms as I quickly checked the guards on my mind. They were all in place, all solid and firmly set up against intruder, and yet Christian had managed to slip by them and speak to me.

I ground my teeth for a moment before deciding there was nothing to be done at the moment about the breach in my mental security. I'd have a little chat with Christian later. Right now . . .

I need you to distract them while I make keepers, I said without lowering my guards, wondering if he would hear me.

It will be my pleasure, he answered with a warm chuckle.

A sudden loud crash at the back of the theater made everyone, including me (but excluding Christian), jump.

"You could have warned me," I grumbled to him.

"Poltergeist!" someone shouted, and a half dozen people went running for the back regions of the theater. Christian turned us so his body was shielding me from the remaining people's view, allowing me to tug two more bobbles off my sweater and covertly turn them into keepers.

I'm going to faint, I thought at Christian. *Lack of consciousness is the only way I could lose the spirits and still remain alive. I'd appreciate it if you could catch me in a suitably dramatic manner, and raise a fuss about me doing any more Summoning tonight.*

I could hear the amusement in his words. *Can it be that you will now find it useful to have a domineering and forceful man in your life? One who will give orders and demand everyone follow them?*

"There's nothing back there!" one of the ARMPITs appeared at the stage and announced with a dramatic wave of his arm. "Nothing at all! It's absolutely clean!"

I used that moment when everyone's attention was on him to bind Alis's and Jem's spirits to my keepers, quickly tucking them away in my pants pocket.

Listen, bucko, you're in enough trouble for being able to get past my guards. If I were you, I'd just do as you're asked and keep the wisecracking to a minimum. Now catch me; I'm going to swoon.

I took a few tottering steps away from Christian, put the back of my hand to my forehead in the best fainting-woman manner, blinked rapidly, swayed, and let myself fall forward. Strong arms caught me before I hit the floor, cradling me to an equally strong chest as Christian's eloquent voice spoke over my head, thick with concern and worry. "Allegra has fainted! It must be the stress of the double Summoning. Quickly, does anyone have water?"

This is ridiculous.

You wished me to be forceful and demanding. I simply complied with your wishes.

I did not wish for you to insist on bringing me to your house. Nor did I wish for you to tell everyone that cock-and-bull story about us being engaged. What on earth were you thinking?

Guarda White was being obstinate about releasing her most promising team member to a mere acquaintance. I felt a more intimate relationship between the two of us would ensure that you remained in my protection.

Yeah, right. Why do I have the feeling you're enjoying all this?

151

His laughter echoed through my mind. *I have a beautiful woman in my arms, and am taking her back to my home, where she and I will be alone and able to indulge whatever fantasies we choose. What is there not to enjoy?*

I had a horrible sense of control slipping through my fingers, and did a double check of all the protective barriers I'd set up to keep my mind from being invaded. Everything *looked* solid.

You know I would never do anything to harm you.

"I believe she is coming around. She's making odd snorting noises. Perhaps if you removed her glasses, Mr. Dante, she would be more comfortable."

"Allegra has sensitive eyes. Bright lights make her uncomfortable. She will be more comfortable with them on."

Christian's breath teased my ear. I turned my head into his neck briefly. *I don't know what sort of cologne you wear, but it has my full approval.*

His laughter filled my mind again.

"Yes, she's definitely coming around. She's smiling. Can you see?"

Cool air wafted over my cheeks. I decided my faint had lasted about as long as I could reasonably drag it out, and started fluttering my eyelids.

"Oh, my, I feel so woozy, so weak. Did I faint?"

You are a terrible actress.

Shut. Up.

I pushed my glasses up from where they'd slipped down my nose, but didn't struggle to get free from where I was slumped against Christian. "Mrs. White? What happened? Why are we in Christian's car?"

"Your fiancé is taking you home. I was worried

about your health, and offered to accompany him, just to satisfy my mind that you have suffered no lasting damage from your experience."

The light in Christian's car—a sleek black luxury model that came equipped with a driver named Philspott—was bright enough for me to make out the calculating gleam in Guarda's eyes.

I leaned back against Christian and passed a wan hand over my cheeks. "Oh, how very thoughtful of you, but I'm sure you have much better things to do with your valuable time."

"Not at all." She smiled in a manner that couldn't help but remind me of a shark. "You are part of my elite team now. No matter is too trivial for me when it concerns you."

What a far from reassuring thought. I managed a weak smile in return.

Guarda leaned forward and pressed my hand. I fought the urge to slide it away from her cold touch. "Your fiancé believes the double Summoning was too much for you. Do you remember anything about what happened before you fainted?"

I made a face as if I were seriously considering the matter. "No, there was just the weakness, and then suddenly I felt myself sliding down into a dark miasma of unconsciousness."

We will have to make sure you take acting lessons before your next performance.

Have you ever had an elbow in your kidney? I'm told it's quite painful.

She made a little moue of unhappiness. "Unfortunately, your loss of consciousness returned the spirits you'd Summoned to their spirit state."

153

"Aw, that is too bad."

Beneath my arm, Christian pinched me.

"That is to say, I'm so very, very sorry that I passed out when I did. I will be more than happy to return to the theater tomorrow and try again."

"Alas, I fear you will do yourself further harm if you attempt such a thing without a suitable resting period, my beloved."

I stiffened at the word. *Have you gone mad?*

There was no capital B in that sentence.

I relaxed again.

"Perhaps you are right, *snuggle-bunny*. Perhaps a day or two of rest will recharge my mental batteries. I'm sure Mrs. White wouldn't wish for me to blow out anything in my brain because I was trying too hard."

Snuggle-bunny?

"No, of course not." Guarda looked uncomfortably aware that I had her in a position in which she would rather not have found herself. Ostensibly along to make sure I was taken care of, she couldn't possibly demand that I go back to work right away. I planned on using the couple of days' grace to do a little investigating into just what ARMPIT was up to.

If you promise never to refer to me as a snuggle-bunny again, I will allow you to investigate with me.

Allow? Allow?

It is a dangerous undertaking. I cannot allow you to put your life in jeopardy for my friend.

Allow, Christian?

His sigh brushed my mind. *I will withdraw the word if you promise not to pursue any investigations without me.*

I thought about it, and decided that he could be of help investigating. *Deal.*

The car bumped into a small building that served as Christian's garage. He had mentioned to me earlier, on the way to dinner, that the only time he kept a driver was in London. He said something about the annoying lack of available parking. It seems Dark Ones have issues with parking lots. He helped me out of the car with a solicitous arm, Guarda following behind as we crossed the small alley separating the garage and his house. I looked up to the top of the three-story building.

Big house for just one guy.

I require both space and privacy in my living quarters.

Don't worry; you'll have both just as soon as Guarda leaves and I can slip back to my hotel.

There are always exceptions to be made in times of necessity.

I glanced over at him as he held the door open for me, wondering if he meant what I thought he'd meant.

I refused to be swept up in his arms and carried up the stairs to the bedroom. "No, lamby-pot-pie, it's much better if I walk. Slowly. It serves to settle my nerves."

You realize, of course, that lamby-pot-pie *constitutes a declaration of war.*

I gave him a mental snort, just to see if I could do it. Evidently I could.

"As you desire, most beauteous of all lotus blossoms. If you will take my arm, I will allow your nerves to settle and yet reassure both myself and Mrs. White that you will not come to any harm in your journey up the stairs."

Have you ever thought of going into politics? You're a natural.

Guarda followed us into a huge room done all in shades of sapphire and midnight. A massive curtained and canopied bed dominated the room, drawing the eye and refusing to release it. I stood stupidly and blinked at it a few minutes, wondering if it felt as heavenly as it looked.

Perhaps you will find out for yourself. Christian's voice danced in my head.

I ignored him and tottered over to sink down in a blue silk–draped armchair. "Thank you so much for accompanying us home, Mrs. White. I feel much better just being out of that building. I'm so very excited about the plans you have for the trust. Might I pop in for a visit tomorrow and have a chat about what you see for the future, and how I might fit into it?"

Guarda's smile didn't even come close to reaching her icy blue eyes. "Of course. There is nothing I would like more. Just give me a ring at that number, and my secretary will set up a time." She handed me a card. I smiled at her. Christian raised an eyebrow. She looked as if she wanted to say something further, but realized that to do so wouldn't be in keeping with her pretended concern. "Well, then, I shall leave you alone so you might rest."

"You may be assured that I will see to it that my little kumquat spends the entire night in bed," Christian said with a smoothness that put the silk bed hangings to shame.

You and what army?

"Oh, you silly Mr. Fuzzy-wuzzy," I chirped in return, making myself faintly nauseated in the process.

Guarda looked between the two of us, then nodded her head and allowed Christian to escort her out of the room and, I assumed, the house.

As soon as the bedroom door closed, I leaped out of the chair and commenced pacing and hand wringing, ignoring the great behemoth bed and all that it represented. Christian, I knew, was planning a seduction. It was in every warm caress of his mind against mine, every touch of his body to mine, every sultry-eyed, heated glance. What was worse was that after the kiss that ended with me almost sucking the tongue from his head, I could no longer trust myself to stay calm and cool, as I had been with every other man. Somehow more than just my mental guards failed me when it came to Christian. All my honorable intentions, all my determination never again to let a man have any part of me, just seemed to evaporate under of the influence of those dark, tortured eyes.

The solution to my problem, I decided a few moments later, was to not let myself be alone with him. If he did what I expected him to do—insisted I remain in his house for the evening—I was in grave danger of succumbing to the siren lure of his desire. Therefore, I simply wouldn't put myself in a position where temptation could raise its ugly head.

By the time Christian returned to his room, I was talking with Jem while trying to keep an eye on Alis.

"So you were a waiter in a restaurant? How very interesting. Did you enjoy your job?"

"Not likely," the sullen teenager snapped. "Why'd

that man at t'other place 'ave bits an' bobs stabbed through 'is face, then? Was 'e wiv one o' them travelin' shows?"

I smiled brightly at Christian's frown before turning back to the ghost. "You mean the man in the black T-shirt with his eyebrow and nose pierced? That is a fashion common today amongst young people, particularly young people who are rebelling against conformity and society."

Jem didn't look like he believed me. I smiled again. "In other words, he was thumbing his nose at everyone in authority."

"Oh, aye." He nodded, and his spotty face lost a bit of its sullenness as he thought this over.

Christian strolled over to me with the grace of a panther who has spotted a particularly succulent bit of prey.

A comparison more apropos than you know, malý váleèník.

I ignored his silky voice in my head as I turned to him. "You don't happen to speak Welsh, do you? Alis seems to be rather uncommunicative, and refuses to answer me when I try to ask her if she'd like to be Released. I think she's trying to summon enough psychic energy to push over that blue-and-white vase. She seems to be particularly angry at it."

Christian paused long enough to cast a quick glance over to where the squat little woman was standing with her hands on her plentiful hips, nose to rim with a Chinese vase. His eyes turned back to me, and he started forward with a look that raised every hair on my neck.

"No, I do not speak Welsh. Do your inhibitions regarding voyeurism include spirits?"

I started backing up and nodded quickly. "Yes, yes, they do. So if you're thinking what I think you're thinking, you can think again. You couldn't possibly wish to damage my psyche by kissing me or ... or ... *anything else* in front of them. I'd never forgive you."

"Then I advise you to bind them to your keepers in the next thirty seconds."

"Ye don't 'ave to do nuffin' for me. I'm goin' t' 'ave me a look around town an' see 'ow it's changed." With those words, Jem stuck his head through the wall so he could see the street below.

I looked from him to Christian, then made a break for the door, but he moved faster than I could see and had me pinned up against the wall before I could blink. He looked deep into my eyes and let me see every emotion he was feeling at that moment. Then he slipped into my head and fed me images of exactly what he was planning to do.

To me.

All evening.

My knees buckled. "Christian, I can't, really I can't. That's not to say I don't want to, although part of me thinks it's really a bad idea because there's no future for us, and I will admit the rest of me is in the agreeable camp, but I can't."

Jem sniggered. I glared at him until he stuck his head through the wall again. Alis ignored us and started screaming at the vase.

"You can." Christian's eyes were hot enough to steam drapes. I swallowed hard and tried to remember why I couldn't give in to the demands of my body. Control, that was it. I couldn't give up control. Not even for what promised to be a night of extreme, never-ending pleasure would I give that up.

If we can do this without your giving up control, will you allow me to love you?

His breath was on my lips as he pressed me against the wall, his body hard and aggressive and, if the pressure against my groin was anything to go by, extremely aroused. Could I share myself if it meant I didn't give up control?

Yes, yes, a thousand times, yes! screamed my body.

He's a man, and all men are fiends, shouted the wounded part of my mind.

It came down to whether or not I trusted him. Would he respect my needs and not strip control from me, or would he lose himself in the endless desire I felt stirring him, blinding him to his promise?

I stared into his eyes, a heated, burning red-brown, and hesitated. Christian was absolutely still, not touching me with his mind, his body solid and warm, but undemanding against me. He was letting me make the choice unswayed by lust and desire and all of the other erotic emotions I knew he could rouse with just the merest touch of his lips.

Could I trust him? I'd never trusted another man. Was he so different that I could trust him?

I took a deep, admittedly shaky breath, ignoring the delightful sensation of my breasts pressed up against his chest. "If you can promise me you won't try to control me, then yes, I would like to see just how comfortable your bed is."

Jem, watching us with a sneer universal to teen-agers throughout the ages, snorted and wiped his nose on his sleeve. Alis flung herself into the middle of the vase and jumped up and down.

We ignored them both.

A slow, seductive smile curled Christian's lips. *I will never ask you to do anything against your desire. If you are uncomfortable with anything we do, you simply need ask me to stop and I will. That I promise you.*

My body sent up a silent cheer of victory as I slipped out of Christian's embrace and gathered up the two keepers. "Jem, Alis, time to go nighty-night. I'm going to be . . ." I glanced over my shoulder at Christian. The look in his eyes made my tongue cleave to the roof of my mouth. "Busy for a bit," I croaked.

Christian smiled as the ghosts shimmered, then disappeared, his smile turning positively wicked as he stalked toward me.

You, my sweet, passionate innocent, are going to be busy for a very . . . long . . . time.

"Gark," I said, and meant it.

Chapter Nine

"And so we commence," Christian said, his voice rich with satisfaction, desire, and just a hint of very flattering longing.

Now that I had committed myself to this, now that I had agreed to do everything my body ached to do, I felt uncomfortable, awkward, gauche. I didn't know what to do. Should I be the one to start things rolling, since I had made such a big deal about being in control? Or should I wait until Christian made the first move? The problem was, none of my past experience could be called on for help. All of the other men I'd been with—

"You will forget them," Christian said as his fingertips brushed my jaw. "There is you, and there is me, and there is no one else."

I started hyperventilating. What a *stupid* time for a panic attack!

"I'm sorry, Christian." I gasped, wrapping my arms around myself. "I'm very sorry, but I don't think I can do this."

"My brave one, my goddess," he murmured, gently enveloping me in his arms. His hands stroked my back as he nuzzled my hair. "You are distressing yourself to no purpose. If you are not ready for this, we shall simply wait until tomorrow night. If you are not ready then, we will wait for the following night, and so on until you feel the time is right."

"I'm only here for a little more than two weeks." I wheezed into his collarbone, the shaking within me slowly abating at the gentle strokes of his hand on my back. I pressed a little closer to him, wanting to breathe in his wonderful masculine scent.

"Do not worry about the future when the present holds such promise."

I shivered with the feeling of his soft breath in my ear, finally pulling a little bit away and looking at a spot just to the side of his face. "Thank you for understanding. I think I'd like to . . . er . . . give it a try. The only thing is"—I swallowed back a lump approximately the size of Rhode Island—"I'm not quite sure what to do next. Should I . . . um . . ." I looked at the bed.

He smiled and pulled me toward the armchair, tugging me down onto his lap. "Why don't we try this first? It was enjoyable at the restaurant; it should be so here, too, yes?"

I gave him a watery smile, relaxing against him. He was giving me a choice, and had said he would stop at any time. Maybe this wouldn't be so bad after all.

Your faith in my ability to stir your passion humbles

me, he murmured in my mind, pulling me forward and kissing my lips until they parted for him.

The day you're humble is the day hell will freeze over, I answered, kissing him back.

I have been to hell, his mind whispered into mine. His tongue teased my lips until I had to send my own out to tell his to stop fooling around and get down to proper tongue work. *It is not a very likely place to freeze.*

No comment. I giggled.

He kissed me thoroughly, let me kiss him just as thoroughly, and then engaged in a bit of a tongue tussle as we tried to outdo each other and push the fire burning between us to new heights.

By the time we finished I was squirming against him, my fingers tangled in his hair, tugging on it in silent demand that he take care of the ache that he had started.

"What do you want, my demanding one?" he asked, his lips nuzzling and nipping at an hitherto unknown sensitive spot on my collarbone.

I released the earlobe I was gnawing on and looked down into his ebony eyes. "I want to touch you. And I want you to touch me."

His tongue painted a line across my collarbone. "It shall be as you order."

He stood up with me in his arms, letting me slide down his body until I was once again on my feet. I took a quick moment to assess my feelings, and decided I was in no danger, not threatened or feeling stifled as I had with other men. Christian had done everything he promised, holding back his own natural tendency to be the one in charge to allow me the time to proceed in a manner and a pace that left me burning with desire and wanting.

"You're a very clever man." I smiled against his lips.

One glossy eyebrow rose. "And you have only just discovered this?"

His head dipped to take possession of my mouth once again, and I sagged against him, welcoming the solid strength of his arms, since my legs had apparently gone boneless and turned to jelly when I wasn't looking.

"Do you wish for me to undress for you, or would it please you to undress me?"

I rubbed up against him, feeling wanton and wicked and extremely like a temptress who was no better than she should be. "Which would drive you wild with excitement?"

His hands spread out to cup my breasts. "Definitely the latter."

I leaned into his hands for a moment, astounded that breasts could feel so good in a man's hands, then pulled back and gave Christian a wicked smile. "Then that is what we will do. Let's see . . . where shall I start . . . tie."

"An excellent choice," Christian said as I kissed his neck, his hands sliding up around my hips. I stepped back.

"No."

Both eyebrows went up at that. "No?"

"No. No hands. I get to undress you without you touching me."

One side of his mouth quirked up in question.

"If you start touching me again, I won't be able to

concentrate on driving you wild, and I very much want to do that. So no hands."

He dropped his hands, his eyes turning the heat up a notch. I fanned myself. "It's getting a bit hot in here, isn't it? Okay, so I was at your tie. Um . . . right, one tie, blue." I set the tie on the chair, then stepped back to consider him, ignoring the obvious bulge in his pants where men are wont to get a bit bulgy. "That's a very handsome jacket, but I think it'll have to go as well."

"I am perfectly agreeable with your decision."

I slipped his jacket off, tugging it down over his arms and laying it carefully across the back of the chair. I turned to eye him. "Shoes next, I think."

I knelt down and untied his shoelaces, pulling off first one shoe, then the other. I refused to look up. I knew what was at eye level. "Well, while I'm down here, we might as well do the socks, too."

He obligingly held up his foot while I pulled his sock off. I let my fingers trail down the long length of his feet, then repeated the action with his second foot.

"You have nice feet."

"Thank you. I have few complaints of them."

"Some men have hairy toes and ugly bits, but yours are nice." I gave both feet a little pat, then without looking at his midsection, stood up. "Vest next."

"Most assuredly so."

I slipped the vest off his arms, making sure to touch as much of him as I could. I looked at him and tipped my head to the side. "Are you wild with excitement yet?"

He shook his head. "Not yet. You will have to try harder."

Ah, a challenge. I loved a challenge. I smiled to myself. "Shirt, I think."

He saw the smile and answered it with one of his own. "I look forward to that with the utmost expectations of enjoyment."

"Button one. Why, look, there's skin behind it!" I kissed the exposed hollow of his throat. He sucked in a big wad of air. "Button two. Oooh, chest hair. Nice." I kissed the bit of chest I'd uncovered, and moved down the line. "Button three. More chest hair, imagine that."

"I'm imagining, I'm imagining." He groaned as I licked a trail down the vee of flesh I'd bared. His hands were clenching and unclenching at his sides. I grinned up at him. "You're being so good, I don't think it's fair of me to tease you anymore."

"If you stop, I'll die," he said, his velvet voice rough with emotion.

"Oh, well, I wouldn't want that," I mumbled against his chest as I unbuttoned the next four buttons in quick succession. I crouched before him, holding on to his hips as I laved his belly button, watching with delight as his stomach muscles contracted under my touch. I stood up and tugged his shirt out of his pants, trailing my fingers across his chest.

"Hand," I ordered, holding out my own. He put his hand in mine. I looked at it. It was a large hand, long-fingered and sensitive. "Cuff link one." I switched hands. "Cuff link two. And now . . ."

I slid my hands up his belly, over the planes of his

chest, over his shoulders, then down his arms, pushing the shirt off as I did so, pressing little kisses along a line to his collarbone. It was so much fun, I spent a little time doing that, but there was still more package to unwrap. I picked the shirt up and tossed it onto the chair, turning back to face that part of him that I'd been avoiding looking at.

"I'll say one thing, you look a lot better without the cuts. Will you tell me what you were doing there that night?"

"Later," he said, his beautiful voice thick with unspoken emotion.

My stomach wadded itself up into a little ball, feeling not at all like a stomach should feel. I stood looking at him, wondering if I were going to throw up, or if it was just a level of arousal that I'd never felt.

"Allegra, if you do not wish to do this . . ."

He really was going to give me an out; I could see it in his eyes.

"No, I want to. I guess your belt is next."

He said nothing, but his eyes spoke volumes.

I stepped forward and bit my lip as I unbuckled his belt, pulling it free from his pants and setting it on the chair with the rest of his clothes.

"That leaves just your pants. Are you . . . um . . . wearing underwear?"

His eyes darkened. "I shall let you determine the answer to that question."

I looked deeply into his eyes and told myself it was up to me. I didn't have to do anything I didn't want to do. I placed my hand on his zipper and felt him jump. The part behind the zipper, that is. "I would say no on the underwear question."

His eyebrows rose. It took both hands, but at last I managed to unbutton the waistband and grab the little zipper tab, pulling it down as I stared into his eyes.

He boinged into my hands.

"Oh," I said as I looked down, thinking that when I'd seen him before, he must have been really cold. "My. Um. Okay. I'll just . . . um . . . hoo!" I tore my eyes from his genitals and gently pushed his pants down his hips, carefully avoiding hitting my face on his erection as I tugged the material off each leg.

"Well, I guess that's it," I said a bit breathlessly as I tossed his pants onto the chair, unable to tear my gaze from his rampant parts. A thought suddenly intruded on my visual examination. I wetted my lips. "You're not going to want me to . . . um . . ."

Christian tipped my chin up. "I don't want you to do anything you don't desire."

Instantly I felt better. "Good. Because I've never really liked . . . well, good. Can I . . . would you mind if I just touched you?"

"I would very much enjoy that," he said gravely. I glanced quickly at his face to see if he was laughing at me, but there wasn't anything there but desire and want and approval.

He was hot and silky and hard.

"Um. You're not . . . er . . . circumcised."

"No, I'm not."

"Oh. I noticed, because that bit just there isn't anything I've seen before. What am I supposed to do with the extra bit?"

"What would you like to do with it?"

169

I contemplated the extra bit. "Well . . . does this do anything for you?"

The veins stood out on his neck. "Yes, yes, it does. You may do that anytime you are struck with the desire."

I smiled, rather proud of myself. I can honestly say it's not often I've made a man's eyes cross with just two fingers. I let my fingers do a little more walking, even daring to investigate the surrounding scenery. It was all very enjoyable, much more than I had ever imagined. Christian was just . . . right. It felt right to touch him.

"Are you finished?" Christian inquired politely as I gave his penis a fond pat. I looked up, concerned. His lovely, rich voice suddenly sounded as if he were gargling marbles.

"For now, unless you don't want me to do that again."

He took a deep breath, closed his eyes, then opened them back up. "I can honestly say that the possibility of you repeating your actions will remain at the top of the list of events I fervently pray will occur. Frequently. Daily, if not hourly."

"Oh," I smiled, pleased with myself. "Good."

"And now," he said, taking another deep breath and making an effort to smooth out the marbles to his usual silky smoothness, "I believe it is my turn. Would you enjoy it more if you undressed yourself, or would you prefer for me to do it?"

My breath caught and held as my mind squirreled around and around with the question. I reminded myself that I'd done things with Christian that I'd never enjoyed before, and that remaining in control did not mean one had to be a coward and take the easy path. "I think I'd like you to undress me. If you'd like to, that is. I don't want to force you."

He swooped down on me with a noise deep in his chest that made something in my belly respond. His hands were everywhere, touching me, teasing me, plucking and pulling and unzipping and sliding my clothing off with such heated touches and whispered words of pleasure and little love nibbles that before I could catch my breath, I stood naked before him.

All of me.

Including my bad leg.

"Eeek," I said, hunching over and trying to cover up the length of scarred flesh.

"I did not eek when you stared at me—stared for at least an eternity—thus you are not allowed to hide yourself from me."

"You're telling me what to do," I told my kneecap, my arms around my leg.

"I'm simply pointing out that what was fair for you is fair for me, Allegra."

I looked up as the teasing tone faded from his voice. He held his hand out for me. "Let me see you."

"My leg is ugly."

"Only if you believe it to be. Let me see you."

Oh, how I wanted to believe he wouldn't look at all the ugly white, twisted tissue and not flinch. *If anyone can do it, Christian can,* an optimistic part of my mind said.

"Okay. I'm going to straighten up. But if you stare at anything below my waist for more than two seconds, I'm leaving. Deal?"

"As you like."

I put my hand in his and let him haul me upright. His eyes burned into mine as he pulled me up against his body, never once looking down at the rest of me. *There is no part of you that I will not worship as is your due. You are beauty and grace and everything a man can desire.*

I shifted as my nipples hardened against the soft brush of his chest hair. I caught an echo in my mind, a thought that I suspected he did not intend for me to hear.

And you are mine.

I decided to let it go. He had kept his word, was making me feel desirable and excited and wanting more from him than I'd ever wanted from a man, and all without feeling as if I were directed, controlled, just a bystander in the event. I made a seductive little purring sound I didn't know I could make, and rubbed up against him. "You're poking me."

His hands stroked up my behind to wrap around my waist, pulling me tighter against his arousal. His breath was hot on my ear as he kissed a hot path up my neck. "I wish to make love to you; I wish to join our bodies and minds in the manner of Moravians. If you tell me to stop, I will, but understand that I will likely die in the process."

I slid my fingers through his hair and licked his lips. I had no need to hesitate over the decision. I knew then that I could trust Christian to hold to his word no matter how intense things became. "Yes, please."

He kissed me, his mouth taking possession in a way I had no objection to, scooping me up and carrying me to the mammoth bed, laying me down on cool satin sheets that rubbed erotically against my skin. He moaned as he followed me down on the bed, his hands and mouth stroking my breasts and belly until I was squirming with need.

"I'm sure foreplay is a very good thing, and I will be sure to appreciate it another time, but you know, I think right this moment I want something a little more substantial," I said, all without breathing. Christian was nibbling my belly, his hair trailing down my skin, leaving rivulets of fire behind. I squirmed against him as he looked down at the really personal part of me, then up to my face.

"Command me."

I blinked and squirmed a bit more. "What?"

"Tell me what you want me to do."

I made an exasperated noise. "This is your revenge, right? You want me to command you to make love to me? You want to hear the actual words?"

"I would know exactly what you want me to do, yes. I am yours. Tell me what you want of me."

I sighed. "Okay, fine, whatever. I command you to make love to me. There, are you happy now?"

"Make love to you how?"

I stopped stroking his arm and poked him in the shoulder. "Do I have to draw you a picture?"

He shook his head, causing his hair to feather out over my belly. I shivered and tried to will him up my body. "Just tell me what you want."

I rubbed my legs up alongside his legs, uncaring for the moment that the scars were plainly visible. "I want to feel you, all of you."

"Yes? Where?" he asked as he slid forward along

173

my body until his mouth was level with my breasts. He paused to pay tribute to them. I arched my back and parted my legs wider, sliding them up his thighs.

"I want to feel you pressed against me."

He moved up until his mouth was on my collarbone. "And?"

I want to feel you inside of me.

His hands cupped my hips as he moved up higher, the hard length of him parting those delicate parts of me that I'd previously considered purely functional.

There was a delicious sort of stretching as my body accommodated his, and then he opened his mind to me, flooding me with the feelings of heat and tightness and overwhelming pleasure that he felt. I wrapped my legs around his hips as he started to move within me, kissing his neck and clutching at his back as every tiny little atom of my body joined with his in absolute ecstasy. I drowned in his pleasure and fed him my own, pushing us both higher as our bodies danced in a rhythm that left us both straining, moving to please ourselves, moving to please each other, pushing our bodies together harder and faster until I felt us bursting into a white blaze of rapture. I heard Christian sing my name just before his teeth pierced the flesh beneath my ear. I arched against him, still locked in our shared orgasm, driven past that point by the exultation he felt as he feasted on my blood. What should have been a forbidden, repulsive act was instead erotic, wild, carnal, and built within me a need I hardly dared put a name to.

His tongue was hot on my neck, pulling me back from the euphoria our joining had brought.

I lay trembling with wonderful little aftershocks,

holding tightly to him, reveling in his ragged breath and heaving chest, warm and safe and for the first time in my life, truly at peace.

What have you done? I asked, a languid hand lazily stroking the hard curves of his behind. *What have you done to me?*

He lifted his head and looked down at me, his lips brushing a gentle salute on mine, his eyes burning red and gold and brown, more variations of color than I'd thought existed. Slowly, ever so slowly, his lips curled up in an extremely smug, thoroughly male smile. *The expression is, I believe, "rocked your world."*

I bit his shoulder as he rolled us over. "You bit me."

"You bit me, as well."

"But I didn't guzzle down your blood."

"I did not guzzle, I never guzzle. I sipped. Carefully. Worshipfully. Gratefully."

I looked up from where my cheek was pressed against Christian's heart. The bed might be the very height of comfort, but he was *much* more comfortable. "Worshipfully, eh? What did I taste like?"

He smiled one of his patented lazy smiles. "Like a woman who doesn't know the depth of her own passion."

"Beast," I said, settling back down on his chest.

His hands were warm on my behind. "And have I captured Beauty?"

I shifted upward until I had my chin resting on my hands, stacked together on his breastbone. "I might be inclined to answer that if you answer a few more of my questions first."

His hands trailed up my back, making random little swirly patterns that were sending shivers of heat out from my belly to every point on my body. "Would I be correct in guessing that the first question was what I was doing in the basement of the inn, naked and covered in ninety-four cuts?"

"You would." I nodded, breathing a little heavier as his hands moved downward again to paint circles on my behind. "Ninety-four? How do you know there were ninety-four cuts?"

He closed his eyes. "Because I made them."

I frowned up at him, waiting for the rest of the explanation.

"Christian?"

"You've worn me out with your lustful demands. I'm sleepy."

"Vampires don't get sleepy. Tell me about your plan in the inn."

He gave a gentle little snore. I turned my head and took one pert little brown nipple in my mouth. His eyes shot open. I pulled away long enough to say, "If you value this nipple's life, you'll finish answering the question."

He sighed in mock regret. "I have unleashed a dragon."

"I have always been a dragon; I was just hidden in an innocent maiden's form. Why did you cut yourself ninety-four times and lie bleeding, if not to death, then at least to a weakened state that had to be dangerous?"

"Because I had arranged through a contact that you do not need to know about for Guarda White and Eduardo Tassalerro to hear that another Dark One had been caught and was being held in an extremely weakened state in the basement of an old, abandoned inn."

"Weakened, hence the need to appear as if you had lost lots of blood."

His hands slid off my behind, lower, to the tops of my thighs.

"Exactly. Unfortunately, just as White and Tassalerro arrived to examine the bait, a plucky Summoner came to save me from the horrors of eternal torment."

His fingers slid between my thighs, heading into an area that had me opening my eyes up very wide.

"Eep."

"There is something deeply erotic about a woman who mutters sweet nothings of the eep caliber into the chin of her partner."

His fingers delved. They parted. They stroked. They did things that I had no idea fingers could do in the parts in question. Oh, I *knew* they could, I just didn't know they *could*, if you get my drift. I shifted and squirmed and wiggled around on him, feeling him harden beneath me as his fingers moved to a seductive dance in my heated flesh.

I sat up, ignoring the stab of pain in my leg as I straddled him, my thighs on either side of his hips as I looked down at the man beneath me. His eyes were open now, hot with need and passion, bright with longing so strong it stripped the breath from my lungs.

I wrapped my fingers around his hard length and leaned forward, swirling my tongue around the previously abused nipple. "Tell me what you want, Christian."

He moaned. *You.*

I stroked him as I kissed my way over to his other nipple. I suckled on it for a moment, scraping it gently with my teeth, enjoying the sound of him sucking in his breath. "Tell me what you want me to do to you, Christian."

His hands shifted to my hips, gripping them as he lifted me straight up in the air. I looked down. He was poised beneath me. *I want you, Allegra.*

I reached down and teased him, pushing back the extra bit of skin and running my fingers around in investigative circles. *You want me how?*

He lowered me as I directed him where I wanted him, his hardness nudging aside all the now tingly bits of me to push into the welcoming heat of my body. *I want you around me, in me, joined with me. I want to feel our hearts beat together, our breaths merged until they cannot be separated, our minds one.*

Yes, I cried as I sank down upon him, sobs of pleasure catching in my throat. The darkness within him swirled around us and in us until he was torn between the joy of our joining and the pain of his torment. I moved upon him, finding a rhythm that I knew through our joined minds pleased him as much as it did me, and fed him my pleasure as I accepted his. Despair shadowed us until I opened my heart and took it into me, molding it, warping it, changing it into an intense sense of satisfaction that sank deep into our bones.

You are light, you are salvation, Christian breathed into my mind as our bodies quickened the pace, racing now for that final moment of completion so perfect it brought tears of happiness to my eyes. *You take my pain and give me only joy.*

I opened my eyes, wanting to see his as we reached our climax together, wanting to see deep inside him to the emptiness I knew I could fill.

You were created for me.

His eyes were an impossible, glowing midnight, so filled with emotion it almost hurt to look into them. Ecstasy coiled tighter and tighter within me until I felt as if I were going to fracture into a thousand pieces. Beneath me Christian's need built, raging through him, burning hot and hard, burning just for me. I leaned down over him, offering myself, wanting, *needing* him to take what only I could give him.

I cannot live without you.

His teeth pierced the skin above my breast, the sensation of pleasure so strong it pushed me over the edge until we were one body, one mind, one being as we succumbed to the power of our passion.

Beloved, his mind echoed in mine as we burned bright for an eternity. *You are my Beloved.*

Chapter Ten

We lay on our sides, our arms and legs twined together, our bodies slick with perspiration.

"I had no idea Dark Ones sweated," I murmured against his shoulder, too tired to even trail my fingers over the chest that lay pressed against me so warmly.

"Dark Ones can do many amazing things. Sweating is just one of them."

"Mmm. So tell me, oh amazing one, how does a nine-hundred-year-old Moravian stud muffin go about helping an exciting, exotic, wild American sex goddess to get rid of the four—count 'em, four—ghosts in her possession?"

"Stud muffin?"

I kissed his Adam's apple. "It's a term of endearment. It is supposed to convey appreciation and awe for your unspeakably fabulous sexual prowess."

"Ah. Then I will accept that term."

"Very gracious of you. Any ideas on what I'm going to do with my little foursome while I'm trying to figure out what Guarda White and company are doing and where they're holding your friend? I can't just leave them at the hotel, and I hate to keep them bound down to the bobbles. It can't be very interesting, or in the least bit fun."

"The hotel question, at least, is moot."

I looked up at him. His eyes were a sleepy, sated dark oak. "What do you mean, moot? Moot in what way?"

"Moot as in, while you have been having your wild, exotic, exciting way with me, I've had your things moved from the hotel to my home. They should be here now."

I pushed back from him until I could get enough distance to rally a really quality glare. "You what? Without my permission? Did it ever occur to you to ask me if I wanted to be moved from the hotel?" Fury built within me as I punched the pillow good and hard. "Dammit, Christian, this is exactly what I'm talking about! You can't just waltz into my life and take over! I will decide if and when I want to move in with you!"

He smoothed a strand of my hair back from where it was caught on my lip. "Guarda White will be watching you very closely. If she found out that you were not my fiancée—and I can assure you that she will be having both of us followed in an attempt to find out more about us—you would be in a very dangerous situation. I cannot allow you to put yourself in danger for me."

I ground my teeth both at that horrible word *allow*

and his high-handed action. "I can understand and even agree with what you say about Guarda. I wouldn't put it past her to send some detectives digging into our pasts. But I do object, most strenuously and strongly, to your making decisions without my knowledge and consent. I will not tolerate it, Christian; I simply will not tolerate it!"

He lay silent for a long minute, the struggle within him visible in his beautiful eyes as they darkened. "I did not see my actions in quite that light. It is difficult for me to remember that you do not wish for my protection without asking for it. For that I apologize. I should have discussed it with you first."

I blinked at him, stunned that he was willing to admit he was wrong. "Really? You admit you were wrong?"

He tugged me down until my lips rested upon his. "Yes, I do."

"Have you ever had to apologize to anyone before?"

His lips feathered across mine. "Never."

A now familiar warmth started deep within me as his hands got into the action. "It didn't hurt too much, did it?"

"Terribly. I need comforting."

"Men. Such babies," I said as I pushed him onto his back and kissed the objection right out of his mind. "You really brought my stuff here? Esme's bobble, too?"

Christian groaned and slapped a hand over my mouth, but too late, as I saw to my horror.

"Oh, my gracious heavens! You're both naked! In bed! Together! I shouldn't be seeing this, should I?

Don't look, Mr. Woogums; it isn't at all fit for you to see."

I stared in horror over Christian's biceps at Esme as she stood in bewildered delight next to Christian, her hand held over the cat's eyes. Dark as it was, I could see her examining Christian from head to toes.

"Oh, my dear, how very fortunate you are. How very fortunate indeed!"

The dream came on me just as the dawn lightened the gray, sodden skies over London. Once again I was in a house, my footsteps echoing before me as I walked down long, empty corridors, aware that I wasn't alone. This time I knew it was Christian who needed my help.

I stepped through an archway to a solid steel door, the lock enhanced by a heavy bolt. I ignored the lock and pushed open the door, entering the room to find myself with a group of people, staring at the figure of a man lying still and silent on a hard metal table. It was Christian lying on the table, his eyes empty and soulless as Eduardo drained the blood from his body.

"She will not come for you," said a small, dark-haired man standing at Christian's feet. "She will not save you, not now, not ever. She is lost to you. If I cannot have her, I will have you."

"You must choose," Eduardo said to me. I shook my head, refusing to make the decision.

Christian turned his head until his eyes met mine. A sob of protest caught in my throat as I tried to push forward, tried to stop Eduardo, tried to refute the second man. I *would* come for him; I *would* save him.

"You will trust me," Christian ordered, his eyes full of sorrow and pain; then he held his arm out to the second man, who bent over his wrist, baring fans that sank cruel and deep into Christian's flesh.

My scream echoed throughout Christian's high-ceilinged bedroom, not in the least bit muffled by the curtains that he had drawn around the bed. I lay frozen in the bed, disoriented by it, by the room, and the strangeness of a warm body lying spooned protectively behind me.

Christian's hand slid up from my hip to tighten around my belly. "Allegra? Were you dreaming?"

My heart was beating wildly, the foul taste of the nightmare still filling my mouth. Suddenly feeling as if I were suffocating, I pushed at his arm until he released me, then sat up on the edge of the bed and pushed the curtain aside, breathing deeply as I hunched over, trying to catch my breath and tell myself that not every dream I'd had turned out to come true.

"Allegra?"

Only ninety or so percent actually came to pass the way I'd dreamed them.

"What is wrong?"

"I'm okay," I mumbled, not wanting him to see me like this. I had suffered nightmares and occasionally night terrors ever since I'd started training as a Summoner. It was the main reason that I didn't sleep nights—the nightmares were less likely to come if I slept after the sun was up.

"You are not. You are shaking like a leaf in a wind-storm, and I can hear your heart beating madly from here." His warm hand touched my back. "It was a dream?"

I nodded, hugging my knees to my chest.

"I take it that it was not a dream in which you relived our recent agreeable activities?"

I shook my head.

The sheets rustled as he scooted over until he was sitting next to me. He slid his arm around me, but I pushed away from him, sliding a few feet down the bed. "No, please, don't touch me."

His pain lanced through my mind at the words. Even sickened as I was by the nightmare, I felt it necessary to reassure him, but I couldn't face those knowing eyes. I turned my head until I saw his knees, and addressed them. "It's not you; it's me. I always feel . . . *tainted* after one of these dreams. I don't want you to touch me until the feeling is gone."

"Do you have such dreams frequently?"

I didn't want to talk about the dream. I didn't want to think about it; I wanted to wipe from my memory the sight of Christian's face as he gave up his life to save me. I wanted to forget him, forget the dream, just go back to being who and what I was before I ever came to this horrible country.

Liar, I scolded myself.

I dropped my chin to my knees and squeezed my eyes shut tight, not wanting Christian to see me cry. He'd want to comfort me and if he comforted me I wasn't sure I would ever find my way back to my solitary life without him.

Why do you want to live alone when you can have Christian? my mind asked me.

I told it to get stuffed.

The dream was a warning. My dreams often are; they show me what will happen if I don't take steps to direct fate to a more pleasant path. I had no idea who the second Dark One was, nor why Christian ordered me to trust him when he was clearly sacrificing himself for me. . . . A sob caught in my throat as the memory of Christian offering his wrist replayed itself in my head. I scrubbed at my eyes and rocked silently as inside me a battle raged. The need to be with him, to take his darkness and fill him with something else warred with the knowledge that in order to save him, I would have to sacrifice everything I held dear.

Without saying a word, Christian rose from the bed and went into the en suite bathroom. I'd been in there earlier and goggled at the marble bathtub, the gold fixtures, the hand textured walls. It was a bathroom that could inspire anyone, but it was rather odd that Christian should have the urge to go in there right at the exact moment I was having a meltdown. I sniffled into my knees.

"Come, I have drawn you a bath," he said a few minutes later. I peeked up at him through damp strands of hair. "I thought you might enjoy it."

A bath suddenly sounded heavenly, only . . . I hugged my knees even tighter.

He turned around and walked to a huge wardrobe, pulling out a Chinese red silk robe. I accepted it, sliding it on quickly as I headed for the bathroom. Christian might have a body that made him think nothing of parading around nude—and heaven only knew I certainly enjoyed his parade—but I did not care to be seen marching about in my birthday suit.

I paused at the door and looked back at where he stood. "Thank you."

He accepted my thanks with a slight nod.

It took me a long time to scrub the aftereffects of the nightmare off my skin, but when I emerged from the bathroom in a cloud of jasmine-scented steam, I had come to several decisions. The first was that I would ignore the fact that Christian had used a capital *B*—I could tell by the inflection he used that it was a capital—when calling me his Beloved. I was sure that slip of the tongue was due more to the fact that we seemed to be very compatible when it came to a physical relationship than to any notion that I might be the sole person who could salvage his soul. We were good together, I argued to myself, but not *that* good.

My second decision was that I was going to have to ignore Christian's previous request that I not see Guarda alone. He'd told me earlier that he didn't think it was safe for me to meet with her by myself, and bemused as I was by the fact that I was at that moment draped over his chest, I hadn't objected to his request that I wait until he'd risen for the night before keeping my appointment with her. That was predream, however. Postdream, I knew what would happen should Guarda and Eduardo ever find out just who Christian was—and I would move heaven and earth to see to it that did not happen.

I stood by the side of Christian's bed, watching him as he slept, and decided that my third decision—that I would accept his invitation to stay with him—was sound. There was really no reason to make myself miserable by cutting off all contact with him. Be-

sides, I told myself as I slipped out of the silk bathrobe and into the bed, it was much easier to keep
tabs on him if I were staying here.

He murmured sleepily as I snuggled up against his
back. *Are you better now, Beloved?*

I ignored the Beloved and slid my hand over his
hip and up his chest, pressing my cheek against the
warm flesh of his back. He felt solid, strong, invin-
cible, but I knew that could change in an instant.
"Much better, thank you for understanding."

*Will you tell me of this dream that left you so dev-
astated?*

"No."

He turned until I was pressed against his chest, my
head tucked under his chin. I sighed and allowed his
heat to sink into me as he tossed a heavy thigh over
my legs. *I did not ask to pry, malý váleèník. I want
only to help you.*

"I know you do." I yawned, snuggling a bit closer
so I could melt against him. "But it's okay now. I just
want to go to sleep."

His breath was slow and soft on my hair as we both
drifted off into sleep. Just before I let sleep claim me,
I felt the faintest echo in my head.

You have much to learn of trust, Beloved.

"All right, we have a couple of ground rules that I
want to go over before I leave. Jem, please stop picking your ear and pay attention. I'm sure there's nothing in there you haven't seen before. Esme, can you
ask Alis if she'd leave off waving her hands through
Christian's vase long enough to listen? Thank you.
Now, since I have told the couple who takes care of

Christian's house that I was leaving some very valuable equipment in here that mustn't be disturbed, they have promised not to come in. As long as you stay *in this room*, everything will be fine."

I ignored the faint nudging at my mind.

"There's a bloke there wot wants ye," Jem said, glowering at me. I was starting to get used to his perpetual sulk, figuring it was just part and parcel of a teenage male, even ghostly teenage males. I nodded at him, then took a closer look at his face.

"Whatever have you done to your eyebrow? It can't be . . . You didn't . . . Is it pierced? Why did you do that? More important, *how* did you do that?"

He slouched aggressively at me.

"And what happened to your powdered wig? Didn't you have a powdered wig? I *know* you had a powdered wig!"

He sneered.

Someone behind me nudged my mind again.

"Esme, is it possible for you to change your appearance if you desire?"

She sat with ladylike elegance in the leather chair behind Christian's desk. "Why, yes, dear, of course we can. Anytime."

"But . . . but . . ." I looked from her ratty slippers to her nightgown and bathrobe. "But if you can change your clothes and such . . ."

She smiled. "There will come a time in your life when you learn to value comfort over fashion. Although I hope for Christian's sake that time doesn't come anytime soon. You're *comfortable* enough now."

I cleared my throat and looked away, feeling a bit

of a blush burn my cheeks. We'd had a terrible time getting Esme from Christian's room once she decided that it was her matchmaking efforts that had made the difference in our relationship. Christian had to decline her offer of lovemaking advice three times before we finally convinced her to go haunt his study, the room I now stood in.

The ghost behind me nudged me again. I gritted my teeth and ignored it.

"Okay, so the rule is that you must stay here in this room, and no investigating anywhere else in the house. Christian will be up once it's dark, and I'll be gone until then, so you're just going to have to amuse yourselves as best you can until then. Need I remind you—Alis, would you *please* stop trying to knock over Christian's vase! I doubt if you can summon the psychic energy necessary to have a physical impact on it, and all that arm waving is a bit distracting. Where was I?"

Behind me, a book flew off the bookshelf and hit the desk. Esme looked at it with interest.

"Um . . . oh, yes. Need I remind you that if anyone misbehaves—"

A second book flew off the shelf.

"—the punishment will be the keepers. Since I've heard from you all that you don't like being bound to a bobble and stuffed in my pocket, I trust you'll all behave so I won't have to take that action."

A red rose materialized out of the air and fell to my feet.

"Oh, my, how romantic!" Esme said as the cat limped over to sniff it.

"Wot're we supposed t'do then, while yer off? Just

sit 'ere an' watch t'old loony bat at them big fancy bits?"

I stepped over the rose and picked up the remote control to the television hidden in an oak armoire. "I'll turn the TV on, but low. You can watch it, or stare out the window, or pick your toes for all I care, just as long as you do it in this room."

Jem dropped his habitual sullenness long enough to stare in openmouthed surprise at the TV. "Wot's it?"

"It's a television. Oh, I don't have time to explain it to you. Esme, you've seen one, yes?"

"Heavens, yes. The maid who used to do my room turned it on every day. Mr. Woogums and I became quite the devotees of *Coronation Street*."

Two more roses materialized and fluttered down at my feet, accompanied by a big push at my mind. "Good, you can explain what a TV is to Jem. Alis, what *is* your problem?"

"She was a housekeeper, dear."

"So?"

"For a man who owned a sizable china collection. He insisted that she be the only one who attend to his things, since they were so valuable. It's only natural that she should hate the sight of objets d'art."

"Hmmm." I watched her for a moment. "You don't think she could focus enough to actually do any damage?" Ghosts, when focused, can sometimes rally enough psychic energy to interact in our world in a physical manner, as demonstrated by the roses that were appearing with regularity at my feet. I knew Christian's vase and a nearby delicate bust of a Greek goddess that had also attracted Alis's attention must be valuable, and hated to think of her inadvertently destroying them.

Esme tore her eyes from the TV and looked thoughtful. "I doubt it, although the gentleman who's trying to get your attention certainly could."

At her words, the jade green–and-blue vase lifted up three inches off its plinth and tilted at a rakish angle.

"Put that down!" I snarled, reaching in my pocket for my chalk and ash. "Carefully, or I won't Summon you!"

The vase settled down with a soft murmur of antique china on highly polished wood.

I drew a circle, hurried through the wards, spoke the words, and pushed away the annoyance of having to Summon a pesky, pushy ghost when I needed to be leaving. I had a difficult enough time dragging myself from Christian's arms after only a couple of hours of sleep; I didn't want to be here when he awoke and noticed my absence.

As I sneezed and got to my feet the air shimmered and collected itself, darkening into the figure of a swarthy man with dark, curly hair, a short, pointed beard, glittering blue eyes, an Elizabethan ruff, a scarlet-and-gold doublet, and what surely must have been a greatly exaggerated codpiece. I grounded the spirit and gathered up my coat.

"*Mi amor!* My beautiful one! You 'ave at last succumbed to my charms and you draw me forth!" His voice was a pleasant tenor with a heavy Spanish accent. I pegged him for one of the Spanish courtiers who hung around Elizabeth's court before the armada took a drubbing.

"What's your name?" I asked as I shoved my arms into my coat.

He kissed his hand to me. "I am Antonio de Gutierrez, Count de Seville and your most 'umble servant."

He made a deep, flourish-laden bow.

"You have ten seconds to explain why you insisted I Summon you."

"*Mi corazón,*" he said, his hand over his heart, his eyes filled with amorous longing. "You 'ave only to ask, and I will attend. I saw you in the arms of that peon, that Dark One, and I knew you were meant for me. You are a Summoner! You have the same fire in your 'eart as I 'ave in mine. Who else could 'ave brought me forth from the dark and dismal existence I 'ave suffered these many centuries?"

I shook a small, squat candle at him. "Look here, no one—I repeat, *no one*—is allowed to watch when Christian and I . . . er . . . when we're alone together. Everyone got that?"

Esme nodded. Jem floated in a cross-legged position about six inches away from the TV. Alis started screaming at a small ceramic cat that sat in one of the bookcases. Mr. Woogums licked his private parts.

"Good. Now, as for you . . ." I turned back to Antonio. He flung himself toward the door and struck a seductive pose before it. "I don't have the time to stay and hear your story, or figure out what it is you need to move on, so this is going to have to be quick. Either you agree to stay right here, in this room, without stepping spectral foot from it, or I'll bind you to this candle."

He stared at the candle. It had herbs mixed into

the wax, and had a pleasing scent reminiscent of frankincense. "You could not find something a bit more masculine? A bit more dashing?"

"No. It's either the candle or stay in this room without leaving. The choice is yours."

He made a pretty pout, which quickly turned into a full-frontal leer. "I will agree to your demands, my fiery one, but it is only because I live to please you."

"You're dead," I pointed out as I grabbed my purse. "All right, everyone, be good. I'll be back as soon as I can. And remember the bobbles! The first one of you who steps out of line will be bobbled for a whole week!"

Esme gasped and put a hand to her cheek. Alis and Jem ignored me. Antonio upped the wattage in his leer and waggled his eyebrows in a manner I was sure he felt was breathtakingly provocative.

"*Mi corazón*, would you not care to 'ave a little discussion with me in a private little room I know of? It would not take long, perhaps 'alf an 'our or so. You will take off your clothes, and I will take off my clothes, and then we will—"

"No! Now stay here and behave."

He gave me a look that had he been alive would have melted steel. "You do not know what you will be missing, but me, I will be patient. Soon you will be mine! Soon you will look at me and demand I pleasure you as I 'ave pleasured so many other women." He stopped suddenly, muttering something under his breath. "Women that meant nothing to me, nothing at all. I cannot even remember them, so dazzling is your beauty."

I shooed him away from the door with an exasperated sigh. He posed next to the Greek bust, stacking his hands on top of it and resting his chin on his hands, donning an expression that would have been irresistible had he been living.

"Oh, for heaven's . . . Antonio, you're dead. I'm alive. Even if I wanted to, and I can tell you that Christian is more than enough man for any woman, there is no way I can be yours. The sooner you get that idea through your head, the happier we'll both be. So stop giving me those seductive little looks and put your codpiece on ice. I've got more important things to do than to beat off a five-hundred-year-old Romeo."

"Antonio, not Romeo," he said mournfully, looking at me with wounded puppy-dog eyes.

"Gah!" I shouted, then made my escape before he propositioned me again.

Chapter Eleven

"Good night, Nelly," I snorted as I closed the door, locking it with the key Christian had given me earlier.

"I beg your pardon, miss?"

I hurriedly slipped on my glasses and smiled at Turner, one of the two people who took care of Christian when he stayed in London. "Nothing. Is my taxi here?"

He nodded and flicked away a molecule of dust that had dared to land on the banister.

I had a feeling that Christian's servants didn't exactly approve of me, but since Christian had told me earlier that they thought the same of him, an eccentric novelist who kept odd hours, I wasn't overly worried how they viewed my sudden, sunglass-wearing appearance any more than I worried about Roxy's claim that he kept a houseful of servants to act as dinner on the hoof, so to speak.

Christian informed me that he always ate out.

I spent the time in the taxi mulling over just how I could get the information I wanted from Guarda without her knowing what I was up to. Of prime importance was the need to find out where Sebastian was being held, but I couldn't think of a way to go about asking that without giving everything away. I decided I'd tackle the ghost that Guarda held. It made sense that wherever they were keeping the ghost was likely to be the same place that they were holding the captured Dark One.

A ghost could be bound to a location that was not his or her original haunt in three ways: the first was to bind the ghost to a keeper and deposit the keeper in the location, the second was for a Summoner to invoke the ghost's name, and keep the Summoner prisoner (thereby trapping the spirit as well), and the third . . . well, the third was something I really didn't want to think about. It involved cursing the spirit to forever remain in the location. There was a way for a Summoner to Release a cursed spirit, but as it involved calling up the demon that was used to enact the curse, I had little knowledge and even less experience in that area.

I hoped the answer was as simple as the keeper, and tried to clear my mind of all thoughts of Christian and the now five ghosts that I had sneezed up.

Ten minutes later I was ushered into a quiet, spartan office done in neutral taupe and oatmeal tones. There was a slight tingle that heralded a ward on the door to Guarda's office as I passed through it, but as she had called out an invitation for me to step into the office, the ward allowed me to pass without slowing me down. Still, I made note that she was powerful enough to keep a ward active on a door for what must be a great length of time.

"Allegra, how nice to see you again." She rose and came around a huge desk to greet me. I held out my hand, assuming she wanted to shake it. "Oh, would you mind if I didn't? I'm so sensitive these days, and it unnerves me to touch others when I have to do a Summoning later. I mean no offense, of course."

"None taken," I said, more than a little surprised that she was also a Summoner. She felt to me more like a psychometrist, someone who knows things related to an object just by touching it. A Summoner who could also tell the history of an object with just a brush of her fingers was a very powerful person—perhaps that was why I was instantly wary of her. "I'll just sit here, shall I?"

I sat on the taupe and muted green striped chair when she nodded, trying not to squirm when she sat on the edge of her desk and examined me closely. "You look rested."

I thought of the night I'd spent doing anything but resting, then quickly pushed it from my mind. Even with my guards up, I didn't want to leave any untoward thoughts of Christian around where Guarda might pick upon them. She had gently felt around the edges of my mind twice since I'd walked through the door.

"Thank you, I am. I feel much better, although Christian did make me promise him that I wouldn't Summon today, just to be on the safe side."

She stood up and walked back around her desk, but not before I saw her eyes move quickly to a black glass etching on the wall. I opened my mind up a little and felt the presence of someone behind the wall. It was Eduardo; I was willing to bet my life on it. The hair on the back of my neck rippled uncomfortably. I hate being spied on. "Ah, your fiancé. What did you say his surname was?" She picked up her pen and poised it over a piece of cream paper.

I sucked on the inside of my cheek for a minute. "I don't believe that ever came up, and to be truthful, I'm not sure why you're asking now. I like to keep my private life private, Mrs. White. I'm sorry you were so concerned about me last night that you were forced to come to our home, but I can assure you that I normally keep my business and personal affairs separate."

She set the pen down and leaned back in an expensive leather chair dyed the same color as the muted green stripes. "I see." She watched me for a minute, tapping her finger on her chin before finally coming to some decision. "I must tell you, Miss Telford, we at the Trust take our role very seriously. No amount is spared to ensure that the research conducted under the Trust's eye is as exacting as possible. We apply the same practice to the researchers who are members of the Trust. For that reason we investigate the background of each member thoroughly before admitting them to the inner circle. You will agree, of course, that such precautions are necessary to keep out people who might have philosophies different from those that govern the Trust."

"Yes," I drawled, wondering how much investigation she could have done on me in just one night.

Quite a bit, as it turned out.

"It is for that reason that I made sure the background check into your past was treated with the highest priority."

Oh, rats. I had a sick feeling I knew what she was going to say.

"Our investigation revealed that your employer in the West Coast UPRA office believed that you were staying at a hotel in Mayfair. A check of that hotel provided confirmation of the fact that until eleven o'clock yesterday evening, you were registered there. Despite having a reservation for the room that still had two and a half weeks to run, your account was paid up, your things were packed, and you were checked out."

I tried to stay calm and not fidget, but it wasn't easy under the influence of Guarda's pale blue eyes. They both dominated and seemed to invite confidence. I couldn't decide which feeling I disliked the most.

"In addition, your employer informed my investigator that this was your first trip to England. I find it somewhat unlikely that you met and accepted a marriage proposal from your fiancé in the matter of a few days," she said mildly, but there was no mildness in her eyes. They were compelling me to reveal my innermost thoughts, something I struggled against with a rising sense of panic.

"Um . . . well, about that," I said, thinking quickly. "As a matter of fact, we aren't really engaged. Not formally. But . . . um . . . Christian and I met a few days ago and we really hit it off, and, well, you know how these things can be."

"No," she said quietly. "I do not. Tell me."

I waved a vague hand around and tried to look mortified that my relationship with Christian was being bandied about. It wasn't too hard to do. "It's all a bit embarrassing to admit to someone that you've hopped into the sack with a person you've just met, so Christian said we were engaged. That's all."

"Is it?"

I slapped an innocent look on my face and met her gaze without wavering.

Much.

"I believe that it is not all, Allegra. I believe that there is something more you have to tell me regarding the two spirits you Summoned in the theater."

Oh, poop. How did she know about Jem and Alis?

"Um . . ."

"Eduardo and Steven both examined the building the theater is in from attic to basement. They could find signs of only one spirit remaining. Thus the spirits you Summoned must have either been Released, which would have taken far longer an amount of time than you had available, or . . ."

She looked at me with her icy blue eyes, demanding that I tell her the truth. Her mind gave mine a little push at the same time, which served only to tick me off. I hate it when psychics get pushy.

"Or what?" I asked, feigning disinterest.

"Or you bound the spirits into keepers when my attention was elsewhere, and smuggled them out of the theater after you pretended to faint. Since that seems to be the most reasonable explanation, I have come to the reluctant conclusion that you have not entered into the spirit—if you will forgive the expression—of the Trust in a manner at all consistent

201

with furthering the tenets we hold inviolate."

I ignored the prickling on the back of my neck and dug up a smile. "Well, that's one theory, yes."

"Do you have another explanation you would care to make?"

I shrugged, trying for the graceful nonchalance that Christian always seemed to have. I didn't quite pull it off. "I'm not sure I have to explain my actions to you, Mrs. White. I have agreed to think about joining your organization, but as you know, I am already employed. I would have to seek and obtain a leave of absence from UPRA before I could commit myself. I'm sorry if my little white lie about Christian has led you to question my actions or intentions, but I can assure you that the furthering of knowledge about ghosts and other spectral entities is my number one priority. I do not keep ghosts against their will. I do not make it a habit of hiding information from my employers. I can tell you in all honesty that I do not have any spirits bound to keepers."

She reached across her desk to press a buzzer, a purely unnecessary action, since I knew full well that Eduardo had been watching the entire conversation. "I am willing to overlook this incident in order to further our working relationship. Regardless, I find myself in a position of needing to protect a valuable resource. For that reason I have arranged accommodations in the town house where the other Trust members have gathered. I am certain you will be very comfortable there, the staff is prone to spoiling the Trust members. We will, of course, collect your things from your acquaintance's home and bring them to your new rooms. Ah, Eduardo, there you are.

Miss Telford and I were just having a discussion about the future."

"Indeed? I gather the confusion over the missing ghosts has been cleared up?" He smiled a white, toothy smile at me, full of false bonhomie and dark thoughts behind his gray eyes.

I smiled back, hoping his phony white teeth rotted from his head. He knew full well that the question of the ghosts hadn't been settled. "Why, yes, I believe it has. You might try finding a psychic who has a little more delicate touch, as you and Mr. Rick didn't seem to be able to feel the ghosts."

It was a dig, and it scored points, but oh, how I was to pay for my folly.

"And as for your accommodations, Mrs. White, I much appreciate the offer, but I'm quite comfortable where I am. Young love and all that," I simpered.

"I am afraid I must be quite insistent on this point," Guarda said in a tone of voice that brooked no further discussion. "We have only your best interests at heart, of course."

I have never been one to take orders. Not since my rebirth into a self-aware, confident woman, that is. I made a faux moue of regret. "Alas, I must be just as insistent. I am certain that such a situation would not at all suit me, perhaps even going so far as to stifle my abilities, leaving me unable to practice those very arts that you would find so attractive."

Subtly would never be said to be my middle name.

Guarda and Eduardo exchanged glances. A little ripple of power in the room raised goose bumps on my arms. I started to get a bit worried that they might be serious in their attempt to keep me under their control, into the belly of their ARMPIT house and away from Christian. I figured it was time to focus their attention on something else. Perhaps if I appeared to rethink my objections and seemed amiable, I would have an opportunity to escape without damaging our tenuous relationship, a relationship I needed if I were to figure out where Christian's friend was being held. Then again, perhaps Guarda was too smart to be fooled by a sudden about-face.

"Well," I said with a little laugh that sounded forced even to my ears, "let us not get our knickers in a twist, as the English say. I'm sure we can work something out regarding the accommodations. I am very cognizant of the importance of the Trust; perhaps if you told me more about its day-to-day workings, how many members there are, what research projects you have under way, what locations you use, et cetera, I might be more willing to give up an extremely interesting companion for a solitary bed in your town house."

Guarda sent a glance fraught with significance to Eduardo. I cursed the fact that I hadn't a shred of mind-reading ability in my body, and chastised myself soundly for being so quick to dismiss Christian's objections to my meeting Guarda alone.

"Yes, of course," she said, steepling her fingers as Eduardo perched on the edge of her desk. She didn't look too convinced by my performance, but was obviously going to give me the benefit of the doubt. "The Trust is, as you know, made up of several influential and important people who have a profound interest in paranormal research. Our headquarters are here, in London, where we have the town house and a research facility, in addition to three other houses in various locations around the U.K., where we spend time conducting experiments into a variety of related paranormal fields. Our primary focus is, of course, spirits and spirit activities."

Three houses, hmm? I put on my best tourist face. "That sounds fascinating, especially the part about the houses. I assume the houses are active, yes? I love active sites. I'm dying to visit the Tower of London, but I bet you guys have been all over that. Where exactly are these houses? I haven't had much of a chance to see England, really, other than at night, and generally my touristing is limited to sites with known phenomena."

Eduardo gave me his phony smile again. "One of our houses is a converted abbey just outside of London. The second is a house in an area in Scotland that has seen several bloody battles; the third is a small cottage in Cornwall that has tremendous activities around the solstices. We believe there is some druid influence there."

"Druids, really, how very fascinating. What exactly are you doing with the spirits that your Trust members Summon?" I turned back to look at Guarda and prayed my tone sounded chatty and not in the least prying. "You mentioned that you wish to keep the ghosts available for research for a little time before Releasing them—what sorts of research are you conducting?"

Guarda ran through the usual litany of tests: spectral analysis, aural dissection, ion and EMF examinations, as well as personal histories and interviews regarding their time bound in spirit form. All pretty standard stuff except the last two. What bothered me was that she was lying, and lying big-time, lying through her teeth.

Summoners have a very good grasp of who is lying and who isn't. It's something to do with our sensitivity to minute environmental changes (a ghost's arrival is always heralded by a slight change in the room temperature and air density). My theory is that our acute awareness of the physical environment is what allows us to detect people in a lie so easily, but other Summoners have other theories.

All I knew at that point was that Guarda was lying to me.

"Fascinating. Well, this has been a really interesting discussion; thank you for being so open with everything. I will think over your offer to stay at the trust house, and will let you know my decision in the next few days. In the meantime, I promised a friend I'd go check out a cold spot in his basement, but I'll be here bright and early tomorrow morning and we can see about Summoning those two missing ghosts at the theater."

I rose as I spoke, but neither Guarda or Eduardo stood with me. "I'm afraid we can't allow that, Allegra," Guarda said slowly, then pulled out a desk drawer. I gasped in horror as I looked over her shoulder, and quickly sketched a protective ward in front of me when both she and Eduardo turned to look at the spot I was staring at. I had no time to do more than sketch the one ward (one to each compass point is recommended for a truly dangerous situation), but I was hoping it had the power to stop a bullet should Guarda be reaching for a gun.

"Sorry," I said when they turned to look back at me, Guarda's hand holding nothing more dangerous than a sheaf of papers. I slumped in relief and came up with a feeble excuse. "I thought I saw something. Boy, what a boob I am, eh? I guess it's a good thing I'm not on tonight!"

A handful of papers couldn't hurt me, right? Right. Not with a ward guarding me, they couldn't. Behind my back I sketched a second ward, then held my hand tight to my bad leg and traced a third. In order to be fully protected from harm, I needed to trace the fourth, but I couldn't do it with Eduardo standing there watching me with those cold gray eyes.

"As I was saying, I'm afraid you represent too great an asset to the Trust to allow you to go traipsing around damp basements on mere whims. If you had cleared the site through the Trust, we would, of course, be happy to have you investigate it after the proper preliminary work was completed on it. You must allow us to be overprotective of our little charges," she added with a horribly insincere smile.

"Of course," I answered, my stomach knotting with concern. I could feel the waves of hostility rolling off her. Once again she tested the guards on my mind, but they held without the slightest bit of give.

"If you will just sign these few papers, everything will be official and we can pay you your first honorarium."

"Oh? How much is that?"

She glanced at Eduardo. "Five thousand pounds for the first month's work," he answered smoothly.

I just about dropped my purse. That was almost $7,500! Just for one month?

"Gark," I said, then suited action to thought and dropped my purse.

Right on top of a small bud vase containing a perfect yellow rose. The vase was knocked over, breaking the delicate glass and sending the water racing toward Eduardo's hind end. He leaped up off the table with a nasty word.

"Oh, I'm so sorry!" I gushed as I turned my body sideways and quickly traced the last ward. "How clumsy of me! Such a pretty rose, too."

"Never mind, leave it, it's quite all right." Guarda's mouth was white with tension, but it was nothing compared to what I was feeling. Now that I was protected, shielded from the influence of Guarda's power, I could feel the threat in the air. It was positively thick with malevolence. She held the pen out to me, but I shook my head and backed away, clutching my purse to my chest.

"I'm sorry, I couldn't. My contract with UPRA says I can't work for any other organization without their consent. I will have to contact my boss to get permission to join you before I sign anything."

"We will call him now. Anton Melrose is his name, yes? Give me the number and you may speak with him."

The power rolling out of her manifested itself in me as nausea. I swayed a little, then moved slowly backward until I had the chair between me and her desk. "No, it's . . . uh . . . Wednesday! Anton always plays golf with the Archbishop of . . . um . . . Fresno on Wednesday. He won't be in the office today."

Eduardo fairly snarled at me. I stepped backward again. "Then you will resign your position. We will see to it that you are more than adequately compensated financially."

"Oh, I couldn't do that," I lied as I took another step backward, praying the wards would keep him from reading my lie. "I owe Anton everything. I couldn't possibly just quit like that. I couldn't!"

The air behind me stirred. I whirled around, blinking with surprise at the woman who entered the room.

"Is there a problem?" the hermit Phillippa asked, giving me a large berth. "I can feel your anger all the way down the hall, Guarda. What is amiss?"

She stopped next to Eduardo and the three of them looked at me. I collected my jaw from where it was hanging around my knees, and thought fast and furious. If Phillippa was here and on friendly terms with Guarda, that meant she was a part of the Trust. It also meant that Guarda was likely to know that I had Esme and Mr. Woogums as part of my entourage, and that I hadn't figured out how to Release them.

All of which added up to some pretty bad trouble for Allegra the Summoner.

Beloved? Christian's voice was sleepy, but infinitely reassuring in my mind. I wasn't alone! *You are frightened?*

Very, I answered, twisting my fingers into my purse. *I've done something stupid.*

I felt his sigh even before his words caressed my mind. *Foolish, perhaps, but never stupid, Beloved.*

"Um, Phillippa, what a surprise. I hadn't expected to see you here."

I'm in Guarda's office. With Eduardo and the hermit

I told you about. I think they want to force me to go live in their town house. They don't seem to be inclined to let me walk out of here, Christian.

His silence was almost as loud as his second sigh. *I believe I will withdraw my objection over the word* stupid.

"Indeed." The hermit turned to Guarda. "She is speaking to someone who is at a distance from us. With whom has she had contact?"

My eyes widened. How did she know I was talking to Christian? And could she tell who he was? The need to protect him was very strong, strong enough that I closed down my mind to him.

I understand, Allegra. It is still daylight; I cannot come to rescue you.

I swallowed hard. Christian seemed so normal to me, I'd forgotten that he couldn't go out in daylight.

I will send help.

Just the touch of his mind in mine reminded me that I was not a victim; I was a woman in charge of her life. I raised my chin a notch and stared down my nose at Phillippa.

"Really? How very interesting." Guarda looked at me with speculation, then edged around her desk and approached me. I backed up until she stopped a few feet away from me. The ward I'd sketched in the air suddenly flared to life, glowing a shimmering gold in the pale, watery light of a rainy November afternoon.

"Wards!" Guarda hissed, then shot me a look of loathing that I won't soon forget.

Phillippa walked a circle around me. As she

reached each ward, it burst into light, fading when she passed its range of protection.

"She is guarded," Phillippa acknowledged. "Still, there may be a way."

Uh-oh. I didn't like the sound of that. I prayed Christian was going to summon the fire department or other emergency service, because I had a worrisome notion that whatever Phillippa was planning, it wasn't going to be fun.

"Um. You know, I think I'll just be leaving. We can talk about this whole Trust thing another day. My fiancé will be waiting for me."

They ignored me to huddle together and speak in tones so quiet I couldn't hear them. I knew as soon as I neared the door that Guarda had done something to it, had warded it so that it would not allow anyone to pass through the door whom she wished to remain within, but I gave it a shot anyway. None of the three even bothered to as much as look my way as I struggled to press through the invisible wall that denied exit to me.

"Hell's bells," I snarled to myself, and took a step back to collect myself. A ward could be undone if you studied it and determine how it was made. Every person who drew wards did so by following a basic format, then personalizing it, adding a word here, a gesture there, something that didn't interfere with the basic function of the ward, but which made it unique and impossible to remove unless you had the time and leisure to examine it closely. It wasn't actually the ward itself that provided the power; it was the belief the person drawing it had in his own abilities. That was why infrequently drawn wards, like the one

I used on Christian at Joy's house, were likely to dissolve after a short amount of time. I hadn't used them enough to have complete faith in my ability to draw them.

Guarda's ward, however, glowed silver when I pushed myself into the doorway, and was of such a complex design that it would take me hours to unravel.

Allegra.

The voice was loud in my head, compelling, demanding, filled with absolute authority. It was *not* Christian's silken tones.

Against my will I turned around slowly. The four wards around me glowed gold, but I ignored them to blink at the scene before me. Guarda and Phillippa stood together, unmoving as they watched me with eyes that were empty, as if they were looking inward on themselves. Behind them Eduardo sat on the desk, his head tipped back, his eyes closed, his hands stretched forward to hold . . . I gasped and tried to back up. I couldn't; my feet were frozen, locking me in place as I stared in horror at the three of them. Eduardo's fingers were pressed to the base of both their necks.

They had formed a triumvirate, the most powerful force known to modern psychics.

And they had breached my defenses.

Chapter Twelve

You will cease struggling against us.

I tried to take a deep breath, but the protective crouch I'd assumed as the triumvirate's joined mind slammed into mine made it impossible to breathe deeply.

You will recognize that we are stronger.

I took lots of tiny little breaths instead, and struggled to focus my attention on something trivial and innocent, something that couldn't be used against me or be corrupted by the power flooding into my mind.

You will tell us what you have done with the ghosts you have in your possession.

The bits of broken bud vase erupted into powder.

I forced my attention to my shoes. The toes were scuffed. I wondered how it was possible to scuff the top of the toes when it was the soles that made contact with the floor.

A small muted green pillow on the love seat beneath the etched black picture exploded in a flurry of foam bits.

The triumvirate's power was increasing, small tendrils of it leaking out into the office.

You will tell us with whom you were speaking.

I pushed the bits of foam away from my feet. It wasn't as if I had made a habit of scraping the upper part of my shoes against things. Yet it was the tops of my shoes that were scuffed.

Allegra Telford.

There was power in a name. Pain shuddered through me as I fought to resist their unspoken command and tucked my head between my knees, praying help would arrive soon. I wasn't sure how much longer I could hold out against the triumvirate's strength.

Books began flying from a glass-fronted bookcase. Straight through the glass.

Help will not arrive to save you. You must yield to us. You cannot do anything but yield.

My inner voice screamed in agony at the sheer volume of power that was being thrown at me. It was like standing directly in front of a jet engine's fan, shards of power piercing me and weakening both my mind and body. Shoes, I desperately told my screaming self. Shoes were what was important. What did they call the little plastic tips on the ends of shoelaces?

Books struck my body. The triumvirate was directing the power leaks, forcing them into a pattern that would help them and weaken me further. I couldn't believe anyone had enough control that they could direct the leaks, and yet with every blow I had proof.

I started to wonder if I was going to make it.

It is no use. You are not strong enough. You are not good enough to resist us. Until you came to England you were a failure, unproven, tested and failed. Do not destroy yourself trying to prove you can best us. No one can. We are all powerful.

For one moment I listened to the words shouted in my mind, and in that moment I found myself walking toward the threesome.

No! I screamed, grabbing the back of the chair to keep from moving closer to them, flinching every time a book slammed up against me. Another power leak had manifested itself as a whirlwind inside the office, bits of paper and foam from the cushion whirling around us, occasionally hitting me in the face. I clung to the chair and tried to lecture myself. If I gave myself up to them, if I answered their call when they summoned me, my wards would be dissolved and I would be at their mercy.

I am strong, I grimly told myself. *I lived through hell in my life, and I've overcome it. I could last here a little bit longer, just until . . .* I erased the image of Christian my mind had wanted to draw even before it formed. I wouldn't give him to them.

You will tell us who you believe will save you.

The little plastic shoelace thing has a name, I screamed to them. *I know it has a name; I just can't remember what it is.*

Two windows looking out onto the street below

shattered, the faint tinkle of glass hitting the pavement sucked up by the howling of the wind within the room.

We have run out of patience. We will tolerate this no longer. You have brought this upon yourself. Allegra Telford, the forces of life shine strong within us.

Panic filled me as I clutched the chair even harder. Those were the first words of grounding, of the way a Summoner bound a spirit. Why were they saying it to me? It couldn't work on a living person, could it?

The power of life binds you to us.

I looked down on myself. It felt like a hundred little ropes were tied to various points on my body, and were slowly snaking outward to form a solid connection to the triumvirate. I started slapping at the invisible ropes, breaking them off, terrified that they really had the power they claimed over me, but as each rope snapped, another formed.

You are lost, my inner voice screamed. *Give in now while you still have your mind!*

Until you are released, you will heed our command.

A heavy book flew into the back of my head, making me see stars. I fought desperately to stay conscious, to keep the remainder of my strength focused on the wards, but I knew it was a lost cause. The wards burned brilliant gold now, filling the room with warm light that seemed to be instantly absorbed by the blackness that seeped out of the triumvirate. Cracks started to appear in ancient symbols, showing a bright, blinding white through the gold. I had no idea how they had twisted the words of grounding to affect me, but I wanted out of there, out of that room and away from the power that was being thrown at me. I knew the limitations of my abilities, and they couldn't stand much more.

Suddenly Eduardo's eyes opened, the gray of his irises glowing with an eerie inner light. I clung to the chair, knowing that the second he turned those eyes on me, I was a goner. I could feel that the grounding was unfinished, but I knew he was about to say the last words, to bind me against my will to them. I just didn't have the strength needed to feed power to the wards and keep my mind focused away from their control.

You can do anything you want, a soft voice soothed me.

Christian?

Ah, it is her fiancé she speaks to.

Oh, hell, they'd heard me!

It is all right, Allegra. You are not alone. They cannot harm you. I would not allow that.

He poured power into me, draining himself to give me the strength that I needed to face Eduardo and fight the grounding, filling me with strength and re-assurance and a belief in me that warmed my heart. I pulled on his power, reinforcing the wards until they were whole again, and the hundreds of little cords stretching from me to them were dissolved.

By the triumvirate, you are thus bound.

I braced myself, but the final words of Eduardo's grounding couldn't penetrate the reinforced wards. I almost cried in relief.

Your connection to Christian has doomed him. We have seen your thoughts. We know now what he is. You have sealed his fate.

I fell to my knees at the smug satisfaction in the

triumvirate's voice, the wards once again glowing gold and white. Despair filled my heart at their words because I knew that what they said was true, knew that I had failed. My dream wasn't a warning; it was a glimpse of the future.

A future I had just made sure would come true.

Beloved, you have more faith in yourself than this. I do not believe you have doomed me. I know you are my salvation. You are everything light and good; you take my darkness and you make me whole. You have more power than you will ever realize. Do not listen to their lies. You know what is within you. Hold tight to that.

I shut out the triumvirate's voice that was screaming in my head and focused on Christian's words. He was right; I was strong. I'd done amazing things. I had survived my own hell, I had Summoned ghosts, I had taken darkness and made it light. That was not the description of a woman who would buckle before a triumvirate.

With grim determination, I got to my feet and faced them, the air full of paper and bits of debris, the wind howling its fury that had a source within the three people facing me.

You have no future without us. If you do not join us, we will destroy you. We will destroy everyone you care about. We will damn you to an eternity of suffering.

"Been there, done that," I ground out through my teeth as I pulled more of Christian's power to keep from giving myself over to them, slowly, painfully restoring my wards. Loud noises outside of the room finally penetrated my consciousness, blessedly also drawing a bit of the triumvirate's attention. I wrapped my arms around my stomach, trying to catch my breath in the moment of respite.

Someone pounded against the door; then it splintered and was kicked aside, the ward guarding it shattering as the triumvirate's focus wavered. Several policemen poured into the room, stopping almost immediately at the scene that met their astonished eyes. Books still flew around the room, caught now in the whirlwind generated by the three people forming a triangle. Two policemen didn't duck in time and were struck by books; another just escaped being beaned by a small potted plant.

A hand reached out from the mass of blue-suited bodies and pulled me backward, out of the room. I looked up. The hand belonged to a very large man with glittering yellow eyes.

Christian had sent Raphael.

"I think I'm going to be sick," I told him. I assume I must have been green, because he immediately shoved me over to a chair in the hallway and pushed me down so my head was between my knees.

"Stay here."

I mumbled that I wasn't going anywhere.

Beloved?

Thank you, Christian. Thank you for everything. I appreciate it more than I can ever tell you.

Allegra, I hear your thoughts. You cannot protect me from Guarda and Eduardo. You cannot leave me. Without you, I have no life.

Reluctantly I closed Christian out of my head and stayed in the chair, rocking with pain and sorrow and the knowledge that my heart had been healed just

in time to fall in love with a man whom I would lead
to destruction if I didn't give him up.

Sometimes life really sucks.

"Thank you for taking me home with you," I told
Raphael later as he drove through the rainy, crowded
streets of London. "I really appreciate it."

"Joy was nearly out of her mind with worry. She'll
want to make sure you're okay. And besides, it's still
daylight; Christian . . ." He made an odd little abrupt
gesture.

I stopped my horrible introspection long enough
to look at the man who had called in every favor he
had with the Metropolitan Police to save me. "Why
do you have such a hard time admitting to yourself
what Christian is? You've known him for over a year,
haven't you?"

"Yes, but . . . some things are difficult. It's just not
natural, just like you and your . . ." He made the odd
gesture again.

I smiled and stuck a hand out of the blanket he'd
wrapped around me in an attempt to stop the shaking. I patted him on his arm. "I know, sometimes it's
all so hard to take in. One minute you think you have
a handle on everything; the next people are telling
you to believe in ghosts and vampires and werewolves."

"Werewolves?" he asked, his eyes getting a bit pan-
icky. "You know werewolves?"

I couldn't help but chuckle at him. "No, I don't. I
don't think they exist, not really."

His strange yellow eyes lost their worried look.

"Then again, I didn't think vampires existed, either,

but I have more than ample proof how wrong I was there," I mused, fingering the faint mark just below my ear.

Raphael was back to looking worried again. "What . . . uh . . . what exactly were those people in the office?"

"Psychics. Very strong ones. They'd formed a triumvirate, a sort of focus for their combined psychic power. It's almost impossible to overcome a triumvirate's power; there's something about the pyramid that becomes stronger just by being. This particular one was more powerful than anything I've ever felt." I rubbed at a bruise on my forehead. "It almost felt as if . . ."

"As if what?" Raphael asked, cursing under his breath as a car shot out in front of him.

I didn't want to put into words the feeling I'd had that one of the three had been tapping into a dark source of power. "It doesn't matter."

He glanced at me, and I had a brief feeling that those yellow eyes of his could see straight through all my guards and protection. "Ah."

"How did you get to me so quickly?"

His mouth twisted in a wry grin. "Joy can be very persuasive when she wants to be."

"But how did she know? Oh, Christian must have called her."

His wry grin turned into a grimace. "Yes, without bothering to use a phone."

"Oh." I let that thought sink in. If Christian could speak to Joy as easily as he did me . . . I sighed and rubbed my forehead again. It was too much to figure out until I had some time to myself. I needed to put some distance between what had happened before I was able to figure out all of the ramifications. "So what'll happen to them? Guarda and Eduardo and Phillippa? They weren't arrested, were they?"

Raphael shook his head and maneuvered us through a roundabout. "No grounds for arrest. Some friends of mine in the yard just had them in for a little interview regarding their source of funding. Seems Mrs. White has been suspected of doing a little money laundering."

"Money laundering?"

He smiled, and suddenly I had a glimpse at what it was that had attracted Joy to him. "It was the only thing I could think of to get in there quickly."

I grinned back at him. "Well, I truly am grateful for your help."

He murmured something about it being his pleasure as he peered out through the rain-streaked window. The rest of the ride was spent in silence.

"I wish there were some way to repay you for your help," I told him a short while later as he delivered me to the door of his building. "I would have been in serious trouble if you hadn't come when you did."

He smiled. "Don't mention it. Your taking Christian's attention away from Joy is repayment enough."

The answering smile faded from my face. I straightened up and waved as he drove off. I couldn't tell him that I wouldn't run the risk of diverting Christian's attention any longer.

"Oh, man, what a horrible muddle," I said, rubbing the ache in my forehead. I sighed again and pulled the blanket around me as I waited for Joy to buzz me into the building. I felt like someone had taken a baseball bat to me, both externally and mentally. I was abused, mentally raped, drained and heartsore. I was such a mess that I burst into tears the second Joy opened the door to me, and didn't stop crying for twenty minutes, ending up in a fetal ball on her couch, a box of tissues at hand, blankets heaped over me, two worried women hovering just beyond my view as I cried out the pain of knowing Christian was lost to me forever.

"That baby has addled your brains. She doesn't need coffee; she needs a stiff belt."

"Alcohol never solved anything, Roxy. Coffee and chocolate, however, can work miracles."

"Don't go all teetotaler on me, missy; you're just saying that because you can't drink anything stronger than a Shirley Temple now."

I sniffled one last time into a tissue and looked up. Roxy and Joy stood next to the couch, Joy with a steaming cup in one hand, a bowl of something that look chocolatey in the other. Roxy held a bottle of whiskey. My decision was quickly made.

I took the cup from Joy, poured a sizable slosh into it from Roxy's bottle, and scooped up a handful of chocolate-covered almonds. "Thanks. This'll work just fine."

"Oh, good, you're done with the water show," Roxy said as she pulled a chair over to where I sat. "Now you can tell us everything. And don't leave out any of the good parts, the way Joy does. First off, did you and Christian do the nasty? I bet Joy you wouldn't be able to hold out against the scrumptious Mr. Dante for very long."

"Oh, for God's sake." Joy whomped her friend on

the arm. "Will you stop prying into things that aren't any of your business? Just ignore her, Allie. She was raised by wolves and has no manners."

Roxy just grinned at me. "So? Did you?"

"Roxy!"

I swallowed the mouthful of almonds and washed them back with spiked coffee. "I will tell you what I told my ghostly friends: the subject of physical relations between Christian and me is off-limits."

"Atta girl," Joy praised me as she lowered herself into an armchair.

"Well, you can at least tell us about why Christian did the mind-meld thing with Joy and had her getting Raphael worked into a frenzy. What was all that about?"

It said a lot about my wounded, exhausted state that I didn't even consider shielding them from the truth, as I might under normal circumstances. People not directly involved in paranormal research usually don't take hearing about things like powerful psychics and ghosts and such without a lot of distress. I've found it's easier to pick and choose a few things to tell the general public, and keep the unvarnished truth for the experts. Unfortunately, I was too tired and sore to think rationally, so I spilled all of it to Joy and Roxy.

"Wow," Roxy breathed when I was finished. "You have five ghosts now? Bring them here, would you?"

"Another time, maybe." I smiled wearily.

"That's right, another time. You just sit there and rest, Allie." Joy glanced at the window. "The sun should go down in about an hour, Christian will come and get you then."

I was shaking my head even before she finished speaking. "No."

"No, what?"

"No, Christian will not come and get me. I don't want to go with him. I was hoping I could stay here with you for the night, until I can find another hotel."

Joy glanced quickly at Roxy. "Allie, I know Christian is very concerned about you; he asked me just a few minutes ago how you were feeling, and—"

I sat up straight and pushed the blankets off me. "He what?"

"He was concerned; he said you weren't talking to him and he wanted to be sure you hadn't been hurt—"

"That . . . that . . ."

"Man," Roxy supplied helpfully.

"*Man!*" I yelled, snatching another tissue and blowing my nose. "How dare he question another woman about me? How dare he pry when it's clear I don't welcome his concern! How dare he—"

"—be so much in love with you that he chafes at the fact that he couldn't be the one to save you?" Joy finished.

"I can save myself," I snarled at her, immediately feeling ashamed because it's not a nice thing to snarl at a pregnant woman. "I didn't mean to attack you, Joy; I'm just angry at Christian. And he doesn't love me. I'm not his bloody Beloved; you are."

"You know," Roxy said thoughtfully as she popped a chocolate almond into her mouth. "That sounds awfully jealous to me. I think maybe you're not being quite honest with yourself or Joy. Or Christian, for that matter."

I glared at Roxy.

"Rox, you're not helping matters."

"Well, I'm trying to!" she argued, and took a swig off the bottle of whiskey. "Look, Allie, this thing between Joy and Christian just isn't important. So they can do the mind-meld, big deal. You only have to get Joy and Raphael together for a couple of minutes before they're going at it like rabbits. Joy couldn't give a hoot about Christian, not in the way you do. She punched him in the nose once, almost broke it. Not to mention kneeing him in the happy sacs."

I stared at Joy, who nodded. "Christian can be a little overbearing sometimes. So can Raphael, but it looks much better on him."

"You hit him? You hit Christian?"

"*And* she stomped on his foot. He limped for a week afterward. It's 'cause she weighs as much as a draft horse."

We both ignored Roxy.

"It's not something I'm proud of," Joy said at last, not looking in the least bit contrite.

I nodded, sucking on an almond. I wondered if I would ever get so mad that I could punch Christian in the nose.

"I fervently pray you do not. I do not wish to experience that again."

I stared at the man leaning elegantly in the doorway, my eyes opening wider as I looked beyond him to the window.

It was still daylight out.

"Christian, what on earth are you doing here? I told you Allie was all right!" Joy gave a little grunt, hoisted herself out of the chair, and bustled around the windows, closing the drapes and shutting out the weak daylight.

I looked back at Christian as Roxy turned on the lamps scattered around the room. "You shouldn't be able to do that, should you?"

He shrugged and peeled off his coat and hat. "No, but I did. I believe I owe the gain in tolerance to daylight to you."

I shook my head. "I'm *not* your Beloved, Christian. Joy is, only she has other priorities."

He ignored my protest and kissed Joy's hand, kissed Roxy on the cheek when she threw herself into his arms, and then sat next to me with the casual possession of longtime lovers. I wanted to push him away, but it felt too good when he tugged me against his side. I closed my eyes for a second and let myself melt into him.

Why did life always have to be so difficult?

If it weren't, you wouldn't appreciate what you have, Christian answered.

Go away. I'm too tired to cope with you.

"Poor Allie, she's been through so much. Christian, she's asked to stay here for tonight. I'm sure you won't mind, and won't pressure her into changing her mind."

"Allegra knows I would never force her to do anything she does not want to do." I rallied enough strength to snort at that. He ignored me. "If she wishes to spend the night here, she shall."

I looked up at him in surprise. I had expected him to at least make a token objection.

"I don't imagine Raphael will be too pleased to have us both move in with you, but if Allegra insists on remaining here, then here is where we shall stay."

I opened my mouth to object, then snapped it shut again. *I don't think you were invited.*

Christian looked at Joy. "That is, assuming that your invitation extends to me, of course."

Joy smiled at him, her eyes full of laughter. "But of course! If you would be more comfortable with Allie at hand, then you're more than welcome to join us."

"If anyone suggests having a pajama party, I'm leaving," Roxy said, standing and pulling her friend toward the door. "Come on, Mama. They can't talk if you're sitting there mothering them."

Joy made an exasperated face as Roxy gently shoved her through the door. "I was *not* mothering them; I was being supportive and concerned. It's what friends do. I'd be happy to give you lessons."

The door closed on Roxy's retort, which I suddenly quite desperately wanted to hear. Anything was better than being smashed up against Christian's side, feeling his warmth sink into me, wanting to bury my face into his neck so I could inhale that wonderfully spicy scent, wishing I could forget the world and just spend the rest of my life in his arms.

That sounds like an excellent plan to me.

Eavesdroppers never hear good of themselves, I snapped.

Mmm. I don't believe having you think of me as the sexiest man on earth is hearing ill of myself.

"I haven't thought that all day, and get out of my mind."

He started kissing my neck.

"And you can just stop doing that, too." He nuzzled

the sweet spot below my ear and I shivered with plea-sure. "It's . . . it's . . . it's not going to change my mind. I'm nothing but danger to you, Christian. Oh, Lord, you really shouldn't, not . . . Oh, yeah, right there." All of my aches and pains were forgotten as he worked around the back of my neck, delivering hot little kisses on my nape, making all sorts of things inside me go up in spontaneous combustion. "I . . . um . . . I won't bring you anything but more torment. You have to understand why this thing between us isn't going to work out."

He stopped kissing my neck long enough to turn me to face him. "I know you feel responsible for me, *malý válečník*, but in truth you are not. If you leave me now, there will be nothing left of me for Guarda and Eduardo to torment."

"Now you're exaggerating," I told him, allowing myself just one, swift little barely there kiss to show him that I appreciated the fact that he thought he couldn't live without me.

The kiss turned into a smoldering inferno of pas-sion the second my lips met his. I fought giving in to the need that rose within me in answer to his longing, then told myself I'd been through a lot, and deserved a little reward. I threw everything I had into my kiss, running my hands over his chest and up to where his hair was once again confined.

I like it loose, I chastised him as I pulled it free from the leather thong.

Then you will have to see to it that it remains that way, he answered.

I heard the door open behind me.

"They're kissing," Roxy called down the hallway.

"No, really kissing. Tongues and everything. What? Oh, all right. You sure have become a prude lately. . . ."

The door closed.

Christian's tongue danced a fiery dance around mine, melting my flesh and bones until all that was left was pure emotion. Tears streaked my cheeks as I kissed him harder, deeper, wanting to lose myself in him.

I would not have that, he told me as his thumb brushed away my tears. *I could not love a woman who was not strong enough to be whole on her own.*

His lips parted from mine, turning to kiss the wet tracks of tears.

You said I complete you; are you not whole?

Not without you, he answered.

But I am complete without you?

He kissed one eye, then the other. "You are whole, perfectly finished as you are. You are a little warrior. Without me, you would still exist. You would laugh, you would learn to love, you would have a satisfying life. You would seek and achieve success because you cannot do otherwise."

I stroked the hair back from his face and looked into his eyes. "You've lived for nine hundred years, Christian. I'm sure you've had relationships with women in the past, and I'm sure they've ended. You survived that, you will survive me."

His eyes, warm, so full of something that I wanted to believe was love, but wouldn't allow myself to acknowledge, studied my face. He opened his mind to me so that the pain and torment that were within him were also within me. He spoke, and it felt as if I were speaking. His thoughts were mine; mine were his. We were one; we were joined together in way so profound it scared the life out of me. *If you leave me, I will have no future. I am not as strong as you are, Beloved. I cannot face the thought of a future without you completing me. If you turn your back on me, I will end my existence rather than live knowing I have failed you.*

"You haven't failed me," I whispered, hot tears welling up in my eyes at the knowledge that what he said was true. His agony of almost a thousand years of despair was as real as anything I'd ever felt, and I knew with my heart and soul that what he was telling me was the truth. He would destroy himself rather than face a bleak future that held nothing but the misery of the past.

I don't know why I thought I had a choice in this. I didn't; I couldn't. Either I left Christian and he would kill himself, or I stayed with him and Guarda and Eduardo would do the job for him.

In the dream Eduardo had told me I must make a choice. Silly me, I thought it was a choice between my own survival and Christian's—not a choice of how he would die.

Why do you believe we will be so easily overcome?

I sniffed. He handed me a handkerchief. I wouldn't allow myself the intimacy of speaking into his mind. "I don't mean any slur, Christian, but if Guarda and Eduardo could overcome your friend, what's to stop them from overcoming you?"

"Sebastian has not found his Beloved."

"So?"

"Is it not true that two are stronger than one?"

I thought about that. "Oh. I guess so. You're saying that a Dark One who's found his Beloved—"

"One who has Joined with his Beloved."

"—is more powerful than a solo Dark One, but that means squat in this case. I'm not your Beloved."

"You are. I was incorrect earlier when I said you weren't. I know now that you are the woman I have waited for, the one who holds my future in her hands, the Beloved who can redeem my soul."

"I'm not! I'm not a soul-saving sort of person; I'm a Summoner. That's all I am."

"There is nothing that says you cannot be both."

"But—"

He took my hand and kissed my palm. Little streaks of fire shot up my arm. "You have already started to heal my soul; you have ever since I met you. That is why I am able to tolerate the last hours of the sun. The hunger within me has diminished, changed so that I crave only you. That, too, would not happen unless you were the woman intended to make me whole again."

"You crave me?" I looked at him suspiciously. "You crave us together, you mean? Sex?"

"That is part of the hunger, yes."

I had a momentary glimpse into what he needed from me. There was the hope that I would salvage his soul, there was an intense desire for physical joining, and there was a deep, dark thirst for—"

"Blood. Oh, I see. Dark Ones only dine off their Beloveds, eh?"

"You will be all I need, all I will want. The act of taking blood from another has become repugnant to me."

He watched me closely to see how I would take that news. I felt for one horrible moment like some sort of deranged cow, fed and pampered so I could donate blood on a regular basis, then thought, really thought about what Christian was feeling. I knew from experience how intimate—how erotic—it was for him to feed off me. Did I want him doing that with anyone else?

I most certainly did not.

Still, there were questions to be answered. "Why did you think Joy was your Beloved? Why did you think I wasn't? Why did you change your mind?"

He ran a long-fingered hand through his hair and leaned back on the couch, taking me with him. "Joy once said that she thought it was possible for there to be two women with, as she put it, their wires crossed: one who was born a Beloved, but who was never meant to fulfill that role, and another who was not born to it, but who would grow into it. I did not think it was possible at the time, but now"—His eyes lightened to a beautiful warm reddish brown with gold flecks that made his eyes seem to shimmer with light—"now I believe she was right. You were not born to be my Beloved, but you are she. If you choose to stay with me now, to help me overcome my darker self, there will be only one more step before we are truly Joined."

Ick. I knew what that meant. A blood exchange. I pushed down the pesky little thought that when we made love, I had a deep, forbidden, primitive urge to taste his blood even as he was drinking mine, and instead focused on the here and now.

"All right, letting the Beloved question go for a

minute, how can you expect me to believe that you and I have enough strength, even working together, to face the triumvirate again? They almost did me in, Christian, and that was with you pouring your power into me. I felt how weak you grew doing that; you were giving me everything you had."

He kissed my palm again. I fought back the shiver of pleasure that his breath on my sensitive skin triggered. "Once we are Joined, we will be as one. You will complete me, and in return you will be made immortal."

"Even immortal, I can still be hurt. You said yourself it was possible to kill a Dark One, and your friend is proof that you can be held prisoner against your will."

"Sebastian was not trapped by Eduardo and Guarda. There was another's hand in it, one who was able to blind Sebastian because he had no Beloved. A Dark One who is redeemed would never make that mistake."

"Don't tell me: When you're redeemed you become even more perfect than you are now?"

A smile flirted with his lips. I wanted to flirt with the smile. "Nothing so arrogant, Allegra. It is simply that a Moravian who has Joined would not do anything that would endanger his Beloved. She is everything and all to him. He lives for her happiness. He would take no chances with his own life simply because he must live to protect her."

I gave in to my desire and let my lips flirt with his smile. "Now why do I find that statement a bit questionable?"

He tugged me closer, until I was sitting on his lap.

That is because you have never had a Dark One of your own. I promise I will make the experience one that you will never forget . . . or regret.

The door opened again. I stayed where I was.

"Now she's sitting on his lap. No, wait, they're kissing again. And he's got his hand on her boob. Will you stop yelling at me? Geez, Joy, I'd appreciate it if you'd make up your mind! Either you *want* me to see what they're doing, or you *don't*—"

The door closed again, rather firmly this time.

I smiled into Christian's mouth. "You know, you're not giving me any choice. What you're doing is called emotional blackmail."

His smile sobered instantly into something that filled me with sorrow to see.

Guilt. He felt guilty about telling me the truth.

"If there were another way, Allegra—"

"You've let me see into that thick head of yours," I said, running my fingers through the cool length of his hair. "I know what you're telling me is true, just as you know I could not let you destroy yourself. So I guess it means we're going to have to work out some sort of a relationship."

I fisted my hands in his hair and tugged until he tipped his chin up. I nibbled on his neck, gently biting the tender flesh around his Adam's apple. *There are going to be some rules, Mr. Arrogance. Lots and lots of rules.*

"Rules can be good," he said, lowering his head until his lips teased mine. "I particularly like the one that says I must make love to you until you beg me to stop."

"I have a very high tolerance for lovemaking," I

warned just before he claimed my mouth.

A short while later the door opened behind us.

"Guys, I think you might want to put some clothes back on. Joy's gone to pee—for the five hundredth time today—but she's coming in to check on you next. So . . . um . . . guys? That is you two under those blankets, right? That looks like your clothes on the floor. Oh, boy, Allie, you really need to get yourself some new underwear. Yours looks like the kind my grandmother wears. I didn't know they still made—"

Christian closed the door on her without ceasing doing what he was doing. I moaned into his mouth and gave myself up to the sharp stab of pure pleasure as our bodies and minds once again merged into one.

There had to be a way to save him from the fate my dream predicted. There just had to be.

Chapter Thirteen

"All right, what do you think of this?"

"I don't like it." Christian's silky voice was a bit sulky.

"You sound like Jem. How about this? I just bet a great strong man like you would appreciate this."

"No."

"You didn't even try it!"

"I don't have to try it to know I won't like it."

"You are *such* a baby. All right, how about this? I love this; I'm sure you will, too."

He looked suspiciously at me. "What is it?"

I waved the spoon under his nose. "Mole chicken."

He made a face. "I don't believe I could eat the flesh of an animal."

"Just try it. For me."

He grimaced and took a tiny little morsel of mole-covered chicken from the spoon. The look on his face as he chewed it was priceless.

"I take it that's a no."

"I do not want any more animal flesh."

"Okay, fine, strictly vegetarian diet, no problem. I'm not a big cow eater myself. Now, let's see . . ." I looked over the dining room table, which was covered in more than a dozen different take-out cartons. "You were go on the Greek pasta salad."

"I liked the wine."

"But the hummus didn't strike a strong chord with you." I pushed the red-pepper-and-olive hummus over to my side of the table. I wasn't nearly as picky as Christian was. Then again, I hadn't just been given the ability to eat after nine hundred years, either. I suppose that gave him the right to have such definite preferences.

"The wine was very good."

"And the Cantonese beef and the mole chicken are out. Same with the ribs."

"I *enjoyed* the wine."

"But you haven't tried the vegetarian fried rice yet. Here, try some rice."

"I believe I could have more wine without suffering any ill effects," he told me as I poked the spoon at his lips in an attempt to slip a few morsels of rice between them.

I sighed and set the spoon down. "You said you would be able to ingest only tiny bits of food and beverage at first, Christian. You did not say that being with me would open up the door to your becoming a wino."

He frowned. "Wino?"

"One who drinks copious quantities of wine."

He looked at the petite sherry glass that I had found to serve him little thimble-size swallows of various wines so he could see what he liked and disliked.

"I suspect that it would take more than the teaspoon or two of wine you've given me to qualify for the word *copious*."

"No one likes a drunk vampire. Now try this rice and I might let you have a sip of a Gewürztraminer."

He selected an individual grain of rice and nibbled on it. "Passable."

I poured him another swallow of wine.

"Okay, so that leaves the spaghetti, which you won't like because it has dead cow in it, and sage roasted potatoes, which I can personally attest to as being nummy, and the—"

"Why are you avoiding the inevitable?" he asked, the sherry glass dangling from his elegant fingers.

"I told you, I don't need anyone to help me take a bath."

"You are bruised; I can feel your pain when you move. Why will you not let me soothe your aches in the warmth and comfort of a bath?"

"Because your sort of soothing involves bare flesh, and I know you around bare flesh; you're going to want to make love, and I just don't think that's a good idea now. It's a good thing Joy interrupted us when she did. Until I get a few things straight in my mind, you're not going to touch me, and that means no bath."

He smiled.

"I'm serious, Christian."

His smile deepened.

"Don't you think what you're thinking!" I shook a fork at him.

"If you ask me to, *corazón*, I will tear 'is 'eart out and dance on it." A disembodied voice floated down the length of the table.

I made a face at the air as it gathered into the translucent image of a randy Elizabethan courtier. "I thought you guys were watching a movie?"

"The others would not let me watch it."

"Really?" I frowned. Esme had discovered that if she focused her attention, she could push buttons on the remote. The freedom to channel-surf had quickly made her and Jem giddy TV addicts. "Why?"

He waved his hand. "They objected to it."

"What was the title?"

He pursed his lips and gave me the wounded-puppy dog look. "I cannot remember. I believe it was a movie about explorers. Someone's visit to a place called Dallas."

"Someone's visit to Dallas?"

"*Debbie Does Dallas*, was, I think, the title. It looked to be most amusing, but Esme said it was not appropriate for her cat. Bah!"

I snorted out the sip of wine I was taking, and coughed and sputtered for a good minute until I got all of it out of my lungs. Christian helpfully patted me on the back until I could breathe again. Antonio took exception to that. He puffed up his chest and stalked over to Christian.

"Oh, no, not again," I moaned, having seen enough male posturing earlier when we had arrived home to last me a lifetime. "Look, it was bad enough

240

that you two had to go *mano a mano* a couple of hours ago, filling the entire house with enough testosterone to choke a horse, but if you don't mind, Antonio, Christian and I are trying to have dinner. Go back and watch whatever movie the others are watching."

" 'A!" Antonio waved his hand at the food and scoffed. Loudly. With one hand on a hip and a sneer on his face. " 'E is as dead as I am; 'e cannot eat. And yet you, *mi amor, mi corazón*, you prefer this monstrosity to me? No." He shook his head, his curls trembling violently. "It cannot be. I will not accept it. I will challenge 'im to a duel of honor for your fair 'and!"

"Christian is not dead; he's just not . . . well, quite human. He's a slight variation on human, that's all."

"I don't care, I still challenge 'im. 'E 'as stolen my true love. 'E will die for that crime."

With a ghostly whisper of steel, Antonio pulled the rapier from the scabbard that suddenly appeared at his waist.

"Oh, for heaven's sake, I don't believe this. . . ."

Antonio waved his rapier about in manner that, had it had been real, would have decapitated Christian, me, and three of the candles in the center of the dining table. "Do you accept my challenge, you 'ideous dead one, or are you too cowardly to face me like a man?"

Christian smiled at Antonio as he rose to his feet. I groaned and made a mental note to find a way to Release Antonio before Christian really lost his temper with him. Not to mention *my* temper.

"Where is Antonio . . . Oh, here you all are. What's

going on?" Esme asked as she materialized in the dining room. "Oooh, you're fighting a duel? Over Allegra? How thrilling! Jem! Alis! You must see this; Antonio and Christian are fighting over Allegra."

"No," I started to say, but it was no use. Before the word left my lips, Jem and Alis popped into the dining room. Mr. Woogums jumped onto the table and limped over to smell the barbeque ribs. "Now, listen here, everyone, there is not going to be any . . . Jem, what in heaven's name have you done to yourself?"

"You insist on badgering my Beloved even when she has asked you to leave," Christian said, ignoring the audience that had lined up against the far wall. Alis spotted a series of Dresden antique statuettes on a shelf and moved in front of them to scream in Welsh. "You are here only on Allegra's sufferance, *ghost*, so I would suggest that you do as she tells you and not persist on this foolish course."

"Have you lost your mind? You can't go around dressed like that," I told Jem. "You look like a punk rocker. How many eighteenth-century waiters do you know who have a purple mohawk and a ring in their nose? I just bet you the answer is none!"

"You are the dead coward most extraordinary," Antonio taunted Christian, pausing long enough to blow me a showy kiss and materialize a red rose right in the middle of my kung pao chicken.

"Is that a tattoo? Who gave you permission to give yourself a tattoo? Of a naked woman, Jem? You're only fifteen! If this is the sort of thing you're going to do if I let you watch TV, you're going to find yourself watching the kiddie channel for a very long time, I can tell you that!"

Christian sighed and raised one hand to Antonio. "Need I show you again how much power this dead man wields?"

Antonio's image flickered as if it were a candle flame in a draft; then (and if his expression was anything to go by, much to his surprise) he dissolved into nothing.

I blinked at the Antonio-less air. "How did you do that?"

Christian shrugged and pulled my chair back. "Call it a perk."

"He's not going to do that to us, is he?" Esme asked nervously, picking up her cat. Jem leaned forward to admire his new look in the glass of a picture. Alis jumped up and down and waved her arms through the statuettes.

"No, he's not going to do that to you. You can all go back to Christian's study. Quietly, please. I don't want the Turners woken up. Hey," I said as Christian gently scooped me up in his arms. "Wait a minute. You have that 'You need a bath and I'm just the man to give you one' look on your face."

"Ah, Allegra." He sighed happily as he carried me up the stairs. I waved to Esme before the door closed behind us. "How little time it has taken you to learn my ways. You, my Beloved, need a bath to soothe your aches and heal your pains, and I am just the man to see to any other needs you might discover while sitting in the warm, oil-slicked water."

It wasn't what he said; it was the erotic, oil-slicked, watery images he was projecting into my mind that had me all quivery inside. "You're dominating me again," I said a tad bit desperately. "You know I don't like that."

He pushed open the door to his bedroom and walked straight into the bathroom. "Then we shall take turns. I shall dominate you until you get into the bathtub, and then you shall dominate me until I make you scream my name with pleasure three times."

Three times? My knees sagged as he stood me up. "Um." There was a reason I had for not wanting to have sex with him. A good reason. I just wished I could think of it.

We do not have sex, Christian thought at me as he turned the taps on full force, then examined a couple of bottles of bath scents and oils. *We make deeply arousing, soul-scorching love.*

You just have to love a romantic vampire.

"You prefer the jasmine, yes?"

I nodded, unable to summon up one good reason why I shouldn't tear off his clothes and make him scream *my* name out three times.

"Shall I undress you again?"

"No. You will leave the room and let me get into the tub by myself."

He raised a glossy raven eyebrow. "Beloved, I have seen your body. You have nothing to be ashamed of."

"Yes, but you haven't seen my body after it's been pummeled by a bunch of flying books. I'm bound to be bruised, and if you're going to want to touch each bruise—and don't tell me you aren't, because I can read your thoughts, too—then we'll be here all night. So just go do something for a minute and let me get into the tub by myself. Then, if you're good, you can come back and sit over there on that bench and talk to me nicely while I soak away the stiffness."

With a grin that didn't fool me for a minute, he bowed over my hand, then strolled out of the bathroom. As soon as the door clicked closed I ripped my shirt off, skinnied out of my pants and shoes, tore off my bra over my head without even pausing to undo the clasps, and had my underwear and socks off before I could take a breath. I sank into the deep water of the tub, sighing loudly with pleasure as the jasmine-scented steam seemed to ease away the aches of my bruises.

"It has been exactly one minute, and upon reviewing your response to me last night and this morning, I have come to the conclusion that I *am* good; thus I have returned."

"Naked," I pointed out as he stepped into the tub. "I noticed that you're naked and . . . um . . ."

He looked down on himself as he sank into the water at the opposite end of the mammoth tub. "Aroused?"

"Very." The water was about nipple high on me, which made me slouch a bit so my breasts were covered by the water. Christian *tsk*ed and moved toward me until his thigh slid alongside mine.

If you do not wish me to soothe your bruises, you must distract me.

I thought about that for a minute, then remembered that it was my turn to dominate him. I smiled. "If you insist."

He watched with interest as I gathered up the sea sponge and picked out a soap I liked (it smelled spicy, like him), then scooted my way over to him, plopping myself down so I sat on his thighs, facing him. Unfortunately that meant my breasts were out of the water, but I figured I'd just have to work harder at distracting him so he wouldn't notice that they were a little on the small side.

I like them just the way they are, he said softly, his hands just as soft as they cupped the aforementioned breasts.

A man will say anything when he's about to be soaped up and washed off.

His fingers stroked lazy circles around all the sensitive parts of my chest. I leaned forward into his hands as his mouth closed onto the wonderfully ticklish spot beneath my ear, shivering just a little as the warm water lapped around us with tiny, oil-slicked erotic movements.

"No more," I murmured into his hair.

"No?" He pulled back from where he was nuzzling my collarbone.

"Not for a bit. This is my turn. I get to drive you wild." I smiled a special wicked smile that I kept just for him and soaped up the sponge. "You, sir, need a bath, and I'm just the woman to see that it's done properly."

"You are so arousing when you give orders," he said, his half-closed eyes giving me a look that went straight to my groin. I just smiled and soaped up his arm, running my fingers along the slick surface of his skin, feeling the hard muscle flex and tense as I made soapy little finger designs along the flesh. I leaned forward to nip at his lips for a second while I soaped up the second arm, kissing him properly and biting his lower lip until he gave me what I wanted and opened his mouth.

He groaned into my mouth as I stroked the soapy muscles on his arm in time to the gentle little dabs of my tongue around his lips.

"Now for your chest," I said, pulling away. The water came to just above his belly button, which left me a delectable amount of chest to play with, and play with it I did. I soaped, I swirled, I spread my fingers across the muscles and through the chest hair, and watched his skin ripple in response.

"I like your chest," I murmured into his mouth.

"I like you liking my chest," he answered, his hands on my hips, tugging me forward.

"Not yet. First I have to wash you."

"I am not certain I will be able to survive such a delight."

"You'll just have to give it your best shot," I answered just before taking him into my soapy hands. "I have decided I like this extra bit you have."

His head tipped back and his eyes closed as I explored his hard length, letting my fingers dance on him as he had done earlier to me. I was suddenly possessed with a desire that shocked me because I'd never thought I'd willingly want to do it.

I moved off his legs. His eyes opened quickly and he looked at me with a worried concern that touched my heart. I smiled. "Slide up onto the seat."

The bath was so large that it had a broad marble ledge that ran around one side. He looked at the seat, then looked back at me, one eyebrow cocked.

"I know what I said, and I meant it at the time. My ex-husband used to make me—"

He laid a finger across my lips, then replaced it with his lips. "There is only you and me, Beloved."

I bit his finger, then kissed away the sting. "Then move over to the seat."

He did. The water now lapped at his thighs. I put a hand on either knee, sliding my spread fingers up the slickness of his legs, spreading them wider so I could kneel between them.

"Allegra, you do not have to do this. . . ."

"I know," I said, slanting a look up at him. His eyes were hot and filled with passion, his chest rising and falling quickly as my hands slid around his heat. "I want to, Christian. I want to give you pleasure."

"Every breath you take gives me pleasure, Beloved. What you wish to do may just kill me."

"What a way to die." I smiled before lowering my head to him. I relaxed the moment I tasted him. This wasn't like the times in the past. Christian was different; he accepted what I gave and opened his mind to me so I could feel the elation my touch was bringing to him. I swirled my tongue around his flesh and reveled in the way I made his hips move, experimenting until I found a rhythm that I knew was driving him mad with pleasure, then redoubled my efforts until he suddenly pulled me upward along his body, my breasts pressed against his chest, my legs straddling his, the hard, extremely aroused tip of him nudging me open.

Let me love you, Beloved.

I tightened my arms around his head and wiggled my consent. He lowered me with so much gentleness that it brought tears to my eyes. How could one man be so very different from the others I'd known? How could one man care so much that every stroke of his fingers did nothing but push me to higher arousal? How could one man fill me with such joy that I happily merged myself with him in order to show him how much I craved his touch?

You are my Beloved. I can do no less.

I moved upon him, relishing the feeling of such erotic impalement, thrilling in the way he filled me, moving upward just so I could experience again the pleasure of him pushing into my body, joining with my flesh until there was no ending of him and beginning of me; there were only our two bodies and hearts and minds sharing every moment.

When his teeth pierced the flesh beneath my ear, I shouted his name, knowing this was right, it was meant to be, and that nothing would ever change that. He drank from me and my body contracted around him, pushing him into joining me as our bodies burned brighter than a supernova.

His hunger filled my mind as he continued to drink, but now there was another need in his mind, the need for me to take the same from him. His tongue was soft on my neck as he whispered the words in my mind.

Feed, Beloved. I know you wish to. Join with me. Take from me what only I can give you.

I trembled on the verge of another orgasm as he continued to move within me, the scent of him filling me, merging with the desire that he had recognized but which I refused to admit. My tongue swirled over the tendons in his neck, his pulse beating loud in my mind. The thought of tasting his blood teased me, aroused me further, claimed every thought in my head until all I wanted was the taste of him on my tongue.

Yes, Beloved. It is right. It is as it should be.

His finger traced a small line on his neck, blood welling up from it and beading along the scratch. I stared at the ruby drops gathering and felt my body ache in response. I lowered my head to his neck, wanting to lick the wound, wanting to taste him in a way more intimate than anything I'd ever done, needing to take his life's blood into my body and complete the circle. Several drops gathered together and snaked a crimson trail down his neck.

More than anything else I wanted his blood.

A tiny voice in my mind screamed out its objection. If I did this, if I took the final step of Joining, there would be no going back. I would be trapped forever, without escape, without the power to leave him. If I let those tantalizing drops of red touch my tongue, I would never again be completely in control of my life; I would be governed by him.

Beloved—

"No." I turned my head and nuzzled it into the other side of his neck, a profound sense of loss making me sob with frustration. "I can't, Christian; I just can't."

Do not distress yourself in this way. Take only what you want from me, no more. I will never force you, Beloved. I seek only your happiness.

He moved within me again, kissing my neck and urging me to move faster upon him, sharing with me how much pleasure he felt. I gave in to the demands of my body and whispered my need into his mouth. He kissed me, his tongue mimicking the movement of our bodies until I knew his hunger would claim me. I tore my mouth from his and arched my back, trembling as his teeth closed on my breast, the familiar flash of pain dissolving instantly into ecstasy as our bodies and minds celebrated our joining in the most elemental manner possible.

It was just a few minutes shy of dawn when Christian carried me back to the mammoth bed, both of us exhausted, my body still humming with the pleasure he had given me. He'd made me scream out his name four times, not three, but as he had done the same, I was happy. I lay limp in his arms and listened to his heart beat, too sated and contented to question whether making love with him had been the wrong thing to do.

It can never be wrong between us.

Do I have to put up a No Trespassing sign? I smiled into his mind.

I cannot help sharing your thoughts. It is the way of things.

I let that go and just enjoyed snuggling against him, drowsily tracing protection wards on his hip. "What are we going to do about finding the location of those two houses in town, Christian? You don't happen to know any clairvoyants, do you?"

"Yes, but not one you wish to consort with."

I looked up to frown a question at him.

"She is a Guardian."

"Oh. You're right. We don't need to bring a Guardian into this." Guardians are powerful mages who shield those hot spots in the world that are open to the influence of the dark forces. You'd be surprised how many of those places there are. The city of Detroit alone has hundreds of them. "How about hiring a really good private detective to look up the leasing and ownership records of likely houses?"

He stroked one of the sore spots on my back, his fingertips warm as they healed the bruise. "I've already done that. The Trust has covered its tracks in a very clever manner; it was only through a lucky coincidence that I found out who leased the house in Greenwich."

"Poop." I thought about the problem, worrying it from a new angle. "You can talk to your friend the way you can with me, right?"

"It's not quite the same, but yes, we do not need words to communicate. I have tried to reach him repeatedly, but either he is too weak to answer, or he is at too great a distance for me to find him."

"How great a distance is too great?" I asked, wondering if perhaps I was wrong in my assumption that the Dark One was being held in London. Perhaps they had shipped him off to Scotland.

"For Sebastian? A few miles. Three or four, perhaps."

I frowned again, propping myself up on my elbow to look at him. "So little? I was all the way across town and you didn't have the slightest bit of trouble reaching me."

"You are my Beloved. It is much easier to maintain contact with you."

"Still, a couple of miles doesn't seem like a very big range."

He touched a bruise on my shoulder. "The distance can increase if I were to know the exact location of the person I'm trying to contact. The powers of a Dark One are great, *malý váleèník,* but they do have limitations. If I do not know where Sebastian is, when I send out a call, it goes out in all directions until it reaches him. Once he answers I can focus the call so it goes directly to him. Until I know where he is, however, I must blanket the area. That reduces the distance I can reach."

"Oh. Sorry, I didn't mean to accuse you of being weak in the mental department." I snuggled back into him, stroking his chest. "I think our answer is going to have to be something illegal."

"Breaking into the Trust offices and searching for information?"

I nodded and kissed the little dip at the base of his throat. Above my head, he sighed, tightening his arms around me. "I fear that is the only solution I can see, as well."

"We should do it tonight. It's less likely that anyone will be around in the offices. They'll be too busy trying to raise spirits elsewhere."

Christian said nothing.

"Then again, they might expect us to do just that, although I don't think they know what it is I'm seeking. It's possible that if they really do know who and what you are, they will connect you to Sebastian, but we can't be certain of that."

His chest moved slowly beneath my hand, one breath to every five of mine. "Hmmm. You know, with your new tolerance of sunlight, it might be better if we waited until just before dawn. Then Guarda and Eduardo and Phillippa would likely to be heading off to their beds, never thinking that you would be able to get out and about then."

His body lay tense beneath my cheek. I wondered briefly if he was worried about the sunlight. "Of course, there's always the direct approach. I could hire myself a couple of really big bodyguards, and just march into the office during the day. Maybe I'd luck out and Guarda and the gang would be out to lunch or something."

Not only had his fingers stopped stroking me, he didn't veto the last, asinine plan that even I recognized was pure folly. Brute strength was nothing to the power of the triumvirate, and if Guarda had any brains at all, she'd be sure to keep Eduardo and Phillippa close by just on the off chance I came calling.

"Christian?"

"*Peste,*" he swore, gently rolling me off him and getting to his feet, grabbing a pair of black jeans and pulling them on. Tension was visible in every line of his body.

"What's wrong?" I sat up and pulled the sheets up over my chest. "Christian?"

He started for the door to the hallway. "Don't you feel it?"

I stilled and opened myself up to the house. "No, I just feel the gruesome fivesome. They're all in your study. What is it? The triumvirate?"

He spat out a word as he slipped through the open door, leaving me frozen with fear.

Demon.

Chapter Fourteen

"Oh, crap," I breathed, for a moment too terrified at the thought of a demon to do anything. Then I realized that was the man I loved out there about to battle a soldier of some demon lord, and it was my job to be at his side, helping him where I could. Summoners might not be any great shakes at fighting minions of the dark, but we do have a few tricks up our sleeves. I hurried into my jeans and pulled on a sweater, taking time to step into some shoes before dashing out into the hallway and racing down the stairs.

Demons go to ground whenever possible; they draw their strength from the earth, and get weaker the farther they are from it. Therefore, demons will almost always engage you in battle in a basement. I stumbled down the stairs to the ground floor, my leg screaming its protest at the combination of my earlier exercise in the tub and being jolted down two flights of stairs.

"Allie? What is the matter?" Esme appeared at the top of the stairs.

"Demon," I called over my shoulder as I ran for the door to the basement stairs. "Stay in the study and keep the others there."

I tried desperately to remember the little I'd learned of demon lore. What did come back to me had me spinning around on the stairs and gritting my teeth as I forced my poor leg into leaping back up the stairs to Christian's study. I ran straight through Esme, and then Antonio as he drifted through the door, throwing apologies and orders over my shoulder as I scrabbled through my bag. "Sorry about that, Antonio. Esme, bring Alis back in here. You'll be safe here. Where the heck is my . . . Oh there it is."

"*Mi amor*, what is the problem? That one, 'e 'as frightened you? 'E will answer to my sword this time, that I will swear upon my life."

"You're dead, and the problem isn't Christian; it's a demon. For heaven's sake, stay here where you're safe." I gathered up my chalk, the bottle of holy water, and my notebook, and spun around, dodging Alis as I hurried back down the stairs. My leg was screaming, but not as much as my mind. Christian had been alone with the demon for two or three minutes; what was he doing? Did he have experience with demons? Did he know they didn't like water, that if you captured one in a circle, it could be made to tell the truth about who summoned it? Did he know how to draw a circle strong enough to hold a demon? And worst of all, just what type was the demon—one of the weak minions, or a strong emissary of a demon lord?

The smell hit me as I raced down the basement stairs. Demons have a very strong odor, something that has been compared to that of a moldering grave. Never having stuck my nose in a moldering grave, I couldn't say, but I did know the smell raised all the hairs on the back of my neck and made my internal warning system go into overdrive trying to convince me to turn around and get myself out of there.

What I saw as I threw open the door to the wine cellar stopped me dead in my tracks. Christian leaned against the wall nearest the door, his arms crossed over his bare chest, his eyes solid black. Standing at the end of one of the six-foot-tall wine racks was a handsome man in a three-piece suit.

A very handsome man.

An exceptionally handsome man. One with dark blond hair slicked back from a broad brow, dark, sardonic eyes, and a pencil-thin mustache.

It was a demon . . . in Eurotrash form.

Are you okay? I asked Christian. He didn't answer me, didn't even glance over to me, but he held out his hand in warning to keep me from stepping between him and the demon. I could feel the power he was exerting to keep the demon in one place, but I didn't see any signs of containment wards. I had no idea how he was controlling the demon, but decided *how* wasn't important.

"This is your woman," the demon said, its voice making a couple of cracks appear in the cement wall.

I knew Christian wasn't happy having me there

with him in the room with what appeared to be one of the greater demons. Only the upper soldiers in a demon lord's service could cause the wall to crack with just a few words.

"She is not Joined with you. Will you give her to me?"

A hand-size patch of plaster fell off the far wall.

I wet my fingers with holy water and moved next to Christian to trace a ward over his heart, being careful to avoid blocking his gaze.

"She is nothing but flesh and bones, Dark One. You could be powerful, more powerful than you can imagine. I know what you seek. If you give her to me, I can give you more power than the lord who created you."

Two of the ceiling lights went out.

I repeated the warding process on my own chest, then squatted down to draw a circle on the tile floor using the holy water, wondering what the demon was talking about. Christian had told me his father had been the one made a Dark One, not him.

"That will do you no good," the demon told me, its words punctuated by the sound of a bottle of wine exploding. I looked up, quickly tracing a capture symbol with my still-wet fingers, an archaic spell a wizard had taught me in case I ever ran up against a succubus or any of the other minor creatures who were sometimes attracted to haunted sites. It didn't last long, but if you were quick, you could use it to keep the creature held to one place for a few vital seconds.

"It's going to take more than just holy water to hold one of its power," I told Christian. He dragged a fingernail across his wrist, stepping forward to allow the blood seeping from the scratch to drop into the circle. I held out my hand to him.

"Would you?"

He hesitated.

"Christian, we don't have much time. You said there's power in us together; we can't do this singly."

"I don't like it," he said, reluctantly taking my hand. He was aware that if something went wrong, the demon could use our blood to bind us to itself.

"I know, and I appreciate that, but this is our only chance. If we can pull it into the circle, it will have no choice but to tell us what we want to know."

He gave me a look to let me know that he knew I was right, but still didn't want to involve me. I wiggled my fingers at him until he took one in his mouth, swiftly nipping the end of the finger. I held it above the spattered drops of his blood and let my blood mingle with his.

The demon shrieked and broke free from the ward. I was knocked backward by the force of the ward exploding, striking my head on the cement wall behind me. The demon went straight for Christian, even as I screamed out a warning.

The ward over his heart protected that organ, but it did nothing for the rest of his body. Before I could draw breath enough to clear my spinning head, the demon threw itself on Christian, punching its fist straight through his stomach and out his back.

"Dear God in heaven." I gasped as Christian clung to the demon, but whether it was for support or in attack, I didn't know. Blood soaked the demon's arm as he jerked it out of Christian's body, but powerful as it was, Christian hadn't survived nine hundred years without learning a few tricks of his own. I saw his lips moving in a spell as he easily broke the demon's bloodied arm.

I crawled over to the circle and started tracing wards around it. Although the demon was stronger than a mortal man, it was bound by the limitations of the form it had chosen, and while it couldn't be destroyed, the form it used could be harmed to the point that the demon would have no choice but to abandon it and return to its master.

All of which meant I had to hurry if I wanted to capture it before it broke Christian's body to the point where he wouldn't be able to heal himself.

The demon screamed again as Christian snapped its neck. It retaliated by punching another hole in Christian's chest, but this time he knew it was coming and fell backward, pulling the demon with him, ripping out its jugular as they fell to the floor.

I could feel Christian's strength dramatically diminish with each blow he took, and hurried to finish the captivity spell. I had never done it before, which meant the wards were not going to be strong enough to hold the demon, but the circle closed by holy water and our blood should give them enough strength to hold the demon for at least a minute or two.

I traced the last symbol, spoke the last word, and gathered up every emotion I had to feed the power I poured into the circle.

The demon shrieked again, this time a long howl of despair that had chunks of plaster falling from the ceiling to rain upon us. The demon disappeared from where it was struggling with Christian, reappearing in the circle, panting, its eyes glowing red, blood streaming down the front of its expensive Savile Row suit.

I waited just long enough to make sure the circle would hold it, then limped over to where Christian was lying drunkenly against the wall.

There were two sizable holes in his torso that were bleeding sluggishly. "What can I do to help you?"

"Merge with me," he said with a gasp, his silky voice spiked with pain. I held my hands over his wounds, closing my eyes and leaning against him, opening my mind to him and allowing him to pull strength from me.

Dark Ones have remarkable powers of recovery and self-healing, but they can be killed if the damage is too great to repair. Luckily, with Christian's heart— his most vulnerable point—warded, the demon could do only enough damage to slow him down. Still, it took valuable time to heal him, and I was very aware of the demon repeatedly testing the circle to see if it could find any weaknesses. At last Christian pulled my hands from his body and got to his feet. He was still injured, but the worst had been repaired, and at least his wounds had filled in and were no longer bleeding.

"What is its name?" Christian asked, moving carefully to stand in front of the demon. I followed, tracing protection wards on him at all four compass points.

"What is your name?" I asked it.

The capture symbols around the circle glowed green, then black in the air. I threw every bit of power

I had into the circle until the symbols glowed green again.

"You *will* answer me. What is your name?" I asked it again.

"Sarra," it answered, all but spitting the answer out at me. Unfortunately, I wasn't hip with the latest list of demons and who they served. I glanced at Christian. He nodded.

"Who is your master?"

"Asmodeus," the demon snarled, throwing itself toward us. The wards glowed a bright green, but held. Still . . .

I don't think I can contain it for much longer. Do you recognize the name of its lord?

Yes.

Christian took my hand and tugged me until I was standing behind him. I gave the back of his arm a pinch and moved to his side.

"Who sent you here?" I asked the demon.

"One who is protected by my master."

Rats. Names have power, remember? Well, there were very particular rules governing the dark world, and one of them was that a demon couldn't be made to rat on anyone else who was under the protection of its lord. In other words, the demon could not be made to invoke the name of someone under his lord's power; however, the rules didn't stop me from naming names and asking the demon point-blank if that person had sent him.

"Did Guarda White send you?"

The demon snarled again and lunged at a ward that was glowing a bit weaker than the others. I threw more power into it.

"Did Phillippa the hermit send you?"

It spun around, fingernails lengthening into claws, and slashed at the air.

"Did Eduardo Tassalerro send you?"

Christian moved closer to me as I spoke the last name, a protective he-man gesture to be sure, but one that warmed me to my toes.

The demon spat out a few suggestions that were anatomically impossible. A ceiling fan spun to the floor behind him.

I leaned into Christian. "I was sure it was Eduardo."

Few of those people who dally with dark powers make free with their true names.

"Good point." I turned back to the demon. If it wanted to play it right down the line, I would be happy to oblige. "Did the one who *calls* himself Eduardo Tassalerro send you?"

"Yes," it hissed at me, its eyes showing its fury at being forced into revealing the truth.

"For what purpose were you sent here?" Christian asked. I glanced at him. His color was better, and he stood more easily, as if his wounds were continuing to heal. I couldn't spare any of my power to pour into him, but I squeezed his hand to let him know I was concerned. He tightened his fingers on mine in response.

The demon ignored him and continued to test the circle. To tell the truth, I was more than a bit surprised it had held a demon of Sarra's stature for as long as it did. I assumed what Christian had told me about the sum of our power combined being more than the parts added together was the reason, and attributed most of the strength of the circle to the blood we'd spilled to close it.

"Why were you sent here?" I repeated the question. Since I was the one who cast the spell, it had to answer me.

"To capture the woman."

Eek.

Christian tried to tug me behind him again. I refused to move, pinching his wrist to let him know there were only so many dominating moves I was willing to tolerate.

"Can you send it back?" he reluctantly asked me.

I looked at the demon. It sneered at me. The circle was still holding, but I could see signs that it wouldn't much longer.

"Not by myself."

Christian's eyes, glittering black onyx, held mine for a moment, his mind sharing his strength with me.

Then we will do it together.

I squashed down the niggle of doubt and clung to Christian's calm assuredness.

I let myself merge into him, holding tight to him as our power joined, swelling until it filled the room. I calmed my mind long enough to dig through my memory and uncover the long-forgotten spell that would send the demon back to its master. Merely breaking the circle would not be enough; we had to send it from its present location.

I started speaking the words, but before I could finish the air quivered expectantly. Three familiar shapes burst through the door.

"*Mi amor*, I am come to save you! I 'ave you now, you scaly-toothed, snaggle-skinned spawn of Satan!"

Antonio cried as he lunged forward, slashing his rapier about in an extremely dashing, if sadly ineffective, manner.

"I found a Bible," Esme yelled helpfully, then looked down at her empty hands. "Oh, dear, I must have dropped it somewhere. It's not easy keeping your attention focused long enough to move an item that is quite so heavy. I wonder if I left it on the stairs. . . ." She wandered out of the room.

Jem, now wearing a tremendously baggy pair of torn jeans that hung extremely low on his hips, a ripped T-shirt, and a black leather jacket adorned with a skull painted on the back, and sporting one of those greased-back hairdos that the 1950s bad boys wore, all topped off with several heavy gold chains, slouched his way around Antonio. He slid a switchblade from his pocket and flicked it open, sneering at the demon. "Oy! Yer wants a taste of me pricker, then?"

"You dare to sully *mi amor* with your filthy presence, you disgusting piece of codpiece lint! For that you will die!"

Christian shook his head and said something in what I assumed was Czech. I didn't need a translation. I was pretty much saying the same thing to myself, only I doubted if I was as polite as he was.

"Ye wanna rumble? I'm ready t'rumble! G'wan, gimme yer best shot, sucka!"

"Jem is definitely watching too much television," I murmured.

"I found it! I must have dropped it just outside the door. Alis, dear, that isn't china; I'm sure it's just a common ceramic light fixture. Here I come; wait for

265

me and Mr. Woogums. This Bible is terribly heavy...."

Now, here is a curious fact about ghosts. While they can interact with the world of the living only if they concentrate very hard and maintain good control over their psychic power, they *can* interact with one another. This is an important point in understanding just why it was that when Esme backed into the room rump-first, inexplicably dragging one of Christian's antique Bibles rather than carrying it, she wasn't able to see that she was doomed to be on a collision course with Antonio, who was dancing about the circle, hurling all sorts of insults and taunts at the demon.

I saw it, but too late.

"Esme," I yelled in warning as she gave the Bible a great jerk, sending her flying backward into Antonio. Just as Antonio was saying, "Now we will see the color of your guts, you distempered toad-spotted rabbit sucker!" he was knocked forward into the circle, thereby breaking it and releasing the demon. Just a nanosecond before the demon realized it was free, I spoke the last word needed to send it back to the depths from which it came. It turned into a column of oily black smoke that doubled up on itself, sinking into a crack in the tile floor as if it had been sucked down by some giant demonic vacuum cleaner.

Which, I guess, is as apt a description as I'll ever find.

"Well, *that* was certainly interesting," Esme said, rubbing her behind.

Antonio staggered out of the circle, his long curls standing on end as if he'd stuck his finger in a light socket. He blinked several times, and seemed to have some difficulty with the coordination of his legs. "I . . . I . . . I . . ."

Esme helped him over to a bench.

I clung to Christian's hand, breathing a bit heavily as we stared at the faint black mark staining the tile that was all that remained of the demon. Christian started forward toward the mark, but I grabbed him with my other hand and wouldn't let go.

"Beloved, it is over," he said, kissing each of my fingers before gently prying them off his wrist.

Antonio lumbered to his feet again, weaving wildly as he tugged down his doublet, a faint corona of smoke rising from his curls. "You will take your filthy 'ands from *mi corazón* this instant or I will be forced to teach you some manners, you pestilential maltworm, you!"

Christian squatted down to examine the crack in the tile as I held up my hands to show Antonio they were Christian-free, then turned to glare at Esme. "Did I not tell you all to stay in the study? I distinctly remember telling you to stay there. If you had broken that circle before I completed the ritual, that demon would have wiped up the floor with all of you! Do you think I want phantoms living in Christian's house?"

Esme paled even beyond her naturally gray state. A phantom was a ghost trapped in limbo, neither in the spirit realm nor the human realm, with no hope of ever finding Release. Demons had the power to drag ghosts there if they were strong enough, and judging by the holes Sarra had punched through

Christian, it was a fair bet to say he would have had little trouble with my gang of five.

"We came to save you," Antonio protested as his legs gave out and he plopped back down onto the bench. Only he wasn't paying attention, and he ended up sitting midway through the bench, the seat portion resting in his chest. He kicked his legs around and waved his arms until Esme and Jem took pity on him and hauled him up so he was sitting on the bench proper.

"And we appreciate that, but—"

"It was the least we could do for you, after everything you've done for us. Giving us a new home, and television, and taking us on little bobble outings and teas and such. Even Mr. Woogums is enjoying our new haunt."

I raised my hands, then let them fall helplessly. "Look, what you did was very noble, but—"

"Bloody, 'ell, on't no'un come 'round me 'ood and mess wit' me bloods," Jem added in an odd, eighteenth-century "lower-class servant meets twenty-first-century rapper" dialect.

I pointed a finger at him. "That's it, no more MTV for you. And pull your pants up; it looks ridiculous with the crotch down around your knees. Esme, please fetch Alis; heaven only knows what she's up to out there. I will speak to all of you later." I gave them all my best mean squinty eyes. Two heads nodded quickly. Antonio tipped over sideways and made faint mewing noises.

I turned and walked over to where Christian was examining the tile. My leg was too sore, and I was too exhausted after the tremendous outpouring of energy that was needed to defeat the demon, to squat next to him, so I just leaned against him and touched his head.

"Did it break your nice floor?"

Christian took one of my hands and pulled me forward until I was bent over and could feel the air just above the black-stained crack.

My hand tingled as if I were holding a low-voltage electric fence.

"Oh, no," I said, straightening up slowly as Christian got to his feet.

His eyes were a warm red-gold-brown that made me think of comfortable winter evenings before a roaring fire.

"This is going to require the help of a Guardian."

I felt my lower lip quiver. "You don't mean—"

He took my face in his hands and kissed me very, very gently.

"Yes," he said simply. "Now we have our very own portal to hell."

"*Caray!*" Antonio moaned from the bench.

"*Merde,*" I agreed, translating it into French. There just didn't seem to be much else to say.

Chapter Fifteen

It took me an hour, but eventually with Christian's help I warded all the doors and windows on the ground floor to prevent anyone who wished to do us harm from entering. I used a strong ward, one I had confidence in because I used it on my apartment every night, so I felt pretty secure as I limped up the stairs to the bed. I looked over at Christian, who had slowed his long-legged pace for me.

"You look pretty good for someone who's had two fist-sized holes punched through him, fought a demon, and is now moving around an hour after sunrise. How do you feel?"

He ran his hand through his hair (an added benefit to making him keep his hair unbound) and rubbed his jaw. "Like I've spent the day jousting without armor."

Ooh. Little time warp there reminding me just how

old he was. Still, I knew how much energy he'd spent on fighting the demon and healing himself. With the warding and the rising sun draining him of more power, I knew it was imperative to get him to rest. I'd just keep our little discussion short, offer him the opportunity for a light snack in case he was peckish, and then put him to bed. "Yes, well, I do plan to grill you at length about everything you've seen and done during your life, but right now I'm more concerned about our immediate plans."

At the top of the stairs I turned left instead of right, and limped toward his study. He lifted me up from behind, turned on his heel, and marched in the opposite direction.

"Hey!" I protested, punching him lightly in the shoulder. "We have stuff to talk about."

"We can talk in bed. I've fought a demon, remember?"

"If we go to bed, we aren't going to talk, and you know it."

He grinned.

I bit his ear. "Christian, this is serious. If Eduardo is desperate enough to summon up a demon— which incidentally confirms my earlier suspicion that one of the people in the triumvirate had tapped into dark power—it's a sure thing he's not just going to shrug his shoulders and walk away. I can't imagine why, but for some reason he wants me."

"Mi amor!"

"Oh, no," I groaned, dropping my forehead to Christian's shoulder. "Not now."

"Stand and face me, you coward!" I looked down the hall. Antonio had taken up a stand in front of

Christian's bedroom door, and was waving his rapier around. "Now at last we will 'ave this out like men! No longer will you bully *mi corazón*."

Christian didn't even stop; he just waved one hand.

"My dove, my sweet rose, you must see 'ow we were meant to be—*Caray!* I 'ate it when 'e does this . . ."

Antonio dissolved.

"I can think of a number of reasons Eduardo wants you," Christian said as if we hadn't been interrupted, gently depositing me on my feet next to the bed. He peeled off my sweater, shoes, and pants without any further ado. I squeaked and scurried under the blankets while he locked the door and took off his jeans. He slid into bed and pulled me up next to him.

"No, now, talk, Christian; we need to talk. Your hands must remain above my waist at all times. And stop waving that around; you could poke someone's eye out with it."

He laughed and rolled onto his side, fitting my back to his chest so we were spooned together. "All right, my brave *malý váleèník*, what do you wish to do about Eduardo?"

I snuggled back against him, laced my fingers through his where they rested on my belly, and thought. "Well, first of all, we need to figure out why he wants me so badly. Yes, I Summoned up two ghosts under less than ideal circumstances, but there are other Summoners around who are just as good, if not better. So why go to all of this trouble for me?"

He was quiet for a moment, rubbing his chin on the top of my head. "I believe that at first the interest was in you as a person who could be swayed by the research possibilities. It sounds as if they thought they could manipulate you to Summon ghosts for them, and go along with their plans to keep the spirits available."

"For research."

"Possibly."

"Well, I can't imagine what else you could do with a ghost. 'At first,' you said. I take it that means you think there's a different interest now?"

He said nothing. He didn't need to. I knew what the interest in me now was. Pain filled my heart.

Christian's arm tightened around me. *Beloved, it is not your fault. I would have come to their attention sooner or later in my attempt to find Sebastian. It was my plan. You have not betrayed me.*

"They found you through me."

And you have made me stronger than I have ever been, so that together we can fight them. Do you not see that rather than destroying me, you have saved me?

"I think it's a very fine line between destruction and salvation, and I never was one who could color within the lines."

His laughter filled my head, warming my soul just as his body warmed mine. *I would not want to you be any different.*

"That's because you're crazy. And old. You're much too old for me, I see that now. I draw the line at dating men more than five hundred years older than me. Anything past that is just decrepit."

He laughed again and pulled my hips tighter to him. *Do I feel decrepit to you, Beloved?*

"Stop that. We have to talk about what we're going to do. And besides, you were gravely wounded just an hour and a half ago. A man who's had two holes punched through his body and fought a demon cannot— Oh, good heavens. Christian!"

He eased my leg up over his thigh and slid into me. *Now we shall see who is too old.*

"You don't play fair," I murmured into his armpit.

I do not have to. I am a Dark One.

"You are an arrogant one is what you are." I turned my head and spread my fingers through the hair on his chest. "But an arrogant one with many amazing and wondrous talents who makes my bones melt. However, there are other things than your talent that we really should talk about. If you don't mind returning to an earlier, less pleasant subject, what are we going to do about Eduardo?"

His sigh ruffled my hair. "We will guard against another attack, and I will locate Sebastian."

I pinched him.

He sighed again. "And to think I spent all those hundreds of years assuming my Beloved would be a sweet, gentle woman who would spend her days finding ways to please me."

"Dream on, Vlad. You were saying?"

"We will guard against another attack, and then I will—with your assistance—locate Sebastian."

I decided he'd had enough pinching for one day. "Just barely passable, mister. Now, I think that the quickest way to find Sebastian is to give Eduardo what he wants—namely, me."

"No."

"If I let him nab me somehow, he'll have to take me to wherever he's keeping Sebastian, because he'll know you are sure to come riding up on your white horse to save me."

"I refuse to allow this."

"I might even be sure to have one or two of the ghosts with me—I'm willing to bet Antonio would volunteer—just to sweeten the pot and make sure they grab me."

"It is totally out of the question."

"Then, once I'm taken to wherever they're holding your friend, I can tell you where I am, and you can come zooming in with reinforcements and rescue Sebastian, save me from whatever terrible fate Eduardo and Guarda have planned for me, and we'll all live happily ever after."

"This plan of yours is intolerable."

It was my turn to sigh. I rolled over until I was stretched out on top of him, resting my chin on my hand. "Do you have a better plan?"

"Yes."

"Christian, you know the only way to find out where Sebastian is being held is to allow one or the other of us to be captured, and let's face facts—it will be easier for you to rescue me than for me to rescue you. I know my own strength, I know what I can and can't do, and summoning up enough power to rescue two half-dead vampires is not within my abilities. I simply do not have the resources that you have."

"Regardless—"

"No." I put my hand over his mouth. "Rather than arguing about this for the rest of the day, why don't you just recognize that I'm right, and start putting that formidable mind of yours to work on how to keep me safe when I'm in the clutches of the triumvirate and rescue Sebastian at the same time."

I will not allow you to endanger yourself.

I moved my hand and kissed him. *I have absolute faith in you, Christian.*

You are everything to me. You cannot do this.

"I have to," I said, tracing the silky line of his eyebrows. "Don't you see? This is all part of my dream, part of us. If we don't do this—together—our relationship will be incomplete, a farce, a shadow of what it should be. If we are truly meant to be together, we must see this through. We must fulfill the promise that our relationship holds."

I sensed the struggle within him, the need he felt to keep me safe and out of trouble warring with the respect he had for my strength, the pride he had in my abilities. He wrapped his arms around me and held me tightly, his lips moving in a line of kisses on my forehead. *You are going to doom me to an eternity of righting every wrong, of saving every person in need who comes to your attention, aren't you?*

I smiled into his chest, closing my eyes and murmuring a prayer of gratitude that I had found him, knowing that I had asked more of him than he ever imagined, and yet he had been everything I hoped for, and so much more. Maybe giving up a little bit of control wasn't a sign of weakness. Maybe, just maybe, I could remain strong even if I committed myself to Christian. *You told me you were knighted when you were twenty-one. Once a knight, always a knight. The only thing that has changed is that now you have a partner.*

If I didn't know better, I'd say the derisive noise that echoed through my head was a disgusted snort. I traced a ward over us both and fell asleep to the sound of his heart beating strong and true beneath my ear.

We held a war conference that afternoon. It wasn't easy getting Christian to agree to it, since his natural tendencies made him (foolishly) believe he could make up plans on his own and then inform me of my role in them after the fact, but in a scene that had all five ghosts disappearing the instant Christian threatened to lock me in a room and conveniently lose the key, which, of course, I countered with a promise of slow castration, I eventually persuaded him that where he and I together might reign supreme over the triumvirate, other warm bodies would be a welcome addition to help with any minions who might be lurking about.

So it was that an hour after I described to Christian just how I would geld him (with a grapefruit knife and two egg cups), we sat in his comfortable study with Joy, Raphael, Roxy, and the ghosts (minus Alis, who had been left in an empty bedroom with several inexpensive ceramic knickknacks to amuse her). The TV was blissfully muted.

"This is so exciting. I've never rescued anyone before. I want a gun. Raphael, can I have a gun? I think I need a gun."

"Firearms! What an excellent idea," Antonio said. Roxy smiled at him. He stroked his beard and wiggled his eyebrows at her until he saw me watching him.

"No guns," Raphael told Roxy, then shot Christian a martyred look that very nearly rivaled the one Christian was always wearing around me.

"There will be no need for guns," Christian agreed. "Your role will not require it."

She frowned. "Oh? Just what do I get to do?"

"I believe you will best serve our cause by keeping a protective guard over Joy. Raphael will feel easier to know someone is with her."

"A woman who is anticipating a blessed event should always be kept calm and reassured." Esme nodded sagely from where she sat next to Christian.

"What?" Roxy asked. "Why does she need to be guarded? No one wants to kidnap *her!*"

"I could be kidnapped if I wanted to," Joy said defensively.

"I would kidnap you if you were not . . . eh . . ." Antonio waved at her stomach.

"Thank you, Antonio, that's very sweet of you," Joy said, smiling smugly at Roxy.

Roxy rolled her eyes. "He's just being nice to you because anyone can see you're about to explode. I want in on this, too; you can't palm off some stay-at-home job on me. I'm very good in a tight place; I've had self-defense training. I was tops in my class with the bottle of Mace. I bet I could take down at least a couple of this Trust's goons."

"There will be no taking down of anyone, no Mace, and no violence. My company specializes in nonlethal security, and I do not want to jeopardize its reputation because of a trigger-happy vigilante,"

Raphael told her. We all nodded, even Jem, who had dropped the chains and torn clothing, and was now clad in a pinstripe suit and talked like he was a cross between a character from *Tom Jones* and *The Godfather*.

"Maces are very old-fashioned," Antonio commiserated with Roxy. "No one uses them anymore. I prefer a rapier, myself. It is very deadly, yet always looks stylish."

She blew him a kiss. I frowned at both of them. "Christian and I talked this all out and we have a plan. If you will let us tell it, you'll see where each of you fits into it."

"I don't have to stay at home with the beached whale, do I?" Roxy asked suspiciously.

"That's it; you're off the list as godmother," Joy answered, trying to cross her arms over her belly but not succeeding.

"Expectant mothers should never be referred to as sea mammals," Esme scolded. Jem sniggered.

"No, you do not need to stay at home with Joy if you don't want to, although I happen to think she looks charming," I answered. Joy beamed at me. "It's really a simple plan, and I think you'll agree that we have all the bases covered."

Everyone looked at us expectantly.

Go ahead; I'll let you tell it, since it was mostly your plan.

How very gracious of you.

Don't push your luck. I'm still ticked off about that "locked in a room" comment.

Three hours and thirty-two minutes later four of us stormed the ARMPIT offices, clad in jumpsuits and ventilation hats labeled with the name of a natural-gas company, Raphael in the lead with a clipboard and an extremely officious manner. Aided by Christian, master of the mind push, we had the offices cleared out in just a couple of minutes.

"That was fun." Roxy giggled as the last secretary dashed out the door, under the mistaken impression that a gas leak was about to cause an explosion of a catastrophic nature. She pulled off her ventilator and smiled at Christian. "That Vulcan mind-meld thingy of yours sure does come in handy. I bet you could make a killing at the racetrack, eh?"

I grabbed her arm and pushed her toward a row of filing cabinets. "Stop hitting on Christian; you're married."

She grinned and saluted me. We scattered around the offices, combing through both paper and computer files for anything that might lead us to the two houses the trust owned in London.

"Hey, is this something? It's a receipt for some temperature-controlled wine vault."

"Wine vault?" Christian looked up from the computer on Guarda's desk and came out into the outer office. "Guarda does not strike me as the type of person who appreciates fine wines."

We all huddled around to look at the receipt.

"It's in the basement," I pointed out.

"And has a steel-lined door and reinforced walls," Raphael mused. "Unusual, that. More like a bunker than a wine vault."

"What's the address?" I asked.

"It's to the north. Hmmm. Might be worth a look."

Raphael and Christian exchanged glances, something I immediately put a halt to.

"Don't even begin to think what you're thinking," I shook my finger at Christian, pulling on my coat and snatching the receipt from Roxy's hand. "It's all of us or none. Your choice."

"I'd prefer it if someone stayed behind with Joy," Raphael started to say.

"We left her the ghosts; they'll let us know if anyone tries anything." I pushed past Raphael and headed out the door at a fast clip, or at as fast a clip as I could get my wonky leg to move. After consulting with a map of the city, we piled into Raphael's car and headed north.

The city quickly turned into bustling suburbia, then into a prosperous neighborhood of tall town houses. Respectability dripped from every eave, leaving me vaguely surprised that Guarda had chosen such a quiet, sedate suburb to use as her ghost and vampire storage facility. Raphael pulled up in front of one of a line of houses pleasantly situated on a street that curved along a gentle crescent.

"That's number eighteen, down there. The one on the end."

We all looked where Raphael was pointing. The house looked no different from any others on the street.

"Doesn't look very creepy, does it?" Roxy asked.

"Which just makes it all that much more chilling," I answered as I got out of the car. "Everyone know the plan? Roxy, you and Raphael create a distraction at the front door while Christian and I slip in the back way."

"Yeah, yeah, piece of cake. No one can create a scene like I can." She grinned.

"An understatement if I ever heard one." Raphael groaned, but allowed her to grab his arm and drag him off toward the door to number eighteen.

Christian took my hand and tugged me down a narrow alley that ran behind the crescent.

You will conform exactly to our plan, malý vá-leèník. *You will not try to rescue Sebastian by yourself.*

We dodged trash cans and parked cars, eventually coming to the back of the last house on the row. The tiny garden was sodden with the incessant rain, water squelching into my boots. I glanced up at the house, shivering at the dark, blank look of the windows. The house felt guarded, as if it were used to holding secrets inside and never allowing them out. Somewhere in there was a Dark One, kept weak and barely alive for who knew what nefarious purpose. "I've already promised you three times I won't endanger myself, Christian. Just remember to stick to your part and don't get any ideas about throwing yourself between me and any danger we run into. If I need help, you will be the first person I ask for it."

His sigh brushed my mind as he waved a hand at the back door. It clicked open. *My next Beloved is going to be a mild, sweet-tempered woman who will never question me, and will not give me one moment's concern.*

He slipped through the door with me right behind him. We were in a semidark small room, a mudroom by the looks of it. Discarded boots littered the floor, and musty-smelling coats hung haphazardly from a row of pegs on the wall. Christian froze for a moment at the door, the sound of Roxy's high-pitched yelling counterpointed by the rumble of Raphael's bass clearly audible even in the back of the house. Bless Roxy, it sounded like she was out there giving birth to a wildcat. If her histrionics didn't attract everyone within hearing distance, I'd be an imp's aunt. Without even turning back to wave good-bye, Christian melted into the shadows and headed toward what I assumed was the door to the basement stairs.

I peered around the dim light of the kitchen to make sure it was empty, then laid my hand against the wall and stood for a moment, opening my mind up to the house. The spirit I was after was being held upstairs, in a small attic room. On the floor below me I could feel Christian as he searched for his friend.

Christian?

Yes, Beloved? I smiled into the gloom of the kitchen as I started up a dark, uncarpeted stair, Roxy's voice echoing through the house as she accused someone of trying to cop a feel.

Your next Beloved isn't going to love you nearly as much as I do.

I grinned at the stunned silence that followed my statement.

We are going to have a talk when this is over, Allegra. A long, long talk. Preferably in the bathtub.

Be careful, Christian. Whoever it was who helped Eduardo and Guarda trap Sebastian is not going to treat you with kid gloves. You might be a bossy, arrogant sort of vampire, but you're my *bossy, arrogant vampire and I don't want anything happening to you.*

He smiled into my mind. *You are my Beloved. You*

mean more to me than my life. I will do everything within my power to do as you command.

I figured that was about as good as I was going to get. Roxy's voice took on a new level of stridency as I limped to the top of the stairs, then started up the second flight. By the time I reached the top of the third flight, my leg was screaming. The wards I'd sketched around me glowed a soft green, indicating that something demonic was in the house.

Everything okay? I checked with Christian.

Yes. I have located the wine vault. The door is locked and warded, but I believe I will be through it shortly. You have not seen anyone?

Not a soul, I thought, then gave a mental grimace as I hurried toward the room that held the ghost. *I just hope Roxy can keep them busy a little bit longer. Let me know if you need help with the wards.*

Follow the plan, Christian replied sternly. *No deviations. No unauthorized rescues. I will not have your safety compromised.*

I rolled my eyes at the empty hallway, and tried the middle door on the left. It was open.

Unfortunately, it was also occupied.

"Allegra Telford," Guarda said from where she sat in the corner.

"Why am I not surprised?" Phillippa asked, standing to one side of the ghostly figure of a small girl. She had her back to me, so I couldn't see much other than that she was dressed in ankle boots, stockings, and an elaborate knee-length salmon-colored skirt that gathered over a small bustle.

"Maybe you're psychic," I answered, then regretted smart-mouthing her. I swung the door open and smiled a shark smile at both of them. "Well, it's been lovely, but I really have to be . . ."

The ghost turned to look at me. Her expression of despair rivaled that which I felt in Christian. Clearly here was a ghost who wanted to be Released, but who was trapped, forced to remain here, called forth by either Phillippa or Guarda and refused the deliverance she was due.

"Honoria, go to your keeper," Guarda commanded as she rose from her chair. The little ghost's eyes turned to a ratty cloth doll; then she disappeared. A little zing of hope quivered in my mind as my fingers automatically began tracing wards in the doorway behind me. "As for you, Allegra Telford, the time has come for you to understand just who you have set yourself against. Phillippa?"

The hermit nodded and slipped out the door behind me. I didn't have long; I knew Phillippa had been sent to fetch Eduardo, who was no doubt at the front of the house trying to deal with Roxy and Raphael.

Christian?

"You realize, of course, that by coming here you have given yourself into our power."

I felt his concentration as he struggled to unmake the wards on the wine vault door. *I am almost through the door.*

Good. I found the ghost. I should have her in a couple of minutes, but then all hell's going to break out. Can you get Sebastian out by yourself?

He frowned into my mind. *I can, but acquiring the spirit is not according to our plans, Allegra. What are you hiding from me?*

"We are too strong for you. It would be better if you came to us willingly, but if it is not to be"— Guarda shrugged—"we will take you by force."

I set up another level of guards in my mind between Christian and Guarda. *Yeah, well, I didn't plan on falling in love with a vampire, either, but sometimes you just have to deal with what life hands you.*

"Why are you torturing that poor child? Why don't you Release her? What can you possibly hope to learn from a little bitty ghost like that?" I asked Guarda, more to keep her from discovering I was talking to Christian than to hear her answers.

You are up to something, the silky, suspicious voice slid through my mind. *I cannot stop now to investigate, but you will remember what you have promised. Your safety comes first.*

"The poor child is a spirit, a mere memory of a human life. It has no feelings."

"You know what?" I asked, tipping my head to the side and gathering power until it glowed hot in my hands. "I think you're the one without any feelings. Which makes me regret this not at all."

Guarda frowned, falling right into my trap. "Regret what?"

I lunged forward, slamming the power held in my hands straight into her face, sending her flying backward until she hit the wall. Her head cracked painfully on a wooden shelf as she slid down, slumping in an untidy heap on the floor. I wasn't sure if it was the overload of my power shorting out hers, or being knocked unconscious that disabled her, but I didn't stop to question the situation. From somewhere on a floor below me I heard a shriek.

"Drat it all; she's got a sympathetic link to Phillippa. I might have known." I grabbed the doll keeper, stuffing it under my sweater as I spun on my good leg to race down hall toward the back stairs.

Noise erupted from the front of the house.

I hope you have that door open, because you're going to have company any second now! I warned Christian.

He didn't answer, and I didn't have the time to probe further. As I hit the second floor running, a dark shadow to my left lunged toward me. My wards glowed gold and white, allowing me to grab the banister and throw myself down the stairs without the ARMPIT flunky getting a grip on me. He was close behind me, though, panting heavily as he thundered down the stairs after me.

I flung myself off the last couple of steps, my weak leg buckling beneath me and sending me crashing painfully to the ground. The ARMPIT tripped over me, and went flying. I stumbled to my feet, holding tight to the front of my coat, the wards around me lit up in brilliant emerald. Beyond me, the door to the basement was suddenly blown off its hinges, the percussion from the blast deafening the shrieks and screams from the front of the house. I kicked at the ARMPIT as he grabbed for me, limping hard toward the back door, glancing behind me to make sure Christian was following.

A tall, handsome man with filthy dark blond hair and sunken eyes staggered from the basement. He was dressed in rags, his emaciated body thin, far too thin for any human to survive. He stumbled and clutched a chair as he tried to walk toward me.

"Sebastian?"

He looked up, his face gray and gaunt.

"Beloved," was all he said, the word a whisper so faint I hardly heard it.

"Yes, I'm Christian's Beloved," I said, limping toward him.

"No, you don't!" the ARMPIT yelled, lumbering to his feet. "That's ours! You can't have it!"

I snatched up the teakettle sitting on the counter and hurled it at his head, lacing the kettle with my last remaining dollop of power. The ARMPIT never stood a chance.

"Come on quickly; we're out of time," I said as I shoved my shoulder under Sebastian's arm and tried to hurry him toward the door. "We have to get out of here now, before the triumvirate—"

The air within the house shuddered.

"Too late." I groaned, half dragging the vampire to the door. A wave of power slammed into me, ramming me up against the counter. I struggled for breath, struggled to hold on to Sebastian as wave after wave of pain rolled through me. My wards were gone, dissolved under the strength of the triumvirate's power. Sebastian started to fall, clawing at the counter. I wrapped my hand into the shredded cloth that covered his back and fought my way through the pain to make it the last few steps to the door. I knew if I could just get us beyond the boundary of the house, the triumvirate's power would be significantly lessened. The door was warded, but I'd seen the ward before. I half held Sebastian as I untraced it, gritting my teeth against the agony that racked me, sick with the stench of demons. My strength was draining quickly, the last reserves being used to hold Sebastian up and keep me standing against the force of the triumvirate's continuous attack. With a sob that was more than a little mingled with prayer, I freed the ward and clutched at the door, dragging Sebastian through it into the black rain outside.

The windows above our heads shattered, tiny bits of glass pinging around us on the paving stones as a soundless roar of anger filled the night.

"Come on," I cried to Sebastian as I pulled him to his feet, my voice a croak of pain. "We have to get out of here."

Stumbling over what seemed like every stone, falling twice into the mud and rain-soaked grass, I managed to navigate Sebastian through the tiny garden, down the alley toward the place Raphael had left his car. Halfway there Roxy appeared out of the shadows.

"God almighty, you're covered in blood."

"Grab his other side," I said in a gasp, my breath a sharp stab in my side. "I can't hold him up much longer."

She hurried around him and took a bit of his weight, and together we got him step by painful step down the alley until we were at Raphael's car. Sebastian fell into the backseat, Roxy beneath him as she tried to pull him in. Raphael ran down the road toward us, several ARMPITs in close pursuit.

"Get in the car," he roared at me as I stood looking back down the alley.

"I can't; Christian isn't here."

"Get in the damned car!"

I shook my head and stepped away from the open door. "Christian hasn't come out yet."

Raphael can run; I'll give him that. For a big guy, he's incredibly fast on his feet. Still, the ARMPITs giving chase were angry, and that meant Raphael had no time to listen to me explain that absolutely, under no circumstances, would I leave without Christian. Instead he just picked me up and threw me into the back of the car on top of Roxy and Sebastian, lunging into the front seat and slamming his foot on the accelerator as he started the car. All three of us in the backseat were thrown backward as the car shot off, swerving around one ARMPIT as he leaped toward us.

Raphael swore and swerved again, the faint thud indicating that this ARMPIT wasn't as agile as the last.

"It's okay," he said, panting as he glanced into his rearview mirror. I hauled myself off Sebastian and turned to glare at Raphael's head. "Just winged him. He's up and running. We made it."

I turned to look back, ignoring the four people as they ran down the rain-slicked pavement after us. The house stood as silent as ever, its windows staring out into the street with dark, watchful eyes.

I slumped down into the seat, a sharp pain slicing through my heart. "No, we didn't make it. We left Christian behind."

Chapter Sixteen

Roxy had to sit on me to keep me from throwing myself out of the car every time Raphael was forced to come to a stop. I swore and thought seriously of cursing her—just a little one—but in the end Raphael and Roxy ignored my sobs and pleas and threats and drove us to Christian's home.

What Sebastian thought, I had no idea. He didn't look very lucid, and to tell the shameful truth, at that moment I didn't care what he thought. In fact, I would have been more than willing to trade him for Christian's safe return.

"Good evening, Mrs. Turner," I told Christian's housekeeper as we stood on his doorstep. "You remember Raphael and Roxy from earlier today, of course. This is a friend of Christian's." I waved toward Sebastian, apparently lying dead in Raphael's arms. "He's . . . um . . . he's not feeling very well at the moment, and Christian asked if we'd get him settled in one of the bedrooms."

Evidently Mrs. Turner's impression of Christian's eccentricities covered two near strangers appearing at the door with her employer's girlfriend and a nearly dead man, because she didn't even bat an eye as she stepped back and allowed us in. Oh, she blinked a bit once she got a good look at my eyes, but she didn't faint or run screaming from the room, so I figured we were well ahead of the game.

"Will Mr. Dante be along shortly? There is a young lady waiting to speak with him," she said as we started up the stairs.

I stopped on the first stair. "Oh, really? What sort of a young lady?"

"It's a good thing you're not denying your fate any longer," Roxy called from the top of the stairs. " 'Cause that's the most jealous 'What sort of a young lady' I've ever heard."

"Christian has been"—*torn from my side . . . held prisoner . . . forced to endure who knows how many torments*—"detained. Is this something I can help with?"

Mrs. Turner looked doubtful. "The young lady said Mr. Dante had asked her to repair some damage done to a floor in the wine cellar."

The Guardian! I'd forgotten all about her. Drat, what a time for her to come and put a cork in the conduit to hell.

"If it will make you feel better, I'll have a talk with her."

Mrs. Turner didn't look as if she'd feel a whole lot better, but I guess she figured I was the lesser of two evils, because she nodded and bustled off to dust something. I limped as quickly as I could up the stairs.

"This is all I need, a Guardian hanging around just when I need to focus on saving Christian."

"You don't know that anything happened to Christian," Raphael pointed out as he carried Sebastian into Christian's bedroom.

I trailed behind, wringing my hands and wishing I could scream and yell out my frustration and worry. "Oh, sure, he's in a house filled with ghost and vampire hunters, not to mention at least one demon and a triumvirate capable of destroying any of us without breaking a sweat, and I have nothing to worry about? Cow cookies! Christian sacrificed himself for Sebastian; I just know he did. And now he's in trouble and I have to go save him. So if you don't mind setting Sebastian down on the bed, I'll get him tucked in and then be on my way to rescue the man I love." I headed for the door as the last word left my lips.

"What about him? You can't just leave him like this. Even I can tell he's not going to last much longer," Raphael said as he set Sebastian down. The Dark One lay limp and exhausted on the bed, too weak to move.

I stopped at the doorway. *Blast.* I knew he was going to call me on that. "He needs blood."

Roxy and Raphael looked at Sebastian doubtfully. I waved my hand toward him. "It's obvious; I can feel his hunger from here. One of you is going to have to allow him to feed."

"Feed?" Roxy yelped. "You mean . . . *feed?*"

I *tsk*ed. "It's just a little blood. Think of it as a donation to a worthy cause. Look, I don't have time to stand around explaining it to you. I have Christian to go save."

"And just how do you plan to do that?" Raphael asked as Roxy stared at Sebastian in horror. The latter moved in feeble protest under her gaze. "You barely made it out of there on your own; how do you expect to find Christian and free him—that's assuming he isn't staying there of his own free choice?"

I was across the room and in front of Raphael even before I could draw breath. "Christian is strong. He would never yield to the triumvirate. Never!"

"Not them," Sebastian whispered, his voice a frail reed of sound. I glanced down at him, the tatters of his shirt making it possible to see his ribs clearly outlined beneath the tautly stretched skin of his chest. His breathing was labored and slow, much slower than it should be. His sunken, hopeless eyes begged me for a release to his nightmare. I was torn between the need to rush out and save Christian, and helping the friend I knew meant a lot to him.

I stood next to the bed, hesitating, knowing that if I didn't do something, Sebastian would slip away. He needed help, and I couldn't turn to either Roxy or Raphael for that help. They simply did not understand.

I hope you're all right, Christian. I hope you understand that I have to do this first.

Sebastian moaned a wordless protest as I sat on the bed next to him.

"You need blood," I told him quietly, rolling up my sleeve. Roxy moved away from the bed, giving us room as I offered my wrist.

Sebastian closed his eyes, his lips thinned into a tight line.

"Come on," I said, shaking my wrist beneath his nose. "I'm offering this to you of my own free will. Please take it. Christian would want you to."

His breath hissed through his teeth.

"*I* want you to."

He turned his face away from my wrist.

I squished his lips apart and shoved the delicate flesh of my inner wrist up against his teeth. "For God's sake, I've never had to beg anyone to drink my blood. Now will you just take it!"

His hands fluttered against the bed. "Not you," he mumbled against my wrist. "Beloved."

"Oh, for heaven's sake . . ."

"What's wrong?" Roxy asked as I straightened up.

"He won't feed off me. I think it's something to do with the fact that I'm Christian's Beloved."

"Glad to know you've finally seen the light," Roxy said, then tapped her chin as she thought. "You know, I think he's right. You haven't Joined with Christian, have you?"

I shook my head.

She continued chin tapping. "That makes sense. Once a Beloved is claimed, you go into kind of a holding zone, a limbo as far as other Dark Ones are concerned. You're not Joined, so you're not a Moravian, and yet you're not quite human because you've completed all but a few steps of Joining."

"There's just the last one remaining," I admitted. "Wait a minute—what do you mean I'm not quite human?"

"According to what Christian wrote in one of his

books—you really need to read them; you're sadly ignorant of even the most basic Dark One lore, and that's bound to be a handicap when you're married to one—your blood is actually like poison to any other Dark Ones."

I gaped at her. "Of all the ridiculous things I've ever heard! My blood is not poisonous!"

"Not to Christian, no, but just you dribble a bit on poor Sebastian's lips and he'll be stiffer than a three-day-dead dog."

We all looked at Sebastian. He lay so still, so lifeless he almost looked as if he were already dead. I couldn't leave him like that, I just couldn't. Not only would Christian not want his friend to suffer; I couldn't allow it. Not when there was a way to help him.

"Now what will you do?" Raphael asked. I turned toward him and smiled.

He was out even before he saw the punch coming.

"What do you think you're doing?" Roxy gasped as Raphael hit the floor. She looked from his massive body to my small fist. "And more important, *how* did you do it?"

I grabbed one of his arms and nodded toward the other one. "Come on, help me—he won't be out for long. I used a spell to add some wallop to my punch, but it doesn't last long. I'm not very good at casting spells."

Roxy grunted as we heaved Raphael's torso up onto the bed, his head lolling next to Sebastian's thigh. I rolled up his sleeve and dragged his arm up over his head. "Dinner's served," I told Sebastian.

He looked from the wrist in front of his mouth

down to the unconscious man lying half-on, half-off the bed.

"You don't have any other choice," I told him. "I realize you feel weird about dining off of someone who helped save you, but I won't force Roxy, and you turned me down. It's Raphael or nothing."

Sebastian nodded, his reluctance evident even as his lips parted.

"Raphael is going to be *so* pissed at you," Roxy said, her eyes wide as she watched Sebastian's fangs sink into Raphael's wrist. "I mean, majorly pissed. We're talking world-class pissed here."

"Tell him he has to take a number," I said, pulling the rag doll keeper from beneath my sweater and setting it carefully on the floor. "There are a lot of other people who were angry with me first. I might as well do this while Sebastian is filling up."

"Do what? What's that doll?"

I explained about the ghost Guarda had Summoned as I chalked out a circle.

"Wait a second, if she Summoned the ghost and bound it to a keeper, how can you do anything for her? I thought there was some rule that said first come, first served."

"There's another rule that I like better," I said as I pulled out a small pair of scissors, a length of ribbon, and the bottle of holy water. "Finders keepers."

Roxy hesitated for a moment, then came around to where I had drawn a circle.

"Is Raphael going to be all right with him?"

I glanced over to the bed. "Sebastian."

The Dark One's eyes opened, and I was startled to see they were a clear, true blue rather than the grayish black they had first appeared. His lips caressed Raphael's wrist.

"Don't take too much; he's one of the good guys. All right?"

He managed a small nod.

I sat down before the circle and snipped a long strand of my hair.

"I don't mean to be rude, but do you . . . er . . . trust him?"

"Yes." I glanced up at her. "I thought you were an expert on the Dark Ones. You of all people should know that Sebastian feels a sense of obligation to Raphael. He would never harm him."

"Oh. I guess you're right. It's just that Raphael's a friend, and I don't want to see him . . . er . . . drained dry, for lack of better word."

I smiled. "He won't be. Sebastian will take care."

"You can feel that?"

I nodded. "I can feel it."

"Okay." With one last glance at them, Roxy sat down beside me. "So how do you 'finders keepers' this ghost?"

I set the keeper in the circle, my strand of hair laid across the doll's neck. "I've never actually done this, so I'm not sure if it'll work or not. Theoretically it should, but who knows?"

The ribbon was used to bind the doll's hands behind its back. I dug into my bag until I found a length of plum-colored cloth wrapped around a long silver object.

"That's gorgeous. What is it?"

I held it up so Roxy could see the figures of two lovers entwined on the top. "It's a hatpin, really, one of the old-fashioned kind. A wizard friend of mine made it for me. I use it for spells, though."

"Cool. Does he take orders?"

I shook my head, glanced over to make sure Sebastian and Raphael were all right, then sketched a binding ward and closed the circle, the keeper and my hands within it. Using the hatpin, I pricked the doll's heart.

"This pin pierces your heart, I see, so let it now be bound only to me."

"Wow, magic," Roxy said, her eyes huge.

I snipped the ribbon binding the keeper's arms, signifying the spirit's bindings to Guarda being destroyed. "Threads your body first entwined, now find you are bound to mine."

"Why do spells always have to rhyme? I mean, it makes for some fairly bad poetry."

"It gets worse, I'm afraid," I told her as I wove the strand of my hair into the ragged, twisted cloth that made up the doll's hair. "As I am now part of thee, so you will answer only to me."

Roxy groaned.

"Last one."

"Good. I don't think I could survive much more. You really need to take a couple of poetry classes before you do this again. I'm thinking something along the lines of an ode would help."

I used the hatpin to prick my finger, pressing the drop of blood into two marks on either side of the circle. "With my blood I do command you to heed my call and stand."

"Oh, that was *so* lame—Hey! It's working!"

I pulled my hands from the circle as the air within

turned opaque, first light gray, then darker, until the image of a small girl in Victorian dress shimmered in the air.

I grounded the spirit. "What is your name?"

"Honoria Entemann."

Roxy blew out a low whistle.

"Honoria Entemann, do you wish to be Released?"

I swore tears glittered in her ghostly eyes. She hugged the ghostly image of the rag doll to her chest and nodded. "Please."

I stood up, traced the ward of protection, and sprinkled ginseng all around the spirit, focusing my mind and speaking the words of Release. With my eyes closed, I summoned every last ounce of will to urge the spirit to move on.

"That was interesting. Is it actually supposed to do something?"

I opened my eyes. The teary-eyed ghost still stood before me. I swore under my breath and carefully stoppered the ginseng.

"Yes, it's supposed to do something, but I don't have time to figure out what went wrong. Esme, I Summon you."

Esme materialized before us. "Oh, my, you've sneezed up another one! What an adorable, sweet child! Where did you come from?"

Honoria threw herself at Esme and sobbed.

I limped over to the bed. "I didn't Summon her; I cut her loose from Guarda. Are Joy and the others all right?"

Esme stroked Honoria's head. "Yes, she's fine. She beat Antonio three hands in a row at strip poker, but I don't think he minded much. Jem decided to pierce his tongue, but something went wrong and now it's gone missing."

I blinked. "The piercing stud?"

"No, his tongue. He's most vexed about it, too."

I took a deep breath and pushed from my mind the thought of a disattached ghostly tongue. "I tried to Release Honoria but didn't have any luck, and I have to go save Christian just as soon as I talk to Sebastian and figure out what's holding Christian there, so if you could just take care of her for a bit . . ."

"I'd be delighted to. Come, little one. I have the most amazing thing to show you. It's called a television, and if we're lucky, *Buffy the Vampire Slayer* will be on BBC 2. . . ."

Their forms evaporated as I gently touched Sebastian's head. "I think that's probably enough."

Slowly he pulled his mouth from Raphael's wrist, his tongue giving it a final flick as he gently released the arm.

"Wow," Roxy breathed, looking at the faint twin puncture marks on Raphael's wrist. The marks dissolved into nothing as we watched.

I eyed Sebastian. He still looked awful, but at least his skin had lost the grayish cast. "Rest for a minute; then I need to talk to you."

His eyes drifted shut.

Roxy and I managed to get Raphael onto the armchair next to the bed. I covered him up with a blanket, and quickly ran downstairs while Roxy stayed behind to watch over Raphael and Sebastian.

She looked up as I set a plate of pound cake and a glass of apple juice next to Raphael for when he woke up. "You know, I used to think this whole Dark One world was so fascinating, but I have to admit, it's a bit freaky seeing a vampire drinking your friend's blood."

I put my hand on Raphael's forehead and opened my mind up to him. I'm not very good at sensing people's emotions, but he didn't seem to be in any distress. "I think he's okay; Sebastian was careful. Raphael probably won't even know what happened unless you tell him."

She looked faintly sick. "Think I'll pass on that."

I glanced at Sebastian. He was watching us now, his eyes the clear blue of a summer sky, a faint flush of color on his cheeks.

"Can you talk?"

His throat worked as he nodded. "A bit."

He had an accent, but one that sounded slightly different from Christian's. More French, perhaps.

Roxy winced at his words. "Ow. Sounds like you're gargling glass."

I agreed, but felt little remorse in questioning him. I had done what I could to tide him over until he could be helped properly; now it was his turn to help me. "Did you see what happened to Christian when he went in to rescue you?"

He shook his head, lifting one fragile hand to touch his eye. "Couldn't see. Blind."

"Oh, I'm sorry. But you can see now, yes?"

He nodded.

"You do know that Christian saved you?"

His lips stretched into what must have been a smile, but just looked terrible with him so emaciated. "Yes. Knew he would. Brothers."

I stared. Christian had never mentioned a brother, other than having lost one when he was young. "Christian is your brother?"

He shook his head, his long fingers fumbling with the cloth until he found the area over his heart.

"Oh, I see, he's the brother of your heart. Well, good, then you understand why I'm so concerned about him. Is someone holding him?"

Pain filled Sebastian's blue eyes. "Didn't know. Hadn't thought he'd come back so soon."

"Who? The person who captured you? Is that who has Christian?" The air in my lungs seemed to thicken until I couldn't draw a breath.

Sebastian's throat worked as if he had a hard time saying the word. "Asmodeus."

My blood froze solid. Now I was not only not breathing; my heart had stopped as well. It was amazing I could still think. Then again, perhaps I was delusional. Perhaps I had just imagined that Sebastian had named the demon lord, the being who had once been a man and now ruled a dark army of such power that even wizards and mages feared to meet with them. Yes, I'm sure that was all it was—a mistake. Sebastian hadn't just spoken the name of one of the most frightening beings in all of existence.

"A demon lord." I exhaled, air suddenly finding its way into my lungs again.

"Oooh, I've read about them in Christian's books. They're bad news."

The knowledge of what Christian must be going through was dark in Sebastian's eyes, bringing tears to my own.

"I am not going to leave him there to suffer as you

303

have suffered," I vowed, closing my hand around his fingers. His hands were weak, but I could feel the strength that they once held. "You have to help me, Sebastian. You have to tell me everything you know about Asmodeus, and how he came to be in cahoots with Eduardo and Guarda." I grabbed the tattered remains of his shirt and shook it to drive home just how serious I was. "You must tell me exactly what happened to you, how they caught you, how they kept you so weak you were unable to escape or even answer Christian's call, and most important, you have to tell me everything you can remember about Christian saving you!"

"Allie, honey, I think you're choking him. I know you're deafening me, and if you don't want Christian's housekeeper to come running to see what all the yelling is about, I'd suggest you lower your voice as well."

I looked down at Sebastian and realized I had gripped the cloth in such a way that he was strangling. He made no protest, though, just watched me as if I had a right to throttle him.

"I'm sorry," I said, releasing his shirt and smoothing it down. "I didn't mean to yell at you. You don't have to look at me like that; I'm not blaming you for what happened."

"He wouldn't have been there but for me," Sebastian replied, his voice a raw croak. I couldn't tell if it was with the pain of knowing Christian had felt him worthy of a sacrifice, or if I had damaged his throat while I was shouting at him, but either way, I couldn't let him suffer needlessly.

Roxy hurried over to Raphael when he moaned in

his sleep. "I think he's about to wake up. He looks pissed even sleeping."

I nodded to let her know I heard her, then turned back to Sebastian. "Christian isn't the type of person to stand in the shadows and not right a wrong," I said slowly, smoothing the blanket over his chest.

"Rozzy?" Raphael tried to sit up, rubbing his face. "What happe'd?"

"I told Allie you were going to be mad. Are you okay? You look a bit blurry-eyed to me."

Sebastian's fingers picked fretfully on the blanket. I patted his hand. "Especially when someone he cares for is in trouble. Christian has so few friends, I know they mean everything to him; he would move heaven and earth to help those he loves. . . ."

Especially someone like a woman who could redeem his soul.

"Feel blurry-eyed. What hit me?" Raphael was sitting up straight now, shaking his head and feeling his jaw gingerly.

I looked at the pain in Sebastian's eyes and was filled with shame at my own selfish desire that kept me from Joining with Christian, as I should have. He had said all along that once we were Joined, we would be more powerful together than we were separately, and yet he'd never pushed me to take the last step, never once made me feel pressured into doing it. He seemed happy with me just as I was, and yet I knew that it was my fault that he was trapped in that house, and I was sitting here safe and sound with Sebastian.

"Uh, that would be Allie. But she had a really good reason for decking you."

"No," I swore, my fist tightening around a handful of blanket.

"You *didn't* have a really good reason?" Roxy asked. She peeked at Raphael out of the corner of her eye. He was trying to stand, and after three tries he at last made it to his feet. "Er . . . I thought we were ixnay on the ampirevay eedingfay."

"We are. I had a very good reason for striking Raphael. I'm saying no, I will not let Christian suffer because of my stupidity."

"If you punch Christian like you did me, you have a hell of a nerve saying you won't let him suffer," Raphael complained, wiggling his jaw.

"She put a spell on you to make her punch more powerful," Roxy said helpfully. I glared at her. "What? I didn't want Raphael to think he can be bested by just anyone."

"That's reassuring to know. Now, if one of you would care to tell me why it was necessary to knock me out, I'd be grateful."

"I needed to feed," Sebastian said simply. "You saved me."

Raphael's yellow eyes darkened as he stared at Sebastian. "I *what?*"

"See? I *told* you he was going to be pissed!"

I held up my hand to stop Raphael. He had a bit of a "wild bull about to charge" look in his eyes. "Raphael, I'll explain it all to you later. Christian is my number one priority now. All right, Sebastian. I want everything, every last thing you can remember. Start at the beginning, when you were captured, and don't leave out a single, solitary—"

The door to the bedroom burst open in a huge

blast of wind. I stiffened as the wind swirled around us, bringing with it a familiar scent.

"You fed my blood to a vampire? You knocked me out and fed my blood to him? Without even bothering to ask me how I felt about it?"

"Oh, Allie, child, we have trouble," Esme said as she spun through the door, caught in the spectral wind.

"You stood by and let her knock me out and feed me to the vampire?"

"Well, honestly, Raphael, what was I supposed to do? She's bigger than me, and she knows all sorts of cool spells. And besides, it's not like you *need* all that blood. Didn't your mother ever teach you to share?"

Honoria clung to Esme, her ghostly gray eyes huge with terror. I looked from her to Esme's pale face and worried eyes.

"It's *my* blood! I don't think it's asking too much to have a say in how it's dispensed!"

"Trouble?" I asked, the word weak on my lips. I didn't want to know. I just didn't want to know.

"I think I'll have that explanation right now, Allie," Raphael growled, stalking toward me.

I had as much on my plate as I could deal with. One more thing . . .

"I'm sorry, dear, but it seems the demon is back. The lower part of the house is filled with demon smoke. And I think the basement has been sucked into H-E-double-toothpicks."

. . . would break me.

Chapter Seventeen

"Oh, sure, the minute Christian needs rescuing, earth-shatteringly important emergencies suddenly pile up on me. First Sebastian, now a demon. What next? The apocalypse?" I grumbled as I stuffed my things into my bag, leaving the holy water on top, where it was handy.

"I'm so very sorry to ruin your evening," Esme apologized.

"So just what does Esme mean when she says the basement is now part of—"

I slapped a hand over Roxy's mouth. "Never, ever say the H-word when there's a demon in the house."

Her eyes were huge as she nodded her understanding. I released her mouth. "I have no idea what's happened down there, but I guess I'll be finding out rather than saving Christian, like I *should* be doing." I slung my bag over my shoulder and headed out the bedroom door. "Blast that Guardian! Just what the . . . *dickens*"—we also don't say the D-word when minions of hell are about—"does she think she's doing?"

"How would I know? I'm just a handy feed bag to hang around the neck of any visiting vampire."

I stopped at the top of the stairs and looked at the man following me. "Look, Raphael, I appreciate your offer of help, but about this you really have to trust me—a situation involving demons is no place for a human."

"You're not human?"

I gave him a wry smile as I limped down the stairs. "According to Roxy, I'm no longer strictly human, no. And even if I were, I'm a Summoner. I practice magic as my business. I won't be likely to fall into any of the demon's traps, as you might."

Raphael looked disbelieving as I approached the door to the basement. Esme was right; the lower half of the house was filled with demon smoke, a sign that the Guardian had either Summoned the demon to banish him forever, or something had gone badly awry. Given my luck, I was pretty sure it was the latter. Perhaps the Turners had already gone to sleep and would remain blissfully ignorant of the evening's events.

I glanced at Raphael. Even as angry as he was with me for allowing Sebastian to feed from him, he was still prepared to stand by my side and fight. He really was a nice guy, and I had made it one of my rules that I never allowed nice guys to become demon fodder. "If you won't listen to me, maybe you'll listen to Joy."

He frowned. I nodded. "Think about her—is she going to want you to risk your life and eternal damnation unnecessarily? Or would she tell you to let the experts handle this?"

"Well . . ."

I have never been able to do a strong mind push on anyone, but I tried now. I put my hand on his arm and focused on what I wanted him to do, giving him a push into agreeing with it. "I think Joy needs you more, Raphael. She loves you; I'm sure she wants you home. Right now."

He blinked, a faint frown between his brows. "I . . ."

Well, pooh, in for a penny, in for a pound. I put my other hand on him and mentally shoved. Hard. "She might even *need* you."

His head snapped up and he turned to bellow up the stairs. "Roxy! We're leaving. *Now*, woman! I don't have time to wait for you!"

Raphael was dragging a protesting Roxy out the front door as I opened up the door to the basement. Thick white smoke boiled up the stairs, a noxious barrier I had to push my way through to reach the basement.

"Hello?" The demon smoke was thick enough to choke a horse, which meant that us almost-humans were coughing like six-pack-a-day smokers. "Um . . . Guardian? Are you down here?"

I swam through the offal-scented smoke and peered around the basement.

"I'm sorry, but the wine cellar is off-limits," a voice called out from the heart of the smoke. It was a young-sounding voice for a Guardian. Very young.

310

"There's a . . . erm . . . gas leak. It would probably be best if you were to evacuate the house, Mrs. Turner."

"My name is Allie, and I've heard the one about the gas leak before." I headed for the open door to the wine cellar, out of which the smoke was pouring. I gagged a couple of times before I made it into the room, but what I saw once I got there had me rubbing my eyes.

In the center of the room Sarra the demon hung upside down by one leg, its arms bound behind its back, its suit scuffed-looking. Beneath it, crawling around an intricately scribed circle, a woman with short, curly red hair drew binding symbols with a gold stick.

She looked up as I fanned away the smoke that was billowing up from the crack in the tile. "You're a Summoner. Hullo. I'm Noelle. Did you know that you have mismatched eyes?"

I walked around the demon. It glared at me. "Yes, I know. Why do you have Sarra strung up by one leg?"

She drew another symbol. It flared bright green as soon as the stick lifted from the circle. "It was getting a bit stroppy with me. The Hanged Man always teaches them a few manners. It's retaliating with the smoke. Are those spirits I saw yours, then?"

"Yes, they are. There are four others as well. I hate to be a bother, but I'm in a bit of a hurry, what with Christian being held by this one's master and all, so if you could possibly just give me the abbreviated version of what's going on here, I'll be on my way to rescue him."

She leaned back on her heels and sucked the tip of her gold stick. "Asmodeus, eh?"

The demon snarled. A chunk of ceiling fell behind me. We both ignored it. It just never does to give a demon the satisfaction of knowing it's startled you.

"It's a nasty bag of tricks, but I heard through the demonic grapevine that it was weakened and searching for a suitable sacrifice to regain its power," she added.

"Well, it can't have Christian; he's mine. Back to the demon, if you don't mind . . ."

She looked up at Sarra, still sucking the stick. "It's a pretty specimen, isn't it? I like the hair gel. Nice touch. The mustache is a bit much, though, don't you think? Makes it look so smarmy."

"Um . . ."

"I'm destroying it, so I suppose it really doesn't matter."

I blinked and avoided two wine bottles as they flew out of a rack when the demon hissed at the Guardian. "Destroying it? I didn't think you could destroy a demon."

She laughed and stuck her stick behind her ear, brushing off her knees as she stood. "Of course you can destroy them. Don't they teach you Summoners anything? It's fairly easy, just a bit time-consuming, what with drawing all the symbols in proper order, and then, of course, there are the twelve words you have to pry out of them. Duck."

Now I was really confused. "Twelve words? What does a duck—" I jumped aside to avoid the wooden bench that was suddenly hurtled toward us. "Oh. Thanks."

Noelle turned to face the demon, her hands on her hips. "That was not in the least bit nice. Do we need to have another talk about what constitutes acceptable behavior?"

She traced a few symbols in the air and the demon screamed, curling up on itself in agony. I looked at the five-foot-long cracks that appeared in the cement wall. "Impressive. Now, if we could—"

"The twelve words are needed to destroy the demon, don't you see?" Noelle knelt again before her circle, pulling the stick from her red curls. "You have to get them out of the demon before you can destroy it, and naturally they're a bit reticent to give them to you. Makes for an exciting time, though."

"Right," I drawled, more than a bit worried about the Guardian's lighthearted manner. Guardians were highly respected, more than a little feared people in my circle of witches and wizards, and the friendly, freckle-faced woman in front of me just didn't meet my expectations. "Do you mind me asking how long you've been doing this?"

She drew another symbol. "Almost six months now."

"Six months?" I choked so hard tears came to my eyes as I coughed the saliva out of my bronchial tubes. Sarra cackled. The door fell off its hinges.

"My mum is a Guardian, too," Noelle answered quickly. "I have oodles of experience, really I do. And it's not usually too exacting a job, you know? An exorcism here, sealing a portal to hell there, destroying the odd demon or two—doesn't take up much space on the schedule, leaving lots of time for my real work."

I couldn't help but ask. I just couldn't help it. "What would that be?"

"I'm writing the definitive work on werefolk."

"Werefolk?"

"Yes, you know, werewolves, werecats, werebeetles, that sort of thing. They're a fascinating people, really."

I made a mental note to keep Raphael from meeting Noelle anytime in the future. "It sounds fascinating, yes, but I really must be running along. There's only"—I looked at my watch—"two more hours until sunrise, and I have Christian to save. I hate to leave you. Are you sure you'll be all right here by yourself?"

She blinked at me. "Of course. Why shouldn't I?"

I waved at Sarra. "Well . . . that is a demon after all, and a powerful one at that. . . ."

She wrinkled her nose and waved me off. "Don't worry about it; I have the situation under control."

I heaved a mental sigh of relief that yet another catastrophe had been averted, and gathered up my bag to leave.

"Oh, Allie?" I turned at the door to look back at Noelle. Sarra twisted until it was snarling in my direction. I sidestepped the bucket that was sent flying toward me.

"The sacrifice that Asmodeus is bound to be looking for?"

I nodded.

"It won't be that of a Dark One. It'll be his Beloved."

That was it; I had reached my saturation point. Nothing else could surprise me. I had seen it all and heard it all. I stared at her for a minute, then nodded again and numbly made my way upstairs.

Fine. Asmodeus wanted me to sacrifice myself for Christian. Roxy had told me it would come down to my making a sacrificial gesture; she'd just never told me it was going to be to *a friggin' demon lord!*

I pushed open the basement door and stepped into the dark hallway, which was now no longer filled with demon smoke.

Instead it was filled with real smoke.

"There you are," Mrs. Turner said, turning to address me. She was standing by the front door, wearing a pair of wellington boots, a pink velour bathrobe, and an expression that would give the Hound of the Baskervilles pause. A long, thick yellow hose snaked in through the front door, curled around Mrs. Turner, headed down the hall, and disappeared into a door at the far end. "The kitchen is on fire."

"Is it." My left eyelid twitched. She flinched in response and quickly averted her eyes from mine.

"I just thought you would like to know."

"Ah. Is it serious?"

"The firemen are here now. They say not."

"Okay. I'll be back later. With Christian. Or not. It depends on just what the sacrifice consists of. His friend is upstairs in his bedroom. Please don't disturb him." I thought for a moment. "And don't be surprised if you hear the TV turning itself on and off in Christian's study."

Mrs. Turner's lips tightened into a grim line.

"And there might be some screaming and unearthly noises coming from the basement. Just ignore them as well."

She tightened the belt to her bathrobe.

"I'll be off then. If neither Christian or I return by nightfall, would you contact Raphael St. John at St. John Security Services? It'll be in the phone book. I'm sure he and Joy and Roxy will figure out something to do with Sebastian and the others. Well . . ." I looked out through the open door and noticed it was pouring, absolutely pouring buckets, a veritable deluge of wind and rain and nasty little bits of ice. "What a lovely morning. I believe I'll walk to the taxi stand."

Mrs. Turner turned on her heel and marched off to her room, muttering to herself and slamming the door behind her. I traced the most powerful protection ward I knew into the wetness on the rain-slicked front door, and headed off into the raging monsoon to save the man whose life had become so inexorably bound to mine.

"Hi. I'm Allie. I think you have something of mine," I said to the ARMPIT who opened the door to the Trust's London house. "He's about six foot one, has long black hair, and favors O-negative."

The thin blond woman pursed her lips and moved aside so I could enter. I stopped at the boundaries of the binding ward and gave it a good look. It was different from the ones I'd seen before, much more intricate. I doubted if I would be able to undraw it without time to study it. I pushed through the ward and entered the house, my four accompanying wards immediately burning green.

"Those will not help you," Phillippa said from

where she stood at the foot of a long, curved staircase.

"Probably not, but I feel better with them anyway. I don't suppose you'd be at all inclined to take me to wherever you're keeping Christian?"

She strolled past me, throwing open a pair of double doors. "Keeping Christian? We are not holding the Dark One prisoner, if that's what you believe. I will ask him if he wishes to see you."

"You do that little thing," I said, probably a mite more testily than was wise, but I was alternating between terror at being in such close contact with something of terrible power the likes of which I'd never felt before, and anger that Christian was being held by such rotten people. I edged around her until I could peer in through the doorway to the room beyond. She *tsk*ed in an annoyed fashion and went off down the dark hallway toward the back of the house.

"Ah, the Beloved has arrived," Eduardo said behind me. He leaned lazily against the newel post at the bottom of the stairs, then strutted toward me, ushering me into what looked like a library. The walls were ceiling-to-floor books, with two large desks set up at either end of the room, the long center wall backing a cluster of wine-colored leather couches and chairs. Above a marble fireplace two huge broadswords were crossed, surrounded by a number of smaller swords and wicked-looking daggers.

Someone clearly had issues, and I was sure I knew who it was.

"Most unusual eyes. I see why you kept them hidden. I should like the opportunity to examine the relationship between their curious colors and the range of your abilities. I must confess, Allegra Telford, I had expected you earlier."

"I was held up. I had to feed the Dark One you've been starving, and then there was a little trouble with a demon that you sent earlier."

He tutted and waved me toward a chair. I rested my bag on my hip and stood where I was, my arms crossed, ready to move quickly if the need should arrive. Eduardo seated himself on one of the couches, crossing his legs so as to display a pair of pale salmon socks. I don't know why I found them so funny, but just the sight of them had me snorting silently to myself.

"Ah, yes, Sebastian. I thought he might enter into our discussion."

"If you think I'm going to give him back in exchange for Christian, you're crazy. I wouldn't leave a goldfish in your care."

Eduardo waved a languid hand. "But my dear, we have no further need for Sebastian. You may do with him as you will. Once it was determined he would not suit, his role simply became that of bait. It brought us exactly what we wanted."

I thought furiously. "Why would you prefer Christian over Sebastian? They're both the same, both Dark Ones, only Christian—" I stopped dead, Noelle's parting words ringing in my ears.

Eduardo nodded. "Christian has a Beloved; Sebastian did not. Hence the need to wait until Christian tracked poor Sebastian to this location."

"Wait a minute," I said, seeing the mistake in his statement. "You couldn't possibly have known that

Christian had a Beloved when you nabbed Sebastian, or even when you realized Sebastian didn't have one. I've only known Christian for a few days."

"We were prepared to wait." Eduardo shrugged. It was a poor imitation of Christian's elegant move. "Until such time as a Moravian who had Joined with a human came into our sphere."

"But why *you*? Why do *you* want a Beloved? What exactly do *you* have to do with the demon lord."

"Asmodeus," a familiar, silky smooth voice said from the doorway. I turned with a gasp, my heart beating madly as Christian entered the room, followed by the swarthy man I had seen in my dream.

Christian?

"Ah, there you are. You see, Allegra Telford? We are not holding Christian prisoner. Far from it; he is a cherished guest."

I started toward Christian, but stopped when I saw his eyes. They were black, but not the glistening, shining onyx of Christian in the throes of passion; no, now they were a flat matte black, a black with no depth, a black that held hopelessness and nothing else. He had decided.

There was death in his eyes.

No, don't even think it. We'll find a way out of this.

I wanted to throw myself on him, to kiss his beautiful lips, to hold him in my arms and reassure him that everything would turn out all right, to merge myself with him and give him every ounce of love that filled me, but I knew it would do no good. Not now, anyway. Not yet. Not while *he* was here.

I turned to the man who stood before the unlit fireplace. "I take it you are Asmodeus?"

He inclined his head, standing patiently while I examined him. He looked like any other man dressed in black, with dark hair and eyes, but there was something surrounding him, an aura of coiled power that alerted me to the glamour. I had no idea what hideous shape he really claimed, but I knew it was not that of the innocuous man before me.

"Christian will not answer you," Asmodeus said. "He has given me his word not to, and if there's one thing of which you can be sure, it's that Moravians are sickeningly true to their word."

"Yes, I imagine honor leaves a nasty taste in your mouth," I said as I set my bag down. It was heavy, and I knew that nothing I had in it would help me against this monster. "I don't understand why you have made a deal with Christian, however. He can't save you. You need a Beloved's sacrifice, not a Dark One's."

I walked over to the nearest desk and started thumbing through the papers, just to annoy Eduardo. Christian's eyes followed me, but he would not answer me, would not touch my mind with his. I ached to merge with him, but knew it would do no good. He was clearly trying to protect me from Asmodeus the only way he knew how—by giving the demon lord himself instead.

Men can be so stubborn.

"It is as you say. However, the sacrifice must be a willing one; it cannot be forced. Thus"—he gestured toward Christian—"you must come to us. And you have, as I knew you would."

I set down the papers and walked over to the demon lord, pulling my arm from my coat and holding it out for him. "What, you want a little blood? Go ahead, dive in. I have plenty to spare."

Asmodeus looked deeply into my eyes, and for a second I saw beyond the glamour and beheld his true self. I staggered backward, feeling as if someone had just kicked me in the chest.

We were in a *whole* lot of trouble.

"A genuine offer, but alas, as you know well, I cannot partake of the blood of a Beloved who has not yet Joined."

I tipped my head at Christian. "I assume he wants us to take the last step. How do you feel about it?"

He stared at me without speaking, his eyes dead and cold. I smiled at him, then turned back to the demon lord. "Christian doesn't seem to be too keen on the idea, and I'm getting the feeling that saving him isn't going to be worth my life, so you know what? I think I'm just going to be trotting along."

"She lies," Eduardo hissed, leaping to his feet as if he were going to tackle me to stop me from leaving. Which, I had to admit that, given the events of the past few days, he might very well do. "She is his Beloved whether or not they have Joined. She will not leave him here; she cannot."

"Watch me," I said, shoving my arm back in my coat and picking up my bag.

The demon lord moved so fast, I didn't even see a blur. One moment he was standing next to the fireplace; the next he was in front of the door, his fingers on my chin as they tipped my head up so he could peer into my eyes.

"You intend to leave Christian here?"

There was nothing I could do to save him by myself. I knew that after taking a peek at what Asmodeus was made of. There was only one way to escape the demon lord's power, and that was to Join with Christian, and if I did that while the demon lord was around, he'd manipulate me into sacrificing myself to save Christian. Therefore, I couldn't save him now. I needed help. So I could honestly answer Asmodeus's question. "Yes, I will leave him here."

I knew he could see the truth in my eyes, could feel that I was not lying to him. I poured a bit more determination into my intention. His fingers tightened on my chin, his eyes burning into mine as if he were trying to sear his way into my brain.

"You will not offer yourself to save his life?"

Pain slashed through me, making my heart weep tears of blood for the other half of my being. It had to be done. There was no other way.

"No, I will not," I said, my head pounding with each word of betrayal. It would do no good, my inner voice shrieked, trying to stop my soul from rending itself in two at my treacherous words. A sacrifice now would accomplish nothing; it would only end with us both dead and damned to an eternity apart. I couldn't risk that, not when there was the slightest ray of hope that we could pull off a miracle. "I will not offer myself to save his life. I make no sacrifice."

Asmodeus dropped his hand as if his fingers were burned. For a moment his eyes glowed with an ominous black light; then he turned wearily to Christian.

"She has refused you, child of the darkness. She has repudiated you. She will not redeem your soul, will do nothing to save you from the torment that she knows will commence the moment she leaves. What say you to this?"

Christian's eyes never left me. For one second, for a fraction of a second, I thought I saw hurt so deep it almost brought me to my knees, but it was gone instantly, the dull hopelessness all that showed in his eyes. I dared not speak to his mind, not with him under Asmodeus's power.

"It is her choice," Christian said finally, his voice so beautiful that tears pricked in my eyes. I blinked them back. "It has always been her choice."

Love welled up within me, love for a man who had made the ultimate sacrifice in order to give me a chance to escape with my life intact. What a wonderful, loving, *stupid* man, I thought to myself, and firmly squished down every last bit of love I felt for him lest Asmodeus detect it and know I was bluffing my way out of the house.

"This can't be. She's his Beloved," Eduardo argued to Asmodeus. "She has to sacrifice herself; you said it was impossible for her not to. If she doesn't sacrifice herself, we don't get that." Eduardo pointed rudely at Christian. "We've already lost one vampire; I won't have us cheated out of another one. What good will the attraction be without any ghosts or vampires?"

"Attraction? What attraction?" I asked, edging past Christian toward the door. I sent him only one tiny glance, a little one while Asmodeus's attention was on Eduardo raving before him, but in that look I packed every bit of love I had.

He blinked.

"She is not Joined. She cannot be forced to Join

with him, and she refuses to sacrifice herself. Unless she does either, she is useless to us."

"She's lying—"

"Attraction? Like what, a haunted house or something? A spectral Disneyland? That's it, isn't it, you guys are capturing spirits and Dark Ones and who knows what else to turn them into a paranormal zoo?"

"She does not lie," Asmodeus said to Eduardo, then turned in a dismissal as clear as any I've seen.

"But you can't know—"

"I know!"

I stepped back, ostensibly out of fear of Asmodeus, as he turned to address Eduardo, but really just so I could bump into Christian. I touched my fingers to his hand. Instantly Asmodeus's head snapped around to look at us.

I swallowed back a lump of pain as I looked into Christian's eyes. "I'm sorry; it's just not working out like you said it would. You were right when you said I could exist without you. I'll see you around." I tossed a glance toward Asmodeus. "Maybe."

Without waiting to see if he believed me or not, I walked out of the room. Eduardo sputtered a protest, but was quickly silenced. Evidently Asmodeus had a tight grip on him as well as Christian, because the ward made no protest when I pushed my way through it into the gray light of a rainy London morning.

"Right," I said to myself as I waved down a black taxi, refusing to think of what Christian would go through before I could return with help. "First things first . . ."

The taxi that pulled up maneuvered straight into a puddle next to the road, spraying me from the waist down with icy, muddy water.

"Sorry," the driver said as he reached behind himself and opened the door. I looked from the water running in rivulets down my legs to the gray, sodden sky above.

"It's useless," I told the sun as it tried in vain to pierce the dense cloud cover. "Don't waste your time battling fate. I'm doomed to be wet and miserable until I get Christian back."

"Welcome to England," the cabby said. I sighed and got in the cab, ignoring the pain in my leg and the sense of fatigue that threatened to pound me into a fetal ball of misery.

"Where you off to, then?" the cabby asked conversationally.

I gave him Christian's address, then couldn't help but ask, "I don't suppose you know how to defeat a demon lord?"

He pursed his lips in a soundless whistle as I met his glance in the rearview mirror. "Can't say as I do."

I nodded and squelched my way back in the seat, wondering vaguely how the water had managed to soak the back of me as well as the front. "It's no matter. I think I know someone who does. I just hope she can fit me in between destroying the demon and interviewing werewolves."

The ride to Christian's house was accomplished in record time.

Chapter Eighteen

"Do you know that there is a Dark One upstairs lying on a really big bed?" Noelle asked as she came down Christian's front stairs. I peeled off my wet coat and sniffed. Only the faintest smell of smoke—both demon and wood—lingered.

I almost smiled, so happy was I to see Noelle. She was such a nice, normal woman in a world that seemed oddly shy of normalcy. "Yes, his name is Sebastian. I hope you didn't wake him; he's been very ill."

"I didn't go into the room, just peeked in when I was checking for imps."

Well, she was *almost* normal.

"Good." I set down my bag, well away from the lake of water that was forming at my feet. "I take it we're imp-free?"

She nodded, her fingers tracing the carving on the

side of the banister. "Yes, but there's a very confused mouse in the pantry. It was sharing its home with an imp."

"Ah. Well, as I don't know the name of any good mice therapists, I guess it'll just have to work things out on its own. Would you mind coming into the study for a couple of minutes? I have a little proposition I'd like to make."

"Sexual or professional?"

I stopped midway up the stairs. "Do I look like I'm about to make a sexual advance?"

She let her gaze wander from my sodden feet, up to my jeans, with mud and water splashed up to my waist, up farther to my damp sweater that had been pulled out of shape when I stuffed the doll under it, finally coming to my face. I had a feeling the long hours with no sleep, not to mention the battle to save Sebastian, and the wear and tear on my nerves at seeing Christian willingly submit to Asmodeus had left my eyes a bit bloodshot. My eyes are not attractive at their best, but bloodshot and tired . . .

Noelle shuddered delicately.

"That bad, eh?"

She gave me a small smile. "I'm sure you've seen better days."

I turned and trudged damply up the stairs, ignoring the pain in my leg just as I always did, suddenly feeling the weight of the world bearing down on me. Life seemed so intolerable without Christian. I knew just how impossible it was going to be for me to live without him. Either we managed a life together, or . . .

"I'm not going down without taking a few of them with me," I said in a growl as I pushed open the door to Christian's study. Esme bustled toward me, Honoria leaping up and following quickly behind.

"Oh, Allie, I'm so relieved to see you! Poor Honoria was beside herself with worry—well, we both were, naturally, but I see you've brought a friend with you. Hello, I'm Esme Cartwright. You must be that nice Guardian who's taken care of the demon and imps. Allie, why are you so damp?"

"I didn't know we had imps," I protested as I collapsed with a wet noise into Christian's chair. "Esme, Honoria, this is Noelle. She is indeed the Guardian Christian called. I take it you finished with Sarra?"

Noelle nodded and took the seat opposite the desk, smiling at Honoria. "That's a very pretty doll. Does it have a name?"

Honoria scooted behind Esme until just the tips of her soft brown curls peeked out from behind Esme's bathrobe. "Bettina."

"That's a nice name as well. Is Allie going to Release you and Bettina?"

I sighed and slumped over the desk until my forehead was resting on my arms. Water rolled off my hair and puddled around my wrists.

"She couldn't do it," the little ghost had the nerve to snap. She came around from behind Esme and pointed at me, stomping a petulant booted foot. "She said she would, but she didn't, because she's too stupid to know how to do it properly."

"Now, Honoria, a lady never speaks to an elder that way."

I glared at Esme over the top of my arms. She hurriedly added, "Especially one who has tried so hard to help you, as Allie has."

"I don't care, I think she's stupid. Stupid, stupid, stupid!" Her little-girl voice rose up into a screech that seemed to pierce the tender flesh of my brain. I narrowed my eyes at her.

"A return to Guarda and her little games can be arranged, you know."

Honoria threw herself against Esme and bawled.

Wearily I pushed my wet hair off my face. "I suppose you should meet the whole gang. Antonio, Jem, Alis, Mr. Woogums, I Summon you."

All four popped into the room.

"*Mi corazón!* You 'ave Summoned me to your side again! My 'eart, it beats only for . . .'Ello. What so charming red curls you 'ave, my lady." Antonio made a deep court bow.

"Ornh! Ah aghn ahnnh ahah ahah ahah arnuah!"

Jem was wearing a blue-and-red skintight spandex outfit, blue boots with gold flames licking up the sides, and a blue black and-red mask fitting tightly over his head.

I grimaced. "Don't tell me, you've been watching one of those wrestling shows?"

"Aaaangh."

"Tongue still missing?" I asked Antonio.

He quickly dragged his eyes from Noelle and blew me a kiss. "Alas, I fear it is so, my little water sprite. We 'ave looked 'igh and low for it, but the tongue, it is 'iding. We cannot find it. And who might this beauteous lady be?"

"Are you Mr. Woogums?" Noelle asked him.

He looked appalled. Quickly I made the necessary introductions. Noelle turned her bright, interested eyes from Antonio's leer to Esme comforting Honoria.

"I used to look like you," I told her, suddenly feeling a bit tetchy and peevish. "I used to be professional-looking, and on top of everything and with it and all that. Nothing rattled me. Well, not much. I had a plan, a life plan. I knew where I was going, and how I was going to get there. Now look what I've turned into." I sat back and the leather protested with a rude, wet sucking noise. "I fell in love. This is what happens when you fall in love. You end up wet, with a houseful of ghosts, and a man who thinks he's responsible for everyone's happiness but his own. Taking it all into consideration, I highly advise you against falling in love with anyone, mortal or not."

She grinned at me. I sighed. She was too cute; some guy was bound to snatch her up and make her wet and miserable, too. "Esme, would you show Alis to the ceramic room? Her screaming is making my head pound. Then perhaps you all could watch some TV quietly. I need to talk to Noelle about rescuing Christian."

"Rescue? Why would you wish to rescue that dead one? I for one am enjoying 'is absence."

I batted Antonio away from where he'd perched on the edge of the desk.

"Ooh, a rescue! Mr. Woogums and I dearly love a good rescue. What can we do to help?"

"Nothing," I said, too tired even to collapse and fall into a stupor. "There's nothing you can do. You're just ghosts."

"We may be ghosts, but we are extremely 'and-some and dashing ghosts," Antonio said as he strutted through the middle of the desk, twanging his codpiece suggestively at Noelle.

"That's right, I'm sure we can do something to help dear Christian." Esme nodded.

"Ahng wahaaaaaan," Jem added.

"I've never rescued a Dark One before," Noelle said slowly, a little frown appearing between her eyebrows. She even frowned cute. "I'm not absolutely certain that it's in my job description."

I stared at her.

"That was a joke."

"Oh. Ha, ha, ha."

"And I hate to contradict you, but if you're serious about rescuing this boyfriend of yours, your friends here might be very helpful indeed."

"There, you see? Even the nice Guardian says we could be of help!" Esme crowed. "I'm sure I'd have no problem overcoming a fiend or two, and Mr. Woogums would be happy to bite someone if only I can teach him how to focus his energy properly."

"I shall bring my rapier. I am most dashing with my rapier," Antonio told Noelle. He demonstrated with a few moves that would have left her without the ability to bear children had the rapier been made up of anything other than air and psychic energy.

Jem adopted a crouched wrestling pose and cracked his knuckles. "Eee oong anh."

"We shall all be able to help," Esme said with great satisfaction as she drifted toward the door. "I'll just fetch Alis back. I'm sure she'll be delighted to pretend the bad people are made of ceramic and yell at them."

I pounded my forehead gently on the desk.

"You know, they have a point. You might not think they can be of help, but just their appearance can give you a few seconds of diversion."

I stopped pounding long enough to look at Noelle. "I haven't told you what I'm up against. It's not just a few Summoners and the odd triumvirate or two. I have to get Christian away from Asmodeus, the demon lord, the demon master who I am fairly certain turned Christian's father and thus has some sort of connection to Christian."

Noelle frowned. "Oh. I'd forgotten you'd mentioned Asmodeus. That is a bit of a sticky wicket."

"How sticky a wicket is it?" I asked as Esme ushered Alis into the room, shushing her and whispering in her ear.

"Well . . ."

I sighed. I didn't have time or the energy to cope with much more. "Let me put it to you this way—do you know if it's possible to defeat a demon lord?"

She nodded. "You can defeat anything, if you go about it properly."

Well, that was hopeful. Kind of.

"Okay, next question: Do you know *how* to defeat a demon lord?"

She shook her head.

"Do you know someone who does?"

She shook her head again.

I started to get a bit desperate. I knew that because I had the overwhelming urge to giggle. I must have been more tired than I thought, because a couple of giggles slipped out as I asked, "Have you ever heard of anyone defeating a demon lord?"

She smiled as my giggling grew stronger. "No, I haven't."

I gave it up and just sat back in the chair and howled, wiping tears from my already damp face as I laughed the laugh of the mentally and physically exhausted. Esme hovered with a worried look on her face, Honoria snickered, Jem demonstrated his prowess by wrestling a chair to the ground, Alis (restrained by Esme's warning) honed her ancient-crone glare until it could split stone, and Antonio seated himself on the arm of Noelle's chair and proceeded to ask very personal questions about her preferences in men. By the time he got to whether or not her sexual partners had to be technically alive, I had managed to gather the few wits remaining to me and arranged them in a formation where I could think again.

Esme had detached herself from Honoria long enough to pat me on my right shoulder. "Overtired, poor child."

My arm went numb.

"Perhaps you'd better tell me everything from the beginning," Noelle said, leaning forward with her elbows on her knees despite the fact that Antonio was not very subtly peering down her blouse.

I thought about the strength I'd need to tell her everything, decided on an abbreviated version, and quickly hit the high points of the last few days, intimacies with Christian excluded.

She chewed on a fingernail. "Hmm. Very sticky. This triumvirate you mentioned is clearly being fed by Asmodeus. That might work to your benefit."

I rubbed my aching forehead and tried to follow

her thoughts. "You mean that feeding them would weaken him? I can see that, but what good is a weakened Asmodeus going to do me when I have the triumvirate breathing down my neck? I barely managed to get Sebastian out without bringing the house down around our ears, and that, I'm positive, is only because Christian was distracting Asmodeus enough that he couldn't throw his power into the triumvirate."

She sat back, apologizing as her arm slid through Antonio's thigh. "Asmodeus is by far the more powerful of the two entities."

I nodded. "Right. So it makes sense to take him out first. I understand that, but the triumvirate—"

"Is made up of humans."

That stopped me cold. I looked at it, prodded it, and decided it was good. Then I realized what her meaning really was, and the little bit of common sense that had remained with me tossed up its hands in despair, packed an overnight case, and headed off on a long, long vacation. "You mean I call up a demon to take care of the triumvirate?"

She nodded.

"Oh, my!" Esme's eyes were round with worry. She scooped up Mr. Woogums and hugged him and Honoria against her ample breast. "Are you sure that's wise?"

"Pish." Antonio snorted, patting his chest. We all turned to look at him. I had never actually heard anyone say the word *pish* before. It was a bit frightening. "I will protect *mi corazón* from any demon. I am 'er courtier most brave."

"It's perfectly safe as long as you keep the demon

334

under your control," Noelle said slowly, considering me with a critical eye that didn't seem to like what it saw. "I think, upon reflection, that it would be a good idea if I were to accompany you on this venture. I should hate to think what would happen if a demon you raised were to run amok through London."

"Earthquakes, mass 'ysteria," Antonio said.

I glared at him.

"Rain of locusts, the sky set afire, the oceans turned to blood," Esme added.

"Yes, thank you, I think we get the picture," I said. "What exactly would the demon—"

"Ehn wahnah ahgha mwaaaah," Jem said with a sorrowful shake of his head.

"Oh, yes, definitely a plague or two," Esme nodded. "And you're absolutely right about the rats."

I glared at them all, then turned my gaze back to Noelle. "What exactly would the demon do?"

She told me.

They had to carry me to bed after that. The exhaustion and Noelle's suggestions were just too much for my poor little brain. Fortunately, between the two of them, she and Antonio were able to get me into Christian's bedroom and onto the bed beside Sebastian without either of the Turners noticing, or Sebastian waking up.

I dreamed of Christian encased in a block of ice, standing in the corner of the bedroom, just watching me as I lay sleeping. The ice turned to glass, and I knew that if I reached out for him, if I tried to touch him, the glass would shatter and pierce his heart. I rose from the bed and stood before him, my arms empty, my heart torn apart by the need I had for him and the knowledge that in order to free him from the glass I'd have to give up everything I had fought for.

I wept tears of blood and watched him until his image faded away into the dull gray of the day.

Joy and Roxy woke me up three hours later. I was disoriented at finding them in Christian's room, even more so when I realized the person lying in bed, tucked in under the covers, was Sebastian, not Christian.

"I'm sorry to wake you, Allie, but Noelle said not to let you sleep any later than noon."

"You met Noelle?" I pushed myself into a sitting position and looked down at Sebastian. His face didn't look nearly as wan and gaunt as it had earlier.

Roxy waved toward a metal apparatus standing next to him. "Noelle arranged this. It's an IV; isn't that clever of her? She even got the blood from one of the blood banks."

"We met her when we stopped by to see how you were after last night. She's taking a shower."

"Oh." I rubbed my eyes, the feel of the dream's blood tears still heavy upon my cheeks.

"You look a bit muzzy yet. Come on; we'll get you into the shower, then let you have some of the soup Mrs. Turner made. What a very odd woman she is," Joy prattled as she bustled me out of bed, out of my clothes, and into the shower even before I gathered together the thought to protest.

A half hour later I was washed, dressed, and fed. Fifteen minutes later Roxy and Joy stood at the door of Christian's house and waved us off as Noelle and

I climbed into a cab. Ten seconds after that I realized I was squishing one of the bobbles and spent the rest of the cab ride frantically resuscitating a flattened yarn bobble.

An hour and seven minutes after waking up, I stood with Noelle outside the Trust's house and prepared to raise my first—and hopefully only—demon.

Three minutes after that I looked at my demon and burst into laughter.

"What?" the demon asked, turning its head 360 degrees to examine itself. "What's so funny? Why is the Summoner laughing and crying at the same time? I don't see what's so funny. I'm a demon; where's my respect? Where's the fear and cowering before me?"

"Erm . . ." Noelle examined it from the tips of its shiny patent leather shoes to the top of its big pink bow. "Demon, what is your name?"

"Oh, right, like I look like I fell off the stupid truck?" it asked, its pudgy little hands on its flat hips. "You can't ask me that, Guardian. Go read the rule book. Sheesh. Amateurs."

I wiped my eyes and hiccupped a couple of times, blowing my nose on the tissue I stuffed away in my bobble-free pocket. "Okay, I think I'm better." I looked at the demon and felt my lips twitch. I couldn't help it; the sight of it was too much for my fragile nerves. "What is your name?"

"Tirana."

"Who do you serve?"

"Oriens. Now would one of you mind telling me why neither of you is averting your eyes from my dreadful presence, so monstrous that my very being is unbearable to humankind?"

Noelle snickered, quickly converting it into a cough.

"Well, possibly," I said, feeling my lips twitch again. "But maybe first you would tell us why you chose to manifest yourself in the form of Shirley Temple as last seen on the 'Good Ship Lollipop'?"

The demon twirled around, its big pink sash fluttering as it smoothed down its dress and frilly little petticoat. "My grotesque form isn't making you sick with fright?"

We both shook our heads, Noelle with a hand over her mouth to keep from laughing out loud. "Shirley Temple at her pinnacle was frightening," I finally told it, "but not in the sense I think you mean."

The demon's little golden curls bobbed as it stamped its foot. "It's that Morilen! He told me that this form would strike terror in the hearts of humans! Well, he'd just better hide behind the legion of Paymon, because when I get back to hell—"

It's never pretty when a demon swears, but it's positively ludicrous when the demon in question is an exact duplicate of America's little sweetheart.

"Have you heard of Tirana?" I asked Noelle while the little demon was stamping around cursing its companion.

"No, but Oriens is the weakest of all the demon lords. I would say,"—she paused a moment to watch the demon jump up and down on a late-blooming flower—"that you have raised one of the lesser demons. In fact, I'm fairly certain it's the bottom of the barrel, demonically speaking."

My shoulders sagged for a minute. I couldn't even raise a proper demon; I had to get the runt of the litter. How could I possibly save Christian with a demon that wore lacy ankle socks and a big pink sash? It just wasn't possible.

"I think it says a lot about the purity of your spirit that the worst type of demon you can raise is . . . well . . . Tirana."

I took a little comfort in that fact until the cold, watchful gaze from the house had me straightening my shoulders, the knowledge that somewhere within the house the man I loved was being held strengthening my resolve.

"Right. I can do this. Tirana, stop trying to squash the flower; you'll get your nice shoes dirty. We have work to do. I command thee to my will."

"Command, schommand," it groused, obediently following me.

Noelle touched my arm gently as I started up the walk to the front door. She pulled an amulet off over her head and slipped the chain over mine, then traced a symbol on my forehead.

"For luck," she said with a half smile.

I fingered the amulet. It was warm and gave me a sense of serenity that was greatly lacking in my present state. "Thanks."

"You remember what I told you?"

I hoped so. I was busy almost the whole of the cab ride trying to desquish one of the ghosts' bobbles, but I felt pretty confident that I had remembered her instructions.

"I wish I could go in with you."

I gave her a little smile that I hoped looked more sincere than it felt. "I know, and I appreciate all the help you've given me. You'll wait here?"

She nodded.

I turned and faced the house again. I could feel Asmodeus inside, gathering his power. My hand closed around the bobbles as I cleared my mind and gathered my own power. The amulet seemed to hold the power, magnifying it slightly. I raised my chin, held up my hand, and commanded the door to open, then marched into the dark, gaping maw of the house armed with a borrowed amulet, a demon that looked like it should be dancing with Bill "Bojangles" Robinson, five helpful ghosts and one petulant one, and a heck of a lot of determination.

The doors to the library had been thrown open. Guarda, Phillippa, and Eduardo stood in the middle of the room in a triangle, not yet a triumvirate, but capable of forming one with just a touch of Eduardo's fingers to the women's necks. Asmodeus stood to the left of them, Christian to their right.

I smiled at them all. "I hope it's no bother, but I've changed my mind. I'd like Christian back, please."

The front door slammed shut behind me.

Chapter Nineteen

"How very curious," Asmodeus drawled as he stepped forward. "I had not thought you would return, but when we saw you arrive I realized just how clever you had been."

"She lied; I told you she lied," Eduardo said with a snarl.

"She did not lie; she told the truth . . . the truth as it was at that moment. Yes, it was very clever indeed. I almost regret that such a keen mind and undaunted spirit should be lost to give me new life, but alas, that is the way of things."

I had been watching Christian while Asmodeus circled around me, but suddenly the amulet glowed red-hot, making me jump. One of my feet stepped outside of the circle Asmodeus had been about to close around me.

"Tricky," I told him, trying to calm my racing heart.

If he had been a second faster, I might even now be trapped within the power of his circle. "But not tricky enough."

He smiled and I lost a few years of my life keeping my eyes on his. "It was worth a try."

I looked from him to Christian. He stood silent and still, his face pale, his eyes dulled with pain and suffering. I thought of the dream warning and knew I couldn't look to him for help until I freed him from his bonds.

"Tirana, come forward. See thou that human?" I pointed to Eduardo. As the strongest of the triumvirate, he was my target. "Know thou what my will is?"

Tirana sighed and crossed its chubby little arms over the ruffled bib front of its dress. "Can we skip the hokey medieval-speak and just get to what you want me to do?"

"Destroy him," I said simply.

Eduardo shrieked and reached for Phillippa and Guarda. Tirana leaped for Eduardo and was immediately thrown backward. The protective ward in front of me burned green, then white, then a shimmering silver as the triumvirate blasted me with power. I braced my legs apart, lowered my head, muttered a protective spell, and gathered my power. The amulet glowed silver with the wards as I gave my power form, then quickly turned it and slammed it into Eduardo.

The sudden wave of my power rocked the triumvirate. I threw my head back and laughed with the joy of it, unleashing the full power of my love for Christian, power that flowed in a silver stream from my hands to pour over the triumvirate.

"Never underestimate the power of a ticked off Beloved," I told them, giving them a dose of my determination and willpower, and a healthy dollop of respect for the living and the dead. Phillippa screamed and crumpled.

My joy was short-lived. Eduardo snarled an oath and hauled a limp Phillippa back into place, pounding me with wave after wave of excruciatingly painful raw power. It was tainted as he was tainted, foul, draining me by the very nature of its dark source. I fought it with everything I had, but the combined power of the triumvirate would overcome me in the end. I withstood it for a moment, my eyes on Christian. He watched me silently, impassively, apparently not aware or not caring that I was being torn apart by the people he had given himself up to. It was useless, a hopeless attempt at rescue that was doomed from the very start. I couldn't beat the triumvirate and Asmodeus together. For a moment I considered the possibility of just giving in.

Thoughts of Christian filled my mind. Memories of him, of his love for me, of us together merged with those of the ghosts, and how they had so bravely prepared to fight Sarra for us. They were more than just ghosts; they were my friends.

"I am not a quitter," I said through my teeth, then shouted the next few words. "I will not let the monsters win."

I dredged up every ounce, every minuscule morsel and shred and iota of power I had, everything from the beating of my heart to the breath that filled my lungs, gathered it, formed it, and prepared to channel it to the target. I cleared my mind, holding it on the image of Eduardo even when it screamed in protest. I knew that what I was doing was professional suicide. To focus my power through my own mind would fry out every psychic circuit I had. I would never Summon another ghost, never cast a spell, never see a ward, never again understand the beautiful balance between nature and magic. I was killing a part of myself that I had crafted so painfully from the shards of my broken past; I would be giving it all up, but one glance at Christian gave my resolve new meaning.

I understood now what it meant to love someone more than my own life.

Christian's name was on my lips as I released my power, the force of it blinding me, throwing me backward, pain unlike anything I've ever known rippling through me, gathering strength until it burst out in the form of psychic power, ripping into Eduardo and leaving him shrieking and begging Asmodeus for help.

My power was spent quickly, trickling to a thin stream, then stopping. I staggered, so weak I could hardly stand, my mind and body and even my soul numb with what I had wrought.

The demon lord gave me a pitying smile. "And so now it begins."

He turned to Eduardo and started feeding him power.

I opened my hand and stared down at what I held, then threw my handful of bobbles on Asmodeus. "Spirits mine, I Summon you."

All six ghosts materialized and leaped straight for the demon lord, taking him off guard. He yanked his power from Eduardo to protect himself, which opened Eduardo's weakened self up to attack by Tirana.

I threw myself at Christian, half knocking him over, half dragging him down to the space between one of the couches and the wall.

I lay panting on him, exhausted, my last shreds of strength worn away, my fingers shaking in his hair. "Christian, quickly, we have little time. We have to Join now while everyone is distracted and weak."

His dull black eyes stared unblinking at me.

I shook his head. "Come on, snap out of it! We have to do this now, right now! Only Joined together will we have the power to defeat the demon lord."

His eyes were dead, his flesh cold. I shook him again, sobbing with frustration. I knew the ghosts couldn't drain enough power from Asmodeus to keep him from us longer than a few seconds.

Please, Christian, please. If you love me, come back to me. We can fight this together, only together, but you have to come back to me. Don't leave me alone. You promised you wouldn't leave me!

I felt his mind stirring, but it wasn't enough. His eyes were still dead, his body unresponsive, his inner self locked in a nightmare that he had permitted in order to save me.

I slapped him as hard as I could, but it did no good. His open eyes didn't even blink. "I will not let him have you. You're mine, do you hear me? Mine!"

He lay passive while I kissed him, sobbing into his mouth as I bit his lip hard enough to draw blood, licking off the hot bead of his blood before I pulled out my silver hatpin and slashed open a wound on my wrist. I held my bloody wrist to his mouth and willed him to drink. Behind me, around me, around us the air was filled with screams as Tirana tried its best to fulfill my command and destroy Eduardo. Shrieks from the ghosts told me that Asmodeus had recovered from the surprise attack and was taking his vengeance on them. I sobbed out a prayer as I held my wrist over Christian's closed lips, praying for the souls of my spirit friends, praying for Christian to open his mouth, praying for me.

A ruby red drop of my blood welled from the cut and slowly trickled down my wrist, where it hung for a second, swaying gently with the beat of my pulse; then it swelled and fell.

Christian's lips parted just as it was about to strike his mouth. The drop of blood disappeared into the dark depths within.

The couch was ripped away from the wall and sent flying across the room, where it exploded in a maelstrom of leather and wood. Asmodeus stood above us, his glamour shredded, his true form visible. It was awful, truly horrible to behold, a parody of a human, a twisted frame that once was made up of flesh and bones and now was bound together by misery and hatred, a crown of deceit topping long, grizzled locks that snaked around his twisted body with a life of their own.

"Now you will fulfill your destiny," the demon lord screamed, reaching for me. The amulet burned bright for a moment, then shattered, falling from my neck. He hauled me forward, his long teeth black with sin as they were bared above my exposed throat. I clutched at the hand that was choking me, but had nowhere near the strength to pry his horrible fingers from my neck.

You certainly do seem to relish dramatic scenes, a warm, silky voice spoke into the shattered remains of my mind. *We're going to have to talk about this as well.*

In the bathtub? I asked, wanting to weep and sing at the same time.

As you command.

Asmodeus's head snapped around as Christian rose to his feet. If I weren't being held by my throat six inches off the ground, I would have cheered, Christian looked so beautiful. His eyes were a beautiful deep mahogany, licked with gold and glittering brightly as he stalked toward us with an elegant grace that made my heart beat madly. His mind merged with mine and suddenly I had the strength to tear myself away from Asmodeus, my body—our body— filled with power that seemed to flow from our joined souls as we turned toward Asmodeus. His fingers tightened around my throat. I broke his grip, surprised to find that a ring he wore came off in my hand, our power flowing in a sweet rush that gave me the strength to push myself away from the demon lord.

Christian smiled as I took my place next to him, reluctantly pulling himself from my mind.

"I told you she was too strong for you," he told Asmodeus, taking my hand and giving Tirana a curious glance.

"It was all I could raise," I explained as Eduardo, the victor in their battle, spun the little demon into the air, its curls spinning madly, lengthening, stretch-

ing, reaching out as if they would snare Eduardo.
Phillippa lay at Guarda's feet, unconscious or dead,
I wasn't sure which. Guarda stood with her hands
outstretched, her eyes blind as she continued to feed
Eduardo her power. I looked on the two of them
almost benignly now, secure in the power and
strength our Joining had given us. It wouldn't take
much for us to overcome them.

"You overestimate both the woman and yourself,"
the demon lord hissed through broken teeth, drawing my attention back to him. "Better, you underestimate my power."

With a horrible expression that I was sure was
meant to be a smile, he disappeared, just turned to
vapor and disappeared before our eyes. Christian
sucked in a big breath and closed the two library
doors, taking one of the broadswords and sliding it
through the handles beneath the doorknobs.

"What are you doing that for?"

"He has summoned his legions."

I glanced back at the broken triumvirate. Tirana
had a grip on Eduardo and was struggling with him.
Guarda continued to stand blind, draining herself to
feed Eduardo.

Christian plucked the second broadsword from
the wall, weighing it in his hand. "Can you take care
of them?"

I blinked. "Yeah, no problem. Um, what legions?
Why are you standing like that *Highlander* guy in
front of the doors? What—"

Something huge crashed into the door, cracking
one panel. An unearthly wail rose from outside, a
wail that Tirana matched inside the room. I slapped

my hands over my ears and watched as Christian braced himself, his sword held in both hands as the doors were battered down before us.

I really was getting tired of demons.

A hand clamped down on my shoulder, yanking me backward as Christian swung at the first demon through the door. Guarda wasn't blind now, although fury and hate twisted her features until they were almost unrecognizable. She spat out something at me in German, clawing at my hand until I realized she was trying to get Asmodeus's ring that I still held.

"I've had just about enough of you and your obnoxious little gang," I yelled at her as I pried her fingers off my hand. I stomped down hard on her foot, jerking my hand free, clearing my mind, and preparing to blast Guarda and Eduardo out of the house and down the street.

My brain gave a little whimper and shut down, leaving me standing cold and helpless, without a single wisp of power to aid me.

"Oh, crap," I said just before Guarda sprang at me. I panicked, leaping aside, almost directly into the path of a demon that was attacking Christian, but stumbled over the carcass of one of its fallen kin, slipping on the slick, black demon blood and falling painfully to my knees. Above me, the broadsword sang as Christian yelled for me to get behind him. A small, particularly ugly demon lunged at me as I scrambled back, for once not about to lecture Christian about his protective nature. Guarda turned from where she was trying to pull Tirana off Eduardo, and threw herself over the body of a demon toward me. I reached for Christian, intent on merging with him to tap into our joined power so I could disable Guarda and Eduardo, but the second my mind merged with his I realized just what Asmodeus had meant.

We have to get out of here, I yelled into Christian's head as he gutted an elongated demon with one stroke, decapitating another on the return swing. *You're almost out of power and I burned up all my circuits. There's no way we can fight off everyone.*

Guarda jumped onto my back, screaming in my ear. I threw myself backward, slamming her into the marble mantelpiece over the fireplace, grabbing one of the daggers and slashing at the arm she held around my throat. She shrieked and released me.

If we leave now, Asmodeus will allow the demons to run free in London. They will kill and destroy as they hunt us, Christian said into my mind. I knew he was almost at the end of our Joined strength, knew also that he had been drained of blood earlier, so he was running on empty now. The power I'd felt in our Joining was the last of his reserves, not the glorious, endless wellspring I'd assumed it was.

Tirana flew past me and crashed into a wall, but was instantly on its feet, its curls standing out in a golden halo around its cherub face adorned by a snarling mouth and sharp, pointed teeth. It screamed a warning of vengeance and threw itself back onto Eduardo, knocking Guarda down in the process. I used the moment of respite to consider our options.

Downstairs, the room they built to hold Sebastian. He said it was specially constructed, warded, protected to keep him inside. We can use that as a bunker, turn the wards to protect us.

No. I will not go there again. He staggered slightly to one side as a demon flung itself at him, shredding his shirt and leaving a trail of blood across his chest.

We have to. It's that or die here. I felt his indecision, felt his horror of the place, and knew then that he must have been locked in it during the hours of the day I was dealing with other matters. *I'm sorry, my love, but we have to go there. I need quiet to see what remains of my abilities, to assess the damage, and you need blood.*

I kicked at a demon that reached for me, stumbling backward when Christian beat the creature off, then turned and thrust his sword downward, throwing the last of his power into the stroke. The carpet beneath my feet caved in, taking Christian and me with it as we fell to the stone floor below. A startled demon peered down at us from the gaping hole in the library floor.

Quickly, Beloved. This way.

I took the hand Christian offered and allowed him to heft me to my feet. My bad leg buckled under me, but Christian's hand was strong, his fingers warm around mine as he swung me up onto his shoulder, the broadsword still in his left hand as he kicked debris out of his way and raced for the vault.

Demons poured down into the hole after us, terrible, tortured shrieks following them that told me the demons weren't too choosy about who they attacked. It was difficult to summon up much pity for any of the triumvirate, so instead I yelled at Christian to go faster, waving my fists at the demons that scrambled after us.

The door to the vault was metal, just as Sebastian

had said, inscribed with wards of containment. The wards were broken now, but still etched into the steel, their presence a testament to the pain of the men who had been held inside.

"Can you ward it?" Christian asked, his back to me as he waved the sword at the oncoming demons.

I tried clearing my mind and gathering strength to draw a ward, but there was nothing there. The ward would not draw.

"No," I cried, sick with the knowledge that I had lost it all, lost all my abilities.

He slashed at the nearest demon, driving it back, then yanked open the door and shoved me inside, slamming the door behind us.

"Is there a lock?" I asked as he threw himself against the door to keep the demons from opening it.

"Not on this side."

"Poop."

"A very polite way of expressing it, but certainly appropriate."

"What are we going to do?"

The sound of a bolt being thrown home outside the door and gales of demonic laughter answered the question.

"It would appear our problem is solved, at least until one of the demons realizes that although we cannot get out, they cannot get in," Christian observed wryly as he eased himself away from the door, prepared for it to spring open.

It stayed locked.

I looked around the small, lead-lined room and felt the hair on the back of my neck rise. In a corner stood a metal table, confinement straps dangling over the sides. It wasn't the table that was so horrible; it was the imprinted fear and anger and pain that clung to it that had me clutching Christian.

"Did they do something to you there? Did they torture you there?"

He said nothing but his eyes darkened. I leaned into him, merging my mind with his, reading there all that he had suffered as Eduardo had drained his blood from him, gloating over Christian, taunting him, tormenting him with the knowledge that he could not save me.

But you did, I told him as I rained kisses down on his face. *You saved us both; I see that now. I didn't understand at first, but now I know why you gave yourself over to Asmodeus. You knew it was the only way to make him believe I would not sacrifice myself for you.*

He stood passive for a moment, taking my love, letting it seep into the parched corners of his soul; then his hands were on me, fitting me tightly against his body, his lips searching out mine as I welcomed him into my body, my heart, my being. His tongue teased mine, tasting me, remembering me, immediately going into an arrogant, ordering-my-tongue-around mode that melted me against him.

"How long do you think they'll keep us locked in here before they figure it out?" I asked breathlessly.

He started backing me toward the far wall. "Long enough," he answered, nuzzling my neck. I let my legs go all boneless, running my fingers through his long, silky hair. . . .

"Drat." I unclenched my hand in order to use both

hands on Christian. A small, metallic ping sounded just as I was about to kiss him until his fangs rattled. We both stopped and looked at the gold ring on the floor.

Christian stilled, his arm tense beneath my hand. I blinked, rather stupidly, I admit, but hey, I'd been through a lot. I was allowed to blink stupidly if I felt like it.

"Is that what I think it is?"

I nodded, staring at it, still blinking. Stupidly.

"Asmodeus's ring. How did you get it?"

"I don't know. It just suddenly came off his hand when I was trying to stop him from strangling me. I forgot I had it."

Christian looked at me. I looked at him. Not stupidly, but with growing dismay. "I can't, Christian. I can't."

"It's a personal item, a talisman of power. Why can't you?"

There was nowhere to sit but the floor, so I sank down onto the cold stainless-steel floor next to the ring and wrapped my arms around my legs. I'd have to tell him; he would know the next time we merged. "I fried my brain when I attacked the triumvirate. I tried, I really tried to deal with Eduardo, but it's gone, it's just gone, I can't do magic anymore. I couldn't even ward the door, and even a *child* can draw wards."

Christian squatted next to me, his hands warm on my shoulders as he turned me to face him. "Allegra, you haven't fried your brain. You've drained yourself, yes, but you haven't permanently damaged yourself. You can't; you are my Beloved. You are immortal now."

"If I'm so immortal, why does my leg still hurt? And I bet you my eyes haven't changed."

"Being granted immortality does not mean your physical flaws are obliterated."

"It's also no guarantee of the quality of brainpower. Part of my brain is dead, Christian, the good part, the only part of value. Now all I have left worth anything is my blood."

His fingers brushed a strand of hair out of my face with a gesture so tender it made tears come to my eyes. "Do you honestly believe that I would pick a woman who had nothing to offer me but a means of sustenance?"

"You're just trying to be nice and make me feel better," I accused. "You're going to say something sweet and endearing and wonderful that will melt my heart and make me see things that I'm too stupid to see now, aren't you?"

"Yes," he said, then tilted my chin up and kissed me. *Tell me who you are.*

"Allegra Telford," I said, obstinately refusing to give in to the intimacy he wanted from me.

That is your name; who are *you?*

"Your Beloved."

That is what *you are; who* are *you?*

"Someone who appreciates you in bed."

Allegra, he sighed into my mind.

"Oh, all right. I'm a Summoner. Or at least, I used to be before I burned up my Summoning equipment trying to overcome Eduardo."

And did you overcome him?

355

"No."

Is he here now?

"No, the demons got him. I'm assuming they did; I doubt if anyone could have survived the horde that Asmodeus called up."

Then you overcame him.

"Indirectly, maybe. Hey, are you supposed to be nibbling on my neck while you're grilling me?"

I can do anything I wish to do. I am a Moravian Dark One.

I waited for the other shoe to drop.

And you are my Beloved.

By which, I assume you're implying I too can do anything I want?

His fingers slid up the curve of my waist to cup my breasts. *Anything,* he breathed into my mind as I turned my head and found his mouth.

You have to feed. You are weak, and we need your strength right now. Blood is all I can offer you; please take it.

His tongue was fire in my mouth. The flames licked down my chest, filling me with need and hunger. *You have so much more to offer, Beloved. I believe in you. I believe you can do anything you desire.*

He merged with me then, his thoughts filling my head, my soul cleansing his, our hearts beating in time. His faith glowed bright, absolute faith in me, in my abilities, in us. I smiled as I kissed him, tears streaking my cheeks even as I slid my arms around him, his strength no threat to me, but an aid, a protection, a part of my life that I knew I wouldn't want to be without.

He pulled my hand forward and pressed the ring into it. *Do it, Beloved.*

I stared at it, doubt tugging at me.

I know you can.

The underlying power in magic, as I have said before, comes from the belief of the practitioner in her own abilities. If you don't believe, the magic won't work. I looked from the ring to Christian's eyes, those beautiful dark eyes that now were smiling at me, full of love and pride and quiet expectation that made warmth bloom inside me again.

"Will you still love me if I fail?"

"I will always love you, no matter what you do."

I held on to the belief he poured into my mind as I set the ring down onto the floor, patting my jeans until I pulled a crumbled piece of chalk from my hip pocket. Christian's hand rested warm and solid on my back, a reminder that I was not alone as I drew the circle. It was odd, this knowledge that I could be myself, be everything I had fought for, and still be a part of Christian, but I had no more time for introspection and other mushy types of thought, no matter how enticing they were.

I had a demon lord to send back to hell.

"Why is it never easy with you? Why must you insist on making even the simplest of matters difficult?"

A dull thud from the door reverberated around the small, soundproofed room.

I'm not being difficult; I'm being practical. Now bite me!

"I do not need to feed."

The door shuddered as another thud, louder this

time, echoed into the room. The sword Christian had wedged into the door frame clattered against the metal, giving warning it was about to be dislodged.

Yes, you do. They drained you; I can feel how weak you are. Drink!

"I will not take from you when you need all your strength."

I'm not so hung up on my own independence that I don't realize that your strength is an integral part of mine, Christian. Either you drink my blood this very minute, or I won't do a thing about closing this circle. I figure those demons are going to break through in about five seconds, so either you bite me now, or forever hold your peace.

His fangs pierced the hollow of my throat, sharp needles of pain dissolving into a sensation of intimate ecstasy. He drank deeply, making my head spin with both the pleasure of his feeding and the power that surged through him as my blood gave him new life. The door shuddered, thought about giving, but changed its mind at the last minute and held solid once again. I knew the next blow the demons made would destroy it. It was now or never; either I believed in myself, or I didn't.

I turned my head and bit Christian's thumb, squeezing his finger over the circle until three drops of dark red blood landed next to Asmodeus's ring. Christian's tongue was warm on my neck; then he pulled away. I wiped the smear of red from his lips, using my blood to trace a binding symbol in the middle of the circle, my finger tingling with the familiar sensation of power.

"Asmodeus, sixty-seventh spirit of Goeth, commander of the thirty legions, I Summon thee by the power of thy own talisman. Come forth and be bound under my hand."

The demons were gathering for another assault on the door; I could feel their intentions pounding against us. Christian stood and prepared to defend me.

Belief is everything. I rose to my feet, grimly tracing protection wards around us, daring them to defy me. The wards allowed themselves to be drawn, wavered, then glowed red as power began to grow within me.

"Asmodeus, sixty-seventh spirit of Goeth, commander of the thirty legions, I command thee to appear before me!"

The demons slammed through the door as Asmodeus snarled into view, confined to the circle, held only by a few drops of blood and the combined belief Christian and I shared in my abilities. The demons stopped, unable to move so long as their master was bound by the circle.

"You do not have the power," the demon lord said with a sneer, his ravaged frame growing until it seemed to fill the room. "You cannot hold me, for I am all-powerful."

Christian stood before the demons, his belief in me flooding my mind, turning to power as we merged together, one will, one mind, one spirit. "Asmodeus, sixty-seventh spirit of Goeth, commander of the thirty legions, bend thee to my command!"

"You will not triumph over me! You are not strong enough to—"

"Asmodeus!" My voice cut through the demon

lord's roars with the clarity of a bell, echoing throughout the room, sending the demons into a shrieking fit of cowering. Asmodeus twisted his body upon itself. I took a deep breath, throwing everything I had into the last few words. "Asmodeus, I return thee to the pit that spawned you!"

With a scream that shook the house to its foundations, Asmodeus turned into oily red smoke that hung in the air for a moment before slowly dissolving into nothing.

The demons left nasty little black marks on the floor as they disappeared with Asmodeus, dragged back to the infernal depths with their master.

Christian grabbed my hand and hauled me forward.

"Wait, the ring—"

"Leave it. The house is coming down."

He was right. The house, which shook as we sent Asmodeus back to hell, continued to shake and rumble above our heads. Loud crashes and ominous cracks from overhead had us racing down the small passageway, Christian more or less dragging me up the stairs to the kitchen. We made it through the back door just as the second floor crashed down onto the first, which sent it down onto the ground floor, and that to the basement. I clung to Christian, his hand holding my face against his chest as wood and glass and debris flew around us as the house came down.

I wrapped my arms around him, holding him tight as we stood in the garden and stared at the remains of the Trust house. We said nothing. There was nothing to say.

Epilogue

Christian moved within me, deeper, harder, surging into me, filling me with more than just his body, giving me his heart and mind as well. Water splashed around us as we moved together, the small seat in the tub not designed for the purpose we were putting it to. Despite the pain in my thigh, my legs tightened around his hips as his mouth caressed my nape, licking me, nipping at my flesh as our bodies moved in an ageless rhythm. I scored his slick back as he nibbled my neck.

Do it!

So demanding. His voice was as soft as his hair. I took a handful of the damp, inky black mane and tugged on it.

Do it now!

Have I told you how arousing I find it when you make demands of me?

I flexed my legs, thrusting my hips up to meet his as his hardness plunged into my eager flesh. *I know how aroused you are; it's fairly evident how aroused you are. If you were any more aroused, you'd be poking out my throat. Now . . . just . . . do . . . it!*

Allegra, my Allegra, he sighed into my mind, his teeth teasing the tender spot beneath my ear as his fingers dug into my hips, pulling me tighter to him until there was no way to tell where his oil-slicked flesh ended and mine began. *How could I live without you?*

Do it!

Heat, sharp and sweet, swept down my neck as he claimed every part of me, taking life from me and returning it with a triumphant shout of my name as our bodies burned with a blinding light. I gave myself up to him, and received his exaltation in return.

"Weren't we supposed to be having a discussion in here?" I asked later, once I could remember how to speak. We were lying together in the tub, our limbs entwined, the warm water lapping sensually against us. *Discussion be damned.* I tipped my head back and bit Christian's chin. "You smell good. You smell like jasmine, and Christian, and just a hint of eau du after-sex."

He opened one eye. "You have worn me out, Allegra. Instead of praising my prowess to the stars, instead of writing sonnets to my masculinity, instead of composing odes showering me with praise, you complain of the lingering scent of our lovemaking. I will make note of this aberration and ensure that any women who wish to apply for the position of my Beloved in the future are free from this prejudice."

I trailed a finger around his left nipple. "You think you're so cute with all that 'other Beloved' talk."

His eye closed. "I know I am cute."

I snorted and tweaked his nipple.

"You think I am very cute. You think me sexy, as well. I can read your thoughts, remember."

I hoisted myself up and slid across his body. *You are conceited, arrogant, and domineering, everything I dislike in a man.*

And you are independent, stubborn, and heedless, everything I dislike in a woman.

I slid my hands under his back and kissed his dampened lips. *So why is it that I love you so much?*

He smiled a smug, masculine little smile and captured my legs with his. *Because I love you, and to be loved by a Dark One is enough for any woman.*

I pinched him in a particularly vulnerable spot and allowed him to kiss me with all the sexy arrogance he had.

"There you are! Sheesh, I thought you guys would never show up! We've been waiting forever for you! I would have thought you could have held on to your libidos for just a few minutes, just long enough for you to tell us what happened."

"Roxy, stop being so obnoxious!"

"I'm never obnoxious; I'm just concerned. You weren't here when they came home. Allie looked half-dead when Christian hauled her in the door, and all Noelle said was that she had to go examine the remains of the Trust house to make sure nothing bad was hanging around. What remains? What happened to the house? What sort of bad thing is she looking for? That's all I want to know, just a few simple answers to a few simple questions, and then I can get packed and go home to my husband."

"Not a moment too soon," Raphael murmured into Joy's ear. She elbowed him gently, but leaned into him and twined her fingers through the hand he rested on her belly.

I looked around Christian's study, overwhelmed for a moment with sadness that had tears pricking behind my eyes.

What is it, Beloved?

"The ghosts," I answered, swallowing hard. "I miss the ghosts. They loved this room. They loved the TV. And now with the house destroyed—"

Christian took my hand in his. "We will search for them, Allegra."

"Asmodeus probably turned them into phantoms," I said thickly, turning away from everyone so I could wipe my eyes. Christian pulled me to his chest and let me sob there while he quickly explained the events of day. His voice was soft, low, and true as it wrapped me in a blanket of comfort, but nothing could ease the pain when I thought of what I had asked from my friends.

"I'm sure they'll be all right, Allie," Joy said thoughtfully. "I doubt if this Asmo-whoever had time to do anything to them. It sounds like he was awfully focused on you and Christian."

I sniveled a noncommittal answer into Christian's black sweater.

"Yeah, and besides, they were smart ghosts," Roxy added. "Well, that Jem character wasn't the brightest bulb in the pack, and that wrinkled up Welsh woman was not working on all six thrusters, but other than that, they were a pretty sharp bunch. They wouldn't let themselves be phantomized."

I sniffed and breathed in Christian's lovely scent. It made me feel better just knowing that even if I were guilty of the eternal damnation of six ghosts, at least he'd suffer with me.

Or something to that effect.

"We will go back to the house as soon as the sun is down," Christian said softly in my ear. "We will search for any sign of your ghosts."

I nodded and sniffed again and made an effort to pull myself together. Christian sat and tugged me down onto his lap as everyone asked questions, hashed over the events, and heaped huge quantities of praise on Christian and me for our quick thinking.

I was utterly miserable.

"Hullo? Anyone home? Oh, hullo again, Joy, Roxy. You must be Raphael. Do you know that your eyes are yellow?"

"Amber, not yellow," Joy corrected Noelle.

"Really?" She tilted her head and examined Raphael. "If you say so. Allie, I was checking through the remains of the house for any signs of demons and imps, and I found this."

She held out her hand, the shattered remains of her amulet scattered across her palm.

"Oh, Noelle, I'm so sorry, I meant to tell you that I'd lost it. It cracked under the strain of Asmodeus's power. I'm sure it was a one-of-a-kind amulet, but I'll do everything I can to replace it."

"Don't worry; I have a drawerful of them. After all, it's not the amulet; it's what goes into it."

I gave her a watery smile. "Have you met Christian?"

I tried to get up so he could greet her, but he held on to me with one hand and offered her another. She said something about it being nice to finally meet him, then asked, "What happened to the Dark One who was in the big bed?"

I leaned back against Christian and let myself drift along with his silken voice.

"Sebastian recovered from his ill treatment, a circumstance that leaves me profoundly grateful for your help. I understand you arranged for several units of blood to be fed to him."

"We weren't sure if he'd like it if it weren't on the hoof, so to speak, but he didn't seem to mind," Roxy said. "In fact, he guzzled it all down pretty quickly. Made a world of difference in him, too, didn't it?"

"It did," Joy agreed.

"He left me a note before he left, asking me to thank you for your kindness," Christian added.

"Oh, he's left already?" Noelle asked, disappointment tinging her voice. I stopped wallowing in sorrow and took a good, long look at her. "That's a shame. I've never met a Dark One, present company excepted, and I was looking forward to interviewing him as to the nature of werefolk in Moravia."

"Were what?" Raphael asked suspiciously. Joy shushed him.

"I would be happy to—"

"No, you wouldn't," Joy said quickly, interrupting Christian. "You have lots to do. You have Allie to get settled, and the Trust to dismantle, and all the other stuff. I'm sure you won't have time."

I pushed myself forward on Christian's legs, bristling at the way she told him what he could do. "If Christian wants to—"

"He doesn't want to, though, do you, Christian?" Joy said, her eyebrows wiggling meaningfully.

Raphael groaned and pulled her back from where she had been leaning forward. "No. I absolutely forbid it. One was enough. No more. We're going to have a quiet life from now on."

"Of course we are," Joy said, absently patting Raphael's leg.

I looked at Roxy. She grinned at me. I looked at Christian. He looked thoughtful. Noelle just looked confused. I knew how she felt; I was as confused as she was.

Is it so that all women are born matchmakers? Christian said into my mind.

I looked again at Noelle, an idea dawning in my mind, a slow smile curving my lips. "I'm afraid Joy is right, Noelle. Christian is going to be very busy for a long while. But I'm sure any of his friends, his *Moravian* friends, would be happy to help you with your book." I turned to look at Christian. "Didn't you tell me that Sebastian had gone to track down the other Trust houses and check them for victims? That means he'll be in the country for a bit."

"Allegra . . ."

I ignored the warning note in Christian's voice and smiled again at Noelle. Roxy and Joy smiled with me. She backed up a step under the onslaught of so much smile wattage.

"I'm sure he'd be delighted to talk to you when he returns."

"Erm . . . yes, that's a possibility. Well, it's been lovely, but I must be on my way. Mummy has been called to a terrible Hecatoncheires outburst, and I promised I'd help her."

"Hecatoncheires?" Roxy asked. "What's that?"

"A nasty little monster with fifty heads and one hundred hands. Ta, everyone! Oh, Allie." Noelle stopped at the door and turned back toward me, reaching into her pocket. "Before I forget, I found these as well. I thought you might want them back."

Six filthy, stained, dust-, dirt-, and plaster-laden bobbles glowed softly in her hand.

"The ghosts!" I leaped up from Christian's lap, scooping the bobbles gently into my hand. "They bobbled themselves! They're all here!"

Noelle smiled. "I told you they would be helpful."

"And smart." Roxy nodded.

I set the bobbles carefully in a blue-and-green Venetian glass bowl and called the names one after another. "Esme, Antonio, Jem, Alis, Honoria, Mr. Woogums, I Summon you."

They all appeared, all their dear forms, even the petulant little Honoria looking relatively pleased at being called forth. Jem, the possessor of the sat-upon bobble, was a bit worse for wear, but at least he could talk again.

"Borrowed a tongue," he told me. I didn't want to know where he borrowed it from, so I just thanked him for his help, and told him how happy I was to see him again.

"I was never in my life so frightened; you simply have no idea what it is to throw oneself willy-nilly at a demon lord!" Esme told Roxy. "I was vicious, though; I truly was. I berated him soundly for his cruel actions, and then I lectured him—yes, I did!—about the state he'd let his hair and fingernails get into. 'Just because one is an inhabitant of hell does not mean one has to let oneself go,' I said to him. Well, *that* gave him something to think about, as you might well imagine!"

Antonio watched with sad puppy eyes as Christian, who had been listening to Jem tell how he had Asmodeus in a headlock, followed by a mangler move, strolled over to me and slid his arm around my waist. "You 'ave given yourself to 'im, *corazón*. I was sure you would save yourself for me. We would 'ave found a way to be together."

"I gave my heart to Christian before I Summoned you, Antonio. You knew there could never be anything between us."

Antonio's lower lip pouted for a moment, then sucked itself back in as he straightened up and smoothed down his doublet. "You will have girl children. Lots of girl children. One of them will grow up and see me and know that she is mine, yes?"

Christian started to protest, but I stopped him. "I'm sure any daughters we have would be smitten with you, but you can't mean to stay here, Antonio. I'm positive I can Release you; it's just a matter of having the time to figure out the proper quantities of ginseng. Now that the threat of Asmodeus is taken care of, I can devote myself to working out the problems so I can Release you." I waved a hand to include the other ghosts. "Release all of you."

"No! Oh, my dear, you wouldn't do that to me! To us!"

"I will never leave you, *corazón!* You may grow tired of the dead one, and wish me to comfort you."

"Don't want t'be Released. I want t'see who'll be left on *Survivor.*"

Alis said something incomprehensible. Esme nodded. "She's absolutely right."

Mr. Woogums piddled on the carpet.

Christian sighed in my ear. *I am adding to my list the condition that future Beloveds not have any ghosts attached to them.*

I stepped firmly on his foot and looked at Honoria. "Well? You've heard the others; they refuse to go on. Do you want me to Release you or not?"

She looked around the room, skipping over Roxy, Joy, and Raphael, frowning at Antonio, ignoring Alis and Jem, wrinkling her nose at the ghostly puddle of cat piddle, finally settling her gaze on Esme. "I want to stay with Esme. I want to watch more *Buffy.*"

"*Buffy?*" Christian asked, stiffening.

I smiled at everyone. "Well, I guess that's settled, then. I'm sure you'll all find Christian's castle in the Moravian highlands more than roomy enough."

"*Buffy* as in, the vampire slayer?"

Roxy snickered.

"Christian says the castle is haunted, so perhaps we'll get to meet some new friends!" I added cheerfully.

"The one who slays vampires? *That Buffy?*"

Raphael got to his feet and pulled Joy to hers. "I believe this is our cue to leave. Come along Roxy; I'll help you pack."

She trailed Joy and Raphael out the door, pausing to pat Christian on the shoulder. "I'm sure she's too young yet to learn how to focus her energy. I mean, it must take a great amount of concentration for a ghost to be able to wield a hammer and stake, don't you think?"

I pushed her out the door and closed it, then opened it and stuck my head out, saying, "Thank you all for everything!" before closing it behind me again.

Antonio eyed Christian's chest, his fingers stroking his beard. "A 'ammer and stake. Why 'ave I never thought of that?"

"I will be happy to give you something to think about," Christian warned as he started toward Antonio, who promptly drew out his sword. Alis wandered over to her favorite vase and started yelling at it. Esme held Mr. Woogums above the puddle he'd left, and scolded him. Honoria and Jem squabbled over who got control of the TV remote.

I sighed happily and leaned back against the door, my eyes catching Christian's as he withstood Antonio's rapier attack.

We will have them forever, you know, Beloved. So long as we live, so shall they exist.

I know. But somehow, with you standing next to me, I think I can bear just about anything.

Antonio lunged with a particularly cruel thrust to Christian's heart.

He sighed in my head as he waved Antonio's image away. *I would not tolerate this for any other woman,* malý válečník. *Only for my Beloved will I sacrifice my peace.*

I laughed and stepped forward into his waiting arms. "We really are going to have to work on this arrogant attitude of yours."

KATIE MacALISTER

A Girl's Guide to Vampires

Nowadays, finding The One really can be a pain in the neck

Joy Randall should know. She's been looking for the right guy for years. But, as yet, no real man has lived up to the heroes of the vampire romance novels she's completely addicted to.

So when her friend Roxy suggests a holiday to the Czech Republic, Joy simply can't say no. After all, it has everything:

A craggy, romantic landscape
   Tall, dark, handsome strangers
      Immortal, undead, bloodsucking fiends ...

OK, the last one is just in Roxy's imagination. Because vampires don't really exist ... or do they?

Plagued by dreams of a handsome stranger, haunted by a mysterious prophecy, and pursued by three pale, brooding, sinister suitors, suddenly Joy isn't so sure ...

HODDER